A GENTLEMAN'S BRIDE

Noelene Jenkinson

'Why do you want to marry, Miss Gutheridge?'

'I don't. It hadn't occurred to me until I read the Argus.' The words slipped off her tongue before she could retract them.

Obviously amused, James burst out laughing. 'Such honesty. Rare indeed. Charming.' He sobered. 'Then why did you respond?'

'I needed to get out into the country.'

'Needed?' James pressed.

'I mean, I have no particular interest in towns,' Anne quickly corrected. 'I loved the open air and wide spaces of the moors back home. Your advertisement offered that chance.'

'Adventurous of you to leave home without any plans and seek marriage the day after you arrive in a foreign land. Do I detect a hint of desperation?'

CHAPTER 1

'Bridge Farm' near Tavistock, Devon
April 1861'

'Marry Mr. Westcott?' Anne's hands gripped the worn edges of the scrubbed kitchen table so tight her fingers ached. 'Are you serious, Pa?'

'I most certainly am, me girl.' William Gray growled, emphatic as always in his role as head of the family, none of whom would ever think to disobey. Except the oldest daughter before him.

'Never,' she gasped, horrified and obstinate, glaring at the man for whom she had never been the favourite. That enviable privilege belonged to her lovely obedient younger sister, Elizabeth.

'Anne Frances Louise!' her mother Frances Gray reprimanded in an appalled whisper, standing loyally to one side and half hidden behind her husband. 'Manners.'

Why her parents had chosen three names each for all of their children when one would suffice, Anne never fathomed. Especially since they descended from humble tenant cottagers for generations before them. And their names weren't even exotic. Just plain Anne and just plain Frances and just plain Louise. Rather than Annabella or Cleopatra or-

'On account of recent happenings like,' her father interrupted her wayward thoughts and glowered beneath bushy grey brows. 'Mr. Westcott has asked my permission and I've given it. Wisely so in the circumstances.'

In exasperated disbelief, Anne's gaze switched to her

mother whose hands nervously twisted a scrappy handkerchief between rough red hands. She couldn't believe it. The pair of them were plotting to marry her. Why was finding her a husband such a sudden priority?

'What circumstances?'

Her father cleared his throat, plainly uncomfortable. 'You willingly visited Mr. Westcott at Combe Hill, girl. Alone,' he bellowed, exasperated.

'Oh, that,' Anne scoffed with relief, flung her arms in the air and paced across the threadbare rug, careful not to trip on its tattered edges, certain now that once she explained she could safely escape this alarming marital threat. 'It was a duty visit on behalf of our family.'

'You didn't think to ask our permission first?'

She briefly recalled that dismal wet day only weeks before when a tiny knot of local people clad in black huddled together in the churchyard cemetery, sheltered beneath glistening wet umbrellas, and young Mary Westcott and her unborn baby had been formally farewelled from this life. Rumour had it that Arthur Westcott remained surly at the loss.

'I felt sorry for him.'

'A sad affair to be sure,' her father nodded sagely. 'And your concern was admirable but you should have controlled your improper conduct. What else was the man to think then?' he spluttered, wiping spittle from the corners of his mouth with the grubby cloth that lived permanently in his trouser pocket.

Anne stopped pacing and tried to sound mature. 'Well, it's also improper then that Mr. Westcott should want to marry again so soon after his wife's death. Surely he's still in mourning?'

'He's a respec'able yeoman who understood an interest from your visit.' William Gray snapped.

'No, Pa, he misunderstood. I only took him a basket of food I tell you from the larder on behalf of the family. It didn't mean nothing.'

'And went hungry the night because of it,' her usually meek mother dared to mutter. 'Mr. Westcott's situation at Combe Hill is far better than ours. He owns his farm,' she said reverently, as though he were a local God, when all hereabouts knew him a miserly man. A status he had undoubtedly achieved for being so frugal. Nonetheless, still a suffering human being and Anne's heart had gone out to him in his grief. In the future, she must learn to curb her compassion for lost souls.

'He's a man of standing hereabouts and all know it,' Frances Gray continued. 'He's a village elder and on the jury at the quarter sessions. You're eighteen now and old enough to marry.'

'But he's old.' Anne's dismay filled her voice. And ill tempered. All knew it but no one voiced it and her parents wanted her to marry him! 'He must be nearly thirty.'

Her father scoffed, waving an impatient arm in the air. 'I've decided and accepted on your be'alf, else your thoughtless conduct will lay you open to gossip. It will teach you to stop these impulsive deeds with no thought to consequences. As the oldest, you should be setting an example to t'others. Mr. Westcott's offer will solve our problems and take care of you.'

'But I don't care for him. I've told you, my visit meant nothing.'

'Not what 'e says.'

'What did he say?'

'You cared enough to make a secret visit,' William Gray accused in a bluster, his thick brows meeting in a ferocious glare.

'I went in broad daylight,' Anne frantically explained. 'I never called on him for any other reason. I only sat in his kitchen while I paid our respects on behalf of our family.'

'And sat right close to the man and took 'is hands, he says,' her father thundered.

Anne groaned. True. She had. On impulse. Out of pity for him and thought nothing of it because he had looked so forlorn. But how to make Pa believe it?

'We may be poor but I'll not have us ashamed by scandal.'

'He didn't hardly take any interest in my company. He wasn't even polite,' Anne muttered, not understanding all the fuss and devastated by the outcome of a neighbourly gesture she wished now she had never made. Arthur Westcott had seemed to be sunk in a world of his own and virtually oblivious to her presence. Now he wanted to marry her. Had he been more aware than she thought?

He had looked so miserable at the funeral, rain dripping off his broad brimmed black hat. Even knowing his gruff nature, she had felt compelled to personally sympathise. Mary Westcott had been a beautiful gentle-natured woman and would be greatly missed by all, especially her husband Anne would have thought. But wanting to remarry so fast, one had to wonder if he had cared for her so much after all.

Frowning, her quick mind assessed the mundane future that lay ahead of her if she married him, remembering his few mumbled words when he bothered to converse and the long awkward silences in between during her visit. At the time, she had thought it grief and cursed her mistake. She would forever regret her visit if it meant she must now marry him against her wishes.

'You should have considered your actions, you twily girl, before you went dashing off to 'is farm.'

'I'll not marry him,' Anne argued.

Her parents shared a troubled glance. 'A future with Mr. Westcott will see you taken care of and have a better life,' William Gray said gruffly.

Anne bit her tongue against a challenge and stayed silent, well aware of what a life with the dour man would mean. At the time, everyone had gossiped over the unlikely match of such a sweet innocent woman as Mary Carter and grumpy

Arthur Westcott. Perhaps, like Anne, her soft heart had gone out to the man.

'Not enough men to go around, girl. Young women are being shipped off to the colonies for bein' too many of 'em. You'll marry Westcott and there's to be said about it.'

'Why can't I marry a man of my own choosing?' Anne dared to argue.

Despite their good intentions for her, Anne had always struggled with authority and felt no differently now. She resisted her parents' demands for this forced marriage. Truly, they could not love her if they would abandon her to this dismal fate. There had to be another way out of the problem. But for the moment, Anne could think of none.

Glowering, William Gray splashed more cider into a large glass and sculled it in one mouthful. Anne wondered what worse news was to come that her weak father should take refuge in drink once again. Anne hid her frustration and despair. By the end of another session, he would be even more of a useless babbling mess. But for hiding his soft ways with drink, he might be a more stable buttress for his family.

'There's no choosing for the likes of us. You'll be fine as long as you do as you're told. Farming makes us less money each year,' her pa reluctantly admitted. 'We make our rent and barely a living besides, like most cottagers hereabouts. But it's not enough. Only your mother, Emma and I can stay on. Zo,' he pondered, 'You three older children must settle elsewhere. The work's hard and boys are leaving. Lads want men's wages, so it's down to your Ma and me.'

Anne cast a frantic glance between her parents. Their situation must be bad. She had never seen her parents look so old and strained. Barely forty, she knew Pa already suffered rheumatism. 'You're turning me out, then?'

'We're doing no such thing,' Ma gasped, an appalled look on her face. 'You'll be well taken care of at Combe Hill.'

Perhaps because of her rebellious glare, her Pa barked, 'Nought other way to survive.'

'What about Richard? Surely you won't be sending him to the Great Consols?'

'Like as not he's thinking of going to America.'

Anne stifled a gasp of shock. Leave Devon? He'd not said a word to her and she thought her brother would be the most likely to confide in her even before Ma and Pa. She felt cheated he'd not told her of his plans. 'You've already spoken to him then?'

He nodded. Deep down, Anne envied her brother's choice of adventure and while she battled her parents' command to stay here and marry a man she barely knew and didn't really like. There was no question of Elizabeth's future, of course. It seemed resolved with gentle Edward Stokes.

'Could I not go with Richard?' she asked in desperation.

'It's decided, Annie. Your chance is here,' Frances Gray said sternly. 'We've not enough Pounds to feed us all and keep up with the rent. It would be a disgrace to fall behind.'

Anne had no idea how to escape their wishes but they all knew the cause of their dilemma, now grown desperate it seemed. William Gray was a poor farmer and manager. Anne wondered if Ma ever regretted running away with him and daily witnessed her dutiful unspoken heartbreak. Forsaking the security and comfort of a more prosperous family, disobeying them to marry the man she loved but clearly knowing little about him. Pa's carelessness had long meant they always wrestled to survive.

Anne desperately searched her mind for an alternative but failed. She would be leaving with no choice about it. Girls married and boys laboured as best they could. So many with a few pounds saved heeded the call to emigrate. Lucky Richard, she sighed with frustration, not for the first time wishing she had been born a male.

From her deep thoughts, Anne grew aware of an uneasy mood between her parents. Perhaps, despite their joint decision, they had deep reservations about marrying their oldest daughter to an unfriendly neighbouring farmer as much as the victim herself.

William Gray took another draught of cider and murmured gruffly, 'You'll marry the man, girl and no complaint. Our survival depends on it.'

Anne straightened her back and calmly folded her hands. 'Your survival. Not mine.'

She could see her bleak future, chained to a prickly man for whom she could never have respect. To her dismay, she could see no other way but to accept her fate and the unwelcome thought filled her with fear.

With no more to be said, dismissed and blind with despair over her undesirable future, Anne collided with Elizabeth eavesdropping outside the door. Catching her sister's arm and dragging her away, Anne put a finger to her lips, urging her to silence.

Arm in arm they strode across the cobbled courtyard, shadowed and chilled in the weak late afternoon early summer sun. At the far end, their younger brother, Richard, had begun milking their small straggly herd.

'How much did you hear?' Anne asked her golden-haired younger sister as they strode through the orchard beneath the gnarled leaning trunks of the old neglected apple trees, their sheltered sides smothered in lichen.

'Most everything,' Elizabeth confessed in an appalled whisper.

'Elizabeth Gray,' Anne teased. 'Suddenly so bold and eavesdropping.'

'Your voices were that loud,' she reasoned contritely. 'Pa sounded right excited after Mr. Westcott left.' Anne whirled on her sister and stared. 'Did you not see him arrive?'

'No.'

'Ma was against it but Pa convinced her. I wonder they didn't call you in.'

'I'm glad not.' Anne paused. 'I'd run away but where would I go?'

'You'd never!' Elizabeth gripped her sister's arm and

pulled her up as they reached the orchard fence. 'Don't even think it. I should miss you so. I shall have no one when you leave.'

'I suppose moving away is all part of being wed, isn't it?' Anne tried to sound cheerful, although she would feel much better about it if she had some feelings for Arthur. But to have none at all…

'I suppose you'll get used to him,' Elizabeth said encouragingly.

'It's all right for you, Elizabeth Alice Grace. Edward is kind. The few words I spoke to Arthur Westcott, he always seemed unhappy to me as though he were holding a grudge. We don't know nothing about him except he came into the county to farm Combe Hill about four or five years ago.'

'He owns his own land, Annie, and it's a decent house. You'll not be poor like Ma and Pa. It's a chance for a good life and, you never know, you might take to him. In time,' she ended lamely trying to sound positive.

'Maybe. Arthur has a horse and cart. I hope he lets me use it to visit Ma and Pa, and you in the vicarage when you're wed, too.' She hesitated. 'I'm not looking forward to the wedding.' Her voice lowered. 'And even less to being with him and having his children.'

Her sister's pale cheeks flushed. 'Anne!'

She nudged her sister gently in the side. 'You'll be doing some of your own with Edward Stokes one day soon. And be livin' in more willing circumstances.'

'Well,' Elizabeth's gaze fell to the lush grassy ground under their booted feet. 'He's … only just … started calling. Nothing's settled like between you and Mr. Westcott.'

Anne looked aside and caught the rosy blush on her sister's cheeks as they scrambled over the low stone wall and headed across the small sheep meadow enclosed by sheltering banks of earth and stone, their father's small reduced flock of long wool sheep in a distant corner he'd somehow managed to keep. For now.

Forests of oak and larch clothed the hill heights of their small acreage. Clouds pushed by a fierce easterly wind scudded light shadows across its lower slopes covered in thickets of gold-tipped gorse. The prickly shrub gave cover to rabbits, always the source of a free meal.

Anne stepped out faster, invigorated as always by this familiar green walking country. 'You like the vicar well enough, though?' She reverted to their conversation.

Elizabeth remained silent for a time, then admitted with reluctant shyness, 'More every day.'

Anne gasped and her brows lifted. 'Do you love him already?' Her face lit with excitement.

Elizabeth's sweet face softened. 'I don't know, but my heart pounds faster when we talk of him and I stand at the window for ages long before I know it's time for him to visit on Sundays and I can't take my eyes from him when he's around,' she ended in a rush.

'I noticed,' Anne smiled for her sister's joy, hiding her own bitter disappointment that she would now never have the same chance herself to marry for love.

'He's quiet for certain, but when we walk out on Sundays, he talks about all manner of things. His life and the church folk.'

'With Edward you'll be comfortable and well loved,' Anne sighed. 'You'll probably have a housemaid and not have half the chore's Ma does. I didn't see one at Mr. Westcott's house. And Edward will be a good father to your children for certain. He's quiet, like, but stronger than Pa.' Her brow dipped into a brief frown. 'Did you hear them say we'll all have to leave, being money's so tight?' Elizabeth nodded. 'You'll have Edward.' Envy tinged Anne's voice. 'At least sounds like they won't send Richard down the copper mines. Did you know he's talked of emigrating?'

Elizabeth's lovely eyes widened in horror. 'Never!'

'It's true. Pa told me.'

'But we might never see him again.'

The long damp grass dragged at their hems as they trudged to the top of a low rise and paused for breath. Anne shrugged. 'Life's changing for us all.'

The wind caught at their skirts, whipped long hair in their faces and Anne hugged her thick woollen shawl tighter about her. She cast her gaze off into the hazy evening distance. The tor-crowned moor was visible in all its rugged beauty and lifted her heart. Outcrops of grey scaly rock and wide brakes of bracken bowing their ferny tips into the icy waters of a tawny winding brook were familiar to her since childhood.

Behind them, from where they had just come, lay their humble cottage, huddled into the lee of the moor, thatched and built of grey stone rubble.

In the distance, although they couldn't see it, lay Arthur Westcott's larger farm at Combe Hill, remotely nestled into the foothills at the valley's end, housing the tall grim man who had mistaken her visits.

Clearly not loving each other, Anne wondered how they would get on living together. She squeezed the unpleasant thought from her mind. Maybe he'd be nicer and happier once they were wed. Maybe he wasn't as tough as people said. She'd heard he worked his farm boy hard. With jobs scarce, lads grabbed whatever work they could. At least they had a roof over their head and meals.

'It's getting dark.' Anne turned resignedly, letting the familiar outline of their cottage guide them home in the gloom.

Later, as the family shared their meagre evening meal of rabbit and potatoes dipped with small chunks of stale bread in the thin gravy, the family remained subdued, neither talking nor looking at one another. Presumably, everyone knew about the wedding by now but there was no excited talk of it around the table, merely a silent undercurrent of unspoken words.

Emmy innocently chattered, diverting their attention for a time. Richard, his stomach always an endless pit for food, ravenously shovelled in his food.

When the modest meal was over, their Pa's chair scraped on the stone floor and he left the kitchen to move into the tiny parlour by the fire to drink and doze as usual before an early night.

Anne and Elizabeth were left to wash the dishes while Ma, her hands rarely still, settled to her basket of mending and sewing. Later, Elizabeth read to Emmy before bed. Surveying them all, Anne knew, as humble as it was, she would deeply regret leaving this struggling household and its simple security.

CHAPTER 2

'Stand still, Annie,' her Ma admonished as her oldest daughter shifted nervously from one foot to another. 'How can I finish the hem before Mr. Westcott arrives?'

Even seeing the result of her Ma's valiant efforts in completely resewing her own wedding dress, carefully stowed in a chest all these years, with its soft material and pretty lace, Anne knew she was going to a better life but failed to gather any enthusiasm for her imminent marriage.

It didn't help that her reclusive fiancé was about to make another unwelcome visit. She and Arthur had barely exchanged a score of words. Being so stern and unapproachable, Anne made a point of asking polite questions to draw him out when he called, if only to fill the long silent gaps in their conversations, being carefully respectful so as not to anger or offend him.

From his terse responses and lack of smiles, she foresaw her joyless future with grave doubts, dreading the time only days hence when she must leave home for good to be wed in his house and stay.

She had only made one visit to Combe Hill accompanied by Ma and Elizabeth. The house was much larger than the Gary's small cottage, as she knew from her previous ill-fated call with a roomy downstairs and kitchen living area as well as an upper floor with three small bedrooms. It was neat enough considering Arthur had lived alone these past weeks without a woman to do for him.

When the three Gray womenfolk had not even been greeted with a whistling kettle for tea, Anne was crisply instructed by their host and her future husband to prepare it herself and become familiar with the kitchen. She was happy to do so but resented the harsh manner of his command.

Now, Ma pushed herself from her knees on the stone floor to survey her daughter. Anne stood on a small frayed scrap of rug to spare dirt from the hem of her lovely dress and not spoil the hours of work skilfully spent in remaking it.

Although Frances Gray has eloped from her comfortable home on a middle class farm, she and William had married in the local parish church of St. Eustachius in Tavistock. But since Arthur was so recently widowed, both families had agreed it best for a quiet marriage in the groom's house with the Gray's to supply the food afterwards with meat and supplies generously provided by the groom.

It would stretch their existing meagre provisions and funds to the limit. The family never had money to spare. But, already, a few locals and staunch obliging neighbours, barely managing themselves, had gifted precious food rations of their own. Meat they could ill afford to share, a handful of eggs, an extra half pound of butter for the cake. All humbly received by Ma.

'You'll make us right proud, Annie,' her mother commented quietly.

Miserable and resigned, her daughter noted there was no mention of happiness. She forced a weak smile for Ma's benefit. 'You should be keeping this dress for Elizabeth.'

A look of horror crossed Ma's face. 'No. You're my first born.'

Anne thought it such a waste. This precious dress and hours of Ma's handiwork deserved to be displayed at a far worthier celebration. She had no illusions that anyone, including herself, would look on her marriage to Arthur Westcott as anything but a union of convenience.

Yet again, Anne had to wonder why he wanted to marry her. She wished she knew the answer but was too afraid to ask. He had no close family it seemed for he had not invited anyone else to the wedding ceremony except his nearest neighbours the Wilsons.

When Arthur arrived annoyingly early a short time later, Anne was forced to hurriedly remove the wedding dress unaided and spread it carefully out on the bed for Ma to finish.

Meanwhile the older woman ushered her future son-in-law into the tiny thinly-furnished parlour off the kitchen and prodded the few resilient coals back into life broadcasting a veil of tepid warmth into the room.

Anne boiled the kettle, stewed a pot of tea and spread Ma's still-warm scones with a thin smothering of precious butter. Grudgingly, she carried in the tea tray and served their drinks while Ma sat respectfully distant in a corner of the room removed from the fire.

Anne sat poised tensely on the edge of the worn sofa sipping her hot drink, willing Arthur to offer any terse conversation other than the state of his farming.

Watching him with irritation as he slurped his tea in large gulps, Anne wondered if he intended to wear the same dark suit to their wedding. He'd worn it at Mary's funeral, she recalled, and on every one of his few visits since.

'Vicar's coming at eleven the day,' he muttered, looking not at Anne but into the fire.

She nodded politely, making no comment, only thinking that the seven days until the ceremony was too soon. She had been appalled to learn that Elizabeth's dear Edward was obliged to conduct their nuptials. She had begged Ma for any other clergyman to officiate but Frances Gray would have none of it and the usually docile woman of the house had remained adamant and proud to engage the assistant curate for the service.

Anne felt embarrassed of her hasty marriage to a recent widower, and didn't want any stigma to settle about Elizabeth's family. Judging by their present close association, it was likely Edward was to become her brother-in-law in the future. Elizabeth and Edward had such a promising happy life together, Anne didn't want to harm it in any way

At least Edward would be one more friendly face around her on their imminent wedding day.

'Would you like another scone, Mr. Westcott?' Anne held the plate out toward him, still uncomfortable with his previous insistence that she address him by his Christian name.

He grabbed one and ate it.

'More tea?'

He nodded curtly and she refilled his cup. She sensed him staring at her as she poured. She found his habit of constant leering unsettling, with those fleshy lips pulled into a watery smile. If he noticed her mood less friendly since their formal betrothal, he gave no indication. Anne was daily remorseful in giving everyone the wrong impression of her interest in the man and expected she would pay for her blunder for the rest of her life.

For her wedding day in early May, Anne was grateful the weather chose to improve slightly from the cold weather and gale force squalls that had been sweeping across the country in February and early spring, now bringing days of calmer air and a weak watery sun. She hoped it was a positive omen.

The pony and trap borrowed for the day from a kindly neighbour rumbled closer to Combe Hill, Anne seated between her parents, a shawl wrapped about her shoulders to protect her precious dress and provide extra warmth. A small bag of clothes and negligible personal possessions sat at her feet. Her three siblings, washed and smartly dressed in their best clothes, walked alongside.

When Arthur's farm came into view, Anne's heart sank even further. She wouldn't have minded leaving home if it was to a more warm-hearted man. Her new house was large and comfortable by most people's standards hereabouts with a slate roof in good repair, whitewashed stone walls and a grid of small panes on the upper and lower windows.

Some hundreds of surrounding acres belonged to the property. Anne admired the rows of freshly turned red soil as their small party slowly trundled past. She prayed that all would turn out well here in her new life as Arthur Westcott's second wife for it was too late now for events to turn around. Her future was sealed.

William Gray proudly escorted his oldest daughter from the trap and waited with her in the small front porch while Elizabeth and her Ma brought in the baskets of food and placed them on the large kitchen table pushed back against one wall to allow more room for the simple ceremony.

Then Pa importantly walked the bride inside and placed Anne's hand on top of Arthur's who stood with Edward before a small table profuse with a thick bunch of wildflowers, freshly picked. Yellow primroses, buttercups, wild hyacinth and a mass of sweet scented bluebells.

Anne smiled at the small touch of brightness in the otherwise serious mood in the room and inhaled a deep breath of their perfume to see her through the coming ordeal and help forget the feel of Arthur's rough hair skin against her own. For she could contemplate the day's proceedings in no other way.

Anne turned aside to see Elizabeth smiling in her direction then realised, sadly, that perhaps it was for Edward. Knowing her sister had brushed her hair endlessly until it shone sleekly and framed her sweet pale face. Any admired, but especially Edward, would be unable to resist her innocent charm.

Anne pooled all of her happy memories in her mind as Edward's deep voice droned on through the rote service. It sustained her until the moment came to repeat her vows and hear Arthur beside her pledge the same.

To her surprise, for she had expected nothing, he produced a thin gold ring and slid it onto her finger, the only piece of jewellery she was ever likely to own. He must have guessed at her size for it only just fit. Even as she admired its golden gleam in the dim room, she realised as much as their words, this gesture officially sealed her marriage in the eyes of the church, all present and the world.

A deep weight settled over her compounded by Arthur lurching forward to roughly grasp her shoulders to give her a cold wet kiss. Anne bore the minor assault with grace and a forced smile, putting on a brave front for the family who so desperately needed this loveless match although it sacrificed their daughter's happiness. For a brief moment, Anne felt that all light had just gone out in her life.

After restrained congratulations from her Ma and a hearty blustery handshake for the groom by her Pa, subdued celebrations were underway.

Emmy delighted at everything connected with the long excursion from home, being allowed to dress up in her best on a weekday and, now, more food than she had ever seen on one table at any one time, enjoying it all in the happy ignorance of childhood.

For a short prudent time, Elizabeth and Edward gravitated coyly together in one corner of the room near the fire. As she watched and envied them, Arthur's farm lad, Stephen, approached. He was tall and wiry but obviously strong or Arthur would undoubtedly not have employed him.

'Mrs. Westcott. Congratulations.' He kept looking at her hands. Anne thought it because he was shy but there seemed to be something else on his mind and she wondered if he was uncomfortable that she was a new mistress of the house so soon after Mary's death.

'Stephen. I'm looking forward to your company here and cooking for you.'

'I'll eat whatever you prepare, Ma'am.'

'Please,' she urged, smiling. 'Call me Anne.'

'Oh, no, Ma'am. Mr. Westcott won't have it. He don't like it.' He looked over his shoulder to where his employer and her Pa had moved on from cider and were freely imbibing of spirits.

'I see. Of course.' He seemed anxious to leave and started to move away. 'I'll see you in the morn, then?'

'Aye. Daybreak.'

Anne heaved a long sigh. She should have known she would be expected to be up so early. She and Elizabeth had always hugged the covers in the bed they shared back home and rarely moved until Ma bustled in each morning to stir them awake. Anne was apprehensive at the prospect of a new husband and master who she suspected to be hardly as lenient as Ma and Pa. It would take time to learn what Arthur would require of her.

Stephen had barely left her side when a local couple from further along the valley, the only guests of Arthur's as far as Anne could see, introduced themselves.

'John and Harriet Wilson,' the plump haughty wife spoke for them, her silent husband half hidden behind her. 'That's our daughter, Susan.' She indicated a pretty girl of her own age with wheat-coloured hair caught up in curls. 'You'll be well provided for here.'

Harriett wasn't telling her something she didn't already know. Anne looked about her, realising well enough that her surroundings were far more comfortable than Ma and Pa's cottage. The kitchen alone where they were all gathered was twice the size of the one at Bridge Farm, as was the fireplace where she would cook. And there was a lovely long wooden settle with cushions beneath the window.

'Arthur's a good catch, to be sure. Bit of a surprise when he married again so soon. We didn't realise he knew someone well enough from further out the valley.'

In her defence, Anne said, 'I paid a respectful call on him after Mary died as I'm sure you did, too.'

Harriett pushed back her shoulders and folded her hands piously in front of her. 'We heard. Arthur's always been fond of our Susan, he has,' she prattled on importantly. 'Known each other all their lives, they have. Have a chat to our Susan.

She knows what Arthur likes. She can always bring a smile to his face.'

Anne was amazed to hear it but her new neighbour seemed to be telling the truth for the girl in question was doing so now. As the Wilson's went in search of more food, Anne took particular notice of Arthur and Susan's behaviour toward each other. She appeared sweetly infatuated with him, hovering nearby, offering him more food or another glass of drink. There was an air of confidence and familiarity in her manner around him.

Puzzling over the sight, Anne knew she wasn't jealous of their obvious friendship but merely mystified why he hadn't chosen a girl he already knew and, judging by his faint guarded returning smile when she attended him, clearly appeared to prefer.

Richard must have sensed her need for reassuring company but she was so focused on Susan and Arthur she was unaware he had come to stand beside her until he touched her elbow and whispered in her ear, 'A right neighbourly lass there.'

Anne tilted her head aside to smile warmly at him. 'She's being very helpful. She'd make any house a happy place.'

'Maybe.' His brows furrowed he grew pensive. 'But she's worth watching, that one, for all the wrong reasons.'

'Didn't I see you sitting with her on the window bench before?' Anne teased.

'Aye, and listened to her silly twittering the whole time. Don't hurt to know your enemies.'

'Oh dear,' Anne said wryly, 'Harriet gave me the impression she was perfect in every way and the apple of her mother's eye.'

'She's clearly blind in both then.'

Brother and sister shared a loud spontaneous laugh, drawing attention to them.

As they sobered, embarrassed, Richard said, 'You're a married woman now. Wouldn't do to look too happy, eh?

Especially being married to Arthur.'

For the first time since Ma and Pa had decided on this marriage for her, Anne found she could laugh at her situation. She realised reality would soon take over but, for this one light sunny moment, she treasured her brother's efforts to raise her spirits by letting her know he understood her new circumstances.

Anne impulsively hugged him and said urgently, 'I shall miss you all terrible dearly, Richard.'

'Oh, Arthur will let you off the chain, surely,' Richard teased. 'And we'll come visit.'

'Promise?' She clutched at the scrap of hope as though she had nothing else to look forward to in her life. There might be an occasional happy time ahead but she was in no doubt they would be rare and buried deep, and she must search hard to find small joys to make her life worthwhile. Richard's vow gave her courage.

By mid-afternoon when the sun lowered early behind the surrounding hills and daylight grew dim, the guests gradually assembled themselves to leave. At Arthur's bidding, Anne noticed Stephen disappear to feed penned stock before nightfall.

Anne's family gathered for their last lingering farewells, even Ma hugging her newly-married daughter close before climbing into the trap and taking the reins since Pa was too drunk to manage. Emmy nestled between them, yawning. Richard and Elizabeth trailed behind as the trap rattled from the yard, her sister's departing backward glances only for Edward.

The vicar pressed her hands in his, wished them well and mounted his horse, waving a cheery goodbye so that only the Wilson family remained.

Susan made the first move, taking Arthur's hands and drawing herself close to him in front of everyone. 'I shall call on you as always, Arthur.' Anne sensed an unspoken message in her comment but perhaps the long day and her growing edginess at the swiftly approaching wedding night had muddled her perception.

'Susan.' He nodded curtly in response as she stepped back.

With sharp eyes and bobbing a mocking curtsy, she said to Anne, 'Mrs. Westcott.'

The two young women warily took each other's measure. In the moment of a slashing glare of mistrust she was given by the other girl, Anne knew they might be neighbours but would never be anything more.

'Thank you for coming.'

Isolated here, she would have appreciated a genuine friend but, since Harriett was equally frosty, Anne decided she would have to be desperate before she would visit them or seek their help.

Harriett embraced Arthur as though he was a long lost son and Anne wondered how often she would be forced to endure their company.

'Arthur.' John Wilson donned his hat and turned toward their waiting horse and cart, clearly making an unfriendly departure. 'Harriett. Susan,' he barked, surprising Anne that this meek little man should show any sign of backbone with his womenfolk. Plainly of a different mind toward Arthur, for whatever reason. There was so much she didn't know and had yet to learn.

Anne darted a quick side glance at the stranger beside her who was now her husband to gauge his mood and response to John's curt rebuff.

She had hardly spoken to him nor taken particular notice of his behaviour since the ceremony but he swayed and could barely stand straight. He and Pa had obviously taken excess drink.

Reluctantly, Anne slipped her arm through his for physical support, not show, but the Wilson women clearly misunderstood what to them perhaps appeared a possessive gesture and glared, each giving a polite controlled nod as John shook the reins and their cart rumbled away.

Anne helped Arthur inside and looked around the kitchen in its disarray of food and dishes. To keep occupied and because she wasn't sure what to do next, she suggested, 'I should be tidying up here-'

'No. Upstairs,' he snapped.

Anne swallowed back her surprise that in his present tipsy state, he should utter such a crisp clear command, his mind clearly and firmly focused it seemed on spousal union.

'Of course.' She grabbed her carpetbag and waited for his direction.

'Follow me.'

She trailed her husband up the short narrow flight of stairs to the small bedroom they would share. She had seen it only once before on her visit with Ma and Elizabeth after her betrothal. Now she saw it in a much more functional light where she would come to know what married couples shared.

Arthur drew the curtains across the narrow window in the side wall and perched on one side of the bed, a grander wrought iron affair then her parents' box bed. This was higher with a small table and candlesticks on either side, and a tall narrow clothes cupboard on what was apparently going to be her side of the bed.

Annie tried not to stare at how swiftly, despite his intoxication, Arthur stripped off his suit and flung it over the bed end, then removed his undergarments. In the flickering candlelight, she could see his body was strong and fit from outdoor work. A pity his nature was so sour for he might then be a more appealing human being.

He wasn't ugly, far from it. Still handsome for his age, face weathered, grey eyes cool. When he blew out his candle and flopped naked into the bed with a grunt, to her embarrassment, Anne became the focus of his attention in the room.

She struggled with buttons and hooks down the side of her dress and would have appreciated Arthur's help but dared not ask. When she finally managed to remove it, she carefully draped it over the bed end until morning, not wanting to keep him waiting.

She blew out her candle too and made to slip into bed beside him when he growled, 'No clothes,' and realised he meant her to completely undress.

'It's right cold, Arthur.'

When he said impatiently, 'Do as you're told, woman,' her Pa's words rang in her ears, returning to haunt her. If you do as you're told, you'll be fine. Is this what he had meant? She hardly had a choice.

Slipping out into the chill room again, Anne took off her remaining clothes and crawled demurely beneath the covers, shivering at the cold bed linen against her warm skin. No-one, not even Elizabeth, had ever seen her unclothed before. Not that Arthur would see her in the dark and she felt grateful for the tiny mercy.

She had barely settled when he reached out for her and rolled close, pummelling her breasts, moaning and kissing them. Anne lay still in shock, feeling annoyed at his eagerness and sore when he sucked and bit her nipples.

He heaved himself on top of her and pressed a cold kiss on her mouth to which she could not respond and endured with alarm and dislike. He started rubbing his body against her and, after breathing heavily for some time and blowing his alcoholic breath in her face, he roughly pushed her legs apart beneath him with his hands and tried to force himself inside her. But all she felt was his awkward fumbling and soft body. Despite his efforts, nothing of any consequence seemed to happen.

At last, he grew still, cursed and slid aside. Anne didn't move, unsure what to do, listening to his breathing.

'Arthur?' she whispered after a while. When there was no response, she realised he was asleep. Grateful for a reprieve, at least for now, she scrambled from bed and groped about in the still-packed bag until she found a warm nightgown to cover her chilled and trembling body.

Not sure when she would be expected to perform her wifely duty again, Anne fell into an exhausted and troubled sleep.

CHAPTER 3

Next morning, Anne awoke by being roughly shaken. 'Get up, woman.'

Tired and still half asleep in the dark, she roused herself to see Arthur dressing by candlelight.

'Need the fire lit and breakfast for me and the boy. We'll be back within the hour.'

His heavy footsteps receded downstairs. Anne quickly poured freezing water from the ewer into the basin and washed. She ran downstairs to get warm, her first priority to get the fire going. When the kindling had caught, she added logs to the growing flames. She found half a loaf of yesterday's bread in the larder. It might do but she would need to bake more this morning. She knew Arthur kept pigs for lard and bacon, and poultry for eggs. And there were always rabbits.

From the small-paned kitchen window as Anne moved between larder, table and fireside, she saw the men in the yard feeding the pigs and poultry. When Stephen brought in eggs and another armful of chopped wood for the fire, he barely acknowledged her and was gone before she could hardly speak. It seemed everyone on this farm lived in fear of its master.

Anne struggled to keep the fire going with enough heat to cook the breakfast. With a sinking heart, she knew her first prepared meal would be late. Everything was to hand but in her first time finding dishes and food, hurrying so as not to anger Arthur, it seemed she was slower and took longer than she ought, so breakfast was only half ready when the men returned.

With dismay, Anne watched Arthur stride across the yard toward the house, two large dogs at his heels.

She hadn't noticed them before. Perhaps he kept them tied up away from the house or they had been out in the fields with Stephen working the sheep.

As Arthur opened the back door, he bellowed to the panting dogs, 'Sit.' Tramping into the kitchen, he glowered at the half-cooked meal.

Anne wiped her hands nervously down the apron she wore over the plain dress she had donned for her working day. 'Breakfast's not quite ready, Arthur. I'm still finding my way,' she smiled weakly.

'We can't wait, woman. There's work to be done. We'll eat what's ready.'

The lad hovered behind his master in the doorway with a bucket of milk. Anne took it from him and set it in the larder.

'Good morning, Stephen,' Annie greeted him warmly, smiling, grateful for other company besides Arthur. 'Come in and sit down.'

The porridge was still watery and uncooked so Anne served up thick slices of bread and cheese with a few strips of cooked bacon. Thankfully the kettle had finally boiled so she could serve up big cups of tea.

Arthur scoffed it all down without one word or glance at either of the other two seated at the table, nor any word of thanks. 'Going to check the bullocks.' Arthur stood, slurping his last mouthful of tea, his chair scraping on the floor.

As he left, Anne observed his irritation that she had not managed a decent breakfast sooner.

She would be glad of a few hours to herself. On the kitchen table, she kneaded dough for fresh loaves of bread and set them to rise while she made potato pasties for the men's lunches and a stew to simmer for dinner. She caught an occasional glimpse of Stephen about the yard but was basically alone. Later in the morning, Anne took the chance to step outdoors and wander around the house to see what vegetables were being grown, pleased to find a small garden of cales, potatoes and onions.

She realised her life here might be more comfortable than Bridge Farm but grew despondent that this existence would be all she might ever know. Her normally bright spirits dampened at the thought. For all her parents' poverty, there was companionship and warmth among her family. Here, it was quite certain she would get none.

When the men returned for their evening meal, the familiar heavy tension among the three of them persisted throughout supper. No one spoke. Even after only a day in her new life and well aware of her husband's dour and moody nature, Anne wisely held her tongue from chatter, as much as she yearned for the conversation. She wondered if every day and every meal would be like this for Arthur had seemed happy to converse at length with Susan Wilson yesterday. Perhaps when she knew him better, things would improve.

Like a servant, Anne dished up the meal, poured a pot of tea and sliced a thick piece of wedding cake. It would have been a rare treat in her parents' home.

As soon as he had finished eating and slurped up the dregs of his tea, Arthur snapped, 'Go now, boy.'

Stephen mumbled, 'Goodnight,' rose and quietly left the house.

Arthur sank into his chair by the fire, sculling cider, smoking and saying nothing as Anne scrubbed the dishes in a basin on the kitchen table, physically and emotionally exhausted from rising early and the long day of coping with her new marriage situation and duties.

What kind of life could they have together if they never spoke? She would shrivel and die without someone to talk to.

Anne intended to do some minor preparations and be ahead for the next morning but, although it was still early evening, Arthur checked his pocket watch and said, 'Upstairs, woman.'

Uneasy about her second night sleeping with her new husband, Anne reluctantly followed him upstairs once more.

He lashed out with his belt as he removed it from his trousers and caught her with a stinging bite across a bare shoulder and back. Not once but twice.

Anne cried out in pain. 'What was that for?' she whispered furiously, glaring at him across the bed.

'Bein' no proper breakfast. Mind you do better tomorrow.'

'Is that all?'

'Mind your tongue, woman,' he bellowed. 'And I'll not have you speakin' to me worker.'

'Stephen?' Anne contemplated the repercussions. 'Not at all?' When he didn't answer, she insisted, 'Why not?'

'I forbid it, is all,' Arthur snarled.

It appeared her husband wanted her to have no conversation with anyone, including his taciturn self.

As she silently and completely undressed, Anne slowly began to understand the depth of his sour temperament. It ran beyond domination to cruelty. As poor as her parents had been and, despite the fact they had disobeyed her Ma's family and eloped to marry, their marriage, although a constant economic struggle to survive, had been quietly loving and never once violent. Pa might be useless at farming but he had never raised a hand in anger to his wife nor to discipline his children.

Anne looked with growing rebellious hatred toward her husband, feeling no enmity for her parents' insistence on this marriage since they could have had no idea of the true extent of Arthur Westcott's personality.

Despite all threats, Anne's dignity emerged. She might come from cottager stock and a lower social scale than the owner of Combe Hill but she would not abide ill treatment.

She could see danger ahead and, in her innocence, determined she would battle this man for the right to decency and respect. A perilous stance to take since he was a lean wiry man and far stronger than she.

In her own mind, she knew she had done nothing seriously wrong and had tried her hardest all day except for a few minor blunders as she found her way.

Anne favoured her aching shoulder as she wearily struggled into bed. Tonight, sober, Arthur pounced on her the second her body slid in beside him. She turned away, rejecting his kiss and lay impassive beneath him. He might have the right to her body but he would never have her love or respect.

Immediately, Anne noticed the difference from the previous night. His body was large and hard and he urgently thrust inside her, causing a sharp pain. She squeezed her eyes shut and counted to distract herself as he pushed in and out of her hard and fast, gasping and grunting, until he tensed up and stilled, slumping down with his full weight upon her.

Finally, he moved away, leaving Anne to curl up into a ball with a dampness between her legs, feeling bleak and used.

In the night, Anne woke to feel Arthur taking her body again from behind as she slept. She started counting again and turned her face into the pillow to muffle her anguish and dry her tears until it was over.

In the morning, angry at his brutish coldness, she cursed her weakness and vowed never to cry again.

In the following days, that became unendurable weeks, Anne's previous carefree nature soon became overwhelmed by her dismal situation. From a combination of instinct and fear, she made sure she rose before Arthur. A full breakfast was always ready on time but conversation between the three people on the farm virtually non-existent.

Anne set herself a diligent routine of work to keep her hands busy and allow no idle moments for contemplation. She scoured the house clean in every corner, rigorously washed the weekly laundry, and cooked and baked to a worthy standard. Any normal person would have no cause for complaint but Arthur constantly found fault. At which times, Anne felt the lash of his belt on her body or welt of his hard broad hand across her face, but always at night in the privacy of their bedroom.

Many a morning, Anne was aware of Stephen's covert gaze upon her dark sad eyes and bruises. If a rare and brief opportunity arose when Arthur was busy eating and did not see, the lad favoured Anne with a weak understanding smile.

It had long since occurred to her that this must have been what Mary Westcott's life was like, too, and her heart ached for the dead woman and her baby. Cruel though it seemed, perhaps it was a blessing, for no one should have to endure this misery.

Anne realised that Stephen must have witnessed Anne's mistreatment, too. Far from accepting her situation, a scheme was forming in the back of her mind and she kept alert for any small chance to speak to the boy. Her only hope lay in devising a plan to get away from Combe Hill. Permanently. For she refused to continue leading this sham of a marriage and suffering Arthur's increasingly violent abuse.

Extra income on the farm was derived from the purchase of thin bullocks, feeding them up on the lush valley meadows and selling them fat. Soon, apparently, from overhearing a brief terse exchange between Arthur and Stephen, another herd was to be driven to market.

Expectant, and desperate to leave the farm even for a few hours to see her Ma and Elizabeth, and making sure Stephen was still present and a witness after the evening meal, Anne cautiously ventured, 'May I ask you something, Arthur?'

He scowled. 'What is it, woman?'

'While hanging out the washing this morning, I couldn't help but overhear you and Stephen talking in the yard. I didn't mean to listen,' she quickly assured him. 'But you were talking loud and I did think, just this once of course, I might ride along with you as far as Bridge Farm and visit my parents while you're at the market.'

'No.'

Anne swallowed hard and braced herself to persist. 'I'd

not expect you to go out of your way, of course. I could easily walk from the main road down the lane to the cottage.'

'I said no.'

'Are you forbidding me always or just this time?' Anne bravely questioned.

Stephen's dark eyes doubled in amazement that she would dare risk challenging him.

'Did you not hear me, woman?' Arthur turned to his workman and growled, 'Leave, boy.'

Anne knew she had tested his wrath but didn't regret using the lad as a temporary foil for Arthur could, and probably would, still beat her. But she had desperately wanted to try. She longed for the safety and harmony of anywhere but here. If she ran way, Arthur would scour the county to find her and haul her back. Somehow, she must be able to leave the farm sometimes but always with his knowledge and permission.

Stephen had barely closed the back door and his boot steps grown fainter across the yard returning to his loft sleeping quarters in the stable, when Arthur rounded on his wife.

'Can you not obey, woman?' he roared, pushing back his chair at the table and stepping closer to the fire. He took up the poker, set it to his pipe and shook it at her. 'Why can't women obey? You're no better than Mary.'

He stopped short, glowering, as though realising he had revealed too much.

'I'm sure she tried hard to please you. As I am,' Anne declared quietly. 'And I don't see the harm in going,' she dared to argue and turn her back on him to begin clearing away the supper dishes. 'I've done all my work and I've not seen anyone for weeks.'

She'd baked a tender joint of lamb from a recent kill hoping to set him in a better mood for her request. But she should have known better. It was clear but discouraging that Arthur Westcott was a selfish stubborn man and would never agree.

'Enough, woman. Quiet.'

Arthur dropped into his fireside chair and stared into the embers, as always frowning and saying nothing. Although their evenings alone together in silence were tense, Anne learned to blank her mind and daydream as she mended or folded clothes or set dough to rise on the hearth for the morning's bread, until Arthur gruffly announced it was time to turn in for another night. At which time, Anne wisely knew to follow.

More mindful now of marital details, she daily prayed not to conceive his child. She would cherish the baby but not Arthur being the father. So it was with huge merciful relief she noticed her monthly bleeding again, triggering an urgency within her to leave this prison existence. Somehow she must ensure Arthur never touched her again.

That night, when he turned to her again, she tensed. 'Not tonight, Arthur. Please,' she begged. 'I'm still very sore.'

Red with fury, he hissed, 'You're my wife. It's your duty,' and roughly grabbed her.

'I know,' Anne struggled against his greater strength, holding him back, 'but it's my woman's time, too,' she explained, trying to sound suitably meek and hoping he restrained his need at least for a night or two. When he demanded proof, Anne showed him.

'Blast you, woman,' he roared, angered by the evidence, pushing her away from him. She covered herself again in grateful disbelief that he should concede.

Two days later, not having touched her since, Arthur departed early on horseback herding fattened cattle to the Friday market in Tavistock, leaving terse instructions with Stephen at breakfast to check the sheep flocks in the upper meadows.

To her relief, as the lumbering mob departed down the laneway toward the main road, Anne noticed the dogs leaving too. The two snarling unchained animals were usually a deterrent for Anne to remain within the confines of the house yard and vegetable garden beyond, and not stray far.

As well, as though in affinity with her bubbling pleasure, the late spring day was also blessed by a weak sun breaking through a low drift of early morning cloud, shedding warmth and brightness on all below as Anne stood dutifully at the kitchen door and happily watched her husband go.

Stephen left for the fields soon after and Anne carefully observed Arthur's disappearing progress, he and the herd growing ever smaller and further away.

Later, in the guise of taking Stephen lunch should she be discovered by anyone, neighbour or stranger alike who might report back to Arthur, she packed a basket of food and set off. She followed the gravelly lane for a time beside the fields of oats and barley growing higher every day. The low hedges of hawthorn used to keep the stock from wandering up onto the foothills and tor were thick with the heady scent of their May blossom.

Anne tilted her face to the sun, feeling the brush of a gentle breeze across her cheeks, striding out and breathing deeply of the warm and calming air.

After a while, when the lane ended, she climbed over a gate, lifted her skirts and trudged higher across the grassy meadows. She shielded her eyes and squinted ahead, looking for the flocks of long-woolled sheep for, when she found them, she would also find Stephen.

Soon, she saw him ahead, his back to her, tending a lamb. Anne called out as she approached. His head snapped around at the sound of her voice and she waved, returning his smile.

'You're takin' a chance comin' out here even with Mr. Westcott gone,' he warned when she reached him.

'I couldn't resist.' Anne paused to catch her breath. 'I've not been away from the house in weeks.' She eyed the thin young boy. 'And we need to talk.'

Stephen turned away, caught and checked another lamb, its mother bleating nearby.

Seeing him clearly reluctant, Anne said brightly, 'I'll wait over by the hedge until you're ready. You must be hungry soon?'

Knowing the gentle lad, he'd not ignore her for long. It might take a few minutes for him to get used to her suddenly appearing up here. She sat patiently on the lush grass, absently plucking blades, her knees raised beneath her skirt, her eyes eagerly taking in the lazy spring scene of green fields, hills and sheep, waiting for Stephen to join her.

When he eventually did so, he stretched out beside her on the thick grass and hungrily devoured the vegetable pasties, cheese and cider she'd brought along. Anne left him alone for a while until he was almost finished and she could curb her curiosity no longer.

'I'll not keep you long from your work, Stephen,' she began cautiously. 'But I need to ask you something and for you not to be afraid and tell me the truth. Promise me that?' Her voice and gaze pleaded with him.

He eyed her in wary alarm and Anne feared he might leap up and bolt away across the meadow. She needed him to stay long enough to give her the information and proof she needed. In recent days, an alarming suspicion had entered her head.

'Did Arthur beat Mary, too?' she asked gently.

He looked down at the ground and took another mouthful of food. She noticed it went around in his mouth and he seemed to have trouble swallowing. Eventually, reluctantly, he nodded.

'Even when she was with child?'

He nodded again.

'And on the night she died?' Anne caught a tense breath, her question barely a whisper.

His bleak returning stare told her all she needed to know. She groaned and her body heaved with heartbreak for the mother and her baby. Even more for the hidden tragic secret Stephen had been forced to keep all this time.

'Can you tell me what happened?' she urged softly. When he didn't respond, she said, 'I swear I'll not tell a soul but I need to know.'

'They was fightin', as always,' he began hesitantly. 'Mary was a tiny little thing but she was a great one for arguin' and standin' up to Mr. Westcott. You wouldn't think.' He managed a weak grin but soon grew serious again. 'I'm not allowed inside the house unless Mr. Westcott asks me but I could hear Mary callin' out and I couldn't ignore her, could I?'

Anne heard the anguish in his voice. 'Oh, no, no. Of course not.' She rested a comforting hand on his arm. 'Why was she calling out? Was the baby coming? Was she in distress?'

'She was in distress, all right,' Stephen muttered and his mouth set into a thin determined line. He cast her a quick dark glance. 'But not from the baby. I knew her quick tongue would end her up in trouble. I'm surprised she lasted so long.' Stephen abruptly stopped and stared at his new mistress, fear in his eyes. 'I think Mr. Westcott likes his women that way,' he said sadly. 'Gives him more excuse to hit 'em.'

'What happened?' Anne whispered, almost afraid to know.

'When I got closer to the house, I peered through the window first to see what was doin'. Being I wasn't allowed inside,' he explained. 'They were shoutin' and strugglin'. Mary got free and was almost to the top of the stairs when he reached her and pushed her down.'

Stephen closed his eyes and put a hand across his forehead.

'You don't have to go on. I can guess.'

Anne saw his Adam's apple move as he swallowed hard and forced himself to continue. 'Mary rolled over and over, screaming out in pain the whole time. At the bottom, she just lay still and didn't move. Mr. Westcott just looked down at her, sneering, and didn't make a move to help.'

Stephen looked at Anne pleadingly as if seeking her

forgiveness. 'I went in. I had to go in. I couldn't leave her.'

'Any kind hearted person would have done the same, Stephen. You did the right thing.'

'I'm not so sure. It didn't save her anyway. Mr. Westcott was right angry to see me comin' through the door. I reckon he guessed I'd seen or heard something I shouldn't.'

'What did you do?'

He shrugged, looking miserable as he recalled the remaining events of the night. 'I just asked if I could help. He made me leave her. Said not to touch her. That she was gone already. When I asked what happened, he said she fell down the stairs. I'd seen everythin' so I knew he was lying. Thing is, he looked really sad about it but not for Mary's sake, I shouldn't wonder. He threatened me and told me to keep my mouth shut. When I asked him why if it was only an accident, he clipped me with a right heavy thump on the ears and told me I'd end up the same if I didn't do as I was told.'

Anne shook her head in horror as Stephen shook with the distress of remembering and the fear he must have known that night.

'What happened next?' she gently prompted.

'I offered to go get the doctor but Mr. Westcott made me stay while he went into Tavistock for Doctor Harness. I was left sittin' all alone for hours in the house with Mary's body lying dead still on the floor. Blid everywhere. It was his way of knowin' where I was.'

Anne nodded in understanding. 'Yes, I've learned the hard way, too, that Arthur's a devious man.'

'When they arrived back at the house, the Doctor could clearly see she was dead and the baby too. All he did was examine her and shake his head. Mr. Westcott,' Stephen said sourly as though he'd eaten bitter food, 'told the doctor the bruises were from the fall. He made me back up his story. I was that sick with meself being as how I lied to keep me job when I should have known better and stood up to him. If I tell the truth now,' he turned to look at her, 'no one will believe me. I'm just a farm labourer. They'd think I was just causin' trouble. And Westcott would deny it.'

'Why did you stay on?'

Stephen hung his head. 'I need my wages to help my family. Me Dad's dead and me Ma needs every penny I can give her to help with my six brothers and sisters. I'm the oldest, so it's up to me, you see?'

'I understand,' Anne nodded, casting a blank gaze off into the distance, reflecting on her own similar forced situation of leaving home too and marrying to help her family and make it easier for them to survive. Surely Stephen craved escape like her, too?

'The ring you're wearin',' he said beside her suddenly. 'It was Mary's.'

Anne gasped, 'No!' looking down at it on her hand, appalled to think it had been removed from the dead woman's finger.

'Promise me you won't tell a soul what I just told you?' Stephen pleaded urgently.

'Never,' Anne breathed. 'Like you said, it's his word against ours. They'd believe a successful yeoman farmer like Arthur Westcott over us.'

'You have to leave, Ma'am,' Stephen appealed earnestly.

'I plan to but I needed more information first. I had my suspicions which is why I took the first opportunity I could to speak to you. We'll keep each other's secrets for now,' she said in understanding, adding sadly, 'Perhaps the truth can be told one day.'

Stephen nodded so fiercely Anne thought his head might fall from his shoulders. 'Mr. Westcott deserves whatever comes to him.'

The shared confidence heartened them both that they were not alone in this and could weather whatever lay ahead.

CHAPTER 4

With measured trepidation but a much lighter heart, Anne packed up her basket and left Stephen in the meadow, striding downhill and back along the narrow hedged lanes towards Combe Hill.

As she trudged the final distance and entered the house yard around the corner of the barn, her heart jolted with surprise to see Susan Wilson seated demurely in a cart. For a moment, she feared it was Arthur returned early but the woman's presence was almost as bad for the spiteful female was sure to tell Arthur of her absence, raising questions she would somehow need to answer.

'Miss Wilson.' Anne stepped forward forcing a cordial smile. 'How lovely to receive a visit from you.'

She felt positively dowdy against her well-dressed young neighbour, her blue dress picking up the colour of her eyes, the outfit tight over her ample bodice. Anne was amused why she wore her Sunday best on a casual farm visit. She would have thought a simple day dress and shawl more sensible. Her curly blonde hair was tucked up neatly beneath a fetching wide brimmed sunhat tied under her chin with matching blue ribbon.

Susan glanced behind Anne. 'Arthur is not with you?'

'No.'

Susan heaved an impatient sigh. 'Where is he, then?'

'At Tavistock market selling cattle. He won't return until late if you were hoping to see him.'

She looked peeved and scowled, her gaze narrowing into suspicion. 'Where have you been?'

'Taking lunch out to our workman.'

Susan's eyes narrowed and she frowned. 'He doesn't take it with him?'

'He forgot today,' Anne replied lightly, afraid now that word of her meeting out in the field with Stephen would get back to her husband.

'Do you think that's wise with Arthur away?'

'I wouldn't want the boy to starve,' she replied curtly, a fact among many untruths she felt forced to tell during the conversation.

'Of course not but with you and Stephen alone out there, you can see how it might look.'

'Stephen's a boy, a labourer.' Anne gritted her teeth. 'I'm a married woman. I visited him in an open field in daylight. I would be disappointed to hear any suggestion that I would be unfaithful to my husband,' she said piously, dipping her head in pretended embarrassment at the mention of such a personal subject.

'I've always watched out for Arthur's interests,' Susan explained.

'I'm sure he appreciates your neighbourly concern but we both know that Arthur's quite able to do that for himself. Besides,' Anne felt spite rising within her and made no effort to restrain her tongue. 'I'm his wife now and I'm taking care of him so there's no need to feel it's your responsibility anymore,' she pointed out crisply.

Anne's deliberately unkind retort hit its mark for Susan's lips thinned in displeasure. All the same, Anne took no pleasure in stretching the truth but determined not to let this irritating woman get the better of her.

Detaching herself from the simmering annoyance, Anne forced herself to remember her manners and asked sweetly, 'Would you care to come inside for a cup of tea?'

'Of course,' Susan snapped, bunching up her full skirts and stepping carefully down from the cart. 'I haven't driven all this way for nothing.'

It seemed her efforts to impress Arthur by dressing smartly had been wasted and Anne smiled to herself as she moved inside, pitying the woman's misplaced affections for surely if Arthur had preferred her, he would have married Susan Wilson instead. Now that she knew what he was really like, she wished he had.

Susan followed her indoors. As Anne stoked the fire and swung the kettle over the growing flames to boil, her guest slowly removed her gloves and circled the kitchen. 'Arthur prefers his house tidy and efficient. In time, you'll come to learn what he likes.' Her sharp eyes absorbed everything. 'I'm sure you'll improve. Eventually.'

Speechless and livid, Anne could only smile weakly despite the cruel slur, somehow sensing a hidden meaning behind her comment. She smouldered with rage because her house gleamed and a pot of thick vegetable soup simmered in its pot over the fire, its spices wafting tantalisingly across the kitchen, ready for Arthur's supper the moment he returned.

She let her caller chatter on, hardly listening to the local gossip she relayed while Anne set out the cups on the kitchen table. She barely endured the tedious visit, suspecting Susan deliberately lingered overlong, waiting for Arthur. And for the first time, she seriously wondered why. Clearly, if he had wanted to marry the other woman he would not have chosen Anne. How would this spoilt girl have withstood Arthur's demands and the workload in the house? Presumably, she would have insisted he hire a servant.

Perhaps Susan did not even wish to be married, to Arthur or anyone, preferring to play the lady and tease?

'I must say,' Susan broke into Anne's deep thoughts as she poured the stewed tea from the pot into their cups and offered her a hard oat biscuit made this morning for the men's lunches, 'I'm surprised you agreed to marry Arthur. Considering.'

Anne covered her confusion over Susan's mysterious comment by stating, 'Arthur and I both understand we did not marry for love but we have come to share similar feelings for each other.' Loathing.

Anne sipped her tea, aware of a subtle and sinister change in the conversation.

'You don't know, do you? Why he married you?' Susan smirked like a cat basking sleepily in a sunny sheltered corner on a chilly day. 'I understand a respectable sum of money changed hands,' she continued, pausing to daintily nibble the edge of her biscuit, 'and undoubtedly one of Arthur's cattle today wandered away from the herd down the lane to Bridge Farm. He would have made no effort to retrieve it.' She gave a short unkind laugh. 'As I am sure they will do on future trips to market. So you see,' she grew serious and her lips curled into a sour grimace. 'Arthur paid to marry you although I'm sure he realises it was far more than you are worth.'

Anne's heart lurched in disbelief. She'd remained still throughout Susan's accusations but now in disbelief, cried out, 'You're lying.'

Susan smiled smugly. 'I see you have been kept in ignorance in an effort to spare you. Ask your parents,' she ended sharply.

'I would if I was allowed to leave Combe Hill to see them,' Anne blurted out angrily without thinking, to her immediate regret.

Susan slowly raised slender eyebrows. 'Allowed? Knowing Arthur as I do, I can hardly believe he would keep you a prisoner in your own home against your will.'

'A prison doesn't always need bars. And there may be many things you choose not to believe, Miss Wilson, but it does not make them less real,' Anne retorted sharply.

'Dear me. Barely married weeks and already dissatisfied with a far more comfortable life than you left.'

In a horrified fog, Anne barely heard Susan's further chiding remarks as she chattered on about arrangements and deals not being uncommon. Her quick mind raced with shock and disbelief that her parents had really done as Susan claimed. She knew times were hard on Bridge Farm but had they been so desperate for money or was Susan's information just mischievous interference?

Anne wanted to believe it was all lies. That her parents had not received money in a bribe, perhaps, to be rid of her. Stubbornly, she did not want to accept any of what Susan said but Pa's words returned yet again to haunt her. Do as you're told and you'll be fine. Had he known what was ahead for his daughter and still betrayed her for his own gain without giving her the slightest forewarning? Had they used her spontaneous visit to the newly widowed Arthur Westcott only as a cover for what really took place?

Anne did not begrudge them trying to better their situation but at her expense? To be traded like a chattel of no account? She felt worthless and ashamed for herself but deep relief that Elizabeth would marry into happier circumstances and Richard able to choose his own path.

How could Ma and Pa have deceived her? Although poor, they had always lived their lives on higher principles than that. She could only imagine their situation was far worse than they had revealed and their action forced out of desperation.

Perhaps they hadn't wanted her to marry Arthur but he had been persuasive and convinced them? But why would he want to marry her in preference to Susan Wilson? What did he have to gain?

Sunk deep into preoccupied thought, Anne grew aware that Susan had finished her tea and biscuit, gently setting down her cup and rising to stand over her, looking down with disdain.

With a superior look on her fresh pale face, she said, 'Please tell Arthur I called and how disappointed I am to have missed him.'

'You visit was not wasted surely? I can see it has given you much pleasure to plant suspicion around my marriage and cause trouble. Because it is clear, you only wish me ill I insist you do not bother to call on us again.' Whether Susan's allegations were true or not, Anne would never let the woman see how the gossip had distressed her.

Susan's beautiful blue eyes flashed with fire and challenge. Her narrowed gaze focused intently on Anne, perhaps realising she had met her match and her adversary would never cower. Still, a smug smile hovered over her lovely mouth.

Rudely, Anne refused to usher her guest from the house but bid her a terse goodbye from the kitchen. The troublemaker knew her way out.

Shaking with the anguish of Susan Wilson's revelations after her cart had rattled from the yard, Anne waited with nervous impatience for Arthur's return. But later, as the men sat slurping their thick soup and bread at tea, she wisely decided to keep silent and not give Arthur any hint of what she had learned today from both Stephen and Susan, although the temptation was great.

No, she must simply bide her time, stay patient and pick her moment to escape. Stay alert for the first opportunity and seize it. She couldn't even pack her small carpetbag or he would notice and suspect something afoot. Arthur's sly eyes noticed everything so she must leave with nothing. While she despaired that she would leave with not even a change of clothes or money, travelling light would help her escape.

Her chance would come and, however suddenly, she must gather the courage to grab it and flee.

For two days, with a combination of a quick tongue and pathetic but apparently effective pleading, Anne avoided her wifely duties at night but knew Arthur's patience was thin and she could not expect another reprieve.

She had anticipated punishment from him when Susan revealed her meeting with Stephen and absence from the house. Clearly, she had not yet told him or, for some ulterior reason, had decided against it. Anne was certain the hostile woman would tell him soon, placing even more urgency on leaving without delay.

On the afternoon of the third day, with Anne watchful and edgy about the house, Arthur gruffly announced he would be up on the far meadow in the foothills. Anne stilled her tongue from questioning why when she knew all the flocks were still grazing in the lower fields. Perhaps he was going up to check the feed of sweeter grasses that ripened later up there. As summer progressed, he moved the sheep higher.

Within minutes of his departure, Anne glanced from the small kitchen window and noticed Arthur striding purposefully away from the farm in the opposite direction from where he said he was going.

Suspicious, Anne was prompted to follow and see where he went. Stephen had taken the horse into Tavistock to be re-shod so there was no chance to use it to get away, her ideal plan. On foot, Arthur would soon catch up with her and drag her back.

His horrid dogs restlessly prowled the yard. Arthur deliberately kept them lean and hungry. Thinking quickly before he got too far away, Anne retrieved the meat bones she had planned to use for broth and carried them outside, calling softly to the unreliable animals. They stalked her, growling low as she led them toward the barn. She threw the meat inside and the dogs dashed in after it, fighting over the unexpected feast.

Anne swiftly pulled and latched the wide barn door shut, knowing there was no other escape and they could not follow or expose her pursuit of their master.

Feeling proud of herself, she strode determinedly across the west fields after Arthur. He was nowhere in sight but at the other side near a break in the trees she found a pathway leading into the Beech Wood and cautiously followed it, vigilant in case Arthur suddenly reappeared.

Gingerly, Anne made her way along the green leafy trail, her footsteps cushioned by the thick mulch of leaves beneath her boots. She relaxed enough to absorb her surroundings, a restful wonderland not far from the house on the edge of Arthur's acres.

She smiled with delight. Bluebells covered the ground in every direction under ancient spreading oaks and beeches, pockets of dappled sunlight splashing through the dense overhead canopy of leaves.

Her distraction soon refocused when she noticed a small hut off to the right side ahead through the trees. Half hidden by undergrowth, it was clearly uninhabited but Anne stopped to look furtively about and listen for any human sounds before she left the path to investigate.

Stepping high over wildflowers and grass, she picked her way around the exterior walls until she found a small window, frowning to hear muffled voices and sounds.

Brushing aside dust and cobwebs from the lower pane, she peered inside, gaped for a moment and almost immediately stumbled backward. Anne clamped a hand over her mouth to stifle any sound and ran.

As she regained the path and fled back through the woods toward Combe Hill, gasping with shock, her heart pounding, images of what she had seen flashed across her mind. Prim Susan Wilson seated on a low wooden table, the bodice of her dress stripped open to the waist. Arthur sucking her full white breasts. Her eyes closed, head tossed back and moaning, skirts hitched to her thighs, legs apart. Arthur between them, trousers around his ankles, rutting into her like the animal she knew him to be.

As she burst from the trees into the open meadow and sunshine, Anne took a deep breath and slowed her pace to a brisk walk. Her mind throbbed with all the possibilities of if, and how, she could confront her husband with the evidence of his unfaithfulness. At least now she had a reason to leave him.

Yet, the niggling, almost shameful, question arose again in her mind why Arthur bothered with a wife when he and Susan Wilson were clearly practised lovers?

Upon her return to the farmhouse, Anne released the dogs again so numb from shock at what she had just seen that she didn't even care if they set upon her. But the animals were so pleased to be released, they bounded away and ignored her.

When Arthur returned toward evening, Anne saw him with fresh repulsion and set her plan in place. It started with trying to look poorly and taking to the kitchen settle after supper for a lie down. She often sat there mending or sewing at night but Arthur barely seemed to notice, sometimes working on account books at the kitchen table but mostly, as now, drinking continuous mugs of cider, smoking his pipe and staring glumly into the fireplace.

Anne had her eyes closed but when she heard his chair creak and his crisp, 'Bed, woman,' she made no effort to rise.

Instead, she said feebly, 'I'd like to rest a while longer, Arthur. My headache's still strong.' She opened her eyes and, although it sickened her to do so, she smiled softly at him. 'I won't be long, I expect. I'll wake you when I come up.'

She prayed the promise in her voice was enough to convince him she spoke the truth for he had no reason to believe otherwise.

He looked surprised and Anne feared he might insist she go with him now. His hazy eyes, addled from drink, studied her briefly and she held her breath. To her deep relief, he merely grunted and clomped slowly upstairs without her for the first time since they were married. Anne could only attribute his mellow mood to his recent assignation with Susan.

She heard her husband moving about briefly above then the house grew still and quiet.

The fireside logs burned low into embers. Anne grew tense listening for every small sound, the wind outside, the faintest creaking of the house. Each time, she feared it might be Arthur coming downstairs to order her to bed. But after what seemed like hours, Anne felt that surely he must be asleep and she could make her move.

Because she was unable to carry any possessions with her, she had deliberately worn a double layer of clothes and her warmest shawl today after returning from the woods. Rising from the settle, she swallowed hard and moved toward the kitchen door that led to the outside porch. Although the dogs were chained for the night, Anne hoped they didn't bark and alert their master to her stealthy presence.

As she gently pulled back the bolt, cringing with every sound, a quiet harsh voice behind her said, 'Where are you creepin' off to?'

Anne's heart thumped with fright and her spirits sank but she made herself turn slowly and, thinking quickly, said with a casual smile and easy calm, 'Just goin' out for more wood. I was tryin' to be quiet and not wake you. The room's gettin' chilly.'

'No need at this time of night.' His cold eyes flashed with cunning and he reached out, roughly grasping her arm.

Terrified that her chance had been lost, Anne decided the time for pretence was over.

In a low threatening voice she said, 'Don't touch me,' and tugged herself free, backing away from him into the kitchen.

'What's the matter with you, woman?'

With her leaving thwarted, Anne knew her escape would now be hard won and she would need all her wiles and physical strength for a battle she doubted she could win. But she determined to give it her best effort. She wished it hadn't come to this but, whatever the outcome, she would not live another moment of misery and pain with this cruel adulterous man.

She stared straight at him and said, 'I'll not end up like Mary.'

Arthur went still. His eyes sparked in realisation and his face grew red with rage. A fearful combination. Taking one small step at a time, Anne edged closer to the fire and the poker.

'She died from a fall,' Arthur growled.

'That's not what I hear.'

He glared at her for a moment then hissed, 'The boy. I'll teach him to lie.'

He stormed from the house and strode across the yard to the barn. Anne hovered at the back door, a hand clamped over her mouth in horror at what Arthur might do. She heard him call out for Stephen, then raised voices. From the gloomy interior of the outbuilding she heard scuffling and thumping. Suddenly, Stephen emerged, stumbling, bruised and bleeding, and fell on his hands and knees to the ground.

'Run,' she cried out. 'He's behind you.'

He recovered before Arthur reached him and, with one last agonising glance toward Anne, staggered off into the dark. She retreated to the house, knowing Stephen would think she had betrayed him. She hadn't, directly, but would never have a chance to tell him. And, worse, she was now alone with her evil husband with no close neighbours aware of her danger or to hear her cries for help. If she needed them.

Frothing at the mouth with anger, Arthur returned to the house and bolted the door, looming over her. Afraid for her life, Anne had used the few precious moments while he had locked the door to grab the fireside poker.

She gripped it tight and glared at her husband. 'You have no right to hurt another person. For no reason. And a woman at that. Have you no pride or shame? Why do you do it?'

'A wife does as she's told.'

'Don't threaten me. I know about you and Susan and what you did to Mary. I'll not stay here a moment longer.'

He gaped in surprise at her statement. 'You won't get far,' he growled, bulging red veins standing out in his neck. 'If you get away. I'll hunt you down and kill you.'

When he suddenly lurched toward her, Anne raised the poker and swung it wildly at him, catching his arm and shoulder. He doubled over and cried out in pain and anger. When she tried to pass him, he stretched out with his uninjured arm and dragged at her skirt. Held firm, she swiped at him again, twice. Hard across the body. He slumped to the floor and moaned then went quiet.

Seizing her chance, Anne leapt for the door, unbolted it and raced across to the barn. Fumbling in the darkness with haste and dread, trying to remember where she'd seen it, Anne groped about. As her eyes grew accustomed to the shadows, she found the bridle.

'Easy, boy,' Anne softly reassured the restless gelding as she entered its stall and slipped the bridle over its head. No time for a saddle. She must get away before Arthur recovered.

As she hurriedly led the animal out into the night, she yelped in fright. Arthur staggered toward her, hunched over, clearly still in pain but desperate to stop her. In panic as he advanced, Anne dragged herself onto the horse's bare back, gasping and sobbing with the effort, her husband now only feet away. She shrieked as he reached out to grab the bridle but Anne kicked out fiercely with her boot. He reeled back, giving her just enough time to knee her mount into action and ride away.

She had no other plan but to flee and his bellowing words of warning rang out across the night, lingering with an ominous ring on the still damp air. 'I'll find ye, Annie Westcott. I'll find ye wherever ye go.'

His horrifying threats crowded her head as she galloped away, wishing she'd been able to make her escape under a full moon but that was over a week away and she couldn't wait that long. Nor would she be guaranteed of another opportunity. She would have to make the best of it and find her way in the dark. For now, Anne needed all of her thoughts on escaping and what to do next. But she had one stop to make before disappearing forever.

CHAPTER 5

The cold night air stung Anne's face as she crouched low over the horse's neck and galloped down the dark lane and out onto the Tavistock Road. She prayed the horse had enough strength and speed to see them both far enough away to safety.

Terrified, she turned aside to listen but could hear nothing above the sounds of clomping hooves upon the hard earth. She had no doubt Arthur would find some way to come after her before morning which meant she had no time to waste. Despite the hollow dread she felt for her future and not knowing what lay ahead, a burst of elation briefly filled her chest, as wild as the Devon moorland where she had been raised, that she had managed to escape. But, growing serious again, she knew before any chance of pursuit, she must get far enough away so she was never found.

Long strands of damp hair clung to Anne's head and she shivered as she headed south away from Combe Hill along more familiar roads, slowing the horse to a canter to rest him for a while before urging him on faster again.

Soon, she turned down the familiar hedged lane that led closer to the vague black outline of her parents' cottage ahead.

Sliding from the horse, Anne tethered it to a post in the orchard fence and picked her way across the small cobbled yard at the back of the house. How she had dearly missed her home and family.

While everyone else slept upstairs, her parents in one of the two bedrooms, her sisters in the other, Richard slept downstairs on a box bed in the small annexe room off the kitchen.

She tossed a small stone at the tiny high window praying the noise didn't wake anyone else. When there was no response, she tried again. Richard was a sound sleeper. Pacing in the cold and dark, she grew anxious he would not wake and kept an ear to the chill night wind, listening for any distant sounds.

Just when she almost gave up hope, she heard movement and the back door squeaked slowly ajar. Richard appeared, tousled and yawning. Anne flung herself against her brother in relief at the wonderful sight of the dearly loved trustworthy soul. And realised how isolated and alone she had felt these past weeks since her marriage.

'Annie!' He held her away from him in surprise. 'What are ye doin' here in the middle of the night? Why are ye not home?'

'Combe Hill was never home,' she whispered tightly, putting a finger to her lips in warning.

Anne tugged his nightshirt sleeve and dragged him away from the house toward the orchard in case they were overheard.

'What's wrong? Is Arthur hurt?' Richard rubbed his arms, shivering despite it being early summer.

Drawing in a deep breath, Anne related what had passed that night and what she had learned from Stephen of Arthur's past with Mary, Stephen's dismissal and Arthur's infidelity. Listening but not speaking, Richard's brow drew into a severe frown and his mouth dropped open.

'I feel so bad about causing Stephen to lose his job. He relies on the money to support his family but I fear for my life Richard. Arthur threatened me and I have no doubt he'll follow me and carry it out.'

'I'd like to go and beat up Westcott man to man and see how he likes it,' Richard hissed between gritted teeth.

'No, no,' Anne pleaded. 'Arthur's dangerous. Stay away from him.

Richard gripped her arm and his voice rasped with distress. 'Ma and Pa will be heartbroken when they hear what's happened. I swear none of us knew.'

'No one's to blame except Arthur.'

'We wondered why you didn't come to visit.'

'You mustn't tell a soul.'

'Arthur will come lookin' for you, then? It's best if no one knows but me. Less chance of anyone lettin' a word slip, eh?'

'I have no idea where I should go,' Anne said in a small anguished voice, realising the magnitude of what she must face. Alone.

'Sell the horse,' Richard suggested urgently, noticing the restless animal nearby. 'Tavistock is too risky. People will recognise you. Head for Plymouth. You'll get a good price at the pannier market.'

'Plymouth?' Anne gasped. 'I've never been there.'

'It's fifteen miles and far enough away they'll maybe not find you soon or think of looking.'

'But-'

'Listen.' Richard gripped her shoulders and gave her a gentle shake. 'Do as I say. Get back up on that horse and ride. When you've sold him, keep the money for a fresh start. Write to us when you're settled somewhere.'

Anne cast a despairing look at her brother, at his smooth boyish face, thick tousled hair and devilish smile. Deep fear for her unknown future cracked her spirit and, for one of the few times in her life, tears filled her eyes. 'Oh Richard, I'm so afraid.'

'You've never shied from anything, Anne Gray. Stay strong. Head for the tithe barn at Buckland Abbey,' he advised. 'Spell the horse, rest yourself and push on to Plymouth in the morning. But, take care,' he warned gently.

'And, after that?' She looked at him with questioning appeal.

'Maybe this is your chance for a new life, Annie?' he cautiously suggested. 'Ships leave from Plymouth for America and Australia all the time.'

'America,' Anne breathed. 'Is that where you're going?'

Richard briskly shook his head. 'One day, maybe. Westcott would never find you there.'

'Could you not come with me?'

Richard's face lined with anguish. 'I'm tempted but I couldn't leave our folks so sudden.'

Anne mulled over the possibilities. She'd always longed for something more but felt daunted that the opportunity had perhaps arrived and she must finally make the choice. Could she? What lay here for her? A bleak treacherous marriage and a poor but loving family who could no longer afford to keep her.

Oh, the enticement of a better life. Tonight had opened up that possibility. A fork in the road of her life branched ahead and she must decide which path to take. If she stayed, Arthur would hunt her down and find her. Her life would be in jeopardy and she would never be free.

Suddenly, her way was clear and she filled with a strange calm and acceptance to confront her fate. Richard's suggestion made sense. Plymouth was a large and busy town with less risk of being found if Arthur came after her.

She thought of her beloved Dartmoor and Devon with its running waters and remote tors jutting up from vast empty hillsides leading down to lanes and villages. No other land would capture her heart or be as dear. She would miss it and all the people she loved but she could not stay. A lump formed in her throat.

Sensing her distress, Richard slid a comforting arm about her shoulder, rubbing her arms against the cold night.

As if in silent understanding and without a further word spoken between them, Anne quickly and fiercely hugged her brother, clinging to him for as long as possible, as if holding onto her last link before finally letting go. Longing to return home but knowing her future lay elsewhere. It might be years before they saw each other again. Or never.

'Tell Elizabeth and Emmy and Ma that I love them,' she whispered.

'You'll write?' Anne nodded, hesitating to make a move. 'Don't think on it, Annie. It's all dead here. Nothin's goin' on. Pa's losing the farm. He'll be givin' up the cows soon and only have his few sheep. There's nothin' here for us.'

'When will you go?'

'I'll stay till Lizzie's married maybe and then think on it. Write me where you are and I can join you later.'

Anne had always thought herself to be brave of heart but, came the time, she was loath to go. She cast a prolonged glance toward the cottage and took the reins from Richard, exchanging a meaningful glance.

'Go on, now,' he urged lightly, grinning.

Anne buried the precious memory of it within her till they met again. 'This won't be forever. Will it?' she asked as if to convince herself otherwise.

Richard briskly shook his head then cupped his hands. She placed one boot into them and mounted the horse.

'Mind you get a good price for him now,' Richard teased as they moved off.

Anne dared not look back, filled with fear, her throat choked with sobs, overwhelmed by the homeless uncertain hours and days that stretched ahead.

Hours later, wet and weary, the dark outline of Buckland Abbey finally loomed ahead, its square tower barely visible in the night. Unlike Tavistock Abbey which had been stripped after the dissolution and left to decay three centuries before, this Cistercian monastery had become a family residence. Sir Francis Drake had lived there once upon returning a hero from his sea voyages of exploration. The abbey mansion was still owned by family branches but Anne knew little of them.

Keeping to the cover of trees, she dismounted and led the horse to rest in the long tithe barn near the house where once a portion of tenants' crops would have been paid as rent to the abbey and stored here. Inside, Anne squinted until her eyes grew accustomed to the gloom for there were only small high windows and arched wooden beams overhead. The barn was so long she could not see the other end but it was warmer than outside and promised basic comfort.

Anne kept to a corner near the door. Soaked from the misty night air, she spread out her skirt around her to dry. Her hands were numb with cold and she rubbed them together. Anne let the reins slip from her fingers, yielded to heavy eyelids and settled to sleep.

She awoke with a start and scrambled to her feet, peering anxiously outside, relieved to see it was barely light. Leading the horse, she skirted the outbuildings away from the abbey before remounting, wearily refreshed but still damp and hungry.

As the miles slipped by, Anne welcomed the warmth of daylight but wariness gnawed her mind, keeping her alert. She left the widening river Tavy and headed south across country to Plymouth feeling a guarded anticipation for the bustling port town. She encountered more travellers on the road. Carts and wagons loaded with goods and produce for market on this summer morning, other horsemen and pedestrians even at this early hour already streaming along the Tavistock Road.

Once in the busier part of town with brick and stone buildings two and three storeys high lining the road, Anne searched for cheap lodgings. In Old Town Street, she found the Old Four Castles public house where a sign on the front of the building promised good stabling.

She secured a stark attic room. The plump landlady puffed ahead of Anne up a steep narrow staircase, her large body and skirts filling its narrow breadth.

' 'ere for the market, love?' she wheezed, pausing for breath on the tiny landing.

'Yes.'

'What ya sellin' then?'

'A horse.'

The cramped space held only a bed, with a water jug, basin and a candlestick on a small rough table. Suddenly the meagre comforts of home seemed welcome by comparison but she knew there would be many changes ahead in her life and braced herself anew to confront them.

From the buxom woman, she learned the pannier market was located off East Street further down. While the woman caught her breath and rested on the flimsy chair before returning downstairs, Anne posed the question on her mind.

'Always dizzens ships in harbour.' She planted one fat red hand on a hip and with the other brushed back a stray grey wisp of hair from her perspiring face. '*Result*'s just in from London afore it collects more passengers and heads for Australia.'

Anne's interest quickened at the snippet of gossip. 'Australia,' she breathed, awed. So far away. Much further than America.

The landlady nodded. 'Aye, 'tis a longful and months asea without touchin' land. Ise be affeard for sure.' She wiped her brow with a corner of her apron. 'Still, some say it's a good life. If you 'ave the fare.'

Awestruck by the thought of embarking on such a voyage alone, Anne cleared her throat. 'Do you know how much?'

'Hear tell its sixty pounds for a cabin.'

Anne's brief hopes swiftly died and her spirit flagged. 'Such a sum.' The horse would never fetch near that much money. Disheartened, she peered from her tiny window onto the busy narrow street below. It seemed her chance for escape and safety had slipped from her grasp.

'Course it don't cost as much for them what gets help through the Emigration Depot on Phoenix Wharf.' The woman broke into Anne's disturbed thoughts. 'Only a few pounds.'

Upon hearing this new information, Anne's mood lifted and she spun about to face the landlady, freshly inspired.

'Such a difference?'

'You got no privacy in steerage, mind. Them what has a cabin gets it all built special.' The woman scratched her head and eyed Anne with a sharp narrowed gaze. 'Zo, thinking to emigrate then?'

'I'm not sure … ' But even as her curiosity bubbled to the surface, she knew her subconscious and Richard's suggestion last night had already brewed the idea into consideration.

She would need to earn money and support herself in a new place. With Ma's teaching, surely she would find something. Maybe some grand house would take her on to tutor their children as governess. If not, she was competent at cooking and housework. She clasped her hands tight across her waist with excitement and dread.

'Best head down to the Barbican. There's assisted passage to Australia and New Zealand granted to single women of good character,' she suggested, eyeing her young lodger shrewdly. 'Plymouth's the only emigration point in the country. Won't get a better chance nowheres else.'

Assisted passage. Even better. But Australia … 'Perhaps I should wait for another ship? To America.'

The big woman shrugged. 'Could be days or weeks.'

By then her money would be depleted. And there was always the threat that Arthur would find her. Whatever she did, she must act now. Could this ship bound for Australia be an omen? It seemed more than coincidence that the *Result* was in port at the same time as she arrived in Plymouth.

'Perhaps I shall go and make enquiries.'

The landlady's back straightened and her ample chest pushed out importantly. 'Be wise, love. Ship 'as over a hundred passengers already I hear. More'n twenty getting on 'ere in port. Be leaving soon as the tide's right, I expect.'

Anne's heart beat with a new urgency to sell the horse to help fund her fare. As soon as the landlady departed, Anne washed in the small puddle of cold water in the basin. She ran her fingers through her tangled hair, tidying it enough to be presentable at the market, and wiped the worst stains from her dress.

She collected the horse from the inn stables and led him along East Street to the open market area surrounded by long low buildings with narrow verandas. Men were gathered about, buyers in suits and hats, traders in rougher clothes and caps, some with long aprons, standing beside their cart of goods. Anne found herself a small free space to one side of the noisy square and took up a place among them. Many showed interest in her fine animal but none stopped to buy.

Finally, to her relief, two expensively attired gentlemen approached. The older man puffed a pipe and the younger was round faced with thick dark hair and a ready genial smile. 'Excellent animal, Charles,' the elder man said.

The man addressed halted and lifted his eyebrows at the sight of the young woman offering a horse for sale. 'Miss.' He half bowed politely. 'I'm always interested in good horse flesh.'

'He's well bred, Sir.'

The corners of his mouth eased upward in mild amusement. 'Fast?'

'He can outrun anything, Sir,' Anne boldly claimed, knowing nothing of the sort.

The younger gent hinged a thumb into his waistcoat pocket exposing an expensive gold watch and chain. His commanding presence, the fine cut and material of his clothes, and shoes that shone even amid the dust told her he was gentry.

Sensing genuine interest and a potential sale, Anne decided to barter, remembering Richard's words to get the best price for she would need every penny she could get.

Charles concentrated on the horse and carried out a thorough inspection, frowning as he ran his smooth manicured hands over the animal's gleaming chestnut coat and long legs.

Straightening to stand back and survey the animal's well-bred lines, he said, 'Name your price, Miss.'

Anne suggested a sum. The man rubbed his chin. 'High, even for this magnificent beast.' He named a lesser amount. Still far more than Anne had first considered so she agreed.

Charles extended a hand and smiled. 'We have a bargain, Miss ... ?'

'Gr ... Gutheridge, Sir. Ann ... abella Gutheridge.' She snatched a new identity out of thin air, pleased with its more fascinating ring. A new name for a new beginning.

His eyes flickered with indulgent humour. Did he guess? 'Charles Montgomery, Miss Gutheridge. A pleasure to make your acquaintance.' He bowed slightly again, watching her with an astute eye.

Montgomery snapped his fingers. His older companion stepped forward and reached into his coat. Anne's emotions were bittersweet as the cold gold sovereigns clinked together in her hand and her fingers closed around them.

'I shall take excellent care of him, Miss Gutheridge,' Montgomery murmured as she transferred the reins.

Anne watched the horse led away and the distinguished purchaser briefly touch his hat in acknowledgement as the two departing gentlemen wove their way through the milling crowd and disappeared from sight.

Standing alone in the centre of the busy market, Anne felt a frightening sense of apprehension at what she was about to do.

CHAPTER 6

With the coins securely knotted in a corner of her petticoat, Anne left the pannier market and returned to the Old Four Castles to pay her bill.

Carrying no possessions and feeling adrift, Anne wandered to the open area that led down to the esplanade and Hoe. From the hillside vantage point in the grassy park with its breezy views over Plymouth Sound, she was finally forced to confront what lay ahead, awed by the sea's vast emptiness from harbour to horizon.

Anne sat down on the cold grass, inhaled the salty air and hugged her knees. From Ma's lessons, she knew the Pilgrim Fathers had left for America from here two hundred years before. Francis Drake had led his fleet from here to defeat the Spanish. And James Cook had set out from here almost a century before in search of the great southern continent everyone now knew as Australia. Furthest away of all. Since the gold rushes, many people claimed it was the land of opportunity.

With the *Result* in harbour, was that far off land also to be the source of her own personal hope and future?

As much as it pained her heart to leave, Anne resolved to make the most of her life and grasp every opportunity that presented itself. And Australia, it seemed, beckoned. If she was destined to find her future there, then so be it.

A chill gust of wind wrapped about her and she shivered. She would miss Richard and the escapades they shared; her rare and precious walks with Elizabeth when duties allowed. Would miss seeing Emmy grow up and may never see her parents alive again.

Decisively, she stood up, shook out her grass-covered skirt and strode uphill toward town. In Whimple Street post office she wrote a brief departing note to Richard, bought a penny stamp and mailed it, pleased to know that it would make the afternoon delivery to Tavistock and Launceston at five.

Then Anne made her way to the waterfront again, emerging from the narrow cobbled streets and alleys of the busy Barbican to see a forest of masts jutting skyward before her from bare rigged sailing vessels tied up at their moorings in Sutton Pool, one of Plymouth's several harbours.

She walked past horses and wagons being loaded and unloaded, people standing in small huddled groups or sitting on baggage and barrels among baskets and tied bundles of belongings. Winding her way through them, she pushed on to Commercial Quay.

She hesitated when she reached the Emigration Depot on Phoenix Wharf, formerly an old warehouse building, before she nervously stepped inside. After earnest interrogation about her reasons for wanting to leave England and whether she had friends or relations waiting or any potential employment arranged upon her arrival, Anne despaired she might be refused so she created a fictitious aunt who would meet her at voyage end.

Eventually she was granted passage on the *Result* to Australia under what they called assisted emigration and promised a prosperous new future. She learnt that in accordance with the Passenger Act, certain facilities and food ration provisions were provided aboard ship, as well as water closets, lifeboats and medicines. Since their vessel carried over fifty passengers, a surgeon accompanied them as well. Perhaps life at sea might not be as unpleasant and hazardous as the landlady at the inn had declared, after all, Anne thought with relief.

Because officials noticed she travelled light, Anne

gratefully received a small bundle of basic clothes and was informed she was obliged to stay among the other emigrants until the ship sailed. Sleeping and accommodation facilities were provided and travellers isolated until embarkation so Anne moved as directed toward the section for single women, unsettled at her enormous decision among the crowds of fellow emigrants all bound for the same destination.

Cautiously eyeing off those around her, she caught the eye of two women about her own age, one looking miserable and unhappy, the other brightly chatting to her, perhaps to lift her spirits. The forthcoming sea voyage was a daunting prospect for all. Anne liked the look of the cheerful girl with her lightly freckled face and mad tumble of dark ginger curls. With nothing to lose, she crossed her fingers and approached them, trusting they would also be on the same ship. They would be many months at sea and companions would be welcome.

Anne set her meagre belongings nearby, took a deep breath and flashed a sunny smile. 'Good evening. Are you both travelling to Australia?'

'Aye,' the redhead responded cordially. 'On the *Result*.'

'I'm on my own and wonder if I might travel with you both.' Anne glanced between the redhead and her plain dark-haired friend.

Having captured their attention, the sad girl eyed her with apathy but the lively girl scrambled to her feet and willingly introduced herself. 'For sure. I'm Jessie Milne.' She turned to her companion. 'And this is Cissy Reilly. We're from County Wicklow in Ireland.'

Anne beamed. 'I'm Annabella Gutheridge from Tavistock.'

'We're travelling out to meet my brothers, John and Michael. They've been in Australia for over two years now. According to their letters, it's sunnier and warmer than Ireland and right hot in summer but you can find work if you're willing. It's right miserable scratching for a living back home that's for sure. That's why they emigrated in the first place. To go on ahead and see if it really was a better life. Why are you leaving?'

'Same as you really.' Anne shrugged. 'There's nothing at home.'

'Can we call you Annie?' Jessie asked and she nodded.

'They don't mind you leaving?' Cissy asked softly, wide-eyed, making the first tentative contribution to their conversation.

'They can't afford to keep me,' she admitted feeling no shame for the other two girls clearly came from similar backgrounds. On such short acquaintance, she decided against revealing more detailed reasons. Maybe when they all knew each other better.

'Ah, you're brave with no-one expecting you at the other end and no job. Cissy and I are being sponsored by my brothers with Passage Warrants. They got them from the Immigration Officer in Melbourne. Only cost two pounds each. You can do that if you already have friends or relatives in Victoria. We're going to work for an important man in a big house in a place called South Yarra near Melbourne. Soon as they can, John and Michael will come down from up country and visit,' Jessie prattled on, wrinkling her pert nose. 'My brothers didn't stay in Melbourne. They're farm boys so they're working on a sheep station up country.' She looked wistful and sighed. 'I'd love to get out there eventually myself.'

'I'm not going out into the bush,' meek Cissy fearfully announced. 'We don't know what's out there. Could be savages. Johnny wrote about aboriginals and it's far from everywhere.'

'Ah, Cissy Reilly, you're a scaredy eejit.' Jessie nudged her friend good-naturedly and gave a deep melodious chuckle that drew a smile from Anne in response. 'I'll be with you all the time and aren't we going to a big grand house and bein' paid handsome wages. Twenty pounds a year including food and board. Can you believe it?' Jessie gasped. 'It's more money than we've ever seen, that's for sure. Maybe in time we'll be able to save a little and better ourselves.'

'Or get married.' Cissy blushed. 'There's lots more men than women in Australia.'

'I'm staying single. Do you want to be looking after a brood of children, Cissy? Look what seven kids did to me Ma.'

'Wouldn't be so bad,' her glum friend challenged, brightening.

'It's all right for you. You love children.' Jessie's tone turned reflective and she caught one of Cissy's hands in her own. 'Ciss lost her parents and three sisters in the famine,' she explained on her friend's behalf. 'They were right poor. Worse than us. Since she was orphaned and livin' on the next farm, me Ma and Da took her in, and she's been livin' with us ever since. We're sisters, really, aren't we?' Her friend nodded, half smiling. 'But there's nothin' at home. We're startin' on a new life in Australia together, aren't we, Ciss?'

'We'll probably never see Ireland again,' she said barely above a whisper.

'Maybe after we've seen Australia, we won't want to,' Jessie said positively with a smile. 'Besides, don't we have each other? And Johnny and Michael when we get to the other end. Going to take us three months to get there, though.'

'I hope the ship doesn't sink.'

'You're always thinkin' the worst, Cissy Reilly. It'll be a grand adventure. Johnny says it's not so bad and we won't be on board the ship forever. What's ten or twelve weeks to us? We'll be ladies of leisure,' she laughed.

Anne looked on, silently observing the warm and honest friendship the two girls shared, the more confident and easy going Jessie coaxing and teasing her nervous companion into a lighter mood. It must have been dreadful for Cissy losing her whole family, and when she wouldn't have been more than ten years old.

'Do you know much about the ship or when we sail?'

Anne asked Jessie, since she was clearly the chattiest and most informed of the two.

'I expect as soon as all the Plymouth passengers have arrived. Johnny says the bunks are cramped but we can walk up on deck in fine weather. I overheard two ladies talking. There's a Doctor and his wife and son on board.'

'Perhaps life at sea might not be so unpleasant after all,' Anne voiced her relief.

'It's easier for the rich. They travel in their own private cabin and eat with the Captain.' Jessie sounded more amused than bitter. 'So long as we get fed, I don't mind. We'll do just fine. I think we're leaving tomorrow so we best all get a good night's sleep.'

The girls made up their simple narrow beds and settled for the night. Next morning, the Depot was all bustle and instructions and organisation as the extra Plymouth passengers including Anne, Jessie and Cissy were shepherded aboard ship to join those who had started from London.

When they climbed below, they found their steerage compartment was a long low room that ran the length of the ship between decks. They found themselves a berth together aft in the single women's quarters. Four people slept in each so they were able to stay together, Cissy clinging fearfully to Jessie the whole time, Anne noticed, afraid to let her friend out of sight.

'There's no privacy for gettin' undressed,' Cissy whispered.

'We're all in the same boat.' Jessie laughed when she realised what she had said. 'So to speak.'

It was certainly cramped. Anne looked about her in dismay, wondering at the last moment what she had done in deciding to leave all that she had ever known and loved. But knew that, with Arthur's threats hanging over her, she had little choice but to disappear so far away, he'd never find her. At least she now had friends to share the experience and challenge of making a new life. She stifled a brief moment of panic-filled regret when a murmur rippled among the passengers that the ship was about to sail.

The three young women scrambled back up on deck, watching as the crew readied the ship for sea. Sails unfurled, ropes fastened. The vast canvas caught the wind and their ship was gradually pushed out to sea.

As the Plymouth buildings grew smaller and the land shrivelled from view to little more than a line on the horizon, Cissy quietly wept. Anne saw Jessie hug her friend tight for comfort, trying to be brave for both of them. To Anne, Devon seemed suddenly dear. Tears threatened her eyes, too, but she blinked them away, refusing to cry. As Jessie had said, their future would be grand.

As the wind whistled in the rigging overhead, most passengers remained on deck for some time, thoughtful and subdued, reflecting like Anne, no doubt, on lives and families they were leaving behind, probably never to see again. Jessie reached out for Anne's hand in mutual reassurance and understanding.

Life at sea soon fell into a routine. The first weeks were a time of adapting to shipboard life not to mention frequent bouts of seasickness for those unable to endure the constant motion and unsteadiness underfoot. Anne felt distinctly unsettled in the stomach during rougher seas but managed to stay out of bed and eat a little. Jessie recovered soon enough but Cissy, once calmer weather returned and her ashen face had turned pink again, stayed curled up in her bunk as if afraid to leave. She couldn't even face the bread and water served out every day before breakfast.

They became inured to getting dressed and undressed in view of others, hearing quarrels and whispers, feeling the roll and creaking of the ship, steadying themselves with practise, grateful for oblivion at night and release from congestion and monotony.

When the weather was fine, Jessie and Anne cajoled Cissy

to join them up on deck to chat and wander about among the other steerage passengers. Anne liked nothing better on days of brisk winds to stand on the poop craning her neck to gaze up in exhilaration at the fully rigged sails straining overhead before the wind.

Shipboard gossip and news among passengers raced between tongues, Jessie usually among the first to hear the latest. A source of entertainment to break the tedium of their idle time at sea as well as watching the wealthy cabin folk sauntering around deck, the women usually escorted by their menfolk.

'I see the gentry's come out to enjoy the sun again, too,' Jessie said one day as they sat together in a group, eating their dinner of soup, meat pie and pudding.

'Don't know why they bother,' Cissy grumbled, ever the pessimist. 'There's nothin' to see but water. And I'm right fed up with pea soup three times a week.'

'You've salt beef, too,' Jessie reminded her. 'And didn't I make a currant roly pudding the other day.'

Anne and Jessie shared turns at shared cooking in the galley with the others in their allotted small group of ten passengers.

'There's Mrs. Walker and her daughter, Mary. She's older than us,' Jessie said, then lowered her voice, grinning. 'I've seen the Doctor's son, Robert, eyeing off one of the Douglas girls.'

Anne admired them all, so well dressed in their elegant finery compared to their own simple dresses. Although she hated sewing, she had managed to let down the hems and make minor alterations for a better fit in the clothes Jessie and Cissy had given her.

She secretly envied the saloon passengers their extra cabin space, especially living under each other's feet in steerage.

'Do you know who they are?' Anne asked Jessie of two couples lingering to chat at the railing for, in her bright inquisitive way, she seemed to learn everything.

'They're wealthy squatters and land owners. John and Isabella Carfrae. They've a big sheep run in Victoria. And the younger ones are Richmond Henty and his new wife, Agnes. They're only just married in England. His father's in the parliament. The Henty's are a wealthy pioneer family.'

Anne smiled to herself. People chatted easily to Jessie, disarmed by her open friendly nature. She shook her head in wonder. Imagine having so much land to be wealthy from it. Such a contrast from Bridge Farm and its humble inadequate earnings. Maybe in a few years if she worked hard and saved enough, she could help Richard emigrate if he wanted. She gazed down on the gentry group, trying to picture what the country would be like where these people lived. Anne now wished she's given more thought and planning to her future like Jessie and Cissy for she, too, would need work and only hoped she could find a suitable position on arrival.

The *Result*'s progress south across the Atlantic Ocean continued with slight seas and favourable winds. As they approached the tropics, June became July and the air grew warmer. Anne gratefully tipped her face to the sun, feeling lazy and indulgent in the balmy sea air. At noon each day she watched, fascinated as Captain Cow took his compass bearings and the miles they'd covered, and wrote them down.

Trunks and boxes were brought up and passengers allowed a few hours to rummage through, exchanging their warm clothes for lighter ones. Again, Anne's new friends shared dresses and underwear, and a large straw hat that had been rolled up and squashed flat.

The tropics revealed their own individual features. Sudden downpours of warm rain drenched them on deck and sent them laughing and squealing for cover. The scary sight of sharks and the hot stifling air below deck that made sleeping difficult. Most nights, while Cissy endured her airless bunk, Jessie and Anne escaped above.

'Isn't it just glorious, Jess?' Anne sighed in awe as they

linked arms at the railing watching the horizon change into every colour of crimson and gold.

'We can see forever. Makes you think you're the only people on earth, don't it?'

The sun became a ball of fire, growing smaller and sinking into the sea. They stayed outside for hours talking and sharing their hopes and dreams for Australia while the moon rose in silent majesty shedding its glorious light over their vast isolated world until the sky's colours faded and a clear spread of stars gradually twinkled into life across the velvet night sky.

'The earth's a huge place,' Anne said, amazed anew each day by the endless sea about them. 'Will Ciss be all right?' She raised her concern that their other companion isolated herself so much, seeming to lack the strength and courage of an adventurous spirit, perhaps regretting her agreement to accompany her best friend on this long precarious voyage.

'Where we're goin' there's greater opportunities and a more comfortable life than back home, for sure. Cissy's knows that. She'll be fine when we reach land again.'

'I can't wait for land,' Anne confessed, frustrated by the enforced idleness, longing for miles of freedom and solid earth beneath her feet instead of restricted life aboard ship. Despairing of the constant rolling and lurching of the ship, bumping into people and battling to stay upright. Her positive attitude was being tested to the limit of endurance.

'We're halfway there. Its five weeks since we left with as many more still to go but we'll be in Australia soon enough.' Jessie turned nostalgic. 'It's going to be different from where we came from, for sure.'

Anne pondered her own unspoken uncertainty and curiosity that now daily settled in her mind as the ship sailed ever closer to their new unfamiliar destination. Venturing to the bottom of the world, she could only trust it proved all that she'd heard promised and not be disappointed. Whatever happened, she vowed to make the best of it.

But even their liberty was soon curtailed. In August, the ship entered the rough cold waters around the Cape of Good Hope before sailing eastward across the Southern Ocean for Australia. The boxes were brought up again for warmer clothes and passengers could no longer eat or walk on deck. To Anne, it seemed the ultimate deprivation this late in the voyage. She was growing restless enough without being curbed in their tiny shared space, living on top of one another.

They huddled in their berths keeping warm with hot food, occasionally climbing above if the weather cleared enough, almost hidden in their coats and scarves and gloves. The days were drawing in and the frosty air nipped any bare skin. The crew kept watchful for icebergs.

But even Cissy, feeling miserable and nauseous again like many, was briefly lured up on deck one day when a pod of whales was sighted. With a huge sea running, everyone clung to the rails as they watched the gigantic creatures send up high water spouts, occasionally rising out of the ocean to thump back down in a giant spray of water.

'That one's nearly as long as the ship.' Anne pointed to the largest of the three playing in their heavy lethargic way.

The spars howled overhead and the winds blew out the cordage on the masts, whipping them about like a lasso. When it became too dangerous to stay out any longer, the few brave folk who had dared venture above, retreated below again.

The weather worsened before it improved. Passengers frequently received visits by a member of the crew who climbed below to secure portholes and hatchways.

'Be a dirty night,' he would rightly predict.

Sleep was impossible. They could lie down but clutched anything solid about them for stability.

Cissy cowered, terrified. 'What if we've come all this way and we don't make it?' she wailed.

Anne and Jessie shared a long-suffering glance, hiding their own discomfort and doubts.

The normally positive Jessie scowled and snapped, 'We're

all goin' through it. Not just you, Cissy Reilly. Bit late to be turnin' back now so take a hold of yourself and make the best of it.'

Anne saw tears pool in Cissy's eyes at her friend's uncharacteristic icy blast and caught her hand, murmuring inane reassurances, making false promises that all would be well and it would be over soon.

'It can't come ... soon enough ... for me,' Cissy sobbed.

The following day was rough and raining. Tempers frayed with alarm. Everyone stayed in their bunk, gripping tight when the ship sank into troughs before rising again on the mountains of waves rolling across each other in peaks and writhing foam. Crests of waves cut into sheets of spray that flung themselves across the bow and flooded the decks. The vessel shipped water despite being tightly sealed so, not only were most people sick, but wet and cold as well. Anne silently prayed Australia was worth the suffering.

Then, towards the end of August, almost ten weeks since they had left Plymouth, excited rumours swept through the ship. There was talk they were only days from Melbourne. Anne knew land was out there and, after months at sea, felt cheated not to be able to see it.

With the weather eased, passengers were allowed up on deck again. Hatchways were opened and the cramped travellers scrambled above hoping to catch a glimpse of this new country on which they had all pinned their various future hopes.

CHAPTER 7

Melbourne, Australia, September 1861

Anne, Jessie and a reluctant pale Cissy joined everyone else who hurried up on deck to fine weather and a light wind.

'Land,' Anne cried, sighting a mountainous promontory with a round white lighthouse, barely able to conceal her excitement. Australia!

'Trees don't look as green as Ireland,' Cissy moaned.

A pilot from a place called Queenscliff came aboard to guide them through the narrow Port Phillip Heads into Hobson's Bay and on the last day of August, the *Result* dropped anchor.

Dressed and ready for hours, the three young women impatiently waited their turn to be offloaded into smaller lighters and ferry boats and taken ashore. As her feet stepped onto foreign soil for the first time in her life, Anne looked back at the ship that had brought them safely here.

'The *Result*'s going on to New Zealand. Taking passengers to the gold fields,' Jessie murmured beside her.

'So many people. All seeking something,' she replied absently, enjoying the softer warmth in the air.

Each hauling their small bag of possessions, Jessie impatiently tugged her sleeve. 'Come on, Annie. We've hired a hansom cab.'

The three young women lifted their skirts and climbed in, tightly squeezed together. 'Just like on the ship,' Jessie laughed.

Cissy, always lagging behind, looked hesitant and wide-eyed as their horse-drawn cab rattled away from the pier toward town and along a broad unmade road. Anne absorbed the radiant sunlight casting its brilliance over everything, so unlike even the sunniest Devon day.

The women spoke little, taking in their new and strange surroundings. It amazed Anne to realise she was on the other side of the world from home and family. But Victoria would now be her home, and please God she find a job and have a better life.

They had just driven past extensive gardens when the cab crossed a plain single-span bridge yawning over a sluggish unclean river, its edges rough and grassy with punts and small boats tied up along its banks.

Even on this early Sunday morning, the broad streets were alive with people, the clop of horses' hooves and rattling buggy wheels. Impeccably dressed gentleman in frock coats and shiny top hats with elegant ladies on their arms strolled the pavements, and church bells tolled, drawing worshippers in.

Lanes ran between the wider streets. The elegant buildings of brick and stone gave a general impression of spaciousness and grandeur. They noticed a horse omnibus on the main streets before their cab turned into a smaller street and halted before a wooden boarding house behind a paling fence from where, Jessie had told her, their new employers had arranged to collect them the following day.

Inside the humble establishment, the girls met their rough but tidy landlady and were shown to their shared room.

The stout woman eyed them up and down. 'There's a sixpenny restaurant nearby that serves breakfast, dinner at one o'clock and supper at seven. Stews, steak, chops and sausages with dry hash, together with soup and a pudding.'

Anne knew she must start looking for employment first thing tomorrow. Hearing Jessie speak of her brothers made her long for life in the country, and she wondered how she might go about seeking work on a farm.

When Anne mentioned her plans to her friends later over their evening meal, Cissy at least was horrified.

'I've heard it's rough out in the bush,' she said. 'Few woman and nothin' but sheep. And you won't know a soul. Why don't you stay in Melbourne? At least you'll know us.'

Anne was sorely tempted but she had never liked towns. They were exciting for a while but then she always longed for open spaces again. 'I'll be just fine,' she assured her worried companion with a brave smile.

'Johnny says the countryside here isn't anything like England,' Jessie warned, cramming another forkful of mutton stew into her mouth, grateful for the fresh decent food after tedious ship's fare of recent months. 'Only be green a while longer then it gets right hot Johnny says and goes brown. And they're not called sheep farms here. They're called stations.'

Although Jessie painted a strange daunting picture of her preferred destination, Anne remained undeterred.

After supper, the women walked out together on the gas lit streets. Knots of men sat in bars at tables. Other groups of young girls, moderately dressed, sauntered for amusement, too. Occasionally, young men three or four abreast in boots and breeches and smoking, doffed their caps and bid them Good evening, raising a giggle from Cissy and modest smiles from Anne and Jessie.

'Shan't be short of admirers, then,' she quipped.

They used the foot bridges over the water channels to step from the footpath onto the unsealed streets. They lingered awhile in the Queen's Arcade of covered shops and bought a penny coffee from a stall but the exciting day soon caught up with them. Cissy started yawning first so, linking elbows, Jessie steered her back toward the boarding house.

The women crawled longingly between clean rough sheets, appreciating a bed that didn't move. They all woke at daylight and took turns to splash cold water over their faces from the flowered jug on the bedside table. Cissy and Jessie dressed and repacked their bags ready for imminent departure.

Out in front of the boarding house in the crisp morning air, Anne waited with her two friends for the transport that would take them to the home of their employer where they were pledged to work as housemaids.

When the smart carriage and pair of horses with a uniformed driver arrived, the three women hugged and kissed. Anne had their address in South Yarra and fervently vowed to keep in touch.

'You'll have to write first, Annie, so's we know where you are when you get a job.' Jessie said, and because neither she nor Cissy could write, added, 'We'll get someone to read it for us.'

After a flurried farewell of waving hands and kerchiefs, the carriage rolled away. With mixed feelings, Anne watched it grow smaller among all the other vehicles and horses on the street until they were lost to sight. Anne returned to their room and sat on her bed, realising that, for the first time since leaving England, she was now completely alone. She had grown close to her travelling companions and would miss them.

Determined to stay positive about her new life, she breakfasted at the restaurant then sauntered along the streets of colonial shops and broad verandas. A newspaper boy approached her calling out 'Argus Argus' and on impulse she bought one. Returning to her lodgings, she settled down on the bed in her room and swiftly scoured its pages, learning something of the country and its affairs as she read, until an advertisement pertaining to the country caught her attention. She read it again, at first stunned, then amused. Then grew serious over the possibility. Would a true gentleman really place such an announcement? Jessie had said women were scarce out here. Maybe...

She clutched the newspaper to her chest then let her shoulders sag. No, it was too outrageous to consider. She had taken enough risks with impulsive decisions these past months. But the newspaper notice drew her imagination yet again and she read it a third time, smiling. No, the opportunity was far too tempting not to explore and might resolve all of her problems. She lost nothing by trying. It might lead to something else. Besides, if she wasn't successful, she'd keep trying.

Anne borrowed stationery from her landlady and penned a note, immediately whisked away by a delivery boy to its fate. After which Anne could do nothing but sit and wait.

The prospect of getting out into the country, even under the unusual circumstances, was far too tempting to ignore. Doubts niggled the back of her mind all afternoon as she wandered the Melbourne streets to keep occupied, but she ignored them, teasing possibilities keeping her positive. She would be able to ride again surely. The city was interesting but the promise of freedom and lure of more distance from the coast and therefore safety inland outweighed the situation involved. Besides, if she were fortunate enough to be successful, there was no need to make a decision straight away. She would think of something to delay.

By late afternoon when she returned to the boarding house, a letter of reply had arrived and Anne tore it open.

'Mr. James Barratt ... this afternoon ... five o'clock.'

The connecting words of the boldly scrawled message were little more than a blur. Five o'clock. Anne dashed into the hallway to check the clock. One hour. Well, she had made herself available at any time. Mr. Barratt had certainly taken her at her word. She offered up a silent prayer that the interview went well.

Back in her room, Anne swept up and captured her long hair as elegantly as possible with pins. It was no crime for a girl to advance her situation in life and seek security, she told herself. As she poked and prodded with her appearance, she hastily recalled the few scraps of etiquette Ma had vainly tried to teach her, annoyed now that she hadn't paid more attention.

She encountered the landlady in the hallway as she left who raised surprised eyebrows and gave an approving nod of admiration. Anne's confidence lifted and she stepped into her hired Albert cab with fresh determination.

The hooded horse-drawn vehicle bowled along at a jaunty pace, the clip clop of horses' hooves joining all the others that clogged the busy Melbourne streets today, bringing Anne closer to the Albion Hotel in Bourke Street, the designated location for her fateful interview.

Distracted by her forthcoming meeting, her mind wandered. Yielding to temptation, she withdrew the clipping she had torn from the Argus, folded neatly in her small drawstring bag and pressed it open, her eyes scanning the tantalising words.

'To Speculators in Matrimonial Engagements', the heading boldly enticed. 'The Advertiser, a Gentleman Pastoralist, wishes for an alliance with a Lady who can forego the tediousness and formality of courtship. Her personal attractions are the only requisites as the Advertiser's character and philosophy warrants him in saying that he can ensure happiness to a Lady of any description that might offer.'

Anne cast her unseeing gaze out onto the street and wondered for what reason a man would place such a notice. She was hardly high-bred but he did stipulate a Lady of any description so she had nothing to lose. If he was young and handsome, she would consider his proposition. Even if it came to nothing, he might have a position in his house and solve her immediate homelessness or have neighbours or friends who could give her work.

He sounded sincere enough, if a trifle indifferent and unmoved by the idea of courtship and romance. In claiming himself a gentleman, it hinted at respectability so Anne remained hopeful about the imminent encounter.

Of course, if he was a rogue, she would know on sight for she was a sensible judge of character. But there was something intriguing and sad about a man who would use this means of finding a wife. Back home, Pa had said there were too many women and not enough men. Out here, it seemed to be the other way around.

Being a pastoralist meant he lived in the country, a key factor that had lured Anne to consider such an unusual notice in the first place. She knew her hasty response was a risk but she had also considered that, with women being scarce here, maybe that was the reason he had grasped at such a desperate action.

From talk on board ship, she knew Australia was well known for its fine wool exported to England, so the man probably raised sheep. She had heard them called squatters because the adventurous men apparently just rode out, claimed their land and squatted on it. The idea of a man with a strong enough pioneering spirit to do such a daring thing appealed to Anne's own sense of excitement.

In her heart, the countryside is where Anne knew she belonged. Even though Jessie described it as isolated, she was undeterred. Born and raised on the edge of the bleak Dartmoor, Anne had loved every wild tempestuous moment of the climate and her life. She found a great harmony with nature and had already noticed many strange differences in the climate. Here, the seasons were opposite to Devon so that now it was the beginning of spring whereas back home autumn would be spreading its chilly fingers across the moor. The sun was brighter and warmer here already and it was not yet summer. And not least, she had sensed the buzz of hope and opportunity in the air.

Anne was also confident that she possessed sufficient personal attractions to interest a man. Before her doomed marriage to Arthur, she had received two offers back home in Devon. Of course, she had been younger and refused them but that did not guarantee her success today for she was completely at Mr. Barratt's mercy. Her future direction rested upon his decision.

She folded the newspaper clipping and returned it to her bag. It was possible the man was old or bald or ugly. He gave no indication of age. If he was too dreadful, she would make polite excuses and leave.

As her cab turned the corner into Bourke Street, Anne's brow furrowed, hoping her impetuous actions for a chance to live in the country led to work and security in her life.

Virtually penniless and urgently needing money and a home, she uttered up a silent prayer that all went well at the interview.

As the cab driver pulled the horse to a halt, Anne glanced out at the distinguished Albion Hotel. She paid the fare and stepped down, pausing on the road as the vehicle clattered away.

The two-storey hotel had two balconies at either side that protruded over the footpath from the first floor windows. She thought a drape flickered at one but she may have been mistaken. A central arched fanlight window displayed a clock in the centre of the building and inscribed above one of the front doors to the left was the name of John Cleeland, Licensee.

She drew in a breath for poise and straightened the folds of her plain green dress. Lifting her skirts to step over the open cobbled gutter onto the footpath, Anne noticed a Cobb & Co coach and telegraph office next door.

Inside the hotel, Anne approached a pale suited clerk standing behind the front desk. 'I have business with Mr. James Barratt.'

The weedy individual immediately understood for his washy grey eyes lit up and he motioned for her to follow him upstairs. Anne folded her hands calmly at her waist as the young man knocked on a door and waited.

When a deep muffled voice commanded, 'Enter,' he

thrust it open, gesturing for Anne to pass through.

She took two strides into the room, her heart beating fast, before she heard the door firmly closed behind.

Her glance ran swiftly over the comfortable surroundings but her inquisitive gaze was drawn to the male figure across the room with his back to her looking out of the window. He had witnessed her arrival on the street below!

From behind, the gentleman pastoralist was tall with wide shoulders, his dark wavy hair touching his shirt collar. It needed a cut but there was no sign of grey. She tried to guess how old. At least he was superbly fitted out in a dark blue suit with the long coat unbuttoned and casually swept back because of the hand in his pocket. The other held a pipe from which a drift of smoke wound its way lazily upward.

When he slowly turned, a look of wearied boredom on his face, Anne held her breath and their eyes met. She crumbled with relief and all reservations vanished. Without warning, her heart began to race. Mr. James Barratt was the most stunning male she had ever met. Although perhaps thirty, he could still be considered reasonably young. And roughly handsome, with a strong nose and sun-browned face and hands. Beneath his top coat, he wore a vivid blue patterned waistcoat that matched his eyes and a crisp white shirt but no cravat or tie. Despite only just having laid eyes on him, Anne was gripped by a sudden jealousy for her rivals.

At the sight of her, Barratt's apathy seemed to fade and his attention sharpened. He stepped closer across the deep red rug. Captivated by his stunning appeal, and without any sensible reasoning, it suddenly became imperative that Anne be the lady he chose.

Her poise wavered as his riveting gaze never left her face. Against his obvious stature and breeding, Anne felt inadequate and drab but managed to turn on her best smile. 'Good afternoon, Sir.'

'And you are?' He scowled with polite impatience.

Perhaps she had not made the best first impression for she

had clearly written her name on her note. 'Miss Annabella Gutheridge.'

'Of course.' He scowled, shook his head and ran two fingers of one hand across his forehead. 'But I seek a woman, not a girl.'

Distracted by the smooth resonant voice that emerged from the very depths of his chest, she grew alarmed he might turn her away without a chance. 'Your advertisement did say a lady of any description,' she reminded him, disagreeing. 'It didn't mention any age.' The moment the words spilled out, Anne winced at her audacity to call herself a lady.

She folded her nervous hands together in an effort to summon more composure. Going to the country now seemed far less important than that this man should not reject her. Although inclined to be rude and blunt, he was her most immediate means of leaving Melbourne and getting out into the country.

One black eyebrow flickered wryly upward as she squarely challenged his gaze. With a long-suffering sigh, he extended a hand, indicating a comfortable velvet settee. 'All right,' he snapped impatiently. 'I can spare you five minutes.'

James cursed himself for a fool. He would regret this and the five promised minutes would prove to be a waste of time. The girl had to be a decade too young and clearly of modest breeding. But her simple green dress was clean and clung to some rather generous curves for a girl her age. Not to mention the tumble of wavy hair she had failed to fully constrain with pins. It glowed golden in the lamplight beside her.

More annoying still, after a parade in recent days of sour puritans, desperate spinsters and delicate needy flowers who would wilt in the bush, this girl was the first exquisite ray of feminine sunshine worthy of a second glance. Pity she was so young.

His gaze settled on the specimen now seated before him. The tantalising wisps of hair that had escaped curled themselves against her slender neck. Even unadorned, her natural beauty was refreshing. Not to mention her engaging country lilt and the way she rolled her r's when she spoke. He restrained the wild thought that her youth may be an advantage for bearing the large family he planned to secure his vast holdings with sons.

Of more immediate concern perhaps, would they get on? Her lack of fragility appealed. She sat straight backed and tense, and those large sparkling green eyes held his without falter.

He was astounded to feel struck by her presence and seized by a fierce protection. Only because she was so young, of course. A girl of spirit, if not means. Hatless because she probably couldn't afford one but it would be sacrilege to hide that lovely mass of vivid hair.

Like most other women he had met in recent days, she undoubtedly sought security. As expected. Politely patient, he had conversed with all female comers but, without committing himself, equally politely let them leave. Every single one of them undoubtedly living in hope.

Earlier today, despondent at his lack of success, he had considered going next door to book a place on the next coach to Ballarat and return to *Barratt Downs* alone.

Anne bit her tongue and remained silent beneath Mr. Barratt's lengthy scrutiny. She jumped when he finally cleared his throat, rested an elbow on the mantle and said, 'You realise I live up country?'

She nodded. 'I love the country, Sir' she told him, too eagerly. 'I was raised on a farm.'

He chuckled softly and Anne found herself captivated by the deep and lovely sound. 'Indeed.' He paused, contemplating her intently. '*Barratt Downs* bears little resemblance to the pocket-sized green squares of England, Miss Gutheridge.'

Reproached for her ignorance, Anne hesitated, then

ventured, 'Why did you advertise for a wife, Mr. Barratt?'

He regarded her with a narrowed gaze. 'I rarely visit Melbourne and meet few women. Lord knows I have been pursued,' he muttered, staring blankly toward the far window. When he eventually returned his attention to her, he told her honestly, 'I am 30 and want heirs. Sons to inherit what I've built.'

'Or daughters.'

He paused, considering her correction. 'Possibly. If so, I will make sure they marry well and choose acceptably affluent husbands. I trust you keep good health?'

Surprised by the question, Anne assured him, 'Always, Sir,' for she seldom caught cold or other illness.

'Good. I want a large family.'

Anne swallowed. Children. She hadn't thought that far ahead but then, she never did. His pronouncement made her realise the importance and sincerity of his advertisement and this interview. Not to mention the realities and extent of the situation into which she had so casually plunged. She knew what marriage meant and recalled Arthur's unpleasant groping and grunting back in Devon. Surely a gentleman like Mr. Barratt would have more consideration.

Strange enough imagining James Barratt as her husband let alone bearing him a brood of children. She had nothing against babies. She had little to do with them except helping raise her youngest sister, Emmy. She was, however, no longer an innocent and fully aware of her marital duties. She felt her colour rise at his comment for the unwanted memories it raised. At least she was not ignorant as to how children were conceived.

Awkward at his honest announcement, all she could think to say was, 'You like children, Sir?'

'Indeed. I come from a large family myself. I intend to create a dynasty.'

Startled by his revelation, Anne frowned, amazed at his practical businesslike reason for marriage and scrambled to think of a suitable response. She noticed his restless agitation and paused.

He paced the room and drew heavily on his pipe, sending clouds of smoke into the room and stalling any response she may have made.

More entranced by him with every moment, Anne decided to tease him. 'Your wife will be kept busy, Mr. Barratt. I trust you have servants to help.'

'Plenty.' Intrigued by her boldness, James studied her, aware she baited him. 'I trust that meets with your approval.'

'Completely. If I was the lady you chose.' She flashed her sweetest smile, sounding much more composed than she felt in the presence of this imposing man. Her heart had completely let her down and was beating with such erratic fierceness she thought her chest would burst.

'Being a new chum, Miss Gutheridge, you would not know it is impossible to run a sheep station without considerable help. Although labourers can be deuced hard to find and keep.'

'New chum?' she pressed for clarification.

His serious face lightened and tiny lines crinkled up beside his eyes. 'A recent arrival to our shores such as yourself, Miss Gutheridge. Where from?'

Although Anne instinctively felt she could trust this man with her life, she would not confide the true reason for her emigration to anyone and hesitated to provide any unnecessary detail. 'Devon, Sir.'

His lovely dark eyebrows rose with interest. 'Then our families are almost neighbours. I'm originally from Sullington in Sussex. Have you ever been there?'

'No.' Anne had never travelled beyond Tavistock and the Dartmoor until that fateful night only months before when her intolerable life was threatened and her life had changed forever.

James appeared well travelled and adventurous. Eager to learn more and divert the conversation, she asked, 'How long have you been in Australia, Mr. Barratt?'

He stared off into space and puffed on his pipe. 'Fifteen years. I came out in '46 on the *Enterprise*.' The corner of his mouth edged into a wry smile. 'An appropriate name, I thought.'

She shared his humour and smiled, and her heart set up a fresh bout of strange beating at the dashing charm that spread across his face.

'I knew the Hentys of West Tarring who bred merino sheep and had become successful out here, so I emigrated to try my luck. I bought my first flock from them at Portland Bay on the coast.'

Anne's sharp mind filled with excitement at the uncanny coincidence. 'A Mr. and Mrs. Henty were passengers on the *Result* coming out. Are they connected?'

At her snippet of information, Anne claimed his full attention. 'They are indeed. I had heard Richmond recently married in London. You met his wife?'

'No, but I learned they were on board and saw them walking on deck occasionally. I understand Richard's father, Stephen Henty, is a successful merchant and in the Victorian parliament.'

Anne noticed James seemed surprised and even mildly impressed by her information.

'The Henty brothers had been in Portland Bay district, as it was known then, for ten years and were well established further south on the Wannon River when I arrived. The sons all have stations south in the Western District. They are all astute pioneering men. The Sussex coast where they come from is backed by the South Downs and ideal for sheep.' Animated, James asked, 'Where did you live in Devon, Miss Gutheridge?'

Anne hesitated. 'My father is a tenant farmer near Tavistock.'

'Ah.' He silently absorbed her humble origins. 'And you decided to leave?'

Anne nodded.

'Did you travel out to the colony alone?'

To counter her discomfort at his question, she countered, 'Yes. Didn't you?' It had always frustrated her why men had so much unquestioned freedom, yet women were bound by stricter rules.

'Clearly your family was agreeable?'

Unable to meet his gaze, her attention wandered. 'There was little choice.' Not entirely untrue although not in the circumstances James would assume. 'My parents found it hard and sought a better life for us.'

'Us?'

'My brother and sisters. It is always sad when families must part. But I met friends aboard,' she brightened. 'I was not completely alone.'

'And where are your friends now?'

'In service at a Mr. Rochester's house in South Yarra.'

'*Belvedere*.' James announced. 'I know it.'

Anne was continually amazed at how small a place the colony was and how people knew each other. 'They had an assisted passage and had their employment arranged before they left.'

'But not you?' James probed.

Anne shook her head and said carefully, 'I had hoped to seek employment up country.'

'But now you seek marriage and a higher status?' His mockery was not derogatory but a challenge.

Because Mr. Barratt had been bluntly honest, Anne decided to do the same. 'Your advertisement was an opportunity for security,' Anne admitted.

Far from being shocked by her explanation, he inclined his head slightly in silent acknowledgement of her candour. 'My run is remote. You won't see many people. Only the household staff, occasional travellers and drifters. It has been a wet winter,' he added. 'Miners were held up. There were frequent floods and cartage was out of the question. No one can travel when the countryside is in such a heavy state.'

Aware he was making a point about his property's isolation, Anne said firmly, 'As I said, I've lived on a farm. I prefer the country.'

'Why do you want to marry, Miss Gutheridge?'

'I don't. It hadn't occurred to me until I read the Argus.' The words slipped off her tongue before she could retract them.

Obviously amused, James burst out laughing. 'Such honesty. Rare indeed. Charming.' He sobered. 'Then why did you respond?'

'I needed to get out into the country.'

'Needed?' James pressed.

'I mean, I have no particular interest in towns,' Anne quickly corrected. 'I loved the open air and wide spaces of the moors back home. Your advertisement offered that chance.'

'Adventurous of you to leave home without any plans and seek marriage the day after you arrive in a foreign land. Do I detect a hint of desperation?'

'No more than you, Mr. Barratt, seeking a complete stranger for a wife,' she retorted indignantly at his teasing provocation, accompanied by an irritating grin of amusement and superior air. 'If I'm not what you're looking for in a wife,' she said primly, 'I'll consider employment if you have a job for me. You did say hired help was hard to come by.'

His gaze narrowed and he cast her a lengthy stare. 'One step at a time, Miss Gutheridge.'

She wasn't sure what he meant but it sounded hopeful and, at least so far, he hadn't dismissed her.

'Why did you really leave England, Miss Gutheridge?'

His casual tone did not conceal his compelling gaze and, to her annoyance, she found it more difficult with every question to mislead him. Was deserting marriage a crime? She had no idea. His question was unexpected and her reply defensive. 'I believe I'm old enough to make my own way. I've already said my father could no longer afford to keep us.

He only rents a small farm.'

'I'm sorry to hear it,' he murmured, his tone genuinely sincere, his keen gaze settled upon her with kindness. 'Now that we've established our reasons for both being here, perhaps it is appropriate to discuss an … alliance.'

Throughout the conversation so far, James remained standing nearby. Now, he tapped out his pipe and set it down on a small side table before moving over to a large sideboard to pour himself a brandy from a crystal decanter.

Anne watched him swallow a mouthful of the golden liquid, his posture straight, his manner assured, and admired the wealthy educated man of the world, feeling young and inadequate alongside him. She despaired that he could possibly consider her a suitable candidate for any union with him. What kind of mismatch would it be?

She cringed at the memory that it could be no worse than her marriage to Arthur. In fact, despite being strangers, it held the potential for far more comfort and happiness. Both of which, in her desperate situation, appealed. And she justified her actions in pursuing her present course by reminding herself that it was for her own safety.

Deep in worried thought, Anne did not notice James sit opposite in an armchair and stretch out his long legs comfortably before him.

'I'm surprised a prosperous man like yourself found no suitable ladies in your district, Mr. Barratt.'

'There have always been more males than females in the colony.'

'I would have thought the pursuit of a lady would challenge you, Mr. Barratt,' Anne dared suggest.

'Only if you can find one in the first place. At least my method has instantly borne fruit.'

'You have made a decision, then?'

'One or two prospects have … captured my imagination,' he ventured. 'Whomever I choose,' he added with subtle caution, 'they must realise this is a union of … convenience.'

Was he giving her an opportunity to reconsider? Anne's heart leapt with hope and joy. Did that mean she was one of his so called prospects? She felt a fleeting ache of sadness that they had only just met. She might not be chosen and forced to leave.

'Of course.' She straightened her back and tried to appear poised amidst the turmoil racing through her stomach.

'Do you? I wonder,' James murmured, adding, 'I intend marriage primarily for a family.'

Not normally affected by female moods, he noted the fleeting sadness that crossed her expectant face, no doubt caused by his words but determined that blunt truth was the only course open to him, since any potential lady candidate must understand the circumstances he offered.

'You expect love will come later, perhaps?' Anne suggested.

'It's not impossible.' His tone softened.

Anne grew hot at his warm gaze and shifted in her soft comfortable chair. Despite his small interest in her, she believed her personal attractions were lacking and wished she had more time and means in which to be more presentable and attractive to him for she was drawn to this strong handsome man as she had been to no other. Mr. Barratt was so much more manly compared to most other men she had met. Except perhaps for Charles Montgomery who had bought the horse from her in Plymouth. He, too, had been a true gentleman.

Like any young woman she had once held wildly romantic notions for herself but, since her ill-fated marriage to Arthur and flight to Australia, all hopes of any such unrealistic nonsense were dashed. Yet here she sat a world away from the land of her birth to which she would probably never return, in a hotel, facing a stranger, poised to leap into marriage if it was offered, without a scrap of romance. Attraction and liking, perhaps yes, but a man, she sensed, worthy of her deepest respect and who would not mistreat her as Arthur had done. She would be safe and unharmed she was sure.

'You spoke with confidence of assuring a lady's happiness, Mr. Barratt. How do you propose to do that without some sign of affection?'

'My home is comfortable and I have servants.'

Anne despaired. That is all he believed he needed to offer! Was it madness to continue with the interview for the single sake of security which she could possibly find elsewhere? Or should she make her apologies and leave? The most sensible course of action, not what her heart and instinct told her, both proving a powerful force to control.

'Were there no prospects for you in Devon, Miss Gutheridge?'

Anne's spine stiffened at his insinuation. 'I had offers.'

'And obviously refused them.' Because she had no choice, she let him misunderstand without interruption or correction. 'Yet you are here today,' he observed with a direct gaze.

'So are you.'

'I know my reasons. I don't know yours.' He drilled her with an accusing glare.

Undaunted, Anne said. 'What I know, Mr. Barratt, is that marriage is the basis of all decent society.' Although her own past experience of it had left her wary.

'True.' Barratt half inclined his head, watching her closely. 'A genuine alliance is to be desired and although attraction can be a consideration, many unions survive without it.'

'Yes. Indeed.' What else could she say? His motives remained clinical. With her mood dampened and a heavy silent pause between, Anne was still inquisitive to learn more about his home. To break the emptiness, she asked, 'Where exactly is your property, Mr. Barratt?'

His eyebrows flickered upward at her unexpected question. James withdrew a pouch of tobacco from his coat pocket and began refilling his pipe. Anne thought it a calming homely gesture. 'Two days' journey west in the foothills of the

Grampians mountains.'

Mountains. It sounded lovely and not at all as Cissy had described.

'I presume you have sheep?'

'Yes.'

'How many?'

He shrugged. 'About ten thousand.'

Anne swallowed and gaped, unable to speak. He must own half of Victoria.

A playful twist moved across his lips and a chuckle spilled from inside him. The sun shone from his smile, filling her with a flood of warmth, and Anne could neither explain her response nor why the smallest of his movements held such fascination.

James marvelled over her eyes. The colour of gum leaves when the sunlight shone on them after rain. With nostalgic urgency, they drew his thoughts homeward.

'My homestead contains every comfort a lady might require. I don't spend much time there but the house is large and I employ a cook, a housemaid, a job-about boy and gardener.'

'Your property must be large.'

Judging by the awe on her glowing face, James realised that this young woman was no gold digger. Her questions came from genuine interest. She was trusting and possessed spirit. Qualities a squatter's wife needed in the harsh colonial bush. Dare he even consider her?

'*Barratt Downs* is 25000 acres.' His mind wandered pleasantly as he puffed on his pipe. He heard her stifle a gasp at the size of his holdings, no doubt suitably impressed, and he felt a quiet sense of pride for his holding was far bigger than even the landed gentry of England.

'Minus the 640 acres that a wretched neighbour stole,' he muttered.

'Stole?' she queried.

James abruptly stopped in the centre of the rug and glared at her interruption. He hesitated then growled, 'Selected. I carved *Barratt Downs* with my own bare hands and hard work. I will not concede a single acre more. I will build a dynasty of my own and outfox him.'

Anne observed the man pacing opposite as passionate and fiercely protective of his possessions. She wondered if that would extend to a wife. If so, for some reason she found it an exciting thought. With no wife, there would not be the heirs he so desperately desired.

James unexpectedly extended a hand to Anne to help her up. 'It's a busy time of year. Shearing is about to start. I don't have any time to waste.'

Surprised by his sudden action, she accepted, and his large warm brown hand closed around hers as she stood, tilting her face up to him.

She tried to appear gracious in panic. 'Of course. You have a decision to make.' Anne's hopes faltered. Would she be ushered to the door like all the others or asked to stay? Either way, within moments, her life was about to change. Again.

'You are young and healthy, Miss Gutheridge,' Barratt announced frankly. 'Two attributes in your favour. As you know, I want heirs.' His words gushed forth with gruff uncertainty. 'Knowing my terms and our ... situation after such short acquaintance, if I offered you marriage, would you accept?'

Anne's heart leapt. Of all his candidates, she was his choice? She hadn't dared hope ... and was at a loss as to why the positive decision meant so much to her. She knew nothing of this compelling man but there was an indefinable quality about him that provoked her complete trust. As a result of this meeting, she had the chance for something different and exciting. And secure. Voices crowded her head telling her this was madness and she must refuse. But her mind argued, hadn't she obediently married another man against her will on equally limited acquaintance. At least a match with this man was by her own choice.

Although much older than her, Mr. Barratt was a fine looking prosperous gentleman. Reasons enough for any sensible woman to accept. But could she marry and commit her life to him when she was still connected to another man in another country? Perhaps not, but right now Arthur Westcott and her family were far away at the other side of the world and it seemed unlikely they should ever see each other again.

She looked at Barratt, torn between her whirl of thoughts and his powerful presence and unbelievable offer. Hovering on the brink of uncertainty, she hesitated.

'Miss Gutheridge?'

His deep voice interrupted her hectic thoughts. He had stepped so close, she could see his devilishly blue eyes, every weathered line on his smooth brown face. All part of his arresting appeal. She smelt the lingering aroma of his tobacco, a hint of brandy on his breath. So male...

In the past, she had made many decisions on impulse. Would agreement to this unusual situation be her undoing?

Barratt grew impatient 'Do you agree then?' he barked.

'No.'

'Why not?'

'I don't know you well enough for marriage.'

Glaring in shock, James softly cursed. He had hoped to find a wife, marry in a day or so and take his bride home. Blast the woman! He needed a wife and he needed a commitment. He had assumed she would be more than grateful for his offer and eagerly accept. In fact, having met her and been charmed, he was loathe to let her go.

Thinking quickly, he said, 'Would you agree to a period of ... betrothal?'

'No. That means the same thing.'

Swept with irritation at her delay, he snapped ungraciously, 'Have you misled me?'

'No,' she hastily assured him. 'But I do have a suggestion.'

His interest sharpened and his foul mood eased. 'Let's hear it.'

'I can give you no guarantee but ... if I could see your home ... and spend some time where you live, it might help me decide. After all,' she added quickly ignoring his scowl, 'The alliance you seek suggests an arrangement by the parties concerned, not a foregone conclusion.'

'It does no such thing,' Barratt argued. 'My advertisement clearly suggests marriage.'

'All the same,' Anne persisted, 'It would be an ideal opportunity to become better acquainted, don't you agree?' she hinted sweetly.

James privately fumed. He was offering this chit of a thing a share of his substantial wealth and she needed to approve his home! The girl's audacity to suggest his circumstances were anything less than superior and completely adequate were humiliating.

'All right,' he frowned in grudging agreement. 'As you wish.' And tried to remember exactly where in their conversation the balance had shifted to Miss Gutheridge's favour. 'I don't suppose you come with a dowry?' he quipped.

His taunt so offended Anne, she decided to wipe the smug smile from his face. With a rising temper, she opened her small bag, turned it upside down and emptied its contents onto the floor. Her few remaining precious coins fell with a soft thud onto the rich red carpet and briefly rolled around before settling about their feet.

'You are welcome to all I own but, if you prefer an heiress, I will gladly leave,' Anne lied and held her breath. She would be devastated if he dismissed her but she believed he possessed a deep seated goodness and hoped his pride would not allow him to dishonour his word.

'That won't be necessary.' He cleared his throat, Anne

thought perhaps regretting his tactless remark until he added, 'I have no need of an heiress. Merely a woman who can bear me sons.'

James assessed her shrewdly. Her farming background made her more acceptable for country life, even though she was of tenant stock. In Australia, he had never held with class distinction as the measure by which he chose his company. In a young colony still being settled, men relied on each other, sometimes with their life. Wiser to count every man your friend. He was well aware that, in England, Annabella would be considered an inappropriate match. Out here, although it mattered less, some fellow squatters were snobs.

For his present urgent purpose, Annabella's beauty and intelligence, despite her humble upbringing, excelled above all other females he had seen. She had the courage to challenge him which she would need in full measure where he lived.

With the insecurity of squatters' lands now being thrown open for selection, James needed to protect all he had built and, at rifle point, would not concede any more acres to selectors like Munro who had cleverly obtained a neglected corner of his property, securing it as his own selection.

Everything now hinged on Miss Gutheridge accepting *Barratt Downs* as her home. He hoped she adapted quickly and they could be married. His need for a family now he was established and successful was strong. Many of his fellow men, having made their fortunes, returned to England to find a wife. As he had done without success. He winced, the emotional humiliation still fresh.

He needed a wife and sons to consolidate his roots. Miss Gutheridge seemed earthy and, he hoped, willing. He would allow her to settle into homestead life alone during shearing and find her way. She would need to become independent and adapt to his habits and routine.

'If you tell me where you are staying, I will arrange to

have your belongings brought to the hotel,' James offered.

'You want me to stay here?'

'In separate rooms, of course,' he hastily clarified. 'It will be more convenient. The Ballarat coach leaves from next door at six in the morning.'

His explanation was logical. 'Of course.'

Anne gave him the name and address of her lodgings. 'I…don't have much,' she was ashamed to admit, embarrassed over her lowly standing compared to the grander surroundings here and up country to which she knew Mr. Barratt was obviously accustomed.

Now it came to revealing the extent of her penury and, although she despised sewing, she must use some of her time to make new clothes. She eyed the coins lying on the floor and wondered how far they would stretch here in the colony to purchase material and thread.

James eyed her and frowned. 'You have no cases?'

'Just one carpet bag. I planned to acquire more as soon as I settled and found work,' she babbled in uncomfortable explanation.

Upon her elaboration of the extent of her penury, Mr. Barratt's gaze softened and his attitude assumed a subtle shift. Not pity, she noticed, but compassion for her circumstances.

'Shearing takes weeks. It will be some time before you can leave *Barratt Downs*. If necessary,' he added wryly. He moved away from her and paced the carpet between chairs. 'You will need more clothes.' He snapped a glance at her. 'Befitting the climate. Summer dresses, blouses, hats. That sort of thing. It's much hotter here than England.'

Anne despaired. She had little money and, yet again, suffered the guilt of being a financial burden. 'Perhaps I could borrow some?'

James flicked an assessing gaze up and down the length of her. 'Bridget's would fit you twice. And Sarah's would be too short. I'll think of something,' he muttered then stepped forward opening one of two panelled doors at the end of the room. 'I have secured an adjoining room.' He noticed her alarm and reassured her, 'The door can be locked from the other side.'

Anne relaxed, grateful to have her privacy ensured. 'Thank you.'

She swept past him and pushed the half open door wider, preceding him into the next room. At first sight, she gasped with delight. It was as grand as the sitting room they had just left, far superior to anything she had ever slept in before, and certainly nothing like the spartan cramped conditions aboard ship on the voyage out.

Her gaze lingered over the deeply carved mahogany bed head, crisp white linen and lace-edged bedspread and pillows. The rich red carpet beneath her boots, delicate rose-patterned wallpaper, comfortable chair, mahogany dresser and carved mirror. The long window at the opposite side was draped with velvet and lace.

James Barratt gave the impression that acquiring a wife was a tedious business formality, yet he had provided comfort and luxury for the woman he chose.

Anne turned to him, unable to restrain her smile. 'It's lovely. Thank you.'

James shuffled, as though embarrassed. 'I'll arrange for your ... things to be collected then I am going out. Supper is served at seven in our sitting room.'

After he disappeared, all fell quiet, and Anne was given time to think over her rash decision. She restlessly paced, wringing her hands. Had she made the right decision?

She had been in Melbourne for barely a day and was already about to depart for the country and possibly married life.

Later she could apologise and say Mr. Barratt's situation didn't suit and leave. But for now and, if only temporarily, this chance gave her a home and security. Perhaps she had leapt into this new life but was prepared and eager to approach it with a positive mind. Anne only briefly allowed herself to dwell on how much she missed her family. She would write to them when her future was more settled.

Soon, Anne's few humble belongings arrived. She washed for supper and brushed her hair. Checking the small china clock on the bedside table and although she had not yet heard Mr. Barratt's return, just before seven she returned to the sitting room.

She nervously waited but James did not appear. When supper arrived and was laid out on a small dining table, Anne stirred up the fire and lit the lamps, assuming he would not be long.

With the food getting cold and her stomach growling with hunger, she lifted the lids of the domed silver dishes. A tureen of thick soup, hearty meat stew with vegetables and a fruit pie. Tempted far beyond denial, she decided to eat, her enjoyment of such a rare feast diminished by James' absence.

What could be so important to detain him at this hour? Without realising it, Anne had looked forward to spending more time with him to become better acquainted.

By nine, drowsy after the generous meal and weary from the day's events, Anne retired to her room, undressed to her undergarments and blew out the lamp, snuggling blissfully between fresh linen on her large soft bed and fell instantly asleep.

CHAPTER 8

Anne stirred to the sound of light tapping on her bedroom door. Still drowsy, she sat up and clutched the bedclothes against her noting no slithers of light showed at the edges of the drapes.

'Yes?'

James entered carrying a candlestick, already dressed in dark grey trousers, black and white checked waistcoat and white shirt. Without the formality of a coat, he seemed more approachable.

'Good morning,' he murmured, letting his gaze linger upon her, touching his candle flame to her lantern wick, spreading soft golden light into the room.

Anne glanced at the small china clock to see it was after six. 'I've slept in. We missed the coach! Why didn't you wake me?' She began scrambling from bed.

'No,' he assured her quickly. 'We're not leaving today.'

'We're not?' Anne wondered why the delay when yesterday he had been impatient to return home. And she noted that, as yet, he had offered no explanation or apology for his absence last night.

'No. Because immediately after breakfast we're visiting the premises of Alston and Brown in Collins Street where I shall buy you new clothes. I am assured they are the most notable establishment for ladies' fashion.'

Alarmed at the extravagance, Anne protested, 'Oh but I couldn't let you-'

'You can and you will. I have been given a list of everything a lady requires, and we will fill it. We have made an alliance, Annabella. Not a contract,' he drawled, his blue eyes filled with meaning and warmth. 'Any lady friend of mine deserves nothing less. Whatever happens,' he added tactfully, 'They are yours to keep.'

Anne gasped and filled with excitement. 'That is most generous.'

The moment James left her room, she swiftly dressed and washed, working her hair into one long thick braid down her back then joined him in the sitting room for breakfast.

Her only slip to spoil their meal was when she innocently commented, 'I was worried when you didn't return last night.'

James glowered. 'I don't normally account for my movements.'

'Maybe not but how would you feel if I went missing for hours without explanation?' she asked bluntly.

For a moment, James looked stumped. 'I would not permit you to go out on Melbourne streets unaccompanied in the first instance.'

His comment ended the conversation and nothing more was said. Despite the brief moment of tension and being firmly put in her place, James appeared to harbour no ill feeling when, at barely nine he escorted her downstairs and outdoors. He offered his arm and they strolled importantly along the Melbourne streets. Anne's senses peaked, as though something new was born inside her and she became alive as never before.

She had added the sedate touch of her only sunbonnet, borrowed from Jessie, although now crumpled and well-worn from months at sea.

The early spring sky was vivid blue and without cloud. The wide street rolled into the distance bustling with all types of horse-drawn vehicles and carts. Many pedestrians were already underway, fashionable women gliding between shops, a sprinkling of young men loitering on corners.

They turned along Swanston and then Collins Streets

toward their destination. Before they reached it, however, they encountered a crowd of men congregated on the kerb beneath a veranda balcony, shouting and bantering among themselves.

'This is called The Veranda,' James explained.

'What are they doing?' Anne asked as his strong hand at her elbow guided her safely around the noisy rabble. Mostly, she noted, well-dressed cheerful men.

'Buying and selling gold shares mostly. It's an outdoor stock exchange. You can win or lose a fortune here. For those tempted to spend their money freely and courage enough to try.' He leaned closer and murmured, 'We all take a gamble now and then, Miss Gutheridge, do we not?'

Anne smiled weakly and nodded, wondering how their own speculation would develop.

As they entered the brick emporium of Alston and Brown, a male shop assistant hurried forward with a chair. James stated their mission and produced his handwritten list. Once proceedings were underway, Anne began to enjoy it, Mr. Barratt offering his nod of approval or shake of the head whenever she turned to seek his opinion. Seeing his reassuring appreciative looks when she paraded in a number of readymade dresses, was reward enough for the ordeal.

Bolts of cloth, printed and checked cottons, the lightest floating silks were all unfurled before her, filling her with foreign pleasure.

Attended like gentry with respect and deference, despite her obvious lower standing, Anne confidently added white and cream blouses, hats with ribbons, shawls, a jacket and a cape.

She also chose simple styles to be made up from patterns. Then, discreetly ushered into an adjoining room, Anne selected petticoats, drawers, chemises and restricting whalebone corsets, until her head spun and she protested. The mature female assistant assured her they were on the list and must be bought. Gloves, shoes and buttoned boots were last.

Then, finally, James arranged for the packages to be

delivered to the hotel with instructions for the remaining garments, when made, to be sent out to *Barratt Downs*.

While they ate a light dinner, her parcels were delivered. Afterwards, Anne excitedly changed into one of her new purchases. A high-necked cotton dress of polished gold sprigged with greenery. She pinned up her braid, adding a straw bonnet with a dashing dark green feather.

Later, when she accompanied James downstairs and out onto the street, she felt like another woman than the one who had left the hotel this morning. To her further delight, before them stood a pair of beautifully groomed greys harnessed to an elegant waiting carriage.

Anne suffered a moment of anguished guilt at such luxurious attention that she may not decide to stay at *Barratt Downs* and was therefore misleading him. Until she remembered that she had only promised to go and look at his property in the bush and make her decision then.

Anne's doubt was soon forgotten, however, by her warm pleasure in James' company seated next to him in the carriage. How large and strong he was beside her. For the first time since leaving Devon, she felt truly safe and protected.

Having always loved the outdoors, she settled back against the plush cushions to enjoy the ride.

Relaxed now that she seemed content with their outing, James watched Anne's animation with interest. Her cheeks whipped to a becoming blush by the playful breeze. She looked naive and natural, clearly unaware of her physical attraction to men. And, although he might be loath to admit it, particularly upon him.

Enchanting beyond any words he could use, James suffered a minor sense of shame for using this lovely young thing to lift his weary spirits. It was too early to tell, and she had not yet agreed – her caution was understandable, if irritating – but any alliance between them promised compatibility at least. And, for that, he was relieved. Isolated up country, it was imperative their relationship was easy and genial.

Miss Annabella Gutheridge had been a stroke of good fortune indeed. With his deepest desire, he prayed she fitted into homestead life and agreed to stay. He must thank Rosie when they met again for suggesting this irregular but fruitful course of action.

Initially, he had thought it a nuisance leaving the property this close to shearing. Once they returned, he would have little time to entertain her. And he had no doubts, guessing the kind of background from whence she came, that his home would fulfil all of her expectations.

On his instructions, the driver flicked the reins and the carriage moved through the city, crossed the Yarra River and out along St. Kilda Road where it diverged and turned into Gardiner's Creek Road.

Fascinated and impressed, Anne viewed the splendid mansions and charming villas along the route, beautiful homes with names like Como and Bona Vista. Their extensive landscaped grounds gave them a rural air although they were suburbs of Melbourne.

'These belong to wealthy merchants, professional men and financiers,' James said with a sweep of his hand as they passed. He indicated Toorak House where the Governor of Victoria, Sir Henry Barkly, resided.

'They are all so beautiful,' Anne breathed in awe.

'It wasn't always like this,' James said. 'Twenty years ago, Melbourne was only a primitive settlement of tumbledown huts. Before gold was discovered a decade ago, it was most inferior. Unpaved and unlit. When I arrived, it was a miserable town.'

Their progress continued further out and Annabella listened avidly as James continued to talk.

'It changed in the Fifties. A Separation Bill was passed making the Port Phillip colony independent and the Queen gave her name to it. Then, in Fifty-one, gold was discovered. With the population explosion, it was a seller's market and you could make a lot of money.'

Anne turned to him. 'Did you?'

James grinned at her candour. 'Yes, I did. As did all other squatters close to the diggings. We supplied the demand for meat at a handsome profit. Better to get a Pound for a sheep instead of a shilling to sell it for tallow. Within a few years,' he continued, 'Victoria was transformed from a pastoral settlement into a thriving colony. Melbourne has become a great city.'

They had travelled for some miles and were now rolling along the sea road which led to Brighton with a magnificent view across Port Phillip Bay into which Annabella had sailed only days before. A brisk, salty wind blew in from the water across the carriage.

'We can raise the hood?' James offered.

'Oh, no!' Anne shook her head, invigorated. 'I love it.' She sat forward, straining to scan the horizon, her face glowing, her eyes bright.

The driver reined the horses, turned the carriage about and they returned into the city, passing the Domain gardens on the river bank, the sluggish water shaded by willows. The carriage re-crossed the waterway and rattled up Collins Street. At the top end of the wide thoroughfare, James indicated the solid respectable mansions inhabited by medical men who lived on the premises where they practised.

Government offices and the unfinished Parliament House promised to grandly preside over the higher part of town. They passed churches, a massive courthouse and gaol, then turned into yet another broad road.

'This is Elizabeth Street,' James said. 'Our coach takes this route up country to Ballarat in the morning.'

The surroundings became familiar again as they passed the new Post Office under construction, with only the ground floor built and scaffolding raised around the upper stories. All about them was progress.

As their carriage pulled up before the Albion Hotel once more, Anne sighed with disappointment. She gathered up her dress and prepared to alight. James leapt down ahead of her, anticipating her descent and his big, brown hands grasped her firmly, settling on her waist. Swept with confusion at his gentlemanly gesture and the excitement that arose within her, she quickly moved from his hold and crossed to the footpath.

As attractive as she found Mr. Barratt in such a short time, Anne knew it was madness to allow any affection to develop for it was not yet certain she would stay on his property. Shadowed by her past, she must be cautious and it would be unfair to mislead him this early in their acquaintance, no matter that he seemed kind and genuine enough.

On the pavement, James offered Anne his arm to escort her upstairs. Not wishing to offend him, she complied. They stepped into the sitting room to find it already set with a lace cloth, fresh flowers and gleaming silverware, the whole setting bathed in candle glow and warmed by crackling flames from a young fire in the grate.

James shrugged off his topcoat. 'I can assure you we shall definitely dine together this evening,' he quipped.

He moved across to the massive sideboard and poured golden liquid into two glasses from a decanter. Her heart raced as he approached and offered her one, their fingers touching as she hesitantly accepted the drink.

'I don't usually-'

'It's only a nip of brandy. A few mouthfuls won't hurt,' he teased. His goblet glinted in the soft light as he proposed a toast. 'To us. Whatever the future holds.' His voice was warm and his thick, dark eyebrows slightly raised.

'To us,' she echoed.

As the sharp unfamiliar liquid burned a path down her throat, Anne coughed at its effect and withstood his amused gaze. Unable to bear the charged silence, Anne moved stiffly toward the table to place a more comfortable distance between them. She sipped her drink again to moisten the sudden dryness in her throat. A discreet knock at their door interrupted them and broke the charged atmosphere.

'Enter,' James responded and a dinner trolley was rolled into the room. The male servant bowed politely and left.

She cast her eyes over the plentiful food when James lifted the silver lids. For the main course, there was a large, roast fowl with vegetables, and for dessert, a rich, creamy confection with fruit.

'John Cleeland is a splendid host and has never disappointed me yet.'

James held out her chair and she sat down, forgetting her manners, suddenly ravenous from the day's excursions and piling generous servings of food onto her plate, blissfully unaware that James watched her, amused.

'Do you come to Melbourne often?' she asked as she tasted the tender white meat.

'Once or twice a year.'

'Oh.' Anne stopped chewing. 'So rarely?'

'I had hoped to come down earlier,' he explained, 'but as I told you yesterday, our winter was wet and I was delayed. The past two winters were almost rainless but this year the creeks are all running high and the swamps and waterholes are filled. Water is vital to a landholder's existence out here. Unlike Sussex and Devon where they get too much of it.'

James eyed her pleasantly as he ate. 'This season we've had floods. Rare indeed. Many places were inaccessible and it was impossible for the bullock wagons to get through.' He shook his head. 'The whole country was sodden.'

Anne realised that, had James come to Melbourne as originally planned and the weather not delayed him, they would never have met. The *Result* would still have been at sea and another woman free to win him.

'Why did you emigrate?' Anne asked.

His clear blue gaze clouded for a moment then livened. 'I was the youngest son, never destined to inherit. My father is a sheepherder in Sussex but our land would never have supported all of us. So my father spared me some of his Southdown breeders to start my own flock.'

'What happened when you arrived?' Annabella was eager to learn more.

He laid down his cutlery and idled with his glass, reflective.

'The October weather was favourable, warmer than any English summer. I was approached by a settler seeking men for shearing.' He smiled directly at her. It was so wide and warm, Anne's heart skipped a beat. 'I was tempted since he offered me sixteen shillings a week plus rations which was extremely generous under the circumstances.'

'What circumstances?'

'A depression. Wool was only bringing four pence a pound on the English market. Squatting was risky at the best of times but with fluctuating markets and a shortage of labour, the hard times forced men out.'

'But not you.'

'No. Those with capital behind them survived. And some of the more…unscrupulous.' His mouth twisted wryly. 'But I had my small flock and was anxious to take up land so I travelled out towards the Grampians mountains where there were still small pockets of land. I found a beautiful isolated area of about ten thousand acres in the foothills and squatted on it.'

'Without buying it?'

'Yes.'

'That was allowed?'

'Officially, no,' he admitted candidly, 'but men did it. Beaurocracy kills fortunes. If I'd waited, I would have lost choice land. Overlanders were coming down from north of the Murray River and others like the Hentys crossed Bass Strait from Tasmania. Or Van Diemen's Land as it was known then. That part of the Port Phillip District was fertile and well-watered with lots of creeks and rivers, and good rainfall. Ideal for sheep.

'In Thirty-six, after a Scottish explorer named Mitchell discovered the region, there was a mad scramble to claim land. Naturally, those who came first picked the best country. Mostly unmarried young men like myself who started with nothing but ambition to succeed and made wool the foundation of the economy.' His voice reflected unmasked pride. 'You worked the Run yourself with no leisure, no security ... and no women folk for company.' He grew pensive. 'The early days were a rough life and no place for them.'

'You must have undergone much hardship,' Anne said softly, appreciating his humble beginnings. He had known poverty and hardship, too.

'The rewards were great for those that endured,' he brushed off her sentiment as though embarrassed by it. 'I emigrated at the right time. Wool prices rose and the Government introduced fourteen-year leases. That gave squatters the security we wanted and the right to purchase against any bidder. The following years were profitable. Homesteads were built and men could settle down. Many returned home for a wife,' he said, a touch nostalgically.

'All that way? What was wrong with the ones that were here?'

James grinned and it pleased Anne that his good mood seemed restored. 'Women were even more scarce back then.'

When they finished their meal, they removed to separate sofas before the fire and Anne poured tea. She watched in silent fascination as James methodically performed the process of cutting a piece of the dark tobacco from his plug with a small knife. After rubbing it in the palm of his hand, he teased it into shreds and filled his wooden pipe. Having pressed it down, he struck a wax lucifer and lit it, a cloud of blue smoke hazing around him. She set down his steaming cup. With his free hand, he added milk, stirred in three heaped spoons of sugar and drank it immediately hot.

'Have you never wanted to return to England?'

'Sometimes,' James reflected. 'In the early days perhaps, but not now. Australia is my home.' He hesitated. 'Life out here is vastly different from England, Annabella,' he cautioned softly. 'Distances are far greater and neighbours tens of miles away.'

'Who lives nearest *Barratt Downs*?'

He darted her a black look. 'The Scottish selector, Munro,' he snapped reluctantly without humour.

How ironic that the man he despised lived so near. Anne smiled to herself at his grudging mention of the thorn in his side. The canny Scotsman had clearly outsmarted James and he disapproved. Wounded pride she was sure.

'Surely it's important to be friendly with your neighbours. You might need their help.' James grunted and puffed his pipe, 'I look forward to meeting them,' she said.

'You shall not,' he growled. 'I forbid it. They're not of my class.'

Anne bristled at his condescension. 'But perhaps of mine?' she questioned with defiant pride. 'Is Mr. Munro not entitled to the land?'

James scoffed. 'Legally, yes. Morally, no. The land was mine by right of pioneering and possession,' he thundered.

'It sounds as though he merely seized an opportunity. Like you,' she teased.

'He was damned sneaky!' James tapped out his pipe and abruptly stood, heading for the sideboard and brandy decanter. 'My property was nothing but virgin bushland with tribes of wandering blacks when I claimed it.' His voice held a stinging edge as he splashed drink into a glass, his shoulders rigid with anger. He swallowed the liquid in one mouthful and poured another. 'But it's the last bit of land he'll acquire,' James announced smugly. 'Being cut off from the creek will make farming difficult, if not impossible. He'll only last a few years then I'll buy him out and reclaim what's rightfully mine.'

Anne thought his scheme sounded harsh and cruel. Perhaps a man had to be out here to get ahead but it was a side of James she did not admire. He had so much land of his own, why should he begrudge 600 acres to a struggling newcomer? Pride and greed, perhaps. If he continued his prejudice against his unwelcome neighbour, she would think far less of him.

Clearly tense from the turn in their conversation, James turned to face her and pointedly withdrew his gold pocket watch from his coat. 'It's getting late? Are you finished?'

Anne gracefully set down her tea cup. 'Yes. Thank you.'

'We have an early start in the morning. I suggest you retire.' James turned his back and kicked a glowing log in the fire, his hands thrust deeply into his pockets, making her feel like a servant who had just been effectively dismissed.

'Of course.' Anne rose and paused. She had offended him by being outspoken but could not leave without stating her case, remnant memories of Arthur's harsh mistreatment still strong. 'You are neither God nor my master, Mr. Barratt, nor shall you ever be.' He spun around and glared at her. 'Should I decide to marry you, never expect to have any authority over me. My opinions will always be my own. Unless,' she smiled sweetly, 'we should ever find ourselves in the happy place that we agree on something.'

Although astonished by her outburst, James admired her nerve. A woman in the bush needed pluck. Despite her audacity, he was captivated by the defiant sparkle in her eyes and the ruby flush on her face.

Yet he felt compelled to caution her. 'You are still very young, Annabella,' he murmured.

'I am nineteen.' Her back straightened.

He laughed softly. 'And I am ten years your senior.'

Irritated by his smugness, Anne retorted, 'Then perhaps you are too old for me, Mr. Barratt, and you should reconsider your offer.'

James marvelled at the fiery rebellion in her eyes. God she was magnificent but he didn't for a moment believe she meant it. If only she was older and more experienced. He longed for Ballarat and all that it promised. Yet it was the girl's very youthfulness that had appealed to him in the first place. No jaded spinster here.

'Do you wish to be released from our agreement?' he found himself asking.

Caught off guard by his challenge, she looked stunned. 'I am prepared to keep my word. For the moment,' she stiffly reconsidered.

Never before in his life had James been so afraid of losing something and released a breath of relief. To slake his tension, he poured and swallowed another mouthful of brandy.

'Then, as a gentleman, I can do no less than keep mine.'

They glared at each other across the room like wild animals assessing their prey until Anne broke the spell and strode in a rustle of haughty skirts from the room.

CHAPTER 9

Anne sleepily opened her eyes to see James light her bedside lantern and turn up the flame. Although he was already dressed, his dark wavy hair was dishevelled and he hadn't shaved for a rough growth of stubble shadowed his sun browned face.

She felt him study her intently as she rubbed her eyes and propped herself up on one elbow.

'We leave within the hour, Annabella,' he murmured.

Before Anne could respond, he turned and left. She scrambled from bed, fumbled with the frustrating row of buttons on one of her new gowns and hastily completed her toilette.

By the time she appeared in the adjoining sitting room, it was abustle and cold, the fire unlit and James supervising her luggage with a porter. Empty plates, tea cup, a folded newspaper and used serviette lay abandoned on a small table. Anne thought she might go hungry until she noticed another placing was set, with hot food dishes waiting on a trolley alongside.

Anne checked the mantel clock and asked with concern, 'Am I late?'

'No.'

'You should have woken me earlier.'

'Should I?' he replied absently.

'Yes. I'm used to getting up early.'

He glanced at her in surprise but continued organising her many packages and boxes from their shopping expedition the previous day. As James and the porter moved between their upstairs accommodation and the street below, Anne did not hesitate to appreciate the substantial meal of oatmeal, eggs and ham, toast and tea.

As she sipped her last mouthful, James strode in. 'Finished?'

She nodded.

'Then let's away,' he beckoned, pacing with a lightness in his step.

Anne thought that perhaps the edge of urgency in his voice and manner had nothing to do with time but his impatience to return home.

When she reached his side, James extended his arm and escorted her downstairs and out into the dark early morning chill, the cold air piercing her new warm woollen coat. Six splendid horses yoked to the coach, shuffled and snorted, their harness jingling. The large red vehicle had the letters VR painted on the side and its lamps lit in readiness for imminent departure. Anne grew excited at the prospect of the coming journey.

Their driver, a short and hairy middle-aged man with a florid complexion, bellowed, 'All aboard'.

Anne lifted her dress and James handed her up into the coach, both of them wedged shoulder-to-shoulder against their fellow passengers. With no choice, Anne squeezed up against James' warmth.

The hotel porter shut the coach door and cried out, 'All right'.

She heard a sharp whistle, 'Haa! Haa! Git up there!' and the coach lurched forward, the wheels crunching beneath them.

For the first hours, they travelled in darkness along rough roads but, soon, sunrise and daylight introduced Anne to the wonders of the wild and sparsely populated Australian countryside.

'It's a grand morning,' she beamed to no one in particular as dawn broke and gum trees like spectres, tall and slim, flashed past on either side.

At Keilor Plains, the end of the first stage, they lurched to a halt at a roadside hut. The horses foamed with perspiration and trotted free into log-fenced yards upon release from their harness. While the team was changed, passengers took refreshment or exercise, a welcome relief to stretch general soreness and stiff limbs from the rugged jolting ride. Anne was enchanted by the delicious peppermint smell from the bush and the sun-sparkled dew on the trees looked like gems.

Next came places called Melton and Bacchus Marsh and this routine became the pattern of the day with many rough tedious hours between stops. Anne gasped when the coach tilted and hurtled down a slope or rushed through a creek, water splashing over the wheels before the team heaved the coach up the other side. She closed her eyes and prayed the driver safely controlled his straining thundering team, and learned to appreciate the rare smoother stretches over swards of grass.

As the day matured, the air grew milder and lost its chill. The coach bumped and rocked along, faster on the hard road surfaces of the level plains, the driver shouting to his horses and snapping his whip that echoed like a rifle shot through the bush.

Conversation was difficult and, to Anne's amazement, James' head often fell forward and he intermittently slept. But Anne was too excited as their journey took them deeper inland and closer to his home. Few words were exchanged between them all day but she noticed a restlessness about him when they alighted between stops and the faraway longing in his eyes when they were underway again and the coach creaked and swayed along the bush tracks.

It was after midday when they made a welcome stop for a meal at Ingles Inn. A meaty stew, scones, jam and lashings of cream and a cup of piping hot refreshing tea. Anne was grateful for even this barest civilisation.

By mid-afternoon, they were hauling up steep hills

through a place James called Buninyong and approached their final destination for the day. Near nightfall, as dusk deepened and lent a hazy gloom to the fading day, the faint glitter of lights ahead signalled their arrival in Ballarat.

Anne had enjoyed the journey well enough as an introduction to the Australian bush but now, tired and sore, longed to stop and sink into bed.

They raced down Bakery Hill and along the narrow main road which emerged into a broader avenue planted down the centre with trees lined at either side with grand imposing buildings, and gas lamps lit on street corners.

With a grinding of wheels in a haze of dust, the coach jolted to a sudden stop. Finally, life stood still.

James opened the door and jumped down then turned and extended a hand to Anne. On the street, she straightened her rumpled clothes and, glad of the exercise, walked with James to the nearby Baths Hotel.

It was a grand stone building and they were warmly and personally greeted by the proprietor who James introduced as Walter Craig.

'It is very splendid,' Anne whispered in awe as he led them up the narrow staircase to their separate rooms.

'Walter Craig bought this hotel four years ago from the original owner, Thomas Bath. He has rebuilt and extended it into one of the finest in the colony.' A light smile escaped his mouth as he added, 'Many political deals and company floats had their beginnings in the sitting room downstairs. I hope you find it comfortable.'

James loitered awkwardly at the open door to her room until their baggage was delivered. He seemed restless but reluctant to leave. Clearly, some matter lay heavily on his mind so she was surprised when he suggested and ordered tea. They settled opposite one another in deep tapestry chairs before the fire and he commenced the now familiar ritual of filling and lighting his pipe.

Anne pressed him to tell her more of Ballarat.

He shrugged easily. 'Originally this area was a sheep run and swamp owned by the Yuilles, Scottish cousins, but they sold up in the Fifties and William now indulges his love of thoroughbred horses and racing. Ballarat was created by gold, of course,' he continued. 'It served the diggers and became a centre for district squatters. After a rich find at Golden Point, ten thousand people arrived within a month. Our quiet pastures were transformed overnight. The hills were covered with tents and thousands of hopeful diggers.'

'You didn't seek your fortune alongside them?'

Her question remained momentarily ignored as, suddenly distracted, he withdrew and checked his pocket watch. 'No, I didn't.' He grew irritated. 'I was trying to save my sheep after my shepherds deserted me for gold. I suppose some good came of it.' He shrugged, philosophical, less anxious. 'We fenced our runs to keep our flocks in and discovered it was cheaper to employ boundary riders instead of shepherds. The sheep improved when they were left alone to graze.'

'Is that when you sold meat to the goldfields?'

James nodded. 'I kept rams and breeding ewes, and culled the rest to build a stud. *Barratt Downs* now produces some of the finest wool in the district.'

To Anne the achievement seemed to please him more than any money he might have made from it but his attention was still elsewhere. He tapped out his pipe, rose and crossed to the window, as though waiting for someone.

'Is gold still found here?'

'Only half the population of Ballarat are still miners,' he said with his back still turned to her. 'The diggings have worked out. Tents and huts are being replaced by proper homes and skilled men are taking up their trades again.' He glanced around at her. 'There is a large Chinese population here.'

'Really?'

'I employ one on *Barratt Downs*. Choong Lee. He is an excellent gardener but he keeps to himself. He's a lot less trouble than some of the shearers.'

He forced a polite grin but Anne was not fooled. His distraction remained. He was physically present in the room but his mind was captured elsewhere.

At last he voiced his elusive hidden thoughts. 'I'm afraid I must leave you for a while. Unfinished business,' was all her offered.

His explanation was vague but she had no right to details. 'Of course.'

In two long strides, he was at the door. With a hand on the knob and not looking at her as he spoke, he said, 'I should return by eight.' And was gone.

Left alone, feeling abandoned and ignored in a strange town, Anne unpacked and took a bath drawn for her by a hotel maid. From her new dresses, she chose a green cotton and, later, descended the elegant staircase alone to the dining room.

As in Melbourne, she waited but James did not return. When it grew late, she ordered dinner and forced herself to eat. Back in her room, she stood at the front window and drew aside the curtain, watching the gas lit street below for any sign of James' return. Despite the fact that he was a grown man and quite able to take care of himself, alarm overcame Anne's thoughts and she grew anxious.

Deciding to do something, she threw a shawl about her shoulders and hurried downstairs. To her frustration, the hotel clerk was uncooperative but her few remaining coins loosened his tongue. He revealed that Mr. Barratt could be found at an establishment called Rosie's Palace, and gave directions.

Anne wrapped the soft woollen shawl more tightly around her as she stepped out onto the street and into the brisk night air. She gave no thought to being alone after dark and strode down the broad avenue of Sturt Street, continuing at a smart pace until she approached the narrow Main Road.

The number of hotels and taverns increased, with names

like the Western, British Queen and Limerick Castle, but no sign of Rosie's Palace. Further on, she passed a cafe, another tavern, the All Nations Hotel and the Diggers' Arms. Finally, shivering with cold and muttering that she ought not to have bothered, Anne reached her goal and gaped.

From outside at least, Rosie's Palace was past its former glory, an unpainted timber building, and she hesitated to cross the gloomy threshold. She knew exactly what kind of establishment lay behind its doors but drew a deep breath and opened them to a bohemian feast of noise, sights and smells.

In the poor light, thick with smoke, the interior was a collision of colours and patterns. Vivid blue carpet, richly painted walls and heavy dark furniture. Rosie had clearly spent far more money on the inside than out.

Beyond in the next room was a billiard table with lavish upholstered sofas and chairs around the walls, some occupied by two people. Usually a voluptuous half-dressed woman, curled up on a man's knee, her breasts thrust toward him.

Anne was appalled that James would conduct business in such a strange and improper place. She jostled against the women in gaudy gowns and painted faces with bare shoulders and low necklines, feeling self-conscious and overdressed. Intrigue overcame her astonishment as she determined to find James and she stopped the first person who passed; a half dressed blonde in a purple satin gown swinging downstairs.

Anne raised her voice above the noise. 'Excuse me. I wonder if you can help me?'

The female looked Anne up and down with a sneer. 'I doubt anyone in here could help you, love. Lost?'

Anne straightened. 'I'm looking for someone.'

The woman gave a bawdy chuckle. 'Aren't we all, lovey?'

Anne ignored her and persisted. 'Do you know a Mr. Barratt? Mr. James Barratt?'

A noisy group spilled from the billiard salon and staggered between them. An elderly man with a paunch and a cigar clenched between his teeth, a woman on each arm. They tittered, pushed past the blonde and the trio thumped upstairs.

The female in purple lazily eyed Anne. 'Who?'

'Mr. James Barratt,' she repeated loudly.

The blonde squinted in thought. 'Barratt,' she repeated to herself. A spark of interest flickered into life across her face followed by a creamy smile. 'You mean big Jim Barratt, the squatter?'

Anne swallowed back surprise that James was so familiarly known here and nodded.

The blonde planted her hands on her hips and grinned. 'You'll have to stand in line, love. He's with Rosie. She won't take kindly to another woman cuttin' in on her territory. A young one like you might make her feel insecure.'

'I need to see him. Now,' Anne snapped, shocked and humiliated that James already seemed to have another woman in his life and realised what business he had probably meant. For the second time in her life, she was stung with the knowledge of deliberate betrayal by a man. She had assumed James of higher character but it seemed no male was immune from his own lust.

Miserably, she wished she had not come but she would not back away until she discovered whether he was genuine about his promised agreement with her. If not, she would take the first coach back to Melbourne tomorrow and find work. She frowned. But would he have invested so much time and money in finding a possible wife if he didn't intend to proceed and honour his word? She thought of all her new clothes and his polite attention to her. Anne thought not but couldn't fathom why.

The blonde shook her head. 'Rosie won't like it.'

'I don't care. I must see him.'

A look of delicious pleasure crossed the woman's face. 'Strewth, lovey. As you please. Who would have thought, eh?' She flicked her head back, indicating the stairs. 'Double doors straight ahead at the end of the hall.' She caught Anne's arm as she moved past to ascend. 'But I never told you nothing. And don't break no furniture, all right?'

Anne flashed her a horrified glare and, without any further thought or hesitation, climbed determinedly to the upper floor. She found her way along the passage and stood before the wide carved doors. She hesitated, her heart pounding. With a dry throat, a sickness in her chest and a confidence she did not feel, she thrust open the doors without knocking and marched into the room.

James lounged on a plump sofa with a stunning black-haired beauty of a similar age to his own curled up against him, one slender arm draped with casual elegance across his shoulder, intimately entwined. Anne suspected what she might find but still found it a bitter pill to swallow and filled with alarm to discover she felt jealous that this ... siren was the one receiving his attention.

Crushed with envy, Anne gaped at the woman's parted full red lips and flimsy scarlet robe shimmering in the candle glow that barely lit the room. Loose hair spilled in a dark sheen over her shoulders. James' coat and vest were slung over a nearby chair, a number of shirt buttons undone revealing a tanned neck and the hint of shadowed hair on his upper chest.

She stopped and pressed both hands against her waist, feeling dowdy against this loose woman snuggled against James.

Astonished by Anne's abrupt intrusion, he disentangled himself from his companion and sprang to his feet. For a moment, while all three studied each other, the room was blanketed by a silent hush.

'Annabella!' he growled, his voice rough with fury. 'What the devil are you doing here?'

'I came only out of concern,' she whispered, shaking, but gripped by a fateful calm. 'You said you would return by eight.' He checked his pocket watch and cursed, speechless. 'If you did not plan to return, you should have had the decency to tell me.'

'I can explain–'

She flashed a sharp glance at the brunette who had slowly risen and observed the exchange with red lips slightly parted in amusement. 'Seems like there's no need.'

With as much dignity as she could gather under the circumstances, Anne turned and strode from the room leaving the doors thrust wide open.

If he knew such a worldly woman already, what did he want with a humble country girl such as herself, Anne wondered, in shame as she fled downstairs.

Rosie gathered up James' clothes and handed them to him. 'You must go after her.'

'Of course.' Halfway to the door, he turned in anguish and said, 'Thank you, Rosie. Goodbye.' A mountain of meaning lay behind the gentle parting words.

Anne rushed blindly forward, pushing people aside as she stumbled out onto the street, gasping in a breath of cold clear air to fill her lungs. Mortified at the extent and twist in her circumstances, she marched back toward the hotel.

Within seconds, she heard urgent heavy footsteps behind, felt a strong hand grip her arm and was forcibly swung about. The shawl slipped from her shoulder and she pulled it up again.

'I said, I could explain.' James' brows met in a scowl and his jaw clenched.

A fearsome sight but Anne was not cowed. What stunned her was the genuine fear in his eyes. But fear of what, she wondered? That she would reveal his sordid liaison with his Rosie? He surely couldn't fear that he had deeply offended and hurt her?

'I didn't take you for a coward, Mr. Barratt.'

She broke free but he grasped both arms and restrained

her. Pinned close together, they glared in defiant confrontation. Chests heaving, eyes glittering, she was amazed to see desperation line his face. Feeling confused and exhausted, Anne's stiffness relented and she turned away from him, gutted.

'Annabella,' he appealed in an urgent gravelly voice, 'Please listen.'

'I will return to Melbourne on the first coach in the morning,' she announced firmly, still unable to look at him.

'For God's sake, woman, will you listen!' James thundered impatiently.

Startled by his vehemence, Anne whirled back to face him. The genuine pain on his face tore at her heart but she, too, was filled with misery and more upset by this episode than she would care to admit so she hardened herself against his appeal.

When she ceased struggling, he loosened her arms, folded one possessively through his own and said gruffly, 'Let's walk. You'll catch cold.' As they fell into step, he continued, 'I did not tell you about Rosie because there was no need for you to know. I sought to spare you the very embarrassment you have just suffered.'

'You hoped to hide your mistress from me?' she accused, her tone filled with hurt.

'Rosie was my ... close companion,' he admitted carefully. 'I visited her one last time to say goodbye, explaining that we could never meet again.'

'You could have written her a letter,' Anne said.

James' mouth twitched into a smile. 'True. But in the circumstances I felt a personal farewell more polite.'

'What circumstances?'

'I've known Rosie for ten years. She was a good ... friend. I owed it to her. It was not my intention to deliberately deceive or hurt you. As you claim,' he admonished.

His comment registered Anne's own guilt for she also had a confidence of her own she was reluctant to share, and doubted she ever could.

Through the thickness and warmth of her shawl, she felt his hand gently placed on her arm. 'I urge you to continue your journey with me, Annabella.'

His deep pleading voice almost changed her mind. 'You claimed to be a gentleman,' she pointed out with stubborn pride. "I shall have to think about it.'

'That's all I ask,' he said quietly. 'Even gentleman make mistakes.'

Trying not to be influenced by his nearness and touch, Anne broke contact and, with gritty determination, walked on ahead. She sensed James maintain a discreet distance for she heard his reassuring measured footsteps behind her all the way back to the hotel.

Back in her room, Anne locked the door, lit a lamp and sank onto her bed. Still fully dressed and refusing to give way to tears, she lay down numb with shock but failed to sleep.

CHAPTER 10

She must have dozed but, for how long, Anne did not know, until woken by gentle persistent knocking at her door. Thinking it might be James come to apologise or beg, she sat up.

'Go away.'

The tapping persisted.

'Miss Gutheridge? Annabella?' A woman's voice called out insistently.

Puzzled, Anne rose and moved closer to the door. 'Who is it?'

'Miss Yates. Rosie. James' friend.'

Anne stiffened at the woman's nerve. 'How dare you.'

'Please let me in. I must speak with you. There are things you must know.'

At Rosie's enticing words and determined voice, Anne wavered, torn between envy and curiosity that she might learn more about James from this woman, who had held his interest for so long. Relenting, Anne turned the key in the lock and slowly opened her door.

In a whisper of burnished gold silk and a waft of heavy floral perfume, the woman strode past Anne into her room and spun around. 'Thank you.'

'If Mr. Barratt sent you—'

'He did not.'

Her brassy poise and presence dominated the room. She was tall and beautiful in a flamboyant way, confident and without shame. Easy to understand any man's attraction. Despite her vocation, from her every graceful movement, it was clear Rosie Yates had class. It raised the question why a lady of some breeding should have been reduced to, or chosen, such a life.

'Miss Gutheridge ... may I call you Annabella?'

Half in awe of this attractive worldly woman but irritated by her assumption to be so friendly, Anne said, 'No.'

Rosie inclined her head in understanding. 'Miss Gutheridge, then. I regret we met under such ... awkward circumstances.'

She contemplated the young woman before her. Wild strands of wheat-coloured hair streaked with auburn lights floated about her shoulders in charming disarray. Puffed eyes, struggling for composure ... James' choice was admirable. For all he had endured, he deserved happiness at last. She released a long inner sigh. Oh, to regain twenty years.

'Miss Gutheridge, I am a businesswoman. James only sought my company for friendship and need. Many a colonial gentleman has a mistress,' she informed her with a twisted smile. 'But he was never more than that. And never mine,' she admitted wistfully. She drifted aimlessly about the room in a rustle of skirts, closely inspecting her surroundings, and began to talk.

'What I am about to disclose, Miss Gutheridge, is to be kept strictly between you and I.'

'I'm not promising anything.'

'When you've heard me,' Rosie gazed steadily upon her successor, 'you will. James has possibly mentioned he came from Sussex. What he will not have told you,' she paused, running her hand over the thick brocade velvet cover of an armchair and half turned back to Anne, 'Is who he left behind. Being a younger son, James was not destined to inherit his family estate, South Grange. A certain young lady, Miss Caroline Fielding, whom he deeply admired, would not accept him unless wealthy. She led James to believe she would wait for him.

'As you know, he found his vocation and way in life with

great success out here in the colony but when he sailed back to England some years ago and proposed to her anew with high hopes and a fat purse, she refused him, claiming she could never leave England.' Rosie was gratified to notice Miss Gutheridge's face shadow with dismay.

'He had written to Caroline regularly over the years and she responded. I suspect her letters kept him going in the early years and he rightly assumed her continued interest. James' whole purpose in life was crushed and his world and hopes ended when she rejected him. He returned to Victoria a disillusioned man. That's when he began to visit me. As you can imagine, so deceived, he vowed never to marry.

'I tried to tell him that a woman who would not cross the world for her love was not worth having. One must question her sincerity in the first place, mustn't one?'

Anne had listened eagerly to every scandalous word. 'Why are you telling me all this?'

'Because underneath he is a lonely man who needs a wife and family. He was never meant to be alone.' She sighed. 'James would never have married me. I am unsuitable. I am too old to bother with children nor do I want them. Whereas it is his most desperate wish.' She shrugged. 'And hurt so badly, he has no patience for courtship. It was my suggestion he forego it and advertise.'

Rosie noticed the young woman's gaze widen. 'It was your idea?'

She nodded. 'He resisted it strongly but eventually conceded it would be the best course for him.' She studied the other woman. 'You have the energy and vitality to keep him young. He needs you, Miss Gutheridge.' She paused. 'He has chosen well.'

As she intended, the young woman looked suitably flustered by her compliment. 'Nothing is decided.'

Rosie covered Anne with a wry smile. 'Often during the time James and I were together this evening he spoke of you. With much enthusiasm. I have no doubt, although he would

never admit it, he harbours great hopes for a future with you.
There is a lightness and enthusiasm in him I have not seen for
years.'

Anne's cheeks flushed. James had spoken of her? She moved
uncomfortably with the knowledge, once again unsure if she
should stay. She was well aware she was deceiving him but
hopeful that her past was never revealed.

She lowered her head, trying not to look discomforted, as
if James' opinion of her didn't matter. Which of course it did.
His approval was of the utmost importance.

'Don't judge him too harshly,' Rosie pleaded softly. 'Give
him another chance. Who among any of us is without
blemish?'

At Rosie's words, Anne felt burdened by guilt that split
her loyalty and emotions, and questioned her slim reason for
giving James misplaced hope. He had been hurt once before
and she did not want to be the one to do so again. She had
thought it so simple to visit his home in the bush then, after a
suitable time, find an excuse to leave and gain employment
elsewhere. But now her obligations and ties to him, it seemed,
had already grown deep and complicated.

'When you know James better, you will find he is a raw
but considerate man. He felt compelled to visit me and
express his genuine delight in finding you. It was not
necessary for him to come and see me but it is a measure of
the man that he took the time in person.'

Rosie considered Anne for a long moment. 'Cherish,
James, Miss Gutheridge. He has an impeccable reputation in
the Western District. Your association with him, if it proceeds,'
she suggested prudently, 'carries a great responsibility. As his
wife, your attitude and behaviour will reflect upon him in
everything you do. Men may disagree but they depend on a
good woman. Don't let him down,' she hinted wistfully. 'I
give him into your care.'

Anne felt gauche and inadequate before this worldly

female. 'And if I can't?'

A gentle smile crossed Rosie's full red lips. 'He would hardly have chosen you if you were not equal to the challenge.'

Anne acknowledged with envy that Rosie was genuine in her efforts to plead James' case and she admired the woman's courage. But she had also planted seeds of concern in Anne's mind. Before morning, she would need to rethink her purpose in his life. That she might be doing him an injustice by staying and whether or not she continued on to *Barratt Downs*.

Rosie moved to leave and gently rested a gloved hand on her arm. 'I wish you both well.' A touch of sadness lingered behind the dark flashing eyes. Then, in an elegant sensual flourish, she left.

In a confusion of thoughts, Anne changed her clothes, slipped into a nightgown and crawled beneath the bedcovers. Exhausted from the day's travelling and this evening's events, her mind filled with compassion for James' loveless life. The humiliation he must have suffered when Caroline refused him after working so hard for her. Even at the risk of involving him in her past, out here, isolated and under his care and protection, she felt safe.

Next morning, stirred by a knock at her door before dawn for the room was still dark, Anne slid reluctantly from her warm bed to answer it, feeling as if she had barely slept. It was the hotel porter.

'Mr. Barratt asked that your bags be taken downstairs to his wagon or the Cobb & Co depot, Miss, as soon as you're ready.'

Anne clenched her hands at her sides. He was giving her a choice. 'Of course. You may collect them in fifteen minutes.'

'Mr. Barratt said to tell you there's time for breakfast but he's leaving soon.'

Anne nodded and mumbled thanks. She dressed and went downstairs, informing the porter her bags were ready to be delivered, then proceeded to the dining room for a quick meal.

Afterwards, as she stepped outside the hotel and into the fresh crisp morning air, she noticed the waiting wagon out front, loaded with sacks of flour and other supplies, harnessed to a magnificent pair of Clydesdales.

James was bent over the back of the vehicle, unaware of her presence, his broad back turned against her. He wore hard wearing trousers and, even in the morning chill, his blue shirt sleeves were rolled up to the elbows. From behind, he looked more ordinary and approachable, less like the gentleman pastoralist she knew from Melbourne.

She secretly watched him, knowing his past sadness, seeing him anew, his dark hair thick and wavy over his neck, almost touching his shoulders. When he straightened and turned, his gaze caught her movement and snapped in her direction. They stood motionless, staring at each other.

Tension strained his posture and uncertainty ravaged his brown face. He nodded stiffly. 'Good morning, Annabella.'

She managed a fleeting smile and said with teasing lightness, 'It's a lovely day to continue our journey.'

She was given no chance to dwell on the relief that crossed his face because a gangly lad appeared from a lane beside the hotel leading a magnificent bay mare, clearly of fine breeding.

James stepped forward. 'Annabella, this is Will Simmons, my stable boy. Will, this is my guest, Miss Gutheridge, who will travel home with us.'

The bashful youth half bowed, scooped off his hat and crumpled it between his hands, revealing a thick straight crop of straw-coloured hair.

'How do you do, Miss.'

'I'm pleased to meet you, Will.'

Anne wondered if all of James' employees knew of the reason for their Master's trip to Melbourne.

As Will gaped at her, she questioned her choice of the

dark blue dress with lace panels down the front. Was she too formal? And perhaps she should have braided her thick hair to control it rather than letting it sweep over her shoulders and trail in wild locks from beneath her broad straw hat. No matter. Too late now, she sighed.

James scowled and snatched the horse's rope from his boy's slackened grasp. 'Close your mouth, Will, and climb aboard.'

The lad turned red, boots shuffling in the dust before he crammed on his hat and leapt up onto a lumpy sack in the back of the wagon.

Anne's gaze was drawn to James' strong brown arms and hands as he tethered the graceful horse to the rear.

When he finished, he met her gaze. 'Beautiful, isn't she?' He stroked the gleaming coat.

'Will you race her?'

'That depends,' he replied vaguely.

She frowned. 'On what?'

'On you.'

'Why?'

'This is your horse so that will be your decision.'

She caught her breath with surprise and, in the same moment, prickled with annoyance. 'You can't buy me, Mr. Barratt.'

'I bought her before our ... misunderstanding last night,' he quickly assured her. 'A neighbour, Thomas Chirnside, has one of the best horse studs in the district. He bred her for me.'

Anne was confounded by his forethought. 'Oh!'

James slid a firm hand beneath her elbow. 'You ride up front with me. Let's get underway.'

His light touch filled her with alarm and pleasure. The strength of it. The reassurance and giddy sense of excitement that lay ahead. Anne settled beside him on the board seat.

James scrambled up and called out, 'Ready for home, Will?'

'Yes, Sir,' the lad replied, beaming.

'Good lad. We have a long day's travel ahead of us.' James flicked the reins and clicked his tongue,' Get up, there.' Straining at their yokes, the horses heaved them forward, the wagon wheels creaked and they began to move, slowly picking up pace and heading west from town.

Within only a few miles, the countryside opened up before them, bathed in sharp early sunlight. Anne breathed deeply of the fresh strong scent like peppermint in the air from the gum trees she had enjoyed yesterday, too. Brilliant red and green parrots darted like flashes of flame among their sparse branches. Here and there, wattles splashed gold through the bush and Anne marvelled at the extent of the endless grasslands stretching away in every direction.

Her eyes registered the difference between this sprawling green and golden brown country, and the damp and rocky greenness of Devon. In shady places, dew still glistened on the grass but the sparkling diamond drops soon melted.

On the open plains, they followed a deeply rutted track from other bush traffic trying to plough through the muddy roads during winter. They wound among clumps of tall gums, their peeling bark revealing smooth slender trunks. Black and white magpies carolled sweetly overhead. Red and pink heath bells pushed their colour up among miles of knee-deep grasses.

Although still early spring, the strong sun warmed Anne through to her bones, easing her into peace with herself, her companions and her surroundings. In the back, Will sprawled out and dozed on a sack.

They slowed as James steered the rattling wagon down through a shallow creek and the strong horses hauled them up the bank on the other side. After a succession of hills and gullies, they passed through the sleepy town of Linton. He hauled on the reins, stopping on the roadside for lunch and to rest the horses. Anne was beyond grateful to jump down from the hard wagon seat to unfold and exercise her stiffened limbs for a time before pressing on again through the long afternoon hours.

Their lumbering party reached the small settlement of Skipton where James secured small but comfortable rooms in the hotel rebuilt only two years before after the previous one had been destroyed by fire. While Anne clambered down and stretched, sauntering a little way afield down the one main street in the town, James and Will unharnessed the big horses, leading them into a nearby paddock.

They were treated to the warmth of a hearty evening meal seated cosily at a large rough table near a roaring open fire. Although the days were warm, the nights were fresh. Anne tried to stay awake but, yawning, excused herself and retired early, taking a candle to her room, leaving the men to talk on topics new and strange to her, still feeling very much a foreigner in this new country but content.

Next morning, Anne emerged from the hotel after a substantial cooked breakfast into the nippy morning air barely after sunrise to see James bustling about the wagon checking their supplies and Will harnessing their well-fed and rested horses.

Upon her appearance and without delay, the small travelling party pressed on, Anne filled with impatient eagerness at every slowly passing mile to reach their destination. James' homestead. Which he had promised they should attain before dark.

Along the way, she forced herself to concentrate and absorb the lovely green early spring countryside and fledgling hamlets through which they passed. Emu Creek and Streatham on Fiery Creek proved to be only a desolate cluster of houses.

All about them, the mild air was filled with the strong smell of horse sweat and leather. And always, with every turn of the wheels grinding beneath them, the haunting beauty of the distant blue and purple hazed mountains drew closer.

When the sun was high overhead and they approached an immense spread of fresh water, to Anne's immense relief and delight, James reined in the team.

'This is Lake Bolac. We'll stop for lunch and rest the horses.'

Anne jumped down from the wagon into the deep grasses that brushed her skirts and stepped across to the lake's reedy edges. Shielding her eyes, she gazed out across its glittering silver water. Wild fowl screeched and flapped overhead at her approach, skimming the surface in hurried flight.

She crouched down, dipped a hand into the cold water and filled her palm to drink. The icy liquid sent a refreshing chill through her body. She rose and turned to catch James standing at the rear of the wagon, watching her.

He turned away and roused a sleepy Will. They gathered kindling, made a clearing in the grass edged with stones, and lit a fire. As it crackled into life, James and Will squatted at the water's edge, rolled up their shirt sleeves and sluiced their face, arms and neck. When they returned, Will reverently spread out a rug on the ground for Anne.

'Thank you, Will.'

The lad flushed at her charming smile.

Soon, a blackened billycan of water scooped from the lake sat on the coals and began to boil. James tossed in a handful of tea leaves from a small tin and replaced the lid to let it brew. He produced a wicker basket of food procured from the hotel this morning before they left, as he had arranged the day before. The three travellers ravenously ate of thickly sliced mutton and fresh baked bread. Will sat apart, his back propped against a wagon wheel, eating in silence but watchful.

Anne glanced at James. 'How much further?'

'We'll make Wickliffe this afternoon and reach the Downs before nightfall.'

He poured three mugs of hot tea, adding three spoons of sugar to his own. As Anne cupped the mug in her hand and sipped, James settled comfortably and lit his pipe.

'Before white men came and settled here twenty years

ago, this lake was a favourite fishing place for aboriginals.'

Anne glanced about, concerned at the possibility of natives lurking nearby and recalled Cissy's fearful words aboard ship. 'Do they still live here?'

James shook his head, puffing his pipe and sending a trail of blue smoke briefly into the still midday air before it dissolved. 'Very few, sadly. White men have displaced them. Once a year, though, in the early days, the district tribes gathered here for feasting and ceremonies, and to exchange and barter goods.'

Anne listened with interest and hugged her knees as Will poked at the coals, spreading them to cool.

'The Geelong tribes brought stone for axes, aboriginals further north traded Mallee saplings for spears, and red clay found in the Otway hills to the south was used for paint. They brought articles they made themselves. Handcrafts, possum rugs, fishing nets, boomerangs.' Anne queried the last item and James explained. 'A bowed wooden weapon that might be thrown at an enemy but was normally used to kill birds and animals to eat. The natives are very skilled in its use.'

James' easy familiarity and knowledge of the country shone through in conversation. He might have been born here and not Sussex. His brows were shadowed beneath his broad hat and his sharp gaze scanned the land. The only sounds intruding on the tranquillity of their temporary bush camp were the water birds on the lake and the breeze rustling the long lush grass.

James finished his pipe and rose first, ending their sojourn. Anne helped Will pack up while James unhobbled her horse and tethered it again to the wagon. Once more, they clambered aboard and rumbled off, continuing west.

Within two hours and five miles later, they ambled into Wickliffe in the Hopkins River valley, comprised of only a few public buildings, a handful of simple homes little more than bush huts, two stores and a new church.

The Irish innkeeper, Farrell, cordially received them and,

grateful for a break in the tedious journey and a comfortable seat, Anne enjoyed a plate of fresh warm scones and piping hot refreshing cups of tea which the men seemed to prefer drowned in milk and sweetened with excessive amounts of sugar. Anne had begun to give up hope of any decent civilisation and wondered anew what James' homestead would be like.

Seated around a table in a small side room, Anne listened to their discussions over all matters local, especially when talk turned to shearing and the blighter Munro as she heard James refer to him.

'Still, he's a good ringer and all,' Farrell nodded sagely.

Anne wondered what ringing had to do with shearing but decided not to ask.

When James enquired after the Burroughs family at a place called *Rosevere Hall*, Farrell replied, 'Hear tell the women folk are gone to Melbourne now the roads are passable again.'

'Charlotte never liked the country,' James commented, obviously knowing her well.

Long since, James and Farrell, although not Will, Anne noticed, gulped huge swigs of ale, each puffing on a pipe, dense blue smoke fogging the room about them.

When they made their farewells and climbed back into the wagon for the final leg of their journey, James turned the giant horses north-west, heading directly toward the foothills of the mountains, their serrated summits jutting abruptly into the sky. The hulking ranges dominated the landscape now. The slopes were a blue haze and the rocky upper faces glowed orange in the afternoon sun.

At times, kangaroos and wallabies leapt suddenly from the cover of bush and bounded across the track in front of them, startling Anne into surprised laughter at the sight of such unusual animals. Flocks of cockatoos screeched overhead and settled like rows of white stones on the slender gum branches. The lush countryside ran with creeks from the hills and fed distant flocks of grazing sheep.

Late in the afternoon, James nodded ahead. 'Next property is *Barratt Downs*.'

He glanced back at Will and they shared a grin. Anne straightened on the hard seat, anticipation sharpening her interest. Her gaze sought a house in any direction but was unrewarded.

James indicated a peak ahead. 'That's Mount William, the Chirnside's run. Our neighbours.'

'Where my horse was bred?' Anne forgot herself and acknowledged ownership. James cast her a lazy glance and nodded.

It was much later before the wagon jolted through a patch of thick timber. As they emerged from the shade, James reined the horses.

On a slight rise, perched just above a gully and glistening narrow stream, a homestead nestled long and low, it's back to the mountain. Smoke curled from its chimneys in a wispy blue haze and the whole panorama was bathed in the golden light of the lengthening day, sunshine glowing on the sandstone bricks.

The iron roof stretched out over broad verandas and skirted the house. A belt of protective trees – gums, wattles and peppercorns, James told her – circled the quiet garden, the sharp midday sun drenching their foliage with light. A shallow creek wound through the trees at the bottom of the slope.

Clearly, *Barratt Downs* was more than just a home. It was a lovely large homestead in prosperous surroundings.

'Welcome to my home,' James said softly, warmth and pride in his voice.

Large flocks of sheep grazed further out, more animals on one property together than Anne had ever seen before. 'So that's what ten thousand sheep look like.'

'That's only one flock.'

Anne gaped, shading her eyes to search. 'Where are the rest?'

'Being brought in from the outstations ready to be put through the sheep wash for shearing.'

Anne let out a deep sigh. From the moment her gaze first settled upon it, she knew she was going to love this place.

CHAPTER 11

Barratt Downs may have been isolated but was far from desolate, the homestead itself comfortably embedded in an elevated clearing. James started the horses again and the wagon rolled on through an open wrought iron gate.

Before they had even halted in front of the house, an attractive girl burst from the house her boots clattering over the veranda flagstones. Her raven hair was bound in a long silky braid and swung down her back. Will's gaze lingered upon her as he leapt down from the back of the wagon.

'Morning, Sarah,' he greeted her shyly, but his attentions passed unnoticed for the lass only had eyes and a saucy smile for James.

'Welcome back, Mr. Barratt, Sir.'

Will's face shadowed with the pain of her rebuff.

'It's good to be home, Sarah.'

A stout middle-aged woman bustled from indoors, broad hips swinging and wide skirts sweeping the path as she came to greet them. Her silver hair was piled into a bun and neatly held with a net.

'Bless St. Patrick for bringin' you safely home, Sir.' Her pink face glowed as she wiped floury hands on her apron. She inspected the sacks in the rear of the wagon. 'We can certainly use those supplies.'

James climbed down and, grinning, planted a kiss on the hovering woman's forehead. 'I can't stay away from you long, Bridget, you know that.'

Anne was stunned by this light hearted change in their boss. Out here, she saw another side to him, one that was at ease and comfortably master of his domain.

Bridget waved a dusty white hand at him and blushed. 'Sure you say that every time. You've hardly been gone a week and the house was empty without you.' She turned her attention to Will. 'Don't you be standin' idle, Will Simmons, the minute you're back. There's unloadin' to be done. Sarah, fetch Zak.'

The girl pouted but obeyed and reluctantly flounced off around the side of the house.

Anne watched the fond reunion among them, feeling an outsider and yearning to belong. Quietly dutiful, Will untethered her horse from the wagon and led her away.

Finally, James turned to Anne still seated in the wagon and offered a hand to step down. 'Bridget, this is my guest, Miss Annabella Gutheridge. She'll be staying with us for a while and I know you'll make her welcome. Annabella, this is my cook, Mrs. O'Grady.'

She opened her mouth to speak but was given no chance.

'Welcome to the Downs, Miss Gutheridge.'

The greeting was tinged by an air of reservation in the older woman's critical gaze. Logically, Anne understood she must earn her friendship and flashed a wide smile.

'Thank you, Mrs. O'Grady.' Anne smiled. Looking over her shoulder, she noticed James did not follow or wait for the servants but began unloading the wagon himself.

Mrs. O'Grady noticed the direction of her glance. 'The Master has no need to be doin' that, to be sure,' she announced importantly, 'but he's his own man. Always has been and always will be. As you'll soon find out.' And with that, she turned a haughty shoulder and marched back toward the house. Anne guessed she was meant to follow and trotted after her.

As they crossed the broad veranda, Anne noted wicker chairs set out invitingly at intervals beneath. 'How long have you been with Mr. Barratt?' She tried to make pleasant conversation as Mrs. O'Grady ushered her in through the open front door, its sturdy frame etched in glass panels of ruby and gold elevating the large entry hall to a magical status with reflected prisms of coloured light. Green and white floor tiles were laid in a diamond pattern, and photographs and paintings hung on the walls to either side.

'Eight years. Since I came out from the Old Country.' Her musical lilt deepened with warmth and Anne's hopes raised that, in time, they might become friends. 'And every year I'm tellin' the master, it's no place out here for a man alone. Him with a fine house now for a lady wife.' Bridget half turned and scowled at their new arrival. 'Although I am wonderin' at his choice.'

Ah, so the staff did know the circumstances surrounding her presence. 'So am I, Mrs. O'Grady,' she freely admitted. 'So am I.'

Cook raised her shoulders in a sceptical shrug and shook her head. 'He's usually a good judge of character but time will tell, true enough.'

As they spoke, Anne had been led down a long hallway that seemed to run the full length of the house and passed beneath a carved arch about halfway along, burgundy runner carpet laid up the centre of the polished floor cushioning their steps as they walked.

Now, Mrs. O'Grady thrust open a door toward the end on the right hand side and Anne was ushered into a bedroom as large and grand as the ones she had enjoyed in the Melbourne and Ballarat hotels. There was a huge wardrobe, a toilet table and mirror with porcelain trays and a decorative beaded lantern, a bedside table with a china clock and candlestick, and a chair and small table near the window with lace curtains fluttering inward before a gentle breeze. On the opposite wall, a delicate cream coverlet was spread neatly over the lower half of a green floral quilt on the big brass bed.

'There's more in here.' Mrs. O'Grady waddled across the room and opened a door into a smaller room with a large white bath tub sitting proudly on brass legs in the centre, a towel rail beneath a stained glass window, and a wash stand with a green floral china jug and basin that matched the white marble top and glossy green tiles at the back.

'This is lovely, Mrs. O'Grady,' Anne breathed with amazement at such luxury and convenience beyond anything she had ever enjoyed before in her life. 'But are you sure it's for me?'

The cook subjected her to a long scathing glare. 'Master's orders. He must think you're worthy although I dare say it's not what you're used to.'

Fortunately for Anne, a short elderly man shuffled into the room bearing the first of her bags, breaking the tension. His wiry arms easily handled the weight and Anne glanced with surprise at the sight of the long grey shaggy beard that matched his thinning unkempt hair. James certainly employed an assortment of servants.

'This is Zak.' Mrs. O'Grady gave him no other name.

'How do you do, Zak.' Anne nodded to acknowledge him.

The old man, deeply tanned and wrinkled, revealed a faint gleam behind his dark sunken eyes almost hidden beneath thick bushy eyebrows that hung out like verandas over his eyes.

'I'll be gettin' back to me supper, then. Sarah?' She called out sharply down the long passageway. Eventually the girl appeared, looking sullen. 'Help the mistress unpack, girl, and sharp about it.'

'There's no need,' Anne protested. 'I can-'

'Yes there is,' cook bluntly disagreed. 'The master will expect it.' With that, she turned on her heavy heels and disappeared, presumably back to her kitchen. Zak, too, left to bring in more bags.

Grudgingly, the housemaid set about transferring all the lovely new clothes into the wardrobe and dresser drawers. Anne noted her gaze settle upon them all with a sigh of great envy.

When James quietly appeared in the bedroom doorway a short time later and subtly cleared his throat, his imposing male presence caused both pairs of female eyes to turn in his direction. Sarah stopped working to stare but sullen disappointment crossed her face when she noticed his full attention focus intently on his guest standing nearby.

'I hope your room is…acceptable,' he said with a twist of mirth tilting up the corners of his mouth.

'Very much so. Thank you. It is most certainly everything a lady might desire,' she recalled the assurances in his advertisement. 'Have you come to show me around the homestead?' she asked hopefully.

His blue eyes clouded. 'No. I must consult my overseer about mustering for shearing.'

Anne hid her regret behind a false smile of understanding, beginning to learn the demands of his property. She knew no sentiment would be involved in their friendship, whatever path it took. Wasn't she, too, here for her own reasons?

James edged a step further into the room. 'If you need anything,' he said awkwardly. 'Ask Sarah or Bridget.'

'That won't be necessary. I have everything I could want.'

In truth, she could be easily drawn into this country household, if allowed, and looked forward to any times she might become more acquainted with this enigmatic man who had hardened his heart to the world but revealed teasing glimpses of a warmer personality since being home.

'Have you managed a household before?' James asked.

Anne's gaze swept the gracious room. 'Well, yes, but not as grand as this.'

'Then perhaps, only while you're here, of course,' he clarified gruffly, 'you might apply any experience you do have to this house and the staff. That includes Bridget, Sarah and Zak. It will give you something to occupy your time,' he murmured.

Anne held reservations how that authority might be

received, especially by the womenfolk.

'Naturally there are limitations,' he cautioned. 'Beyond the homestead fence is my domain.'

'Of course, Sir.' She bobbed a mocking curtsy and quipped, 'Are you under my control when in the house?'

'If you ever manage that, you will have earned the right,' he softly challenged, turning to pause at the door. 'When I have more time, I will show you the property but that may not be for some weeks.' Then he was gone.

Anne's shoulders sagged and she felt as though a cold draught had swept over her. She would hardly see him. She refused to dwell on the empty days and weeks ahead, and glanced across at Sarah who stiffened warily. 'Sarah, you may leave the unpacking for now and conduct me on a homestead tour.'

The girl, clearly displeased, took the order with poor grace, flouncing ahead of her mistress from the room.

The house boasted many gracious and functional rooms, all fully furnished but hidden beneath layers of dust and drawn drapes. When Anne drew them back, she coughed at the powdery cloud it caused, the whole interior dark, gloomy and virtually unused. In its dismal state, Anne wondered how Sarah occupied her days for it certainly wasn't in cleaning.

By comparison, Combe Hill may have been a humble and unhappy house but Anne had always kept it spotless. Even that brief memory caused a lurch in her chest. James' home cried out for love and attention, and she determined to provide it.

She continued trailing in wonder after the haughty housemaid through the spacious front rooms showcased by lovely bay windows filled with lace and built-in cushioned seats, while French doors in every bedroom led out onto the veranda and overlooked the bush garden with tantalising glimpses through the trees of the blue-hazed foothills beyond. Anne longed to explore.

The cosy drawing room seemed larger because of the

gigantic gilt-edged mirror above the fireplace that reflected everything in its frame. This sanctuary was filled with deep comfortable leather chairs, small tables and lamps, and a connecting library boasted a commendable display of books.

'The master spends a lot of time reading in here, especially during winter,' Sarah informed her arrogantly.

Anne missed the girl's gibe because she was silently compiling an impression of a man's solitary life. Deliberately exiled because of his lost love?

Further down the passageway, the housemaid indicated James' study, its door ajar, and moved on but Anne paused, inquisitive, and pushed it open.

'No one's allowed in there, Ma'am,' Sarah pouted, sullen.

'I won't touch anything.'

The girl glared at her and Anne privately glowed in the pleasure of defiance. Her curiosity brimmed as she entered, running her hand along the edge of a large cedar desk that dominated the room, it's surface covered with orderly piles of papers, ledgers, pens and ink, and a collection of wooden pipes. The familiar aroma of James' pungent tobacco hung intangibly redolent in the air. A battered leather chair was pushed in neatly behind the desk, and wooden cabinets and smaller tables carefully arranged about the room.

Judging by the attention to order, Anne suspected James would be meticulous in the management of his run. She indulged one final glance around his private world before retreating and closing the door.

In the passageway, Sarah fidgeted with her apron. 'There's still the dining room,' she smirked with a fearless glare, dropping any form of address or civility.

Seeing her chance to take the lead, Anne calmly suggested, 'Perhaps you might address me as Miss Gutheridge until we know each other better.' She smiled sweetly adding, 'Now, let's see the dining room, shall we?'

At first sight of it, Anne gasped.

'Cook says it's never been used since the house was built.'

As dim and musty as all the others, Anne thought, what an appalling waste. She strode down its length and flung aside the velvet drapes, releasing a blanket of heavy dust that set them sneezing.

Sarah waved the pall away, annoyed. Anne trailed a finger along the top of a richly carved mahogany sideboard leaving a marked path across the top. The matching dining table seated twelve. Above, a glorious chandelier, dripping with crystal prisms and fresh white candles, hung dull with neglect. All this, Anne slowly turned around, must sparkle.

'Has this room ever been cleaned?'

Sarah's eyes narrowed and she folded her arms defensively. 'The master said it wasn't necessary since it wasn't used.'

'Mr. Barratt never entertains?'

'Not since I've been working here.'

'And how long is that?'

'One year.' When Anne glared at her, she added hastily, 'Miss.'

'Then where does he take his meals?'

'In the kitchen or his study, Miss.'

'Well,' Anne planted her hands on her hips and scanned the potentially magnificent room, growing enthused at the prospect of its rejuvenation, 'I'm sure the kitchen is comfortable but this room was meant to be used.'

Sarah's young shoulders sagged and she glowered.

Anne's fingers drummed on the sideboard in the dust. 'I'm sure two industrious women can have this room cleaned in time for dinner.'

Sarah's gaze widened. 'Tonight, Miss?'

Anne hid her delight at the girl's reluctance. She would earn her wages today at least.

'Yes, Sarah.'

'And you're going to help?'

'All we need is dust cloths, hot soapy water and elbow grease.'

'Shouldn't I unpack your clothes first, Miss.'

Anne stifled a smile at the maid's transparent excuse. 'They can wait.'

The following hours were frantic but rewarding. The cumbersome drapes were carefully removed, taken outside into the rear cobbled courtyard and carefully suspended over the wash line to be shaken and beaten.

Barefoot, Anne clambered onto the dining room table, removing every glass bead from the chandelier for Sarah to wash before being replaced, sparkling. Cook grumbled at the use of some of her precious candles from the kitchen larder but seemed impressed with their efforts.

'I hope you know what you're doing,' Mrs. O'Grady muttered late in the afternoon, bewildered by all the activity as she brought in a tea tray and freshly baked ginger biscuits.

As the day wore on, Anne's optimism and quiet humming received dark looks from Sarah but grudging admiration from the cook.

As the sun set, blanketing the homestead in shadow, Sarah lit the lamps and candles, christening the grand room with soft light.

As they stood back admiring their labours, Anne said, 'Thank you, Sarah. You've worked hard and I appreciate it. It's magnificent.'

A pouting Sarah was forced to nod as she joined her new mistress looking around the gleaming surfaces, the elegant room transformed into life and young flames crackling in the fireplace. Anne sighed with pleasure, hoping James approved. How could he not? This room was made to be used.

She dismissed Sarah to help Mrs. O'Grady in the kitchen and returned to her room to freshen up and prepare for supper. With her window open wide to admit the evening noise of twittering birds and minty perfume from the surrounding bush, Anne wriggled into a cotton gown inlaid with panels of cream lace, struggling to fasten dozens of buttons. Then tussling to pin up her wild hair into a more sophisticated style to look more mature. She wished she had asked Sarah to help and frowned over her desperation to impress James and fit his expectations.

In the end, she gave up, simply brushing her hair until it gleamed and leaving it to fall long and naturally down her back, caught off her face at each side by wide combs. Much less fuss than curls. When she was ready, she stroked a light touch of lavender water cross her wrists, took a deep breath and strode down the passageway to the drawing room.

Anne waited for almost an hour, alternating between sitting and restless pacing in front of the fire before she heard a door slam and the thud of booted footsteps along the hall. She waited nervously to greet him.

As he bowled through the door, Anne's shoulders sank at the sight. His uncivilised appearance, unkempt dark wavy hair and dusty clothes could never betray his masculinity and breeding, but she had assumed he would dress to eat.

He halted abruptly, as if surprised to see her standing there. His intense blue gaze rested upon her for a long time, as though he had forgotten she would be here when he returned.

Covering her self-conscious unease before him, she cleared her throat. 'You're very late,' came out more sharply than she intended.

His eyes still held hers as he stepped closer into the room. 'I return when my day's work is done.'

'Surely you can't see much when it's dark?'

James brushed past her, braced his hands on the fireplace mantel, his back turned, and stabbed at a burning log with a long black boot. 'I know every inch of my property, Annabella. I neither need a lamp nor a map.' He turned a glance toward her. 'I trust you weren't worried?' he teased wryly, perhaps unwisely recalling her impetuous night foray in Ballarat

'Of course not.' Anne folded her hands together to calm them and seem more composed than she really felt.

'Good. Bridget knows I'm usually late.'

Well, she didn't tell me. Then Anne realised she hadn't thought to ask and sighed, feeling young and inadequate.

'I don't live by rules, Annabella, and often have a long ride home.'

Anne moved uneasily beneath his fierce scowl. 'Of course. I shall learn to adapt.' She could understand why he had worked long days over many years to build up his property but, judging by the prosperity around them, she questioned if there was still a need.

To her amazement, his tone softened. 'In future, I will try and remember to let you know my movements on the property for the day, hmm?'

An admirable compromise. His change of demeanour disarmed her so that her stiff spine and shoulders relaxed.

'You look ... lovely,' he seemed obliged to comment in acknowledgement of her efforts.

Anne felt herself blush and raised her chin. 'I thought you dressed for dinner.'

James pushed out a weary sigh. 'There's been no need. I'm hungry. Let's eat.' Noticing her stricken gaze, he barked, 'What?'

'Sarah spent a great deal of time cleaning today.'

'She did?' He passed off her comment, distracted.

Anne pointed to the dirty boots that encased his long strong legs almost to the knees. 'At least, please remove those,' she dared to suggest.

With one hand still on the mantel, he glared in disbelief at her request. For a moment, Anne thought he might not cooperate. Eventually, he shook his head and sat on a chair, muttering, 'I can't believe I'm doing this,' wrenched off his boots and hurled them aside.

He stood in stockinged feed and strode for the door. 'Now can we eat?'

Anne stifled a grin of delight and nodded but when he turned and headed for the kitchen, she called out, 'No, no. This way.'

She beckoned and swept by him, marching along the hall ahead of him to the dining room. Standing on the threshold, she paused and turned for his reaction to the transformation. A warm blazing fire, gleaming tableware and polished surfaces.

Anne winced when he gave her a strange awkward glance, almost of pain. Then his eyebrows flickered upward and he said tightly, 'The house needs a woman's touch. I've never wanted to eat in here alone,' he confessed.

Touched with compassion, for he must surely be thinking of Caroline, Anne slid her arm through his and looked up at him with an encouraging smile. 'Shall we dine?'

As they entered, she noticed Sarah had certainly set a place for each of them. At opposite ends of the table. Probably on purpose. Anne bristled. They would only be able to talk if they shouted! She swiftly gathered up the cutlery from the far end and reset a place to James' left side.

After Sarah served the meal, Anne was horrified to discover the tableware was disastrous. She had assumed the best table service would be in use but nothing matched. There was a chip in the edge of her bowl as Sarah served up Mrs. O'Grady's thick vegetable soup, and when she finished her spit roasted mutton and gravy, discovered a crack as large as a gum twig right across the centre of her dinner plate.

James seemed impervious to the lack, making little conversation and eating everything placed before him but Anne was appalled. She had wanted everything to be perfect, to appear competent and James to feel proud and reassured that he had made the right choice.

She was marginally heartened when James commented warmly that she had obviously been busy today, and then she asked him distractedly about his day. But when he responded briefly about the process of dipping sheep and shearers arriving, her thoughts were elsewhere. She would speak to Sarah in the morning. The girl had mentioned something about old trunks in the shed.

CHAPTER 12

After the meal, Sarah cleared away the dishes, smiling and flirtatious toward James. Anne rose, expecting they would retire to the cosy drawing room before the fire and talk. Instead, he clenched his jaw. 'I have paperwork to attend to in my study.'

'Oh.' She tried not to show her disappointment and rejection.

'I have a property to run. I'm sure you can amuse yourself. I need to organise the wages ledgers for shearing.'

'Oh.'

James looked awkward. 'After a long day, you don't want to retire early?' Anne shook her head feeling dismal. 'Well, there are plenty of books in the library,' he muttered.

After mumbling a vague and incoherent apology, he left. Anne heard the soft thud of his footfall along the hall and, moments later, the solid click of his study door close behind him. Except for a log settling in the grate, the dining room fell silent.

She snuffed the table candles and wandered into the library, idly running her fingers along the book spines and chose one at random. Settled in a comfortable chair accompanied only by the ticking of a mantel clock, she flipped disinterestedly through its pages, not really concentrating on what she read, restless, her energy still bubbling from the day's activities and her new surroundings. She imagined James bent over his desk and smoking his pipe. Did he regret their age difference and his decision? Was he comparing her to Caroline, his lost love, and finding her lacking? Did he not enjoy her company? It had seemed so in Melbourne but, then, he had no work to occupy him. Now, entrenched in running his property again, it seemed she was to be ignored.

Frustrated by her uncertainties, Anne slammed the book shut, left it on a table and strode to her room. Sarah had lit a fire and the flames flickered in leaping lights around the room. Her bed was turned down and her nightdress laid out. Such indulgences and peaceful surroundings. So different to those she had known in Devon.

Although James could be blunt and inattentive, Anne greatly admired and respected him for what he had achieved. All the more reason then not to hurt him further. If pressed, she might one day be forced to reveal her deception but it seemed unlikely that the fact of her previous marriage would ever be revealed and her true past discovered. She had left England for a better life. It seemed she had quite unintentionally landed on her feet and found it. In this young country of opportunities, she must forget her old life and concentrate on the new.

Anne slowly undressed and methodically brushed her hair then sauntered across to the window. She drew aside the lace and velvet drapes and stared out into the darkness of the night but saw only her own reflected image. She returned to the fireplace and dug at the coals with a poker, sending sparks flying up the chimney. She rubbed her thinly-clad arms and paced again until, on impulse, she ventured from her room and down the long passageway, hesitating when she reached James' study door.

She heard nothing from the other side but a pale shaft of light glowed beneath and she raised an arm to knock. She hesitated. Annoyed by her lack of courage, she backed away.

In her bedroom, growing tired at last, she crawled beneath the downy comfort of the thick warm quilt. The long journey from Ballarat and busy day proved more beneficial than a sleeping powder. Within moments, she fell into a deep but troubled sleep.

She woke refreshed and positive to a new day. Scrambling from bed, she threw back the drapes and opened her window. Stepping onto the veranda, she gasped at the chill of the crisp air as it nipped at her sleep-warmed body and the cold veranda tiles under her feet.

She inhaled the strange scents wafting in from the garden and frowned in concentration, detecting lavender. Nearby among the trees, a kookaburra laughed and magpies carolled a beautiful song. In the distance, dogs barked and sheep bleated, the sounds carrying on the still morning air.

She quickly dressed, lured by the promise of her first full day on *Barratt Downs* and the chance to explore further afield. She brushed and tied back her torrent of wild hair with a green ribbon to match her cotton skirt into which she tucked her plainest cream blouse.

Tempting aromas and humming drew her toward the kitchen. The huge warm room loomed into her vision as she peered around the doorway. Dominated by a giant blazing hearth across the far wall and a long oak table set with a bench along one side, there was also a gigantic sideboard crammed with china. Pots and pans hung on wall hooks opposite above a double washing sink set into a scrubbed wooden bench under a large window that overlooked the rear courtyard.

At the far end a large door stood ajar allowing a glimpse of a well-stocked larder.

'Good morning, Mrs. O'Grady,' Anne greeted the cook.

The humming ceased and the matronly woman turned a pink perspiring face from the fire. 'You're up then,' she said brusquely.

Anne ignored the less than warm welcome, drawn to the fireplace. She crossed the tiled floor and held her hands out to the coals. 'I love the mornings.'

'Just like the master. Always away with the dawn he is.'

Anne's shoulders sagged and her smile faded. Were they never to see each other? How did he think they were ever to become better acquainted? 'Will he be gone all day?' She masked her fresh disappointment with a casual smile.

'Aye, that he will. They're still bringin' in sheep from the out stations and down to the wash ready for shearin'. Sarah's set the dinin' room for breakfast.'

'Oh. I can eat in here.'

Mrs. O'Grady wiped wisps of grey hair back from her forehead and frowned. 'Doesn't seem right, Miss. The Master wouldn't be pleased.'

'Does he need to find out?'

Cook gave her a strange look but sighed, relenting. She waddled across to the fire and filled a teapot with boiling water from the cast iron fountain but gasped in horror as she turned to set it on the kitchen table.

'Oh Miss, you mustn't be doin' that.' She scowled to see Anne taking down crockery from the dresser shelves. ''Tis Sarah's work.' She shuffled to the back screen door and bellowed, 'Sarah!'

Soon after, the housemaid struggled inside bearing an armful of wood, an angry scowl across her forehead and stubborn pout on her lovely young lips. She ignored Anne and grumbled, 'Zak's missing again.'

'Mightn't be the drink,' cook snapped defensively. 'He might be helpin' with mustering down at the Wash.'

'They're always stealing him. As if we haven't got enough else to do.'

'Fed the poultry?'

'With bringing in the wood, I've not had time,' Sarah retorted.

'You would if you'd left your bed sooner.'

With a vicious swirl of her full skirt and apron, Sarah turned and flounced out the back door again letting it slam after her.

'What's the Wash?' Anne asked.

'A creek down in the gully beyond the shed, Miss. They dam it up and drive the sheep through before shearin'.'

Feeling ignorant about the property and forbidden from

helping with breakfast, Anne slid onto the kitchen bench, folded her hands in her lap and allowed herself to be waited on.

Mrs. O'Grady set a place at the table. 'Would you be likin' oatmeal first, Miss?'

Anne shook her head. 'Not today. But when I go riding.'

The cook flashed her an alarming glance as she pierced a thick slab of bread with a long fork and toasted it over the coals. 'This mornin'?'

Anne laughed. 'No, I can't. I haven't found the stables yet. I'd like to have a look around the homestead and fields first.'

'They're called a paddock out here, Miss.'

'Oh, I see.' Two boiled eggs were placed before Anne, then toast with fresh butter and homemade jams in small pots produced from the scullery, and a cup of tea continually topped up from the huge pot on the table.

When she had finished eating in silence watching cook roll out pastry on the bench, Anne asked, 'Will you share tea with me?'

Mrs. O'Grady sniffed uncomfortably. 'I've bakin' this mornin' and a roast to set.'

'I realise your work is important, Mrs. O'Grady, but ten minutes?' Anne coaxed, smiling.

So praised, the busy woman seated her large frame alongside Anne on the wooden bench as though she was eating with Queen Victoria. Anne poured Mrs. O'Grady a cup of tea who tutted her disapproval.

'You know that Mr. Barratt and I have only recently met? So I don't know if, or how long, I might stay,' she added tactfully.

Bridget gulped a large mouthful of hot tea, clearly startled by the news. 'You're not to be married, then?'

'Nothing's settled yet,' she continued, looking around her. 'But whether I remain or leave, I plan to be useful and make this lovely house into a home.'

Cook seemed impressed for her haughty manner

softened. 'I'd have to be agreein' with you there, Miss. I'm surprised the Master suggested it.'

'He didn't but I'm sure he won't mind. He seemed happy with the dining room last night. Since you're clearly the most experienced in the household and in charge,' Anne slid in a little subtle flattery, 'Could you tell me about the household routine?'

Bridget's broad chest swelled with importance as she drained the last of her tea and clattered her cup back into its saucer. 'You'll soon get used to it all, so you will,' she said proudly and launched into details. 'I do the cookin', of course, and laundry once a week. Young Will you met yesterday. He's the groom.' Anne nodded. 'Sarah's responsible for the poultry, milkin' and the dairy. Churns butter three times a week. Outside of that, she cleans house and helps me or wherever she's needed.'

'Is she a local girl?'

'Daughter of the blacksmith in Wickliffe, Miss. Big family. Glad to escape, I expect, but no discipline. Only been here a year and can't see her lastin' much longer.' She shook her head and mopped her damp forehead with a corner of her apron. 'Good female help is hard to find and keep, Miss, anywhere up country.' She shook her head sadly. 'And some just don't like hard work,' she confided, leaning closer, as though they were old friends.

'Then there's Zak, of course. You met him yesterday. Job about. Works a long day but not hard. He's an old hand, you know.' When Anne stared blankly, she explained, 'Ex-convict. Done his time and earned his ticket of leave. Don't know why he was transported in the first place. He never said and I never asked. Probably better not to know,' she wrinkled her nose in confidence. 'Been with the Master since the start. Came over from Tasmania, he did.

'And there's Choong Lee, the gardener. Why the master employed him, I'll never guess.' She shook her head. 'Bit of a mystery to us all, he is. Came out for gold and when that finished, the Master took him on. Just marched up to the house one day, so he says, askin' for work and been here ever since. Years now. Long before I came and that's eight years ago, to be sure. But to be fair,' her mouth drew into a thin line, 'He grows the best vegetables a cook could ask for and keeps to himself.'

'Is that all the household staff then, Mrs. O'Grady?' 'Ah, there's dozens of hands work out on the property and more men arrivin' every day for shearin'. Same lot turn up every year. Regular as you like. Some of 'em sign on with the Master year after year.'

'Do you like it here, Mrs. O'Grady? You seem happy?'

The cook's grey eyes misted over. 'I certainly do. The master's like me own family since I lost me own.'

'Oh. I'm sorry to hear it.'

'I wish me Patrick could be here sharin' it all with me still.' She dabbed her eyes with the corner of her large apron and heaved a weary sigh.

'Patrick?'

'Aye. My husband, bless his poor departed soul.' She stared nostalgically across the kitchen and crossed herself. 'A strong God-fearin' man. Could split the biggest block of wood into pieces with a single blow.' She shook her head, sad and proud. 'Kind and hard workin' every day of his life. But the damp and coughin' got to him so it did. We sold up and sailed for sunny Australia but he never made it. He died not a month out to sea.' She pressed her apron to her mouth, clearly distressed. 'To see his body slide into the ocean near broke my heart.'

'I'm so sorry, Mrs. O'Grady.' Anne acknowledged her grief and laid a gentle hand on her arm. 'But I'm sure you have wonderful memories.'

'Aye, I do. So I do. Maybe it was God's will to ease his sufferin'. May his good soul rest in peace.' She crossed herself again. 'And don't I have four fine boys to remind me of my man.'

'No daughters?' Anne teasingly enquired, trying to lighten the mood.

Cook clasped her hands together, her ruddy face beaming, a grey sadness behind her eyes. 'Aye, we had a daughter. Catherine. Fair charmed the boots off her father, so she did. All sweet smiles and dimples and curls.' Her face clouded and she heaved one of her deep sighs with which Anne was quickly becoming familiar. 'The Good Lord only lent her to us, though. She died when she was five months old.' Mrs. O'Grady paused for thought. 'She would have been about your age now. Ah, but there's enough gossipin'.' She suddenly seemed to remember her place and duties, and struggled to her feet.

Just then Sarah returned from the fowl yard with her usual sullen expression and a basketful of eggs.

Anne rose as the girl entered the big warm room. 'Sarah, I need you a moment.'

'What now?' she snapped, setting the eggs in the larder.

'Mind your tongue, girl.' Mrs. O'Grady glowered and her reprimand filled the kitchen with tension.

'Yes, Miss?' Sarah mocked, a rebellious gleam in her dark flashing eyes.

'Follow me.' Anne smiled and beckoned, ignoring the girl's bad manners and resentment of her presence in the house. The housemaid followed her down the passage and into the dining room. Together, they opened all the dresser and sideboard doors and surveyed the dismal sight. 'Is this the best crockery the Master owns?'

The girl gave a careless shrug and flicked aside the glossy black braid that had fallen over her shoulder. 'Yes, Miss.'

Anne lifted plates and inspected cutlery and muttered to herself, 'I can hardly believe it. I'd have thought he'd only have the best.'

'That's all he needs for himself,' Sarah obstinately disagreed. 'But there's more in the store shed. I've never been there myself but Mrs. O'Grady says there's boxes and trunks the Master brought out from England but they've never been opened.'

Anne's hope's rose and her interest sharpened. 'Can you show me?'

Led outside, she shielded her eyes from the glare of brilliant sunshine as they emerged from the shady veranda that skirted the house and framed views of the bush. Through the rustling mint-scented gum trees, the nearby rocky mountains loomed into the deep blue sky.

They crossed the brick paved courtyard past a well and hand pump, and continued through a gate. On the other side, the Chinese gardener was stooped over rows of meticulously cultivated vegetables, weeding. He straightened as they drew near.

Sarah retreated a pace behind Anne. Leaning closer, she hissed in distaste, 'This is Choong Lee.'

A broad grin parted his olive-skinned face and he bowed low. 'Velly pleased meet Missy.' His long loose shirt and baggy trousers flapped in the light breeze, and a long queue trailed down his back beneath his broad pointed hat.

Anne found the little man's courtesy and deference humbling. She smiled and nodded to him.

'Lee's strange.' Sarah's lips curled as they moved on. 'I don't come out here alone at night. Sometimes there's a dreadful sickly smell in his hut.' She wrinkled her nose in disgust.

Maybe time would change her impression but, to Anne, Lee seemed harmless enough and eager to please. She surveyed the shabby hut into which the Chinaman disappeared, ragged pieces of canvas flapping at the open windows. It must be freezing in winter. She felt a great pity for him, living in such a mean dwelling. Even though he certainly looked strange and she'd never seen a Chinaman before, Anne felt resentful on his behalf and said crisply to Sarah, 'Perhaps we should show more respect. Seems to me, Mr. Lee is an important part of the household since he provides much of our food.'

Sarah sniffed and lifted her skirts, walking on ahead through the grass until they reached the storage shed. Beyond, an orchard burst with pink blossom-covered trees and rows of timber and wire fence supports were smothered with the glossy new growth of grape vines.

Anne stared at what Sarah had called a shed. It was, in fact, a substantial stone brick cottage with two small windows either side of a central door, held shut by a propped piece of timber. Sarah heaved the wood aside and pushed it to the ground. 'This was the Master's first home but it's only used for storage now.'

Anne brushed aside a thick film of dust from one of the windows and peered inside. She tried to imagine back fifteen years to when James would have first squatted on this land, working all day and returning to this humble dwelling at night. What hopes and dreams he must have held in the future to withstand those lonely hard years, and the hope he held out that Caroline would join him one day. She looked back toward the gracious homestead. A marked elevation in status that showed how far James had come. Unfortunately alone.

Through the dirty window pane, Anne squinted into the hut's interior gloom. A huge open fireplace that once must have blazed with a welcoming fire covered one wall. Anne felt a nostalgic pang that the hut was neglected and disused, all but forgotten, when it had played such an important role in James' early life here.

A strip of sunlight slashed across the room as Sarah dragged open the stiff creaking door and they stepped inside, brushing at cobwebs drooping with dust. The thick dusty atmosphere made Sarah sneeze.

Standing in the middle of the one-roomed hut, Anne tried to visualise it when James lived here. It must hold many memories for him. Perhaps the reason it still stood. Anne ignored the dirt floor and knelt beside a huge wooden chest.

She unhinged the rusty catches and pushed it open, rummaging through layers of old newspaper to find what lay beneath.

'Porcelain, Sarah. Mountains of it,' she gasped in a hushed voice, afraid to disturb the peace in which the boxes had lain for years. Anne wound her finger through the delicate curve of a cup handle. Sarah abandoned another crate she had prised open and joined her. 'They've been lying here all this time.'

Even the housemaid's apathy faded as, together, they excitedly unwrapped each piece and wiped the dust from the china with their petticoats to reveal a complete dining setting in a delicate blue and white pattern. Anne had never seen anything so grand in her life and turned over each piece to read the label beneath. 'Doulton ware, Lambeth, London,' she read aloud. She knew nothing of fine things but it all looked very special.

'The Master might not want you to use them?' Sarah frowned, her enthusiasm abating, suddenly wary of her find.

Anne scrambled to her feet and thought of Caroline. 'Perhaps there was no reason until now but they'll be on the dining table tonight. This must all be taken up to the kitchen and washed. Fetch Will to help carry the boxes.'

The girl sneered. 'Will Simmons is a weakling. He'll never manage them by himself.'

Anne thought the girl's attitude rude and unkind, and she was certainly a poor judge of character for Will had impressed her at first sight. 'Go and find him.'

With a petulant swing, Sarah marched off toward the stables. When she returned with Will, he trailed obediently behind the scornful maid, his eyes shining with adoration. Sarah ignored him while they loaded baskets and carried the china back to the house. When the heavy carrying work was done, the lad reluctantly returned to the stables.

Mrs. O'Grady gazed on their incredible find with awe and immediately took charge, announcing she would personally supervise all the washing herself.

With the china restoration in cook's capable hands, and hours of daylight ahead, Anne felt housebound. Craving the outdoors, she swept through the kitchen where a red-faced Mrs O'Grady was elbow-deep in dishwater, and announced, 'I'm going for a walk.'

Horror covered the older woman's face and she raised a wet soapy hand to rest on her heart. 'A walk. Alone?'

Anne nodded, smiling.

'May the Good Lord be castin' his mercy on you, Miss.' She crossed herself. 'You can't be knowing the dangers of the bush or you'd not be suggestin' such a foolish notion.'

'I'm only going a short way across the fields,' Anne assured her, edgy to escape.

'Paddocks,' the older woman corrected, scowling. 'And short distance or not, 'tis a blazing sun outside today.'

Anne tried to be patient. 'I shall take a sunhat.'

'It's not your skin I'm thinkin' of. It's the snakes.'

Cook's warning alarmed her but only for a moment. 'I shall be careful and keep in sight of the house.'

'Mind you do or you'll be gettin' yourself lost.'

'I shall be fine. And,' she suggested pointedly, 'There's no need to mention this to ... anyone, is there?'.

Mrs. O'Grady shook her head in dismay and from between thin disapproving lips said, 'The Master'd not be likin' it, for sure, you goin' off alone and not knowin' the bush.'

'The Master,' Anne teased, 'will never know. Will he? I shan't be long. Only an hour or so.'

'Blessed Saints,' Bridget gasped, crossing herself again. 'Tis a mighty long short walk you're takin'.'

'I promise to be careful,' Anne mocked, turning serious. She hurried to her room and found her new straw hat with the wide brim and planted it firmly on her head.

As she crossed the kitchen again a short time later, cook muttered, 'You've no sense under that hat for sure. No good will come of it, you'll see.'

Anne smiled to herself as she pushed open the back wire door, ignoring the woman's dire warnings, still audible even as she crossed the courtyard and hurried out through the back garden before someone stopped her. She smiled and waved to Lee, stooped and tending his vegetables, her spirits lifting, her stride lengthening.

Beneath the cloudless blue sky, as clear as she'd ever seen in her life, and strong sun, Anne restrained herself from bursting into an unladylike run. Soon standing ankle deep in the thick grass of the homestead paddock, she spread out her arms and spun around, elated with freedom.

She lifted up a handful of skirt and tramped across yet another paddock, squeezing between the wires of a boundary fence. As crows aahed and the brisk wind pushed against her face, Anne struck out across the open countryside toward the mountain foothills where she scrambled up among large boulders to a protruding rocky ledge for a better view.

Shading her eyes, she squinted down to the homestead below, nestled amid its sanctuary of natural bush on this blue and golden day, set apart from other farm buildings including a large one on wooden piles further out, surrounded by milling yarded flocks of sheep in smaller pens around the massive iron-roofed shed.

Perched on a rock, Anne contemplated the scene. In spring it was as green and lovely as Devon but with a harsher beauty and the spectacle of endless plains. And it all belonged to James. She realised she could live here, far removed from the rest of the world and her past. But it would mean marriage to James and she frowned over the deceit she would need to do it.

Anne tossed her hat aside and shook out her long hair, immediately whipped about by the breeze sweeping up the hillside, mulling over her future and the moral ethics of the decision she must make. James Barratt was a good and decent man but she had only just arrived. There was yet time to resolve her reservations and troubling conscience.

When she had cooled off, she removed her walking boots and picked her way downhill again, her mind settling on the good fortune from bad that had brought her to this bountiful distant country. She was beginning to understand how early squatters might have arrived intending to stay only a short time or until they had made their fortune but, like James, had grown so fond of it they stayed, never returning to the land of their birth.

With annoyance, she watched slate clouds gather to mar the sky. She dawdled on her return walk, deciding she must enjoy the outdoors as often as possible. She bent to pick small faintly scented pink bell wildflowers and sprays of fine white blooms from woody bushes, ignorant of their names and wishing she knew them.

As the wind grew stronger, Anne looked skyward at the darkening clouds racing before it. The sudden spring shower that swept overhead caught her unaware and the first heavy raindrops fell. The paddocks yawned ahead and she dashed across them as the sharp downpour increased, pelting her with great fat drops in wet bites that hurled themselves against her face and soaked her dress.

Before reaching the shelter of a stand of gum trees, the rain suddenly stopped, the sun already edging the thundercloud with gold. Drenched but content, she plodded back to the homestead.

As Anne straggled into the kitchen beneath the weight of her sodden clothes, leaving puddles of water on the tiled floor, Mrs. O'Grady threw up her hands in the air and clucked in dismay. 'You'll catch your death, for sure,' she cried. 'Praise God for your safe return.' She plucked at the grass and leaves clinging to Anne's muddy hem and caught in her matted hair.

As Sarah entered the kitchen and gaped at the sight, Anne said, 'Put these in a vase on the dining room table for tonight,' and thrust her pretty but drooping bunch of wildflowers at the wide-eyed girl.

As she strode off down the hall, Anne undid stiff buttons and peeled off layers of clothing as she went, calling over her bare shoulders, 'And I'll need lots of hot water, Sarah, for a bath.'

CHAPTER 13

At dusk, having suitably soaked at length in a lavender-scented bath, Anne eagerly awaited James' return and, with Sarah's grudging help, struggled into a gown of ivy green. Even if she wasn't destined to be here for very long, she determined to justify James' faith in choosing her and dress to please him, making full use of her lovely clothes.

She dabbed lavender water behind her ears and clasped a gold necklet at her throat. She towelled and brushed her hair dry then drew it up away from her face, leaving only wisps to trail her face and neck.

As darkness settled and the lamps were lit, Anne swished down the hall in a whisper of skirts, surprised to discover James already in the drawing room when she entered. Although he still wore dusty working clothes and riding boots, the rugged sight of him took her breath away, causing her to halt in the doorway. He really was an extremely handsome and imposing man. And she realised she had missed him.

Her joy was eroded when he growled, 'Why did you move my favourite chair?'

He didn't even comment on her appearance. At the sight of the scowl on his brown face and the grim set of his square chin, she stiffened in defence. 'You said I was Mistress of the house. I changed some furniture that's all.' She understood his resistance since the homestead had always been his sole domain but he had clearly given her free rein.

His warm blue-eyed gaze contemplated her until, gradually, his tense mood eased. 'Yes, so I did,' he conceded

169

gruffly.

'It's much more usable now I think.' She swept an arm to indicate the room, smiled sweet innocence and calmly took a seat.

'Well I don't,' he muttered, 'But I suppose I'll get used to it.' He lounged against the mantel, eyeing Anne closely.

'We could change it back?'

'No need,' he said curtly. He poured a small sherry for Anne and a large brandy for himself.

As she accepted it and James disposed of his in a single gulp, Anne decided it wise to prepare him for the rest. 'I took another liberty today. We explored the cottage.'

'The hut?' He frowned and poured another drink.

Anne nodded. 'The crockery in the dining room was shameful. I didn't mean to intrude on your privacy but I took the decision-' She abruptly stopped her babbling and trailed off, taking a deep breath. 'I have a surprise for you in the dining room.'

'There's more?' His lips curled wryly and Anne relaxed at his show of good humour.

Silence fell between them as Anne sipped her sweet wine, staring vacantly into the fire. When she glanced across at him again, a frown of concentration creased his forehead, as though troubled. 'Sheep behaving themselves down at the Wash?'

He regarded her with surprise but her question was obviously well chosen for he said, 'Yes, but Zak complained that his bones ached which usually means a change in the weather.'

Anne grinned, thinking how welcome the rain would be for the gardens and paddocks. 'He was certainly right.'

James scowled. 'It will delay shearing until the sheep dry out.'

'We could have done with Zak's help today,' Anne blurted out lightly without thought.

'I needed him at the Wash,' James said firmly. 'Zak and

one sheep dog are worth five men. At this time of year, he can't be spared. Will and Choong Lee were about.'

'Yes, Will helped,' she assured him. 'Speaking of Lee, I wonder if Sarah cleaned out the cottage, would you allow him to use it?' Anne realised she was on sensitive ground and James might not appreciate the intrusion.

He frowned. 'He seems happy enough where he is.'

'Have you asked him?'

James glared. 'No.'

With no further comment, Anne probed, 'Do you have any objection?'

He considered her request for a time then said quietly, 'If Lee agrees.'

Anne breathed a sigh of relief. 'Thank you. His accommodation is rather ... humble.'

'It was the only shelter available when he came.' James stared into the fire but was clearly miles away, remembering. 'He was only living under canvas on the goldfields anyway.'

'All the same,' Anne ventured carefully, 'he's getting older.'

'Aren't we all?' he muttered to himself. 'Now,' he said more brightly, setting his empty glass on the mantel to reach out and grasp her small hand in his. 'What's this surprise you have for me?'

Drawn so courteously to her feet, Anne understood Rosie's faithfulness to him for so long. He was irresistibly charming and, judging by her racing pulse at the touch of his hand, she, too, was not immune.

Still holding her hand, their fingers interlaced, they strolled along the hallway to the dining room. Pausing in the doorway, James surveyed the scene. Blue and white porcelain and shining silverware lavishly graced the table. Anne held her breath and waited. When he didn't speak, she glanced up at him, dismayed to see a bleak expression across his face.

After an edgy silence, James sighed, his voice thick with nostalgia. 'Of course. The china. It's so long ago, I'd forgotten.'

He turned to explain and his nearness, the familiar outdoor scent of him, the wavy hair that teased his blue serge shirt collar so enchanted her into silence, she could only gape and listen.

'It was a gift from my mother when I left England. Intended for the lady of the house, one day.'

Anne winced with regret. Oh, dear. Caroline.

Suddenly he grinned and gave her hand a gentle squeeze. 'They obviously assumed it would be much sooner than fifteen years. Mother would approve of your discovery.'

'She would?'

'Of course. Women appreciate these ... niceties. It's time they were used,' he murmured.

Releasing her hand at last, he drew out a chair at the table. Anne took her seat, knowing she had unintentionally dredged up old wounds and unwanted memories. Rosie had sworn her to secrecy but should she tell him she knew so that he at least realised she understood his pain?

Fortunately, he seemed to recover and she was just beginning to relax when James said, 'You wandered off alone today.'

Anne's heart sank. 'I went for a walk, yes.'

'To the mountains,' he scoffed. 'Three miles. Don't deny it. You were seen from the sheep wash. I trust you don't catch a chill.'

'I had a wonderful view-'

'Or could have got lost or stumbled and fell. You must not go out alone again. You're unfamiliar with the country.'

'I love the outdoors. I can't stay in the house all day.'

Sarah entered, interrupting them and set a tureen of soup on the table between them. Sensing the tension between them, and probably having heard their raised voices along the hall, she smirked at Anne as she left the room.

'This isn't Sussex or Devon, Annabella. You must promise.'

'No,' she quietly refused, ladling hot soup into their new

blue and white bowls.

'Until I can spare you more time,' he pleaded urgently.

Anne was appalled and glared at him. 'That will be weeks. I'm not staying chained to the house till then.'

'I must have your word?' he scowled. Frustrated by his demand, she couldn't agree and remained silent, taking up a spoonful of the broth. 'I will not see you come to any harm.'

'I'll take care.' She kept her gaze downcast.

James pushed out a long impatient sigh. 'Annabella Gutheridge,' he ground out in annoyance. 'What am I going to do with you?'

'Ignore me until shearing's over and then we'll see where we stand.'

Anne glanced up thinking he might suggest she leave only to see him shaking his head and a twitching grin hover at the edges of his mouth. When he caught her smiling in return, his gaze settled for so long upon her, she could not prevent a blush.

Alone in her bedroom that night, Anne grinned in the dark. She had made no promises to James so therefore she could undertake more excursions. And they would not all be on foot. The surrounding plains were so vast, they would be much more easily explored on horseback.

Anne's thoughts turned to James' gift of the filly. A thoughtful gesture, as was his generosity with clothes. She enjoyed his company and the joy of anticipation before she saw him but he seemed determined to honour the wording of his advertisement, forego any hint of courtship or romance and remain aloof.

For the moment, she was happy to fill the role of mistress of the house but yearned to go riding further afield. But because James was making such a fuss of her suggestions to venture further from the homestead, she reluctantly decided – if only to keep the peace with him – she must tell him her plans for tomorrow.

At daylight, Anne woke to the loud clumping of James'

boots in the hall. Anxious to catch him before he disappeared for another long day, she tossed back the covers and hurled herself from bed, hurriedly pulling on a robe over her nightdress and running down the hall. Head down, hastily trying to tie the satin ribbons, she slammed up against him. Perhaps having heard her pattering down the hallway after him, he must have stopped and turned.

James steadied her as they collided, her cheeks flushed, her rich golden hair tousled from sleep. Her robe slipped with silken softness between his fingers, her upturned face so vulnerable and enticing, he felt an absurd impulse to kiss her.

Astounded by his strong reaction, he released his grip and stepped back. 'What is it?' He heard her catch her breath and her gaze fixed on him.

'Oh!' she breathed. 'Nothing really. Well ... just ... ' She smiled and her eyes sparkled like the sun on wet grass. Then she straightened and said, 'I'm going riding today. I thought you should know.'

In her innocent flurry of ribbons and lace, he believed she was completely unaware of her attraction so that, momentarily, he almost yielded and agreed to grant her anything she asked. But, for her own safety, he must deny her the privilege.

He resisted the expectation in her arresting hazel eyes and shook his head, bracing himself for another argument. 'You know I can't allow it.'

'Why not?' she blazed with defiant spirit.

'Not until you're more familiar with the countryside.'

She crossed her arms, glaring at him and threatened, 'Always assuming I stay. How can I get to know the place if I don't get out there? And what's the point of having a horse if I can't ride her?'

'During shearing, I don't have the time to come with you.'

'I didn't think you would. I'm happy to ride alone.'

'You're not riding anywhere and that's an end to it. It's

too dangerous.' Unable to bear her disappointment and questioning glare, he said, 'Snakes for one thing,' and turned to leave.

'I can't stay indoors every day,' she protested, trailing after him. 'The weather is too lovely.'

'Other women do.'

Anne scoffed. 'What? Pansy women from England or Melbourne. I'm not other women.'

He paused, letting a small silence fall between them. 'Then you must try.' His voice softened. 'I warned you about the isolation and loneliness, Annabella.' He shrugged, his implication clear.

Anne planted her hands on her hips. 'Have I complained?'

He sighed. 'No.'

She flashed him a gloating smile. 'I am an experienced horsewoman.'

'I can't agree. I forbid it. And that's an order,' he scowled.

'Your final word?'

'Yes.'

She brushed against him as she walked away in the opposite direction down the hall. 'Where are you going?' he barked.

Annabella glanced back over her shoulder and arched her brows. 'To the kitchen for breakfast,' she purred. 'If that is all right with you?'

'Dressed like that?' Her robe had fallen open revealing her shapely young body beneath.

'You're never here and the house is filled with females. It hardly matters, does it? I don't see you dressing up around here either.'

The sweet challenge behind her glittering gaze irritated him but she was right and he privately cursed.

'Anyway, if I am banned from going anywhere,' she said, her voice as smooth as syrup, 'it's useless to dress. Perhaps I shall return to bed.' She patted a hand over her mouth to cover an unconvincing yawn and, in a whirl of flowing robes, swaggered away.

Still furious and barely able to eat much breakfast, Anne ignored her threat and dressed anyway, impatient with buttons and pulling angrily at the knots in her hair as she brushed. Simmering resentment lingered that James should feel he had enough authority over her to confine her to the house. She was not formally attached to him in any way so he had no right.

In Devon, she had walked far beyond the boundaries of their small farm so she saw no reason why she could not get out into the Australian countryside she was growing to love and enjoy it. After all, Queen Victoria was married with nine children and had been ruling the empire for over twenty years so what was a little ride outdoors?

Secure in the strength of sisterhood and an evolving plan, Anne discarded her restricting corset, tucked a floral blouse into a cotton skirt and left her hair to fall in a cloud about her face and shoulders. She slid her feet into boots, grabbed her sunhat and escaped directly out through the French doors avoiding Mrs. O'Grady's potential wrath in the kitchen.

At the stables, Anne found Will feeding the horses. 'Good morning, Miss,' he responded, going red and bashful at her unexpected visit.

'My goodness, Will.' Anne summoned all of her charm and cringed at her tactics. 'You certainly keep orderly stables. Do you manage all this by yourself?' She strolled about, her sharp gaze watching for one particular stall.

He nodded, profusely pleased as she intended. Anne felt uncomfortable using flattery on this trusting employee for her own selfish ends.

'I can understand why you're a valued worker and Mr. Barratt trusts the horses to you.'

Will shuffled his awkward, large feet and didn't know where to look. 'Tisn't anything really, Miss. I love animals.'

Anne spied her filly and sauntered toward it. 'I suppose you know all of them well?' She flashed him a brilliant smile.

'Yes, Miss.' Will fumbled to find a place for his nervous hands and decided they'd do best in his pockets. 'Know each one by name and nature.'

'Course you do.' She drew on every ounce of feminine class as though born to it and not merely the oldest daughter of a struggling tenant farmer. 'So you'll be able to help me.'

'Be my pleasure, Miss.'

She approached her horse and stroked it. 'It's such a glorious morning, I'm going for a ride,' she said with confidence and the expectation that Will would agree, saddle her mount and assist her in every way, hoping James had not instructed him otherwise.

Will's anguished face revealed his struggling conscience and sense of duty against her winning appeal. 'The Master wouldn't want you to go riding alone, Miss.'

'Has he said so?' Anne probed, holding her breath.

'Well ... no, Miss, but-'

'There you are then. It's time this beauty and I became acquainted.' She entered the filly's stall as if the decision was already made and stroked her horse affectionately. As Will wavered, Anne said firmly with natural authority, 'I'm a good rider.'

Will scratched his head. 'We don't have a side saddle, Miss.'

She wrinkled her nose as if taking him into her confidence. 'Just this once, a normal saddle will do.'

Anne only breathed easily as Will turned aside to lift down a saddle from the wall and carry it to the loose box. 'Still don't seem right, Miss.' Will frowned, shaking his blonde head.

'Will.' Anne lowered her voice persuasively, resting a gentle hand on his arm. 'It is sweet of you to be so worried for me and I shall tell Mr. Barratt myself, but I'll be perfectly safe.'

His furrowed brows eased as he led the filly outside.

Anne stroked its gleaming coat and murmured soothing words to gain its trust while quelling her excitement at the prospect of her first ride in the bush. She accepted Will's cupped hands for her foot and was amazed at his wiry strength as he easily lifted her astride. She settled her skirts around her and clicked her tongue, urging her mount forward.

'Keep to the front track, Miss,' Will called out as she trotted away.

Anne waved and smiled, glancing cautiously across to the shearing shed before pointing her horse along the rutted road away from the stables and homestead.

Trotting away with dust lightly raised behind them, she gradually urged the horse into a canter. Sunlight filtered through the thin canopy of eucalypts as they rode along. Although this was their first time together, the horse responded beautifully to her gentle commands, leaping over fallen timber and skilfully weaving through the scrubby bush undergrowth with only the lightest touch of reins.

On a sandy level track, filled with growing confidence and high spirits, Anne set the filly into a gallop. When both were pleasantly exhausted, Anne reined in for a spell. She patted the filly and let her contentedly crop from the new spring grasses.

Anne dismounted and, holding the reins, backed up against the crisp curling bark of a gum tree, listening contentedly to the sounds of the bush. At mid-morning, the landscape was all peace and sunlight. Birds twittered, brittle gum leaves rustled together and a gentle breeze stirred the grasses. Although alone, Anne was touched by a companionable solitude. Far from lonely, she rested awhile, immersed in the unfamiliar scenery, reluctantly aware she must return before she was missed.

She led her horse to a fallen log to remount but the filly shied. Soothing and gentling, she coaxed her closer and tried again. Once more, the horse sidled away, snorting.

Anne almost lost control and wound the reins tighter around her hand. Murmuring reassurances, she glanced about to find any reason for the animal's sudden nervous behaviour.

'There, there, girl.' She steadied her fidgety mount and dragged herself up onto its back once more.

Just when she thought herself safely in the saddle, the horse swerved, Anne unbalanced and only managed to stay on by desperately grasping the mane.

'Whoa, girl. Whoa.'

As she clung low over the horse's neck, Anne saw the reason for the animal's fear. A thick, slithering body darted through the grass ahead but she caught only a brief glimpse of the reptile's rough, crinkled skin glistening in the sun before it disappeared from sight.

The filly reared and Anne was tossed through the air, landing with a heavy thud on the sandy earth. As her head hit the dry leafy ground, she felt the breath sucked out of her chest and her world went black.

Growing conscious, Anne remembered what had happened. Her head throbbed and she lay still until her whirling senses refocused. Gingerly, she pushed herself up on an elbow, groaning at the aches through her body when she moved. Her arms and legs felt heavy and shaky, and her lovely new blouse was torn. Dirt and leaves clung to her clothes, and she spat out a gritty mouthful of dust. All of which she could have endured if she still had a horse. Her filly was nowhere to be seen. It had doubtless galloped off in fright.

Stiff and bruised, Anne struggled to her feet. She hobbled to a tree and leant against it for support. Ants crawled across her fingers and she shook them off. She walked about, forcing her muscles to work and stretching herself even when the pain was so sharp she grew faint.

It was a long walk home but, although her body protested, she had no choice. Anne's only concern was for her valuable animal. She only hoped it returned to the stables and prayed Will had the good sense not to raise any alarm, find her himself and not involve James.

Filled with determination, Anne started walking the long, rutted track back in the direction of the homestead. Limping and in pain, she realised it might take some time. Atop a gentle rise, she slowed her shuffling steps, letting the light breeze cool her hot face. The sun, now directly overhead, beat down with relentless vengeance and she sensibly sought the dappled shade alongside the track.

She didn't know how much longer she continued to shuffle and stagger but eventually heard the sound of beating hooves. Please let it be Will, she sent up a silent prayer. But her worst fear was realised and she filled with dread when a familiar figure astride a black stallion galloped closer. In a glint of sunshine on brass and sweating horse flesh, the blowing horse was reined to a stop. James leapt down, letting the reins fall to the ground.

To her surprise, his blazing blue eyes were filled with fear as well as relief, his first words lending her hope that his concern might outweigh his anger. 'You're hurt!'

'I'm fine.'

'No, you're not.'

'Is my horse all right?'

James faltered at her unselfish question, then nodded and with scowling impatience, said, 'Deuce it, woman. You disobeyed my orders.' He gripped her shoulders.

Bruised, hurting and exhausted, barely able to stand, Anne ached for James to wrap his arms around her and just be held. Tight. How much safer she would feel and less ... exposed. But his hands pinned her to confront him and it was impossible to move.

'It could have happened to anyone,' she said weakly, too sapped to oppose his verbal assault.

'But it happened to you,' he blasted. 'How dare you be so irresponsible and exploit Will's good nature. If you had stayed at the house where you belong, this would never have happened.'

'Exactly,' Anne muttered. 'If I never leave the house, nothing will ever happen!'

'I've lived here for fifteen years. I carved the Downs from the Bush with my bare hands. I know every track and every tree. I can read the signs of the weather and the land.' His grim expression and fierce grip slackened. 'You can't,' he ended in exasperation.

Released, Anne pulled away and stumbled. 'It was an accident. You're making far too much of it.'

'Was my warning not plain enough for you?'

'If you remember, I made no promises.'

He let out an impatient gasp. 'And now you bear the consequences. Now that this has happened, perhaps you will understand why I forbade you.'

Bothered that she had used Will, she needed reassurance. 'You must not blame Will for this.'

'Of course not,' James snapped. 'He did your bidding believing you told the truth but you misled him. Never forget, Annabella,' his voice lowered with a threatening edge, 'who is Master on *Barratt Downs*.'

Seeing a bedraggled Annabella recoil before him, James' instinct was to reach out and comfort her in the aftermath of her ordeal but this alarming episode must serve as a warning so he hardened himself to remain stern.

Wisps of her damp hair clung angelically about her face. Although Annabella Gutheridge was far from a saint, James grew confused, torn between her contrary independence and arresting beauty. Pale when they first met in Melbourne, she had miraculously blossomed since arrival. To his relief, she appeared untroubled with the isolation and bush life but he had sensed a brewing restless energy within her resulting in this horse incident today. As soon as he had time, he must get to know her better and learn more of her mysterious background.

Softening, he surveyed her sweet disorder and shook his head, finally asking, 'What happened?'

Anne sighed. 'I was thrown.'

'There must have been a reason.'

'There was. About six feet long,' she announced wearily.

'Ah.' James frowned, amazed she was not more terrified from the encounter.

Anne forced herself to be brave but secretly craved some show of compassion from him. He irritated her to distraction with his imperious attitude, standing there, dusty and stained from work. Far from feeling repulsed, instead, his simmering maleness caused an edgy stirring in her chest.

He had come after her like a rescuing knight and that was all that mattered. His sharp words she could bear, although at times she sensed he didn't really mean them. Perhaps his blustery way of dealing with a defiant female.

'You should never have come out in this heat.'

'It wasn't hot when I left. I had a sunhat,' she defended lamely.

He looked about. 'Where is it now?'

'Lost.' She grew annoyed at his badgering. 'I was almost home. There was no need to come racing out here after me.' Why on earth had she said that when, before his arrival, she'd felt about to collapse.

James seemed equally alarmed at her explosive torrent of words. 'Your horse returned alone. We could hardly have ignored the fact. Deuce it, woman, don't you see? You might have been lying in the bush seriously hurt or ... worse. We're hours from a doctor out here.'

Anne flinched at his raised voice but detected concern behind his words. 'Do not treat me like a child,' she sighed.

'Then don't act like one! You show no good sense or wisdom.'

Spent from the morning's drama, Anne bore James' hurtful criticism but her resentment surfaced. 'I will not stay back there in that house like some delicate flower. I've lived in the country all my life and always take long walks. And,' she paused for breath, 'Sometimes ... just sometimes, I would appreciate your company,' she announced angrily. 'You're only here now to come looking for me out of obligation. If there'd been no accident, I wouldn't have been missed.'

Her words appeared to startle him. 'You must endure as other women do.' He floundered.

'I love the country and I love your home. I see what you've built,' she implored him. 'But you allow me no freedom to enjoy it. By your own choice, you sought a wife. Since I appear to be your most likely candidate. I expect you to spare me at least some of your time. Am I so disagreeable that you avoid me?'

James stared at her intently, which she found unsettling. Disheartened when he failed to respond, probably shocked by her outburst, she began to walk on until his deep voice came to her with soft amusement.

'Challenging, perhaps. Entertaining. But never disagreeable, Annabella. Never that,' he ended lightly.

She halted her limping steps and turned to face him, catching her breath at the warm expression in his eyes.

'You're being childish. Come here and get on my horse.'

'I am a woman, not a child.' Her teeth clenched in exasperation, her stamina and aching body crumbling with exhaustion. 'If you still plan to marry, you would be wise to bear that in mind. If you want a wife, you need to pay her some attention. You've been a bachelor far too long and had your needs too easily met,' she announced without flinching. James' attention sharpened at her comment. 'Every woman likes a little interest.'

Judging by the confusion in his eyes, James seemed stunned by her outflow of words. She sensed they had just reached a small milestone between them so she awaited his next move.

He had the grace to look mildly apologetic and heaved a

long sigh. 'Perhaps,' he suggested equably, 'I can manage some free time and we'll go riding together.'

Anne listened in disbelief at his promise and melted at his irresistible grin, wishing he used it more often. 'When?' she pressed urgently, stepping closer, her weariness easing, lightened in anticipation and hope. 'Even the shearers have Saturday afternoon and Sunday off.'

'All right. Sunday.'

'Oh, James!.' She eagerly clutched his arm. 'Do you promise?'

Solemn and unsmiling, he nodded.

Standing so close, Anne wondered if he sensed her beating heart. Pumped to excitement by his vow and the now familiar scent of him, the magnetic eyes and smile she was growing to adore. Brimming with joy, she impulsively stood on tiptoe and kissed him on a rough whiskery cheek.

Collapsing with happy exhaustion, she felt herself swept up into powerful arms and onto the saddle. She barely managed to stay upright before James swung up behind her, his chest and legs firmly supportive against her wilting body. His arms reached around her to grip the reins.

Gradually, the gentle movement of the walking horse and blazing opiate sun made her drowsy, and she dozed. In her dreams, she felt warm lips brush her hair and she sighed with pleasure.

CHAPTER 14

Within days, Anne's stiffness and bruising from her riding accident soon eased. Nothing could dampen her high spirits over the eagerly-anticipated forthcoming outing with James the following weekend.

Saturday afternoons and Sundays were passed idly on the run. The shearers read newspapers or books, competed in friendly games of cricket or fished. Only the selector, Duncan Munro, returned home to his small neighbouring property each Saturday when the hum of work in the shed temporarily ceased, reappearing at first light Monday morning.

When Sunday finally arrived, it was imbued with deep spring warmth. To Anne's frustration, it took forever to get underway. She was ready dressed and pacing, awaiting James. The minutes dragged until their departure and it felt as though he intentionally delayed.

Will saddled the horses and brought them around to the front of the homestead, her spirited filly alongside James' impressive black stallion, The General, ridden to her rescue days before.

This would be the first time they were alone socially since Melbourne and Anne's excitement soared as she stepped out in her crisp white pintucked blouse and well-cut dark green riding skirt.

Anne glanced up at the cloudless sky. 'Good morning, Will.'

Flushing, he nodded, mumbling a bashful response. She had apologised to the lad for misleading him but he remained wary, probably cautioned by James. Anne only hoped she continued to enjoy his loyalty.

Her attention was diverted by footsteps crunching behind and James' deep voice. 'Ready, Will?'

'Yes, Sir.'

Anne glanced at the lean, mature man whose roguish blue eyes sparkled over her, smartly attired in a blue cotton shirt and moleskin trousers tucked into his usual black knee-high boots that looked like Zak had given them an extra shine this morning. 'And you, Annabella?'

'Of course.' A generous dash of spirit spiced her reply and she was grateful she had agreed to riding clothes on their shopping expedition to Alston & Brown.

James circled the graceful filly. 'Have you decided on a name for her yet?'

Anne had given the matter thought. 'Yes. Since you told me she is high-born, I shall call her Princess.'

James inclined his head in approval and stepped closer. He clasped his powerful hands about her tiny waist and whipped her easily aloft into her saddle. Against her will, Anne thrilled to his touch, aware that she was growing to love not only this place but also its master, and the growing chaos into which these unwelcome feelings had invaded her scheme of escaping into the country only temporarily before seeking employment elsewhere.

She had grown to appreciate being treated like a lady, even if she had not been born one, which was making it harder to even contemplate her planned break. She had even begun to question the possibility that she could stay and marry James. After all, she could do far worse and, in fact, already had.

Pushing out a sigh of confusion, she watched James turn aside to his mount. He hadn't shown any sign of being affected by their brief physical contact. Perhaps the sun would warm his heart toward her, she thought despondently. Although he had come to her rescue that fateful day and relented to this ride, he had otherwise glowered at her all week. No doubt because she had disobeyed him and she had no idea how to make amends.

They urged their horses forward and James led them away from the homestead where they broke into a canter along a bush track among the trees.

After a time of silence between them, James said, 'You ride well, Annabella.' Pride and good humour showed on his handsome sun browned face.

Disarmed by his unexpected praise, Anne hid her delight. 'No need to look so surprised.'

Further on, he dismounted and unlatched a gate in the fence ahead. After she walked Princess through, he closed it behind them and re-mounted to join her.

'We'll head across to the creek,' James nodded south along the undulating tree-studded grasslands that stretched into the distance. Suddenly, he touched her arm and pointed across the paddock.

Anne shielded her eyes and glanced toward a group of animals virtually camouflaged against the landscape, their long thin legs looking too fragile to support the bulky body drooped with brown shaggy feathers, long elegant necks like a giraffe poised and alert.

Instinct made them wary and they lurched into a swift loping run, heading for the sanctuary of distant bush.

'Emus,' James explained.

Fascinated, Anne watched them swagger away at incredible speed.

'Think you can ride as fast as they can run?' He teased, his hands folded together on the pommel.

His challenge inspired a spark of wicked devilment in response. 'Don't tempt me.'

'I'm trying to.' A lazy sluggish smile accompanied his taunt.

Anne gaped. He meant it. Speechless, she flashed a saucy grin. 'I accept your challenge, Mr. Barratt.'

'To that first stand of trees. I'll give you a head start.'

'Because I am a woman?' Anne's gaze glittered with determination. 'What prize for my victory?' she grinned.

'Or mine.'

'A kiss,' she saucily declared, her lips tilted with mirth.

He scowled and grew serious. 'As you wish.' He held her challenging gaze, knowing as she did, under those terms, neither could lose.

The light hearted banter between them hummed with deeper meaning. Anne let the breeze cool her hot face as her heart raced with exhilaration.

James gripped his reins to control the restless stallion. Anne watched him, tense, and jumped away the instant he flexed his muscles to spur the stallion.

She took the lead, thundering across the grassy paddock at a gallop, pounding hooves churning up the soft turf beneath them. The excited horses tore at their bits and strained forward as they raced each other.

Anne laughed but her confidence was short lived. Halfway to the trees, James drew alongside. Desperately, she spurred on her roan but the mighty stallion, bred for racing and scenting victory, lengthened its powerful stride and snatched the lead.

Anne leant forward over the filly's neck, coaxing her in vain. James and The General easily gained a length, the black thoroughbred pulling further away with every stride, and she was struck with competitive envy that her fiancé possessed such a magnificent beast.

Reaching the trees at the creek's edge, James slowed his horse and walked him about before leaping down and striding across to Anne. Smiling and breathless, she gathered her skirts and James' strong arms lifted her down. On a frivolous impulse, she leaned closer and kissed him, discovering his lips soft and warm, sparking a shaft of pleasure in her stomach.

'Your reward,' she stepped back unsteadily, smiling.

'Is that the best you can do?' His voice turned husky.

Anne's gaze doubled in amazement at the dare. Drawing in a slight sharp breath, she licked her lips and said, 'Be my guest.'

James slid an arm around her waist and hauled her against him. The other hand gently tilted her face to meet his. He smelled of outdoors and sweat and tobacco. When his face lowered, Anne's eyelids fluttered closed and she felt his mouth crush hers in a long moist kiss. She willed it to last forever but James stiffened and pulled away. As their lips parted, the magic ceased. Breathing heavily, all smiles gone, Anne's eyes searched his face but she saw only scowling regret.

'I'm sorry,' James muttered. 'I shouldn't have taken advantage.'

'It was your prize. You were entitled.' Anne flung at him carelessly, stung by his abrupt change of mood and obvious regret at the impulse.

'Yes. Of course.'

'You still think I'm too young,' she accused bluntly.

He hesitated. 'Inexperienced perhaps.'

She remembered what she had endured with Arthur. How could she forget? And ached with regret for her shameful past.

Instinctively, she knew any involvement with James would be different but, as much as she craved it and longed to give her emotions rein, any attachment would be fragile and dangerous while James held back and that same past loomed overhead to haunt her.

'I am stronger than you think. And,' she added quietly, believing the timing appropriate since their friendship seemed to be moving in a new direction, and it couldn't hurt to shake up his detachment, 'I know about Caroline.'

James glared, jaw clenched. Anne saw a barrier of pain and wondered if he was still in love and tormented by her memory, unable to forget. She ached for his suffering but felt it important he knew. Something deep inside, perhaps a legacy of her own torment and abuse from Arthur, compelled her to help him heal.

'Rosie,' he breathed sharply with a bitter curl of his mouth but head held proudly high. 'Is that the only reason you continued on with me at Ballarat? Out of pity?' He challenged coldly.

'No! I was moved,' she added hastily, 'but we all have unhappiness in our past.' She paused. 'Rosie cares very much for you and she believed I should know.'

James turned his back to her, staring off into the distance, clearly uncomfortable with her knowledge of his private life. Any strong man who had hidden his deep sorrow would feel humiliated.

All the same, Anne stepped closer and gently advised, 'If you never let yourself freely love again, James, you won't ever get back more than you give. Your marriage will be empty. Only a front for siring children.'

At her simple words of wisdom, James swung around to face her, gaping. 'What would you know of love?' he growled disparagingly, clearly considering her too immature and her advice worthless.

'I know I can,' she said indignantly with as much poise as she could muster, 'And you're not the only one who's known a nasty version of it.'

'You?' he mocked, but his surprised attention remained riveted on her face.

'Age has nothing to do with misery.'

His narrow gaze made her feel estranged and bleak. 'Is that why you left England?' She reluctantly nodded. 'And why a marriage of convenience appealed?'

Anne shrugged. 'I told you the truth. I wanted to get out into the country.'

'Why?' he demanded curtly. 'To escape from someone?'

If she told him the full truth, he would despise her and she would lose him. Knowing she did not yet wish to leave, her future dangled by a fine thread indeed. Unwilling to reveal details, Anne merely nodded but could not meet his stripping gaze.

James looked away again, whether in anger or disappointment Anne did not know but he remained absorbed and remote for a long while.

Hoping to recapture their earlier companionship and warmth, she asked, 'Is it all *Barratt Downs* beyond those trees?' indicating the distant eucalypt bushland creating a blue haze across the landscape.

'No,' James growled. 'The Munro selection.'

Ah, the thorn in his side. She couldn't have asked the wrong question at a worse moment. At least she had rekindled his attention. 'Is he married?'

'Yes.'

'Children?'

'Yes.'

As if knowing her thoughts, he turned, his eyes blazing. 'Don't even consider it.'

Despite his disapproval, Anne was beginning to enjoy their lively exchange. At least they were talking again if not on the most heart-warming topic for him.

'I heard you talking to Mr. Farrell at Wickliffe and you said Munro was a ringer. What's that?'

Responding to Anne's raised eyebrows, he explained, 'The shearer with the highest tally of sheep in a day.'

She knew it was pushing the limits of his patience, but she could not hide her amazement at this ironic disclosure and restrained a private smile. 'So, you dislike him but you need him?'

'He applied like everyone else,' James gruffly defended. 'It proves he needs me and cannot make a living scratching over the soil on his poorly-watered piece of my land.'

'Why is it poorly watered?'

'Because I made sure I bought up all the land with river frontages,' he claimed proudly.

Anne cringed at his ruthless declaration revealing an

aggressive side of him she had not seen. But his actions had probably also been borne out of the need to protect the interests he had created over the past fifteen years. He had started out with nothing and all about them as far as the eye could see had been hard won. Maybe now that, too, was the challenge ahead for the Munros.

'All the same,' she maintained, 'If the wife and children are at home, I'd care to visit.'

'You will not! Every station is busy shearing now. Not just us. No-one has time for social calls at this time of year.'

Undaunted and defiant, Anne said, 'You may not but I do.'

'Never.' James' deep voice bellowed across the paddocks, carrying on the warm still air like a threatening cloud. 'I will not cross the threshold of that wily Scot and neither will you. He has his corner of the Downs. That's enough.'

'I'm a guest in your house and you may send me away if you want.' How could she utter such a dare? 'But you will not tell me how to spend my days. Your fight with Duncan Munro is not my concern.'

'You would deliberately go against my wishes and socialise with that…Highland thief?' James scoffed.

'You have tens of thousands of acres. Surely the loss of a few hundred hardly matters and Duncan Munro is no threat.'

'This land was nothing before squatters like myself claimed and improved it, and bred stud merinos to develop their fleece into the finest in the country. If any of his scabby sheep stray onto my land, they'll end up on my dinner plate.' He nodded to their horses grazing nearby. 'They are both from the finest blood stock in the country.'

'Given time, I'm sure Mr. Munro intends to do the same.'

'You're defending that Gaelic scoundrel?'

'He's only doing what you did fifteen years ago.'

Her sound argument silenced him into thought and Anne lamented that their moments of harmony always seemed so fleeting. The lovely playfulness of earlier this afternoon was gone and a strained tension lay between them as they rode back to the homestead in silence.

CHAPTER 15

Determined not to be persuaded otherwise or tell James of her intentions, Anne decided to visit Mrs. Munro the next day. With Duncan and James occupied down at the shearing shed on the first day of another shearing week, the womenfolk could become acquainted without hostile male interference. Besides, as she settled in to life on *Barratt Downs* and nurtured the hope that perhaps it could become permanent, Anne felt the need to seek out neighbours, look further afield and find friends.

James usually ate early and left but, today, shared breakfast with Anne in the dining room, seemingly reluctant to leave, preoccupied and remote, lingering over a second cup of tea. Considering the spoonfuls of sugar he loaded into each one, Anne thought his disposition should be much sweeter. Or perhaps he was mulling over her disclosure yesterday that she knew about his lost love, Caroline.

Eventually, he pushed back his chair, wished her a curt and passing, 'Until this evening, then,' and left.

Although she was anxious to set out for the Munro selection, Anne had hoped for at least a smile or touch of his hand after their brief moment of affection yesterday, believing it meant something, so that, when he was gone, a hollow ache crept into her heart as his heavy footsteps receded down the long hall.

Deciding not to let his apathy bother her, Anne strode into the kitchen where, sworn to grudging secrecy, Mrs. O'Grady was packing preserves and other goods from the larder into a large basket.

'Do you know Mrs. Munro's name?' Anne asked as cook bustled about.

'I'm told it's Mary. The master won't be happy about this,' she warned darkly.

'He won't know.'

'I'll not say a word, for sure, but I can't speak for Sarah.' She frowned. 'Where is that girl? It takes her longer every day to do the milkin' and feed a few hens.'

'I'm looking forward to meeting Mrs. Munro. Surely her husband is hardly the rogue everyone claims?'

Squatters are no friends of selectors,' she scoffed. 'They own most of the land and want to keep it all.'

'How much land do they need?' Anne muttered.

Mrs. O'Grady tossed her a shocked glance. 'It's not like England or Ireland out here, Miss. Australia's a big colony, free for the takin'. Most of us come out here for a better life and some like the master to make their fortune. Good luck to them what make it, I say.'

'Have you met Mary Munro, Mrs. O'Grady?'

She looked horrified. 'I've no time for visitin'.'

When Will had harnessed the horse and buggy and Anne saw him bring it around to the front of the homestead, for she had been watching anxiously from the front window, she thanked cook for preparing the basket and hurried out to greet the stable boy.

To her amazement, he suggested shyly, 'It might be wise to take the back road away from the house. The long way round,' and gave her detailed directions. 'You're unlikely to be seen.'

Grateful but concerned for his conspiracy, Anne was nonetheless pleased to have found an ally and friend despite having misled him about her unfortunate ride last week.

'With my luck, Will,' she pulled a wry smile, 'I probably shall but thank you for your advice anyway. Mr. Barratt can only put me on the next coach for Ballarat.'

'I hope not, Miss.' Will looked genuinely appalled and

Anne's spirits lifted to see he meant it.

With the buggy hood down, she bowled away from the house, the biddable hackney soon whisking her along the bush track leading south to the Munro selection. The sun beat down and she soon found need of her sunhat.

There was something exhilarating about a jaunty buggy ride on a crisp spring morning. The satisfying rattle of the wheels on the rough track; the keen bite of the wind on her face; the musty scent of damp dew-soaked grass mixed with the minty gums; and the earthy smell of horse sweat and leather.

The sweet carol of magpies pierced the still air as she passed and always the haunting beauty of the nearby blue-hazed mountains, already flooded with warm morning sunlight, rose up from the plains in the background.

Endless acres of pink heath bells and wildflowers dotted colour through the grass and it was almost an hour later before Anne turned the hackney off the main track onto a narrow bush lane running alongside a small fenced paddock planted with oats. The thick crop would soon ripen and make valuable hay. She eagerly squinted when a bark hut with a wooden shingled roof emerged through a clump of gum trees ahead. A column of smoke drifted from its brick chimney across one end wall.

Suddenly Anne grew uncertain of her reception. Apart from gossip, coloured by personal opinion, she knew nothing of the Munro family. Her own curiosity and deepening desire for friendship had compelled her to come. Hopefully, she would receive a civil welcome and not be turned away.

Anne gasped in dismay at the small crude square shack as she reined the hackney to a stop. It was far worse than James' first hut where she and Sarah had found the crates of china. Anne heartstrings tugged with compassion for the family's hardship to come.

The buggy's raised dust must have heralded her unannounced approach for the straggly family band had clustered around the open door beneath a small front veranda.

A tiny dark-haired woman stood in the centre of the expectant group nursing a toddler on her hip while two thin wiry boys and an older girl, almost as tall as her mother, crowded her skirts. Anne jumped down from the buggy leaving the horse hitched to a gnarled ancient gum, the only tree in the middle of the barren dusty yard.

Carrying the basket over one arm, she approached the huddled group, greeted by a faint smile from the woman and silent stares from the children.

'Good morning.' She paused at the veranda's edge. 'Mrs. Munro?'

The woman nodded. 'Aye.' Her soft voice was rich with a Scottish brogue.

'I'm Annabella Gutheridge, a...guest at *Barratt Downs*.'

'I know who ye are,' she said, her brown eyes studying their visitor with caution.

District news travelled fast, Anne marvelled. Not too different from Devon with Duncan shearing on *Barratt Downs*, he must have learned of her presence at the homestead.

As Mrs. Munro shifted the child on her hip, Anne noticed her gently rounded stomach, swollen with a fifth child, beneath her plain dark dress and full length apron.

Her gleaming black hair, caught off her face with a ribbon, streamed long and straight down her back to her waist. Anne noted the rough work-hardened hands and lines on her young face, revealing traces of former beauty. Anne guessed the woman to be no more than thirty, her once-pretty face gaunt, her huge dark eyes shadowed and tired.

Yet, Anne sensed an aura of serenity about her. Unbelievable in this pitiable situation. Easy to see how Duncan Munro might have been captivated by this delicate woman of wiry strength and clear brown eyes. Anne guessed this tiny soul would be a match for her husband.

'I apologise for my unexpected visit but, as Mr. Barratt's closest neighbour, I wanted to pay my respects.'

'I'm thinkin' Mr. Barratt didn't send ye?' The woman's eyes sparkled along with her quick retort.

'No.' Anne stifled a smile, appreciating her refreshing honesty and humour. 'He most certainly did not. My visit has nothing to do with him. It's simply for a friendly chance to chat.'

Anne found herself the focus of Mrs. Munro's shrewd and lively gaze. 'Men can be proud and stubborn creatures, for sure.' When she gently smiled, the tired lines at the corners of her eyes deepened and Anne's apprehension eased.

Because both arms held the toddler, she gave a curt nod. 'Ma name's Mary, and these are ma bairns. Wee Robbie,' she smiled at the child she held. 'Janet.' She indicated the girl. 'Young Hector and Andrew.'

Ginger haired and freckled, the mischievous boys grinned and nudged each other. Janet offered a shy smile, her long russet hair bound into a thick braid while Robbie snuggled closer against his mother and sucked his thumb, the only child to share his mother's fine dark looks. The others had all obviously inherited their flame colouring from their father.

'It's Robbie's time for sleeping.' Mary brushed a tender hand across his flushed forehead. 'Will ye not be coming inside, Miss Gutheridge, while I put him doon? We can have a wee chat over a pot of tea.'

'Please, call me Annie.'

'I'm obliged for your company. With Munro gone all week, there's never a soul to be seen and no school yet in the district for the bairns.'

Mary turned and disappeared indoors, the children trailed behind, casting wide-eyed stares at their guest as Anne followed. Inside the hut, the earthen floor was hard packed but swept. Behind a hessian partition, Anne glimpsed rough low beds with pole legs where Mary set Robbie down. About her in the one main room, its walls plastered with newsprint, stood a beautifully carved table and chairs, out of place among the packing cases and crates used as benches and cupboards elsewhere.

The two small windows at the front were covered with calico, at the moment drawn aside to admit the breeze, and an open fire burnt low with coals beneath a cast iron pot, a kettle on bricks to one side.

For all its crude simplicity, the room was tidy. Anne admired Mary's efforts coping alone with a large family. Once, James and every other squatter decades before had been newcomers too.

Presently, Mary reappeared and without a word, silently fluttered her hands toward her inquisitive sons, dismissing them from the room. Anne set down the uncovered basket, producing fresh fruit and vegetables from Lee's garden and preserves from Bridget's larder.

Sensing Mary's hesitation at the generous gift, Anne warmly reassured her, 'A token of my friendship,' and accompanied it with a smile.

Mary astutely understood her tactful explanation. 'Then I thank ye for your kindness.' She turned to her daughter. 'Janie, put the produce in the cool safe and the jars on the shelf.'

As the girl reverently put away the food, Mary set crockery on the table and filled a teapot with hot water from the kettle on the fire, setting it on the table to steep. Then she moved to the fireplace and stirred the contents of a huge blackened pot.

She straightened, resting a hand at her back and placing the other gently on the bulging front of her apron. 'Duncan shot rabbits at the weekend so I've prepared a hearty stew. You'll be taking lunch with us?'

Anne noted the expectant query in her voice and eyes. 'I would be delighted. It will give us more time to chat.' And perhaps give James more time to find out she was missing again.

As Mary seated herself slowly at the table, her perceptive brown eyes skimmed her guest. 'You're from England?' She poured two cups of tea.

Anne nodded. 'Devon. From a farm near Tavistock.'

'Do ye miss it, then?' Mary asked, passing her a cup.

Anne heard warmth in her voice and understanding behind the steady lovely brown eyes, perhaps from a touch of nostalgia of her own. 'I've only been out here a short time and, yes, sometimes I miss my family but I've decided that Australia will be my new home now.'

'Ye've not known Mr. Barratt long, then?'

Self-conscious, Anne had trouble holding Mary's sharp gaze and shook her head. 'I met him the day after I arrived.'

Mary raised expressive eyebrows. 'You're a wee bit younger than Mr. Barratt.'

Anne decided to loosen her guard, took a deep breath and launched into a concise explanation of the unusual circumstances under which she had arrived at *Barratt Downs*.

'A strange tale and all. So,' Mary observed her keenly, 'Ye've come to run an eye over your possible new home?'

'There's no ... arrangement between us,' Anne swiftly explained. 'Despite being a proud man, James Barratt is a warm-hearted man underneath. So far, we get along.' Anne paused then changed the subject and smiled. 'Scotland's much further away than Devon.'

'Aye, indeed it is,' Mary agreed. 'Much greener and mair mountains. That's why Duncan wanted to settle here by the Grampians. There's Grampians mountains in Scotland, too, near where we lived in the highlands. But not enough land for Munro there. Only raising his Blackface on a few acres. Here, he's already bought three hundred.' A gentle expression came over her face. 'It was Duncan's dream to come oot here and nothing would keep him from it. If I'd not agreed to marry him, he'd have left me behind in Scotland for sure.'

Mary's unexpected light laugh penetrated every corner of the hut, filling it with warmth. This tiny woman was the centre of her small home, and Anne admired her courage in emigrating to be with the man she loved.

Mary fixed her gaze outside and grew nostalgic. 'I've known ma man since childhood. Our families were crofters and me one of the few people he'd ever talk to. Always scaring away the other girls he was with his loud voice and temper.' Mary returned her attention into the small room and smiled faintly. 'I never minded, feeling aboot him the way I did. Only dream Munro ever had was to own land. Fierce and determined to have a better life he was.'

Anne realised Duncan Munro was no different to James. A little later on his road to success maybe.

Mary's animated face and sparkling brown eyes betrayed her love and devotion for the man who had so naturally become the centre of their conversation. Drawn into reminiscence, the lines softened on her thin tired face. 'And me not giving a thought to travelling away across the world with him.'

Throughout the conversation, Janet sat listening to her mother and studying their elegant visitor, eyes wide, elbows resting on the table in awe, chin cupped in her hands.

'Eighteen fifty-two it was and straight to the Ballarat goldfields. We were more fortunate than most and made a good living.' She looked fondly across at her daughter. 'Janet was born in a tent. Later on, Duncan set up business as a carpenter. He's guid with his hands.' She ran her work-worn fingers lovingly over the table. 'He made this, and he's working on more when he gets time. Now we have our own place.' Mary directed an astute gaze toward Anne. 'Munro'll be fightin' hard to be keepin' it.'

Anne acknowledged her veiled remark with a nod of understanding. As far as she could see, it was time for this new wave of settlers, selectors like Duncan and Mary and their family, to expand the colony the pioneers had begun.

'I wish you every success, Mary. I hope the ... differences between the men folk won't interfere with our friendship?'

'I'd be hoping not. I'd not be Christian or neighbourly if I held Mr. Barratt's unfriendliness against you personally but, at week's end, I've a care to tell Duncan you called.'

Anne scowled, realising James must eventually discover her visit and hoped Duncan didn't forbid his wife from allowing her to call again. She sensed this petite unassuming woman could become a good friend. If she stayed.

The awkward moment of candour was interrupted when the two older boys hurtled through the open door.

'Have ye washed before lunch?' Mary demanded, at which they grew sheepish and returned outdoors.

The women chatted of more general matters during the meal while the children hungrily crammed the rabbit stew into their mouths and soaked up the juices with slabs of homemade bread. It was simple hearty food and, scarcely had the boys swallowed the last mouthful, than they asked to be excused.

At the door, young Hector, thin-lipped and proud, turned to Anne with a lofty glance. 'Ma Dad owns this land now and no-one can take it back.'

'Hector Munro, mind ye tongue,' his mother reprimanded with firm quiet authority.

Surprised by the blunt outburst, Anne responded quickly, 'I know. You must be proud of him.'

Her agreement confounded the lad. Silenced by honesty, he realised this guest was probably no threat or enemy. After a moment's rebellious hesitation under his mother's cool glance, the lad disappeared.

'They're good bairns. Mostly. Just need to mind their manners. We don't get visitors.'

'He only spoke the truth. I hope nothing ever crushes his spirit. The conflict between squatters and selectors is unfortunate. I can assure you Mr. Barratt's views are not mine.'

'Then ye might be havin' trouble. The big sheep men are powerful. Most of the land up for sale and selection was bought back by just a few of them. Doesn't give families like us much of a chance. We're all just trying to raise our families and make a home.'

Anne sat silently, amazed to learn the lengths the squatters had gone to retain their land.

With a heavy sigh, Mary struggled to her feet. Anne Rosie, having forgotten all sense of time in her gentle company. Janet cleared the table and poured hot water from the kettle into a large tin dish.

As they ambled outdoors and paused under the short veranda, Anne grew thoughtful. 'There are plenty of books in the library at the Downs. I could bring some over for the children next time I visit.'

'Would Mr. Barratt approve?' Doubt edged Mary's voice.

'He has given me charge of the house,' Anne grinned. 'They'd only be on loan, of course,' she added, trying not to offend Mary's pride.

'That would be useful for the older children,' Mary agreed.

'I hope all goes well for you and the baby. When is it due?'

Mary rested a hand on her rounded body. 'Two months. Duncan's hoping for another son. There's so much work to be done, another pair of strong arms is always welcome. Come summer, there's harvesting, and more land to clear in the autumn.'

'I don't see what's wrong with daughters, do you?' Anne half-turned to acknowledge Janet standing just behind them in the doorway.

The girl flashed a shy smile toward her mother and Mary slid an arm companionably around her daughter's shoulder. Anne's thoughts moved to James and the clinical manner in which he had chosen her as a suitable breeder for his children. She suddenly longed for the same affection and loyalty as Mary and Duncan Munro clearly shared, despite their poverty. Ironic she should envy a family with far less worldly possessions than the master of *Barratt Downs*.

Anne worried what the future held in store for, every day,

her attraction for James grew. Unfortunately, it seemed her feelings were not returned. At this point, the thought of leaving him was too hard to bear but he had not declared his love and she now knew she could not marry him without it.

Returning her concentration to the present, Anne said, 'I've enjoyed my visit, Mary. Thank you for lunch and your hospitality. Take care of your mother, Janet, until I see her again.' The girl nodded, smiling. 'At the end-of-shearing ball maybe?'

'Aye,' Mary confirmed. 'Ma bairn will have arrived by then but I'll not be doing much dancing.'

Anne hesitated in concern. 'Will you be all right when your time comes?'

'It's not ma first. There's a district midwife and Janet can help.'

'If I'm still here, will you send word and let me know?'

Mary nodded, smiling gently. 'We'll see you at the ball, then?'

Anne donned her sunhat against the warm afternoon sun and set the empty basket on the buggy seat. 'Say goodbye to the boys for me. Whenever they come home.' She laughed, scrambling up and gathering the reins. She clicked to the horse and, with a rattle and a wave, set off for home.

After a short distance, she looked back and waved again, before losing sight of the hut and its occupants still standing in the doorway.

CHAPTER 16

At dinner that night, James was impossibly distracted by the candlelight on Annabella's hair, gilded lighter gold from the sun. His concentration could not resist the turn of her face toward him when she spoke, the dip of her head to eat, and her delicious body tightly encased in a ruby gown.

Every day she seemed happier and more settled and he wondered if she was ready to consider a permanent arrangement. Despite his daily absences, his growing attraction for her fought against his irate frustration over her regular defiance and unwillingness to conform. Including her latest rebellious visit to the Munros.

She had been seen from the shed and word spread. He did not intend to mention he knew, choosing to avoid yet another disagreement of which they seemed to have plenty. It would serve no purpose to lecture. Annabella would not listen anyway. It seemed apparent, the girl needed to learn by experience. If that meant exposure to misadventure then he must conceal his concern and stay alert.

Deep down, to his annoyance, he had begun to acquire a grudging respect for her independent spirit yet also knew it necessary to protect her from the untamed Australian bush and its potential dangers.

Although bested by her stubborn will, James also realised if he checked her freedom, he would crush the essence of the woman that had attracted him in the first place. The one who had so excited him with potential as a challenging mate the first time he set eyes upon her in the Albion hotel. He had denied his feelings and taken escape in the busy season of shearing to avoid her, amazed to discover that thoughts of Caroline faded daily.

In the evenings now, he looked forward to returning to the homestead, captivated anew by the slim golden ray of sunshine that awaited him and who drew feelings from his heart he had not known since his early liaison with Caroline, still embarrassed that Anne knew about her but grateful for Rosie's concern.

No doubt in the years ahead he would thank her strategy in making him confront the past so that he could move on to his future. It had made him see, to his shame, when comparing both women how unsuitable Caroline would have been to share his life.

Whereas Annabella showed interest and the capability to live out here with him, possessing a natural curiosity to explore – not always healthy as she had discovered – and brought his mausoleum of a house to life. For the first time, he truly saw its potential as a family home, remaining on edge that Annabella might not want to share it with him. Despite her wilful nature, she fascinated him and challenged him to redefine his requisites for a wife.

The vibrant young woman seated opposite him at the dining table was proof that any presumptions could be shattered. He had come to recognize the subtle whisper of lavender that drifted about her when she was near. If she had been in a room, he knew.

Dare he expose his heart again to rejection and pain? He had coldly advertised in The Argus, vowing he would never be moved by another woman. He was appalled to remember the extent of desperation he had felt in England and subsequent years upon his return to the colony at Caroline's rejection and loss. Even his deep friendship with Rosie he had never allowed to pass a certain point.

He finished his meal, set down his cutlery on the empty plate with a clatter and, troubled, drained the last of his wine.

'You have been very quiet this evening, James.'

Her lovely green eyes watched him with deep perception and he marvelled that she had been affected by his mood for, in turn, he too was growing increasingly aware of hers and, indeed, affected by them. An undercurrent of unresolved attraction simmered between them these days since their kiss, never repeated or mentioned again.

'I have much on my mind.'

'Shearing?'

'More or less.'

'How many sheep can be shorn in one day?' She leant forward in lively interest.

'Most good men manage seventy or eighty.'

'Has it been a good clip?' He nodded, noting her growing struggle to converse because of his clipped replies. 'How many days are left?'

'Less than a week.' She brightened, clearly hopeful it might mean more of his time. To satisfy her questions, he explained, 'The bullocky will be arriving any day now to cart the bales.'

'It will be a heavy load.'

'Labels must be painted on them first before cartage to the coast.'

'Where is the wool taken?'

'It will be hauled to Geelong then bound by ship for England.'

Her gaze faltered and grew distant but only for a moment before her eagerness and attention returned.

Tempted to relent, James hesitated to reveal his position and expectations. Annabella was a match waiting to be struck. When she flared, it would be with her whole heart. Was it fair of him to confine her to his small corner of the world? Crush the opportunities that lay ahead for a young budding woman of such beauty and energy? Years her senior, he sometimes felt old and jaded. Would she tire of him in future years? All irrelevant concerns if she was not interested to accept him in the first place.

Losing Caroline and parting from Rosie was nothing compared to the devastation he would know if Annabella did not stay. Fearful of her refusal, his anxiety plagued him into tense moods and he delayed their obligatory discussion, knowing it must be soon.

Toward the end of September, the weather turned bleak and wintry, and Anne was pleased she had seized the opportunity to visit Mary Munro weeks before. While the early spring days had been sunny and alive, now, fires blazed in every room of the homestead as icy winds whipped rain across the paddocks. Shearing was delayed and outdoor expeditions abandoned. Confined, Anne restlessly paced and spent hours browsing the library shelves to set aside suitable books for the Munro children to read.

There was no word of Mary, although the baby was not yet due for weeks. Still, she was concerned for her new friend that all would be well and both safely delivered.

When October arrived, the weather improved and shearing progressed, James fully engrossed again in the bustling shed. He seemed distant and reluctant to do more than share light insignificant conversation over dinner after which, to Anne's resentment, he often retired to his study.

He always departed the homestead at first light after which the shearers began another working day. Alcohol was strictly forbidden and, apart from two or three hours each day for meals and smokes, the men laboured tirelessly until six in the evening when they returned to their quarters.

Only occasionally did James join her for the midday meal.

Unhappily, Anne became convinced he regretted their one exciting kiss so long ago, believing her immature and unsuitable to be his wife. Afraid she would be released from any commitment and sent back to Melbourne, she grew miserable at the possibility. To her despair, she had fallen in love with the man and his land, and could not easily leave. Deep down, she also knew that if her Devon past was ever discovered, it would mean the end of her life here with him.

Beneath the constant mental torment, Anne struggled to occupy her mind and days. To Sarah's horror, she had introduced a stricter household routine and led by example pitching in to regularly help when needed. She brooded, gazing into the distance toward the shearing shed, dust clouds rising from mobs of restless sheep. Their endless bleating filled the air, men shouted and whistled to the sheep dogs.

Anne recalled an encounter with Sarah one morning when she had slipped outdoors to pick wildflowers from the home paddock, encountering Lee on the way, and waved. Grinning as usual, the diminutive Chinaman bowed as she passed then hunched over hoeing weeds among his rows of vegetables again.

Irritated to see Sarah sitting idly on the veranda, Anne bit her tongue against a reprimand. Instead, knowing it would be futile, she ignored the girl's laziness and said, 'Have you ever seen the shearing, Sarah?'

She sniffed. 'Never. Who'd want to visit that smelly place?'

Anne bristled. 'Your wages are possible because of those sheep!' And not because you work hard enough to earn them.

Anne's worry also extended to a deepening concern for James. He grew increasingly weary at day's end with rarely a break. Understandable when the entire year's work depended on his wool clip. The shearers, however, unburdened by such responsibility, wandered down to the billabong on warmer weekends for a shave and a swim.

Anne wished James would allow himself more recreation. Once or twice, as a rare treat, he had taken a walk and picnic with her into the bush, and she treasured these precious times together. Although he remained aloof and she did not know if he wanted her to stay.

With each passing day, the sun's sting increased. Although still spring, Anne gradually dispensed with all unnecessary undergarments in the heat, wearing only the lightest cotton dress or blouse and skirt. But always a hat to protect her skin.

Everyone predicted a hot summer, yet December was still six weeks away and Anne constantly sought ways to keep cool.

One pristine midweek afternoon with a clear blue sky and not a breath of wind to rustle even the crispest gum leaf, Anne restlessly wandered the homestead before she seized upon a brilliant idea far more stimulating than sitting in the shade and using a fan. A refreshing dip in the billabong. No shearers would be about during the day.

'Bathing?' Mrs. O'Grady's face registered disaster. 'You'll not be goin' alone, Miss?'

Anne schooled her voice to placation. 'The shearers go down there at the weekend.'

'Can ye swim?'

She could not. 'I won't wade out too deep. I shall keep my feet on solid ground all the time.'

'In your underclothes?' Bridget clutched her throat, aghast.

Anne laughed. 'Of course. I should sink fully dressed.'

Mrs. O'Grady fanned herself furiously with her apron then crossed her large bosom. 'Holy Virgin Mother! It don't seem proper.'

Anne grabbed her favourite sunhat now quite battered from use, and a towel, setting off eagerly from the house. The thought of an inviting dip with cool water over her skin kept her footsteps light as she tramped the grassy path to the billabong. Warmth rose from the earth beneath her feet as she followed the narrow path to the water's edge.

Reeds bordered an island mid-stream where the creek level had dropped and divided in the dry. Anne watched flocks of water fowl paddle in search of food or skim the dark shallows before taking flight.

It was eerily peaceful and private. She removed her shoes and dipped her toes into the cold water, quickly enticed to shed her blouse and skirt, hanging them over a bush and, with a delighted squeal, she surged in, alarming birds nearby who flapped away in a rush of wings.

Invigorated in the heat, Anne splashed herself cool, tilting her head to take in the cloudless blue sky then waded back out onto the riverbank, squeezing water from her chemise and hair. She towelled herself then sat down on it to dry in the sun.

She had just begun to ponder the peace and her possible future with James when she heard rustling, and started. Alarmed, she sat up. The boughs of a wattle bush nearby, aglow with golden racemes, stirred. But there was no breeze! She glanced around. Nothing. She sighed, chastising herself. It must have been her imagination. Probably a bush creature.

Still wary, she reached for her skirt and blouse, pulling them on quickly over her damp underclothes. Again she heard it. The slightest sound, scarcely more than a whisper. Her heart beat faster in the uneasy suspicion of being watched, another presence, and yet, spinning around in a full circle, she saw nothing out of the ordinary. At first.

But, as she stooped to retrieve the towel, she saw him. Dark beady eyes squinting at her from beneath bushy jutting brows. An old gaunt native, his leathery brown skin gleaming, legs apart, feet plunged into the sandy soil, an upright spear gripped at his side. A scant cloth covered his lower body and his ribs were visible on his thin chest.

As Anne stood riveted to the ground, the dusky stranger took a menacing step forward, jabbering words she didn't understand. He lifted the spear above his head and shook it. Cissy's dire words about savages returned to haunt her. Was this man one of them?

Terrified by his threatening pose, Anne screamed and ran. Mercifully, she found the track back to the homestead. Sharp dry grass cut into her bare feet and scratched her as she fled. Her only thought was escape.

Fresh from her swim and sleep, she sprinted, leaping

fallen logs in her path, pressed with a desperate need to survive. She pushed herself faster and heard a spear hum past, missing her but embedded in a tree trunk nearby as she fled.

She cried out but kept running, her heart pounding, her mouth dry. The heat and pain in her lacerated feet increased. Her legs ached. She licked her parched lips and tried to swallow, panting. She must keep going, she must. Would the homestead never appear? She had not thought it so far away.

She tried to run faster but her legs and body tired. Exhausted and running blind, Anne risked a backward glance and stumbled over a tree root. She landed with a sprawling thud on a bed of sand and dry leaves. She winced at the sharp pain in her left ankle. In horror, she saw the native loom over her before she screamed and everything went black.

CHAPTER 17

Anne's awareness ebbed and flowed. She heard faint voices and whispers. When she tried to open her eyes, she saw only blurred images. Her limp body ached all over and, when she slept, was cursed by restless sleep and distorted visions of a strange black face.

Then the heat disappeared and her face brushed with a cool dampness, the sound of a familiar deep voice murmuring nearby.

'James...?' Her stiff lips barely formed the words before she surrendered to sleep again.

Finally her need for sleep eased and her eyelids opened. She turned her head aside on the pillow and focused. She was in her room. Safe from her fearful nightmares. She struggled to raise herself on one elbow and moaned with the effort.

James slumped in a chair by her open window, dozing. Anne melted with tenderness at the sight of him, head bowed, dark hair tumbling over his suntanned forehead.

Greedily, she nestled back against her pillows and studied him, swept by longing, wondering if he could ever love again. Hoping against hope but knowing she had no right to expect it of him. A fine state of affairs falling in love with this man and his country under false pretences. The dilemma spoilt her joy and she pushed out a long sigh of remorse.

Just then, Sarah peeped into the room and her usually sullen face flowered into a smile when her gaze settled on her sleeping master. 'You're awake, Miss,' she said dispassionately, turning her lapsed attention back to the patient and approached Anne's bed. 'Mrs. O'Grady said I'm to see how you're feeling.'

Anne grimaced. 'Sore and my head aches.' She raised an arm to its throbbing.

'Cook will be relieved, Miss. You were so pale when the Master carried you up to the house.'

'He did?' Anne softened anew.

Sarah nodded. 'I heard you scream and when I found you unconscious, I ran to the shed for the Master's help.' She pulled a face and said impatiently, 'He gabbled away to Tommy the way he always does in his language. He sounded furious. I don't have anything to do with the blacks but the Master does.'

Anne sat up in bed. 'James knows the man?'

'The Master's right mad at you for going off like that on your own,' she declared smugly. 'But madder with Tommy for scaring you like that. After the Master scooped you up, he yelled at Tommy. Poor man just waved and gabbled back and disappeared into the bush. Good riddance, I say. That's where he belongs.'

Anne scoffed and glanced across at James. Despite their hushed voices, he hadn't stirred. 'James let him go? He threw a spear. He tried to kill me.'

'He's harmless,' Sarah said airily. 'He shows up sometimes. Lives in the foothills with his tribe. Not many left these days, thank goodness. Don't see why the Master bothers with them,' she muttered, actually doing some work for a change, straightening the bed.

Anne gasped in exasperation and sank back against the pillows at the news. 'You mean I was afraid for nothing?'

'You know now,' she said gruffly. 'The Master brought you in here and won't hardly let another soul near you. He hasn't left that chair since.' Her gaze wandered across the room with envy. 'Said if you didn't come round soon, he'd send Will for the doctor in Hamilton. Mrs. O'Grady's stamping around the kitchen saying it's a woman's place to be looking after you.'

'Now you're rested, cook will be wanting to arrange a bath for you.' Sarah moaned, knowing it was her job to cart the water and turned for the door. 'I'll tell Mrs. O'Grady you're awake. She's been clutching her cross and praying ever since the Master brought you in. You should hear her.' The housemaid pulled a scornful face. 'She's been bellowing at me and Will all afternoon,' she complained as she left.

It was a miracle he hadn't done it before but, at that moment, James roused. Anne quickly closed her eyes and lay perfectly still, her heart pounding.

She heard the chair scrape on the floor, heavy booted footsteps approach, the sound of trickling water and felt a damp cloth gently dabbed over her forehead.

The bed creaked as James sank down beside her. He was so close. Anne longed to open her eyes and watch his tender ministrations. Her nostrils inhaled the familiar scent of him.

The cool cloth was lifted from her skin and strong rough fingers lightly brushed back the hair from her face.

Unable to contain herself any longer, she opened her eyes. His back was turned as he dried his hands on a towel.

'You have a healing touch, James,' she murmured.

He swung around, his dazzling blue eyes filled with warmth and concern, his gaze so intense Anne felt as though he had physically touched her again.

'How are you feeling?'

'Much better, thank you.' She edged herself higher against the pillows. 'You released Tommy?'

He frowned. 'How do you know his name?'

'Sarah.'

'He meant you no harm.' James paused, scowling. 'Long before white men came, this land belonged to his Tjapwurong tribe. In the early days, natives and squatters clashed. The aboriginals are nomadic hunters. When I settled here, we made a pact that Tommy and his people could always have access, camp in their usual place when they returned here in spring and summer from their wandering further north. I explained you belonged to me. He won't threaten you again. He saw you were a stranger and meant me harm.'

In an instant, Anne forgot her quandary and her heart turned over with a rush of pleasure for James and his humanity and goodness that he should have claimed her as his own and spoken of her with such possession. It was the closest he had ever come to hinting at any affection. Was there hope after all? Was Caroline finally edged from her place in his heart?

But James' good humour quickly vanished behind a scowl. Anne watched his struggle before he burst out, 'Deuce it, woman. You wandered off to the creek half-dressed! Will you never listen?'

The impact of his outburst was weakened because his doting blue-grey eyes betrayed his true emotions. Anne wanted to throw her arms about his neck. James cared what happened to her!

Snug and safe in her comfortable bed, Anne smiled back at him. 'Life is for living. Besides, it was very hot.'

His … gaze settled over her and he was about to add something further when Mrs. O'Grady bustled inconveniently into the room, fussing like a mother hen around her chick.

Ignoring the Master's authority, she glared at him. 'Don't you go upsettin' and tirin' her, now. She's been through quite enough for one day, so she has.'

Anne glowed with cook's loyalty and the memory of James' tender attention.

'Miss Gutheridge,' he tossed her a searing glare, 'must learn to accept responsibility for her own actions.'

'Well, she's home safely now and we can be thankin' the Good Lord for that. I've made a broth and you can have it after yer bath,' cook stated crisply. 'If you'll kindly leave, Sarah will fetch the water,' she commanded and marched from the room.

Fired with confidence in the light of James' revelation of affection, Anne decided to test his resilience and draw him out. She turned back the covers and slid from the bed, clad only in her ragged underclothes. Clearly surprised by her daring move, his gaping eyes told her he appreciated what he saw. After weeks beneath the colonial sun, her pale English skin was tinged to a honeyed brown. For, apart from the hottest part of the day, she often ventured outdoors.

Overcome by a new and heady sense of power, Anne slowly unlaced her chemise and, under a veil of innocence, enquired, 'Will you stay and help me bathe in case I grow faint?'

His jaw ground and he stumbled backward toward the door. 'I think not. Sarah can help,' he muttered, too polite. 'I should get back to the shed. I'll see you this evening.' He made an awkward retreat.

Elated that James should at last be affected by her, she decided to force his hand. When Sarah had carried in the last of the water jugs and filled the tub, Anne stepped into the warm soaking water, perfumed with the lavender she loved, and let the heat heal her limbs.

Then, for dinner, because she wanted it to be special, with Sarah's grumbling ungracious help, Anne elegantly swept up her mass of unruly burnished golden hair. She tucked a tiny sprig of heath at one side, plucked from a vase on her dresser, then wriggled into a tawny cotton gown, its light glossy material softly draping her figure.

Viewing herself in the toilet table mirror, Anne blushed at the effect. Surely James would not resist her tonight and make some declaration? She dashed more lavender water at her throat and wrists, took a deep breath and floated down the hallway to dinner.

In the drawing room doorway, she paused. Now the moment had arrived after all her preparations, she would be crushed if he did not honour her with a positive reaction. Against all the doubts about the correctness of what she had done, she felt compelled by something deeper and stronger than she could control. All that mattered was for James to like and admire her.

He glanced up at her rustling movement as he poured brandy into a glass and spilt some on his clothes. Cursing, he stared as though seeing her for the very first time. Expectant turmoil simmered across the distance between them.

'You look…refreshed,' he said, setting down his glass to step forward. 'Are you feeling better?'

The touch of his warm hand covering hers sent her heart racing. 'I've taken a powder for a headache but, yes, I am. Tommy gave me such a fright.'

'Perhaps you should still be in bed?' he suggested but seemed pleased she was not.

His every doting glance raised her happiness. Errant dark waves at his collar lapped their starched edges and she wanted to tidy them. Anne trembled with a heavenly, yet intolerable, ache that ruled all rational thought.

Throughout dinner, a heady undercurrent burned between them. Anne barely knew what she ate for James hardly averted his gaze, drowning her in warmth and confusion. She grew frustrated with his idle neutral conversation wishing it would take a more personal turn.

At the end of the meal, James raised his dark eyebrows, pushed back his chair and rose. 'I believe we have…unfinished business.'

Anne's heart whirled with anticipation. 'We do?'

When he held out a hand, she accepted without question, His fingers firmly clasped around hers sparked a depth of awareness that drew them together like unresisting moths toward light. He led her down the passage and into the drawing room. As the door clicked shut behind her, Anne hardly dared breathe or move.

'Annabella?' His voice was little more than a soft plea.

She half turned toward him, feeling young and gauche before his poised maturity. She tilted up her gaze to meet his clear blue eyes. If she leaned forward just a little she might be kissed for a second time…

Although the hem of her full gown brushed his boots, James kept one pace between them and cleared his throat.

'You've spent some time on *Barratt Downs*, now.' She swallowed and nodded. 'You seem to like it here.'

'Yes. Very much.' Anne responded without hesitation.

There was no doubt in her mind that she had grown to love the homestead and its people. Although she had not spent as much time with James as she would have liked, from the first moment she caught sight of him in the Albion Hotel in Melbourne all those weeks ago she had known a lightness of heart that had not dimmed.

At times, naturally, she had dearly missed her family back in Devon, longed for the walks and confidences she and Elizabeth had once shared, the camaraderie with Richard. But she had pushed to the deepest reaches of her mind her disastrous marriage to Arthur Westcott and his abuse, now little more than a nightmarish memory but one she would never forget.

'You have capably managed my household and befriended my staff. And the neighbours,' he pointed out, not wryly, at which moment Anne was given the first indication that James knew of her visit to Mary Munro.

Anne privately gasped against the knowledge, afraid he was about to ask her to leave. She hid her disappointment that he gave no sign that any commitment between them would be anything other than formal. It seemed he would still consider any alliance a contract.

'You have no reservations about our age difference?' he probed.

'No.' She inhaled a calming breath. 'Have you?'

He shook his head. 'You are a capable young woman. If sometimes rash and disobedient.'

Anne scoffed at his criticism. 'If you mean my ride and tripping this afternoon, they were accidents that would have happened to anyone.'

'Let's not dwell on them, hmm? Because of them,' his

gaze roamed over her so intently that Anne was convinced he would announce his displeasure and dismiss her from his life, 'you have revealed yourself as a woman of courage, spirit and … curiosity. Combined as they are with good intent, I see a woman suited and adaptable to life out here in the Australian bush.'

Anne's amazement was so great she could have been toppled over with the breeze from a fan. She thought she knew this man but his pronouncement was a complete surprise.

James deliberated a while longer before he spoke again. 'Annabella … you agreed in Melbourne to consider my … offer, dependant on your approval of my home. Has it met with your expectations?'

Anne's hopes sank when he reduced their acquaintance to cold hearted realistic facts. 'Of course, James,' she humbly admitted. 'And more.'

'Then, since you seem to approve of my … situation, I need to ask if you are prepared to honour that promise.'

'And what would that promise entail?'

James pushed out a gush of exasperation. 'Being the woman who would stand beside me and give me sons-'

'Or daughters.'

'And make my life complete.'

Anne stilled. 'Would I?'

His compliments were all very well but he had still made no mention of his feelings. Presuming there were any to reveal. Had she misread him?

'Why do you want me?' she whispered, appalled that she was forced to plead for confirmation that their alliance would not merely be a contract.

'I've told you.'

'Remind me,' she dared suggest.

He moved away and paced before the fire, gaze downcast, remaining silent.

'Can I ever hope for even the smallest affection from

you?' she asked softly, ashamed to beg but needing to know.

James cursed, clearly annoyed by her insistence. 'Deuce it, woman. You know I…care.'

'Care?' Anne clasped her hands together in anguish.

Drawn to James by a force stronger than anything she had ever known, Anne still hesitated to blindly step forward into a future with him. She could ignore the legalities of her past marriage to Arthur but to make absolutely sure her leap of faith proved worthwhile before she gave her word to this man, she needed more from James than she realized he seemed able to give.

The unwanted truth almost broke her heart for James could not look at her, nor did he speak.

'Is it Caroline?'

'No!' he snapped.

'Then I am sorry,' she whispered, consumed with utter misery, all hope lost, 'If I'll never be more to you than a means to an end, I won't agree to any … attachment.'

James swung around in shock. 'You have no wish to share all this with me?' He swept an arm about the elegant comfortable room where, despite their differences and his absences, they had spent many companionable hours together.

'I'm not ungrateful. You've been so generous. Fine clothes. A comfortable home. Princess…' she trailed off lamely.

'What else do you expect from me?' His mouth curled derisively, his pride wounded.

'Your true feelings. Whatever they are, I must know.' Cold fear circled her heart despite the warmth in the cosy fire lit room. Oh James, please say it, she uttered up a fervent prayer. Please make my foolish dream come true. He had come to her rescue when thrown from Princess, sat by her bedside today after her nasty fall. The evidence did not signify indifference. Surely he admired her just a little…?

Anne moved closer to the fire and James gripped the

mantelpiece so tight she noticed his knuckles were white.

'Deuce it, woman.' His discomfort grew. 'You know I hold … affections for you,' he reluctantly confessed, sounding bleak.

'But you need me only to bear your sons?'

'Have you no wish to be my wife?' he challenged gruffly, deftly avoiding her question. When she did not respond, his expression clouded with horror. Clearly appalled, he accused, 'You want to leave!'

His strong shocked reaction gave her a spark of hope that he might actually care if she left. 'That has always been a possibility.'

'But...you just said you approved of my home,' he spluttered.

'Can't you see, James, how empty a woman's life would be existing only in a man's life only to bear his...sons?' she put forward tactfully. 'Having no other purpose in his life.'

'You're wrong.'

'I am?' He hesitated so she pressed, 'You see us sharing more?'

'I offered all I have to you.'

Except yourself. Anne's heartache deepened and foolish tears welled in her eyes. Straight-backed and proud, she walked to the door. With her hand on the knob, she half turned back to him. 'I greatly admire and respect you, James, what you have achieved in your life and your kindness to your staff, but I know we would both soon have regrets if any...arrangement proceeded.'

Anne swallowed back her sadness at the vision of James stranding so arrogantly in the centre of the room believing that what he offered was enough. Blue eyes shining, dark hair long, his face a proud mask of composure. If only she knew his true thoughts...

'Deuce it woman. Close the door.'

The bite in his command shocked her and her hand dropped from the knob as though she suddenly felt it hot. She raised an unsteady hand to the cool stones of her necklace and steadied her ragged breathing.

'I admitted I carried affections for you, did I not?' he demanded tersely.

'Yes. You did.'

His eyes narrowed and he stepped closer, standing askance, hands on hips. 'But what of your affections, Annabella?' he asked. 'For me?'

She gasped. 'Mine?'

'My need to know your feelings is equally important.'

Of course! Because of Caroline. How foolish of her not to realise. He had been rejected before and, for that reason alone he would naturally remain cautious.

'I have grown to like you. Most of the time,' Anne ventured warily, afraid of revealing the depth of her feelings too soon, knowing when she did she took the reckless risk of her past threatening her future.

'Like?' he repeated wryly. 'I suppose that is a place to start but I believe we need to move on further, don't you? Hmm?' he prompted when she did not reply.

Beneath his soft seductive taunt, Anne grew flustered.

Suddenly, James' entire demeanour changed. 'Allow me your full attention for, I at least, have the courage to express my feelings.'

In a single stride, he closed the remaining distance between them, pulled Annabella against him so that their bodies were fully aligned, and slowly placed his hands firmly upon her trim waist. Anne instinctively gripped his sleeves for support, the feel of his jacket coat excitingly real and strange beneath her hands.

Spellbound from his touch, Anne focussed on James' glinting blue eyes, his nose and mouth almost touching hers, his ragged breath a feather light caress across her skin.

'Do you have any idea, Miss Gutheridge,' he murmured, 'precisely how much I care?'

She shook her head, alarmed and excited by his actions.

'Then listen carefully and I shall tell you so you are in no doubt.' Anne hardly dared breathe for fear she missed a single word. 'I adore every inch of you.' He pressed her closer and she gasped. 'Every curve of you.'

He dipped his head so that his lips brushed the warm bare skin in the sensitive hollow between neck and shoulder. Previously deprived of any show of affection, except for occasional long glances and the one kiss the day they had gone riding together, Anne's pulses throbbed into life. Glorious disbelief flooded her body from head to toe like a rushing tide at the whispering of his breath against her skin, the touch of his lips to her flesh and his confessions at last.

James raised his head and levelled his gaze. 'Your green eyes remind me of spring grasses. Your smile lights up my heart.' He wound a finger in the wisps of hair that had escaped her coiffure. 'I listen for your voice and footsteps about the house when I return at night. I want to be the man who shares his life with you. I sense a naïve vulnerability that you have been hurt in the past, too. I would hope that we could learn to love anew. Together.'

'You do?' she squeaked. 'Why?'

'Because,' he sighed heavily. 'Because I love you, Annabella Gutheridge, as a man only loves one woman in his lifetime. More than any other woman before you.'

When he held her gaze, she understood his meaning. Caroline. A deep well of emotion lodged in her throat and tears threatened the corners of her eyes. She wanted to shout with happiness and weep at the same time. Instead, she drew strength from the openness in his warm blue eyes and showered him with her broadest smile.

'As I love you, too, James,' she whispered, relieved at long last to release the words she had withheld for so long. Her shaking hands spread across the security of his broad chest.

'Annabella…I hadn't dared hope. I sensed you were growing to love this country. I could only hope you might learn to love me, too.'

His declaration of love was tender and sincere. His head lowered and he kissed her, his arms wound firmly about her. She closed her eyes and clasped her hands behind his neck. Her fingers wove into his thick dark hair, her mind lost in the taste and touch and smell of him.

Too soon, he broke away, leaving her sighing and breathless.

'So,' James beamed. 'Are we agreed we shall marry?'

With a sudden lurching panic in her heart and a split second's indecision, Anne wondered if good sense should prevail before it was too late. Should she refuse James' proposal or gather courage and confess the awful truth and reason for her flight to Australia?

But she knew in her heart, if she did so, she risked losing him. If her life depended on it, she dared not jeopardise this newfound precious love. Her past no longer mattered out here in Australia, surely. That fateful night last May seemed from another life.

'Annabella?' James voice came to her with husky urgency.

'Yes.' She smiled to reassure him. 'Yes, we shall marry,' she repeated to dissolve the last remnants of her own lingering doubt and clung to him tightly as he tenderly kissed her again, sending up a secret prayer that all would be well.

'You must write to your family in Devon,' James innocently suggested.

Should she take the risk? An action she had delayed so far for fear of revealing her whereabouts? Caution always lingered foremost in her mind. Eventually, Anne nodded her agreement but privately decided to defer a letter as long as possible.

'I shall write home to my family in Sussex.' James grasped her hands eagerly. Anne marvelled that, even after fifteen years in the colony, he still considered Sussex home. Would she feel the same way in years to come, unable to release the bond with the land of her birth? 'Mother will be overjoyed with pleasure,' he continued. 'And I shall contact the district circuit minister telling him we wish to be wed.'

They smiled at each other with foolish happiness.

'I am amazed you love me. Why did you wait so long?' Anne chided.

'Because you were so young and vital. Despite your courage in emigrating alone to find a new life – for whatever reason,' he added, pausing, 'you looked lost. You had only just arrived. I didn't want to influence your chances out here but, I confess, if you had declined me that first meeting, I would have been devastated. I loved you from the moment I turned from the window in the Albion Hotel and saw you standing there, beautiful and wild. All the other women I had interviewed paled against you and I knew from that moment there could never be anyone else for me.'

'Why didn't you tell me?' She wanted to beat his chest with frustration.

'Because you are so young, I feared you might regret marriage to an older man. I worried that you might become homesick and wish to return to Devon. I wanted you to be sure before you made your final decision.'

'I've missed my family, it's true, but I've never felt homesick. I have loved the adventure of life in a new country. I love it here and I want to explore more of it. With you.'

James threw back his head and laughed. 'Ah, my lovely Annabella. You will always keep me young. I see an eagerness in you for life and all about you. But I had to be sure. I had to give you time. Fortunately, shearing kept me busy as much as possible. It was agony,' he groaned, crushing her in his arms again, his mouth sweetly upon hers. 'As much as I adored you,' James murmured bleakly, 'I had to be prepared to let you go.'

'Never. I want to be this close to you. Forever.'

CHAPTER 18

'Now I know what a prize I will marry, I must know more about you.' James' lips brushed Anne's forehead as he drew her down onto the settee beside him in the cosy drawing room. But not before he had poured them a celebratory glass of sherry.

Cautiously, in order not to raise any suspicions, Anne talked generally of her parents, her brother Richard, Elizabeth and her beau Edward, and little Emmy.

'Why did you leave England?' It was a question he had asked of her at their first meeting in Melbourne. She had evaded it then and, even now, her mind worked quickly for a reasonable explanation to satisfy him.

To delay, she sipped her wine and stared into the fire, unable to meet his searching gaze. 'I told you. My parents are poor and believed I would find a better life in Australia.'

'I'm surprised your family let their lovely oldest daughter go off alone,' he probed deeper, clearly to draw her out.

Anne decided to give him enough vague information without going into what she considered were shameful details, longing with all her heart to confide in him but resisting. If only she dared.

'I didn't leave England in the happiest of circumstances.' She sighed and, drawing a little apart, turned to face him. Arrested by the deep compassion in his eyes, Anne was tempted to confide. 'My decision to leave my home was…forced, but I don't regret it.' At James' frown of alarm, she hastily added, 'Please, don't ask. Maybe one day I can tell you but not now.'

She allowed herself to be drawn into his arms again and he kissed her upturned nose. 'Is there no way I can help you?'

Anne shook her head, adoring him all the more for his concern and grateful that he did not press her for more facts. 'Tell me about your family,' she appealed, casting her dark thoughts aside and snuggling against him. 'Do you ever long for Sussex?'

He would guess she deliberately changed the subject but tactfully did not pursue her past any further although she had no doubt it would be raised again at some time in the future.

'Rarely, even in the early days. I saw the colony's freedom and potential. My family know I'm settled and that my life is here now. They've had fifteen years to grow accustomed to the idea. I love this country as my own, Annabella.' Passionate warmth filled his deep voice. 'As much as if I had been born here. It will be home for both of us now.'

'Yes,' Anne fervently agreed.

Swept up in the fervour of the moment, James kissed her long and thoroughly again before reluctantly tearing himself away. 'I must go and write to the district minister to ask how soon he can ride out and marry us before Mrs. O'Grady comes in here lashing us with her tongue for our bold behaviour.'

James escorted his fiancé down the hall to her room, lingering on the threshold to say goodnight before retiring to their separate rooms.

In the middle of the night some weeks later, the household was awakened by the thundering approach of a horse and cart, followed by pounding at the front door. The commotion startled Anne from a deep luxurious sleep and dreams of James.

She sat up rigidly in bed, lit a lamp and clutched the bedclothes around her. She heard voices in the passage outside and then knocking on her door. 'Come in.'

James entered, holding a candle aloft. Despite a scowl of what appeared to be irritation, Anne's only thought was how tousled and lovable he looked in his nightclothes and that soon they would not only share a room but their whole lives together.

'What is it?'

'Duncan Munro. It's Mary's time and he wants you to go with him.'

Anne was shocked. 'Me? Now?'

'Apparently Mary asked for you,' he said bluntly, clearly irritated by the identity of their caller as much as for being woken in the middle of the night.

Anne knew it would have taken Duncan equal humility to come here. 'I know nothing of babies or childbirth. She planned to send for the district midwife.'

James ran an impatient hand through his ruffled hair. 'Apparently she's out elsewhere. You don't have to go.'

'Oh, no. If Mary asked for me, I must. I couldn't let her down.' Anne slipped quickly from bed. Seeing the confusion on his face and well knowing his feelings toward the selector, Anne stepped forward and kissed him. 'I want to go. Please understand.'

James' distracted gaze clung to her for a long moment before he growled, 'All right. I'll tell Munro you won't be long.'

'Invite him into the drawing room.'

'No. He can wait outside,' James snarled as he strode away down the hall.

Oh dear, Anne sighed. She had no idea what she needed nor how long she would be away. Suddenly, Sarah appeared in her nightgown and cap, glowering. James must have sent for her.

'Just pack a few of my most serviceable clothes, Sarah.'

'Breed like rabbits, those Munros,' she muttered unkindly.

'That's enough, Sarah,' Anne reprimanded.

Working under the girl's cloud of petulance, Anne hurriedly dressed while the maid packed a small bag. Then she dashed down the hall and out into the cool spring night.

Duncan Munro sat rigidly in the front of his wagon, reins in hand, anxious to leave, his shock of red hair vivid in the moonlight. James stood aside, glaring. At Anne's approach, he took her bag and stowed it in the back of the wagon. To her surprise, he swept her into his arms for a departing kiss and she wondered if male pride had made him so demonstrative in front of his enemy. For whatever reason, his passion clearly breached propriety.

'Take care of her, Munro,' James snapped.

The big Scot nodded and touched his cap but did not speak. 'Miss,' the surly selector grunted in acknowledgement as James handed her up and she settled beside him.

She could see how his big brawny arms would be so powerful behind a pair of shearing blades. Such a physical giant against Mary's slight stature.

Without wasting a moment, Munro whipped the horse and they jolted away. He urged the sweating team into a gallop and Anne clung on desperately as the horse raced and the cart jolted through the bush in the dim moon-washed night.

Looking across at the driver's stern face, Anne yelled, 'Is Mary all right, Mr. Munro?'

'Aye,' he shouted back. 'But she's quick with her bairns so there's nae time to waste.'

Anxiety edged his harsh voice telling Anne that, beneath his rough exterior, gentle Mary was dearly loved and precious to this man.

Later, as night shadows streaked by them on the dark track, Anne shouted, 'I have no experience with childbirth, Mr. Munro.'

'Nae matter. Mary wants ye and Janet knows what to do. She helped deliver young Robbie.' There was fierce pride in his gruff voice. 'A man need sons.'

Men! Anne thought, fired with exasperation. They were eager enough to cast their lust upon a woman and selfish enough to want the result their own way nine months later.

Irritated, she lashed out. 'You have three sons already, Mr. Munro. It would be nice for Mary to have another daughter.'

A surly black glare of dissent was his only response and conversation ceased. The remaining journey was fast and rough, and she ached all over from bouncing on the hard wooden seat.

'Haa! Haa! Giddup there,' Munro roared to the straining horses as the wagon swung dangerously through the gateway toward a faint light in the cottage ahead.

They jolted to a stop and Munro leapt down, nodding toward the hut before tending the frothing horses.

Anne scrambled down and, because he did not offer, grabbed her bag and ran indoors. In one side of the partitioned sleeping area, the two older boys, Andrew and Hector, slept, crammed together in their narrow bed, but young Robbie was awake, kneeling on his bed, rubbing frightened eyes.

'Is Mama sick?'

'No, Robbie.' Janet gently settled him and pulled a thin blanket over his tiny frame. 'She's having a baby brother or sister for us. Hush now and off to sleep with you again.'

The boy's thumb found his mouth and his eyelids soon fluttered down.

From the other side of the petition, Anne heard heavy breathing and moans. Apprehensive for Mary's wellbeing, Anne drew the curtain aside. Mary lay propped up with pillows, her dark hair damp, her forehead beaded with perspiration, her eyes closed. Janet silently reappeared and sat at the end of the rough pallet.

Anne smiled at the girl, seemingly pleased at her arrival, surely only for reassurance since Anne was convinced she could do nothing to help unless told.

'Mary?' Anne whispered.

Her eyes opened and came to life when she noticed her friend. 'Oh, Annabella. Thank ye for coming.' Mary gripped her hand. 'I'm sorry to trouble ye but I fear this one is difficult.' Deep concern shadowed her brow. 'Did Mr. Barratt mind?'

Anne shook her head, even if it was clouding the truth.

'The midwife is away toward Hamilton helping' young Mrs. Wagner with her first. She's been poorly and weak.'

'I only hope I can be of some help to you. Tell me what I must do.' She glanced between mother and daughter, feeling useless.

'We've plenty of hot water, Ma'am,' Janet said. 'Papa saw to everything when the pains started.'

When the girl referred so trustingly of her father, Anne was forced to no longer see him as the wild scowling Scotsman who had recklessly driven the wagon through the night but a husband and father who was master in his own humble house.

Anne admired Janet's quiet competence despite her youth as Mary began panting again.

'They're coming closer.' Janet said softly with a hint of brogue, but less than her parents. 'The baby should be showing soon.'

She and Anne could only wait and watch each time another contraction gripped Mary, each one growing more intense than the last. Anne sat on the edge of the bed and kept a damp cloth to Mary's face. When the spasms lengthened and grew more severe, Mary squeezed her hand, groaning until it faded, breathing easier as it passed, but only until the next agonising wave.

Anne forced herself to composure, sensing calm more helpful than panic. You really needed to love a man to go through this for him and she fleetingly thought of her own future and family with James.

The time between each crippling attack shortened and Anne watched, entranced, as the miracle of childbirth unfolded before her. Mary endured one final urgent push, thrusting a tiny slippery head into the world, followed by the messy body of a baby girl.

Amid her first lusty cries, Mary and Janet eyed each other through weary smiles and tears.

Exhausted, Mary sank back onto the pillows, her face strained with disappointment. 'Duncan so wanted a son.'

Anne grew impatient that after all she had been through and safely delivered of a daughter, Mary considered her man's wants above her own.

Thinking quickly to lighten her mood, Anne mocked their Scottish brogue. 'Och, and doesn't he have three already. What would he be wanting with another?'

Her simple humour drew a weak laughter from Mary and a giggle from Janet, lifting the atmosphere in their small corner of the room.

They washed and wrapped the baby, making Mary clean and comfortable before Anne wandered outside to find Munro. She found him pacing the front porch.

'You have a beautiful healthy daughter.'

A grunt was the only acknowledgement that he heard what she said. 'Is Mary all right?'

Taken aback by his blunt indifference, she sighed and said, 'Yes, but exhausted naturally.'

'Good. She can name the child,' he stated gruffly, stalking away from the cottage into the night.

Angered anew by his attitude and rebuff, Anne returned indoors. Seeing Janet's fatigue, she insisted the girl get some sleep. With only mild protests, she obeyed.

Anne watched the squirming newborn bundle suckle its mother, awed with tenderness as the baby nestled against Mary's bare breast, its tiny hand curled about one of her fingers. A maternal tug pulled at Anne's heart. She wanted to scoop up the infant and cuddle it close.

'Duncan said you may choose her name.' Anne told Mary brightly.

Mary looked up, weary but content. 'He'll be disappointed. He was convinced we'd have a son. We'd only thought of David.' She sighed with a trace of despair, glancing down at her second daughter. 'I shall name her Helen Maree, for ma mother.'

'You have five children now, Mary. Will you cope?' Anne shook her head in wonder at this tiny woman's capacity to manage, thinking of her own situation with servants, grateful, yet aching for this family's struggle, so like her parents back in Devon.

'Janet helps me and the boys are good workers on the farm here for Munro,' she said practically.

When Mary finished feeding Helen and before Duncan returned, a howling wind sprang up outside, whistling around the corners of the hut, pushing through the cracks in gusty draughts. Thunder rumbled and lightning flashed ahead of a sudden spring storm. Soon, rain poured down and dripped through holes in the roof.

Close to daybreak, Munro reappeared, drenched, but in a more untroubled mood. He bent over and kissed Mary then lifted his sleeping daughter for a nurse. He built up the fire with extra logs then settled before it on a mat to dry off and sleep for what remained of the shortened night.

Yawning and barely able to keep her eyes open, Anne gratefully squeezed in underneath a thin blanket on the pallet beside Janet, already sound asleep. She thought of her own large comfortable room and bed back at *Barratt Downs* but barely had time for thoughts of James before she fell asleep.

Next morning, the household stirred late to the sound of steady rain still drumming on the shingles. Anne had already decided to stay and help Mary but the weather change made it inevitable for the bush tracks would be soft and impassable.

With shearing finished, Duncan no longer travelled to *Barratt Downs* but promised Anne to send over young Hector on horseback with word for James to collect her in three days at the end of the week.

Even with her youth and stamina, Anne found caring for a family of seven from daybreak to dark exhausting, and she marvelled how fragile Mary coped. But with Janet's help and the new mother's instructions, they managed.

At dawn, she stoked the fire and fetched water, prepared and cooked meals, washed dishes, fed the animals, tended the vegetable garden refreshed from the heavy rain that had fallen the night Helen was born.

In between constant scrapping and physical tussles, the two oldest boys, Andy and Hector accomplished their chores and helped Duncan out in the paddocks cutting hay and building fences. Janet carted out lunches to them since they left early and only returned at dusk, falling later now with approaching summer.

In the evenings, Duncan conversed little at meals, his stern presence alone enough to ensure obedience from his children who all regarded him with respect. He proved a dour but caring father. Every night, Robbie scrambled onto his knee in a fireside chair but was fast asleep before his father ever finished a story. Anne was pleased to see the Munro's passing on their basic literacy to their children. Perhaps the next generation would not have such a hard struggle.

After baby Helen's last feed of the day, Munro rocked the handmade wooden cradle until she fell asleep. Mostly indifferent to his daughters but indulgent with his sons, Anne found his gesture an encouraging sight.

The day after Helen's birth, Mary was already slowly shuffling about the hut, insisting the exercise did her good but she tired easily and Anne forced her to rest.

Quietly strict, the humble home centred around her and, with her easy smile and gentle ways, brightened everyone's day. She tolerated no nonsense but gave mountains of love to each of her children and complete devotion to Duncan.

On the appointed third day, Anne waited impatiently outside the cottage for James' arrival. The morning passed annoyingly slowly and it wasn't until early afternoon that the raised dust of a horse and buggy heralded a visitor's approach.

James halted with a flourish before the hut. Overjoyed at the sight of her man, so dearly loved and missed, Anne ran to meet him before the vehicle wheels had barely stopped turning. James climbed down, beaming at her eager welcome and kissed her, oblivious to all around.

When they drew apart, he looked over Anne's shoulder where Mary stood at the cottage door, glowing with motherhood. She gave a reserved smile and nodded. James removed his wide brimmed hat and returned her nod of acknowledgement. 'Mrs. Munro. Congratulations.'

Fortunately, Duncan was absent out in one of the paddocks with the boys. On purpose perhaps, wisely avoiding an unnecessary meeting. At least the womenfolk were friends and, for the first time, James was visiting their home. Anne secretly hoped it would not be the last and caught his wistful gaze over their hut, perhaps remembering his own origins and struggles fifteen years before.

The two women hugged warmly. 'Take care of yourself, Mary. I'll visit again when I can. 'Will you be at the end of shearing dance in a few weeks?'

'We'll be looking forward to it. Nothing will keep us away,' she assured Anne with a gentle smile.

James and Anne climbed into the buggy, he clicked to the horses, turning them in the front yard before heading back along the track to the main road.

Immediately Anne returned from the Munro's cottage, she rummaged in the store shed and discovered a cache of material scraps and a length of calico, and occupied the lengthening spring evenings stitching a quilt for baby Helen. No small accomplishment considering her strong aversion to needlework and lack of nimble fingers but, having seen their spare possessions, Anne knew it was desperately needed and would be appreciated.

Despite strained eyes and pricked bleeding fingers, Anne hoped to finish her laborious masterpiece in time to present it to Mary at the shearing dance.

A week later, the calendar fluttered over to November and a balmy feel entered the milder days and nights. Shearing cut out and the men lingered on the property for the end of shearing dance.

The day before the much-anticipated event, following a sharp frosty night, bullocky Bill and his lumbering team arrived. The huge creaking wagon rolled into the property with three mongrel dogs yapping at its wheels and the rugged man himself strolling alongside, wielding a twenty-foot whip, a long unshaven beard on his dusty chin, his grey hair shaggy, his face and arms sunburnt and lined.

The ten bullocks were turned out into a paddock to graze until the wool bales were loaded and got away after the dance.

A legend in the district, Bill was a colourful blasphemous bush character, his appearance causing a stir around the homestead for his arrival meant supplies, newspapers and mail, the first contact with the outside world for months.

To everyone's concern, they learnt that news had reached Melbourne from Sandhurst further north that Burke & Wills of an inland exploratory mission were both dead after crossing the Australian continent from south to north. James read Annabella a full report one evening from The Argus while she sewed.

Although it cast a certain gloom over the homestead, Anne could not conceal her delight in taking delivery of the remaining dresses she had ordered months ago in Melbourne. It seemed so long ago that she had been fitted for them, she had almost forgotten what she ordered. Eagerly, she tore open the parcels and, with Sarah's help, unwrapped and laid them all out on her bed. The young housemaid sighed with bliss, running her fingers over laces, smooth silk and crisp cottons.

Anne clutched first one then another against her and whirled about the room in excitement, feeling a guilty pleasure in the face of their recent bad news. She decided to send over one of her simpler cotton house dresses to the Munro selection for Mary.

With shearing finished, James was more often about the homestead, returning unexpectedly to share tea under the veranda, always accompanied by a huge slice of Mrs. O'Grady's rich fruit cake. In the evenings, they settled in the drawing room re-reading The Argus and mail.

James received a letter from his family in Sussex and opened another larger and more formal envelope. 'From Mr. and Mrs. Albert Burroughs of *Rosevere Hall*,' he told her, and Anne watched with interest as he broke the seal. 'It's an invitation to their annual New Year weekend house party, dinner and ball.'

When he handed her the elegant cream parchment to read for herself, it was the footnote that caught Anne's attention. Their hostess, Henrietta Burroughs, mentioned that a lady and gentleman recently arrived from Devon, England were anxious to make the acquaintance of Mr. Barratt's betrothed.

Anne's mouth went dry with alarm but she managed to ask, 'How would anyone here know where I am from?' hiding her concern behind a forced smile.

James chuckled. 'Word spreads easily in the district. Perhaps one of the shearers or workers passed it on,' he said, unperturbed. 'I may have mentioned it in passing and you can be sure every female hereabouts will have expressed interest in the presence of a beautiful new woman on *Barratt Downs*. Surely it doesn't bother you?' he said, noticing her frown.

'No. No, of course not.' She smiled to mask her growing fear. 'I'm surprised word has travelled about me.'

'Don't be.' He laughed. 'It's the bush telegraph.'

'Do they know my name?'

'I'm sure they do.' James did not glance up from reading his mail and was therefore unaware of the dark cloud of doubt that weighed heavily on Anne's mind and showed on her face.

Over dinner that night, James and Anne discussed the tragic news that two men had reached the Telegraph Station in Sandhurst and sent a dispatch to Melbourne that had been reported in The Argus and which they had both read.

'Robert O'Hara Burke was a Scottish policeman and William Wills an English surveyor,' James told Anne. 'They left Melbourne last year with men and camels intending to cross the Australian continent from south to north, a feat never before achieved. According to The Argus they were the first to succeed from sea to sea but perished attempting to return.

'Inland Australia is a harsh desert, not green and fertile like here in the Western District. Only for explorers like Thomas Mitchell who opened up these grazing lands does the country become known and civilized. Unfortunately, sometimes, at great cost,' James spoke reflectively, shaking his head in resignation.

'How were they found?'

'When nothing was heard of them, search parties followed their trail until it was discovered that all, save one, had died of exhaustion and lack of food. The survivor, King, was only saved when discovered by natives with whom he lived until restored to health. The white men achieved their goal but at the ultimate price.'

Although she had been some months in Australia, Anne was only beginning to realize how young and unexplored this country still remained, the first ships of settlers having arrived barely seventy years before. 'It seems such a waste. Why do they do it?'

'The call of adventure. Any man who heeds it is aware of the risks involved, my dear.' James tried to ease her distress. 'After all, that was exactly how these grazing lands were opened up for settlement.'

When they retired to the drawing room later, Anne was thoughtful as she poured the tea Sarah had brought in for them on a tray and took up her quilting while James smoked his pipe and trawled The Argus.

'Here's something that might interest you, Annabella,' he said from behind his newspaper.

'Oh?' She glanced up from her stitching and he told her of

a new horse race called the Melbourne Cup at the Victoria Turf Club's spring meeting.

'It was overshadowed of course by the Burke and Wills tragedy. Only 4000 attended the first day's races. It carried sweepstakes of twenty sovereigns with two hundred extra sovereigns from the Victoria Turf Club.'

'It sounds a prestigious race.'

'The winning horse, Archer, walked five hundred miles from New South Wales just to compete in the race. Three horses fell, two of them were destroyed, but Archer kept clear of trouble and won by six lengths. Thomas Chirnside was a steward,' James added. 'He's powerfully fond of horse racing.'

'Our neighbour?'

James nodded. 'He has Mount William run. And a chain of others. Director of the National Bank. He's a burly man with a rough tongue but a kind heart. He's settled now at Werribee further south in a rather impressive bluestone mansion. It's a vast estate along the coast of Port Phillip Bay and extends about five miles inland. A splendid tract. More than 80000 acres I believe.'

Anne almost pricked her finger with a needle in astonishment. 'Four times as big as *Barratt Downs*? What a wonderful legacy for his sons,' she murmured, sipping her tea.

'Ah, Thomas is a bachelor,' James murmured. 'Unlucky in love, I gather.'

They exchanged a knowing glance. 'The Melbourne Cup's to be held every year now apparently. What would you say if I promised we should attend next year?'

Anne brightened. 'James, do you mean it?'

He grinned. 'We have much to look forward to in the future.'

A few days later, preparations began on cleaning out the woolshed for the dance.

Indoors, Mrs. O'Grady, who had insisted Anne call her Bridget since their betrothal, supervised cooking preparations to provide a memorable banquet of meats, salads, vegetables, cakes and fruit pies.

Saturday the twenty-third of November was a clear night after a warm sunny day. The woolshed was lit with lamps swinging from the rafters, decorated with gum boughs, and candle wax scraped onto the rough floor for dancing.

At dusk, James and Anne greeted the first arrivals. With love clearly glowing between them, the Master looking dapper in a smart grey suit and his future bride stylish at his side in a pale yellow gown sprigged with leaves and flowers. Young ladies had their hair curled and wore their best dresses. Somehow, the men managed to be smartly dressed in suits and polished boots. Bales of wool provided seating, each stamped with the black imprint B.D. A table along one shed wall creaked beneath its burden of food.

When Duncan Munro and his family arrived, James was terse in greeting but Anne was ecstatic to see Mary and the children again. The women hugged warmly, Anne anxious for another glimpse of month-old Helen, alert in her mother's arms.

'How she's grown already,' Anne exclaimed. 'She's started to smile.'

Bridget, red-faced and fussing, had squeezed her plump body into her best dress. For once, without an apron. Barney, the shearers' cook, arrived and sat smoking a pipe to one side. Choong Lee quietly bowed and assumed an inconspicuous position in a far corner.

Zak drifted about and the shearers entered in a rowdy group with a few district females to capture the bachelors' eyes. Because they were in short supply, the women were promptly swung into dances the moment the trio of musicians struck up its first lively tune.

The young melodeon player squeezed out the music while his fingers ran expertly over the keys. An older man played a quavering violin and a third tapped one dusty booted foot keeping time and rhythm while blowing his mouth organ, lost in the forest of wiry whiskers that covered his face.

The melodious threesome poured out their music into the shearing shed and homestead yard beyond. Children grabbed each other's hands or linked arms and swirled to the strains that filtered outside.

For one night, the cares of everyday life were briefly forgotten and all revelled in the rare social occasion.

To Anne's surprise, Will proved a competent dancer with the young ladies. Except Sarah, who flirted with a dashing shearer, Harry Molloy, the girl no doubt smitten by his dark laughing eyes and cheeky winning smile.

The dancers romped to sets of quadrilles, jaunty polkas and, occasionally, a circular waltz.

Although dancing monopolised the evening, there were also poetry readings from one of the shearers, a hardened gent who held his hat reverently over his chest as he recited and swept forward with a wide flourish to the floor as he accepted his ovation at the conclusion of his renditions.

Two well-imbibed men lustily sang a bush song that almost lifted the roof, and made baby Helen cry.

Eventually, the brisk dancing and merriment resumed, Sarah still partnered by Harry Molloy. Anne noted Will's longing glances in her direction. Later, when Sarah was standing near Anne and James, she suspected the girl hoped to be asked to dance by the Master.

Anne foresaw trouble when Will approached them. Sarah straightened, preened and smiled. But, to her crushing humiliation, it was to Anne that he bowed and requested a dance. Sarah turned red and pouted, giving Anne a black glare before sidling off to sit alone.

'There are lots of other pretty girls here tonight, Will,' Anne hinted as they danced.

He returned her warm smile with a shy grin, understanding her subtle message.

As host, James wandered genially among the crowd,

spending time with everyone but the moment Will and Anne finished their dance, he strolled determinedly toward her, leading her out onto the floor and into his arms where she belonged as a violin quavered out the strains of a waltz.

Not before time, Bridget's magnificent supper was served and the evening drew to a close. James made a brief informal speech thanking the shearers for another season's work and inviting them all to return the following year. He placed a protective affectionate arm around Annabella.

'On behalf of my future wife and myself, I wish you all a safe journey home. As always, those who are…indisposed may sleep here in the barn or over in the men's quarters for the night.'

A ripple of laughter and hearty applause went through the gathering.

Soon, families began leaving, their sleepy children bundled up warmly under rugs against the frosty night in the back of wagons and buggies as they rattled off into the dark. As the Munros gathered to leave, Anne proudly presented a humble but delighted Mary with the baby quilt.

As the last of the lanterns was extinguished in the shed, Anne and James trudged arm in arm across the damp grass back to the homestead.

'This year was the most successful shearing dance ever,' James declared. 'I believe everyone came to see you.'

Next day, although the household was slow to start after the revelry of the night before, the wool was got away. Everyone deserted their work to watch the massive bullocks strain at their yokes, the huge bales stacked four high on the dray, Bill's whip cracking overhead as the cumbersome wagon inched forward, groaning with every slow turn of its creaking wheels.

Anne felt a gush of joy and pride swell in her chest as the load of fleece departed on the first stage of its long journey that would take it down to the coast to be shipped halfway across the world to England.

For the rest of the day, one by one, the shearers straggled up to the homestead to be paid, chatting and smoking under the veranda while James wrote their cheques, then trailed away from the property in a dusty procession for another year.

Soon it would be Christmas and New Year, and a visit to the Burroughs' house party at *Rosevere Hall*. Anne frowned over their mysterious house guests that had asked to make her acquaintance but held her concerns inside and concentrated instead on the festive season to come.

CHAPTER 19

Summer officially began on the first of December and it was hot. But the next day a change arrived with high winds, heavy rain and low cloud draping a grey mist over the Grampians. The late rains throughout the spring had postponed the brownness of the country and there was a rich crop of grass, much greater than in recent years. The weather cleared, however, allowing the small wheat harvest to continue to the beating of cutters in the paddocks and the smell of fresh mown hay.

Then, on Christmas Eve, the district circuit minister arrived unexpectedly, announcing he could marry James and Annabella.

Thrown into a deep and sudden emotional chaos by his surprise appearance, Anne realized her future would soon be irrevocably sealed with no chance to turn back. Not that she wanted to for each day her love for James deepened so that, although a small question still remained in the back of her mind, she anticipated marriage to him with all her heart.

James, on the other hand, strode about the homestead smiling and whistling so that Anne was swept along by his enthusiastic delight at their imminent nuptials. He suggested a double celebration, a wedding and Christmas, to which Anne agreed, upon which he flung out instructions in every direction, turning the homestead and Bridget with Sarah's resentful help into a fever of activity to prepare.

After a wedding eve dinner of cold sliced mutton and fresh vegetables and fruit picked from Lee's lovingly-tended garden, James and Anne sat diligently with the minister in the drawing room while he gathered their personal details for the wedding registration.

Anne thought of telling James about her assumed name but considered she was still the same person and didn't believe it would do any harm. And she would soon be Mrs. James Barratt anyway so what did it matter?

In humble surprise, earlier in the evening, she had graciously accepted James' gift of a triple strand of pearls, apparently an heirloom from his mother's family.

Following a hurried breakfast on Christmas Day, a sullen Sarah helped Anne dress for the wedding ceremony that was to take place under trees in the garden. Their simple luncheon afterwards, over which Bridget had lovingly and laboriously toiled, was to be eaten at long tables laid out with white linen under the broad and shady homestead verandas.

Pride of place in the centre of the bridal table was a two tiered cake that, until their feast, was being safely stored in the cool underground cellar beneath the courtyard at the back of the house.

Sarah lugged hot water from the kitchen to fill the tub, complaining with every load. Anne soaked at length, reluctantly stepping out to dry off and slip into her best undergarments.

The housemaid revealed her skills and neatly braided and pinned up Anne's hair into an elegant swirl then the precious gown she had chosen from among her new wardrobe was carefully removed from its box among folds of paper and ceremoniously displayed upon the bed. An ivory gown edged at the neck and wrists with rich lace to which Anne had fashioned a circlet of fresh wildflowers for her sun bleached hair.

'It's beautiful, Ma'am,' Sarah muttered, enviously fingering the smooth yards of whispering silk.

In her happiness, Anne said compassionately, 'Your turn will come, Sarah.'

'Not out here, it won't,' she grumbled, and Anne's

empathy went out to poor besotted Will, clearly no contender for the housemaid's affection.

When the small mantel clock chimed the half hour, Sarah said, 'Time for your gown, Miss.'

Together they jiggled and worked and buttoned until the silky dress graced Anne's shapely young body and swirled in a gleaming mass about her feet. Sarah buttoned on her light shoes since, fixed securely in a corset for this one day, Anne could not reach her feet, then settled the crown of flowers in place and secured it atop the loopy curls she had fashioned for her mistress.

She stepped back to smugly admire her own work. 'The Master will be pleased for sure, Miss.'

Anne was left to wonder if Sarah had done this for her Master in the hope of praise. As she checked herself in the long cheval mirror her wistful thoughts pondered on the fact that none of her own family were with her to celebrate and they suddenly all seemed so very far away. She hoped Edward Stokes had offered for Elizabeth, and questioned what her Ma and Pa would think of this union. Whereas her farce of a marriage to Arthur had meant nothing, this ceremony with James today meant everything and she knew, no matter what happened, he was her true love for life.

Anne breathed deeply. This was no time for sentiment. She was about to marry the man she loved and offered up a secret and silent prayer that her past misdeeds never returned to haunt and disturb her new life.

Sarah disappeared to ensure all was ready outside. When she returned to confirm it, Anne took the long walk down the homestead passage, through the tiled entry hallway, across the wide homestead veranda and out into the brilliant summer sun.

She walked slowly across the swathe of grass toward James, her love forever. He turned and smiled as she neared, his gaze sweeping her with passion and love. He wore a dark grey suit with a stiff white collar that seemed uncomfortable and a lavish dark blue necktie, his long dark hair damp and smoothly combed.

Her heart raced at the dashing sight of him. Then he took her hands, his face alive with a disarming contagious grin.

Bridget, attired in the same best summer dress she had worn to the end of shearing dance, and Zak, in an old but clean suit, hair and whiskers washed and trimmed, stood beside him as witnesses.

The minister, bespectacled and reverent in a shiny black suit, a solemn expression on his face, opened the Bible in his hands.

A warm and lethargic summer breeze sighed around them, the scents of summer heavy and languid in the air.

The minister cleared his throat and commenced, his deep voice echoing in the open air as he ministered traditional words of wisdom, supervised their formal vows and presided over the final moment when James, his warm hands holding hers, slipped a gold band of marriage onto her finger.

With a lingering kiss to seal their union, James Barratt and Annabella Gutheridge became husband and wife.

The small homestead gathering burst into a hum of vocal life as laughter, smiles, hugs and even more kisses ensued.

Bridget's face dripped with tears of joy as she squeezed the bride, Zak respectfully shook her hand and Will took the liberty of a bold kiss on her cheek.

A combination Christmas dinner and lavish wedding luncheon followed with roast meats, cold cuts of fowl, mutton and pork, vegetables and fruits from Choong Lee's garden, pies and puddings, jugs of cream, Bridget's freshly baked bread and cakes, Sarah's home churned butter and cheeses, peaches and apricots from the orchard, jugs of wine and endless pots of tea.

Seated beside James, Anne's happiness was complete. Eating, feasting and conversation continued through the long hot afternoon and into the evening, long after the late summer twilight streaked red and orange banners across the evening sky. After dark, all parties reluctantly dispersed, leaving Anne and James finally alone.

Apart from the loud chorus of crickets, the warm night had stilled. Mosquitoes and moths hovered around candles and lanterns as James led Anne indoors and closed their bedroom door behind them. Weary but happy, she dissolved into his welcoming arms.

Between wine flavoured kisses, James freed her hair, impatiently unfastening buttons and ribbons on her gown with deft fingers until it slid in a creamy mound around her feet.

James pressed his warm lips on her skin and unlaced her corset. Standing before him, Anne felt cool and free at last.

James swiftly undressed then came to her, his gaze burning over her young seductive body bathed in faint moonlight through the open window.

Anne gasped with deep pleasure as James' experienced hands worked their magical caresses. She leant back as he pleasured her until she was on fire and, with whispered pleadings, begged to feel complete. Lovemaking had never been this ecstasy before.

She combed her hands through his long dark hair as they explored each other until their passion could not wait and James united them as one.

During the night, they made love again, each time falling asleep in each other's arms. It was long after sunrise when Anne awoke, feeling serene and loved, watching James doze alongside. Her husband. Hungry for him again, she kissed him awake, returned his devilish sleepy smile and, in silent communion, urged him to love her again.

For James and Anne, it became a summer of love. Lazy days idly passed together, riding in the cool of early morning before the heat of the day or swimming in the billabong, afterwards making love on the sandy banks.

As the new year of 1862 ushered in, household routine continued about them. Evenings lent respite from the sapping heat. Anne loved this time of day best, when she and James sat out on the veranda gazing across to the hazy blue Grampians, the rocky mountains shadowed with the fiery setting sun behind them. Anne was always entranced by the explosion of hot colours in a last defiant burst, as though the sun was determined to etch a memory until the next night.

Every evening, a mob of kangaroos appeared, aware of nearby human presence but not threatened by it. Standing upright and alert, using their strong tails for balance they pricked their ears before returning to graze. At dusk, they returned with huge leaping strides back into the bush.

James smoked his pipe and Anne wafted her fan, sipping cool drinks and talking about the forthcoming weekend house party at *Rosevere Hall*. He had already told her it was a large and prosperous stud merino Run.

'I shall take great pleasure in introducing you, my darling.'

'What are they like?' Anne tried to remain positive but as the day approached when they were to leave for the neighbouring property, she grew edgy and apprehensive about the visitors she was to meet.

James smiled wryly in reflection. 'Charlotte Burroughs is a beauty as her mother Ettie once was, and young Bessie is sweet.'

'You know them well, don't you?' Again, doubts crept into Anne's mind. These were James' long time good friends and an unusual uncertainty rose within her.

'I've attended events at the Hall for ten years.' He glanced across at her in the twilight. 'The homestead is far grander than *Barratt Downs*,' an edge of apology entered his voice. 'But they're friendly enough, especially Albert, although you may find Ettie … sharp,' he chuckled. 'Their homestead is a showcase of far greater wealth than mine. Although not nearly as grand as Thomas Chirnside's mansion at Werribee.'

'How can anyone wish for more than this?' Anne observed, sending up a desperate silent appeal that her happiness endured.

James reached for her hand and lifted it to his lips, brushing it with a kiss. 'I agree but old Albert's head will turn at the sight of you, just you wait and see.' He grinned wickedly.

'Then I shall be on my guard.'

'You're safe with Albert. He's out of condition and beyond a chase these days. But his son Laurence is another matter.'

Anne's curiosity was raised.

'Known as Lazy Laurence.' James answered her unspoken query and puffed thoughtfully on his pipe. 'Happy to spend his father's fortune but make none himself. He's your age and quite the lady's man.'

'*Rosevere Hall* promises to be interesting.'

'Unlike you,' James continued, 'Ettie and her oldest daughter, Charlotte, both believe living in the Australian bush rather like living at the end of the earth. Ettie constantly invites strays from England to remind her of home and nags Albert every summer to sell up and return to her beloved Kent.'

Anne fell silent, watching the last orange rays glorify the top of the mountains but not really seeing the beauty at all. James' mention of strays from England had set her mind racing again to who the visitors could possibly be. Perhaps they didn't know her at all but merely wished to meet. Still, her foreboding mounted.

Two weeks later, James and Anne set off before dawn in the loaded buggy to make use of the cooler early morning hours. The chestnut pair pulled them briskly along on the hard dry track. Anne should have enjoyed the outing through new countryside with plains stretching as far as the eye could see but her mind was preoccupied with who awaited them at their journey's end.

The January day grew hotter. About midday, they reined the horses and stopped for lunch beneath a clump of aged eucalypts casting welcome if flimsy shade from the heat.

When they continued, a warm wind sprang up and gritty dust whipped about them so that they were grateful when *Rosevere Hall* appeared in the distance ahead, heralded by the surrounding thick belts of trees.

James turned the buggy off the main road and followed the three mile avenue of pines that lined the long drive to the house.

Anne gaped as they emerged at the end and out into sharp sunshine again to catch her first glimpse of the house set in a formal oasis of mown grass and trees, incompatible with the Australian bush. It was an impressive, two storeyed red brick homestead, a forest of chimneys across its acres of slate roof with a square central tower and entrance portico, the whole fully surrounded by a broad colonnaded veranda. As James had advised her, *Rosevere Hall* was indeed grander than *Barratt Downs* and built for show.

Perched, gracious and commanding on a rise, grass and trees sprawled away from the house down to a lake where white swans drifted lazily across its dark cool waters.

Clusters of house guests stood in knots of twos and threes or sauntered about. The womenfolk wore large light sunhats or sheltered beneath parasols against the fierce sun. White and pastel gowns stood out against the verdant tended lawn. Some played croquet, the distant clop of the wooden balls on mallets echoing across the open grounds.

The entire scene depicted an oasis of civilised gentility in an otherwise arid summer landscape, foreign, Anne thought, and unrealistic for Australia. At least, compared to *Barratt Downs*.

James reined in the horses and the buggy pulled up on the wide circular gravelled drive before the house. As they stepped down, Anne's attention was drawn farther out to the undulating hills and grazing flocks of sheep.

Inquisitive heads turned in their direction as a stout couple swept through the open front doors and down the wide flight of steps to greet them.

The woman, slightly taller than the man, wore her dark hair looped in elaborate curls all over her head, making her round face look plumper, her overdone pale green dress all flounces and ribbons. Presumably their hostess, Henrietta Burroughs.

Trailing behind the showy woman, a little man dressed in a beige suit, undoubtedly her husband, Albert, immediately captivated Anne. His ruddy face was fixed with a warm smile, his eyes twinkled with mirth, and she instinctively knew she was going to like him.

Henrietta possessively grabbed James' arm and gushed, 'Darling James, it's so wonderful to see you again. Isn't this dreadful heat exhausting?' she furiously fluttered a beautifully carved ivory fan.

Although she addressed James, Anne sensed her attention was diverted by her presence at his side.

'Ettie.' He kissed her on a flabby wrinkled cheek. 'Surely you're accustomed to Australian summers by now?' he teased. 'Albert.' The men slapped palms in a hearty handshake, 'Happy New Year my good neighbour. Pleased to find you in good health, as always.'

Albert gave a hearty laugh that issued deep from his rotund chest and patted his thick waist that extended his lightweight summer suit. 'Life's been good to us, eh Barratt? Welcome back to the Hall.' He wiped his beaded forehead with a handkerchief then tucked it back into the small top pocket of his vest.

Anne felt Ettie's eyes focus upon her as James turned and sought her hand, giving it a gentle reassuring squeeze. 'This is my wife, Annabella,' he said with proud affection. 'May I introduce Mr. and Mrs. Albert Burroughs.'

She smiled nervously. 'Thank you for your invitation. I'm pleased to meet you both.'

The broad smile on Henrietta's face was apparently reserved solely for James because it swiftly faded as her analytical gaze settled on Anne. 'Mrs. Barratt. We're pleased to make your acquaintance. James quite scandalized the district when we heard he'd advertised for a wife. Still,' she looked Anne up and down, 'We're pleased he found someone to his liking.' Henrietta's effusive personality swiftly cooled but her husband stepped forward and grasped her hands.

'Annabella, what a beauty you are. Welcome to our home, my dear.' He winked at James. 'Barratt, you've excelled yourself and make us all wish we were twenty years younger.'

'You have a grand home, Mr. Burroughs.' Anne glanced behind him.

He beamed. 'Glad you appreciate it, my dear. Took years to build, not to mention a lot of patience and a long purse.' Far from being boastful, Albert's comment contained only genuine pride. He leant closer and grinned. 'And you must call me Albert.'

'Well, it was certainly worth the effort. You must be proud of your achievement.'

'The house is named after our home in England. *Rosevere* means the big moor,' Albert explained. 'Ettie and I are from Cornwall.'

Anne was delighted. 'I'm from Devon so we're practically neighbours.' She didn't feel it harmful to reveal her origins since everyone seemed to know.

'So we understand, Mrs. Barratt.' Henrietta glared at her darkly and Anne's confidence wavered.

'We most certainly are. As close as neighbours can be out here, anyway.' Albert chuckled. 'And how do you find living in the Australian bush?'

'I've come to love it very much,' Anne admitted with enthusiasm. 'Although the summer is much hotter than England, isn't it?'

'After twenty years, you'll be quite acclimatised, Mrs. Barratt,' Henrietta said sharply with a thin smile, clearly reminding Anne she was a newcomer with much to learn.

'Nonsense, Ettie,' Albert chided, flashing his wife a warning glance. 'Have you forgotten your first summer out here? You barely moved from the chaise longue. At least Annabella's still afoot.' His stock body erupted into an uproar of laughter at his wife's expense. When he recovered, he explained, 'When Christmas and our house party are over, Ettie and our daughters retire to our house in Melbourne for the summer.'

Ettie's lips pressed together and she glared at her husband's reproach. Anne wondered why on earth genial Albert had married such a humourless woman. She was clearly of some breeding if, for all her wealth, she lacked a sense of dress, so perhaps she had merely been a good catch. Yet she could not think it of Albert for, despite his wife's abrasive nature, he seemed genuinely fond of her.

Albert placed Anne's hand on his arm. 'Let's go inside out of the sun. Millie will take you up to your room.' He dabbed at the perspiration on his face again, easing a chubby finger between his neck and stiff shirt collar. 'And when you're refreshed, our overseas guests are anxious to meet you, Mrs. Barratt.'

'I shall look forward to it,' she lied. 'And, please, call me Annabella.'

Henrietta had dotingly attached herself to James. 'Charlotte is so looking forward to seeing you again,' she confided in a low voice behind them as they climbed the front steps to the grand entrance but loud enough that Anne could not help but overhear. 'It will be just like old times.'

'Not quite, my dear.' Albert grunted in correction. 'James is a married man now.'

They crossed the broad flagged veranda and entered the cool sanctuary of the huge entrance hall. A gallery of paintings and portraits lined the walls that soared beyond the first floor stairs and landing, streamed with light from a glass domed ceiling. A wide carpeted cedar staircase in the centre drew all eyes upward to stunning effect.

A petite young maid neatly dressed in a dark dress and crisp white frilly apron appeared from an inner door behind the stairs. 'Millie will show you up, then join us for afternoon tea outside under the trees, eh? Everyone else is here,' Albert smiled.

With James' hand at her elbow, they followed the maid to their bedroom suite, one of many opening off the square upper gallery. A manservant arrived bearing their luggage from the buggy and the maid began to unpack.

'How many rooms are there in the house?' Anne asked as she surveyed the dark and gleaming mahogany furniture that filled the room. A four-poster bed, mirrored dresser, wardrobes and small tables, and a white marbled fireplace set with pine cones in the grate, a shining potted palm in front of it on the hearth.

'Over thirty I believe.'

'It is a very grand and beautiful house,' Anne murmured politely.

'Ettie still pines for England. Albert indulges her,' James replied tactfully, mindful of the maid's presence and being overheard.

Presently, Millie finished unpacking, curtsied and softly closed the door.

'*Rosevere Hall* is splendid but, do you know, on first impressions, I prefer *Barratt Downs*,' Anne stated and flashed James a winning smile.

He drew her into his arms. 'Shall we try out the bed and make sure it's comfortable,' he murmured into her ear.

'James!' She pretended to be shocked, winding her arms around his neck. 'I'm all dusty from our journey,' she teased, then asked mischievously, 'Won't we be missed?'

'Not for at least an hour.' He gave a wicked chuckle. 'Do you realise just how ravishing you are?' His lips brushed her ear, then softly trailed down her neck and across her exposed shoulder as he undressed her.

'Only because you love me and make me so.'

He removed her large sunhat and tossed it carelessly across the room. Anne giggled as they tumbled onto the immense soft bed. Hopeless to resist her husband, of course, from the moment he kissed her warm bare skin.

As James made slow and delicious love to her, Anne was vaguely aware of voices and laughter drifting up to them from outside.

It was much later before Mr. and Mrs. James Barratt returned downstairs, refreshed after their siesta, to join their fellow guests.

CHAPTER 20

'I hope you will be there to catch me if I faint,' Anne muttered ungraciously as they descended the carpeted cedar staircase, having unwillingly surrendered to Millie's insistence as she helped her dress that she simply must wear the required layers of petticoats. Anne thought them hot and ridiculous in the climate and only relented because the maid assured her it was quite improper to go without.

James kissed her on the nose and chuckled. 'Persevere my dearest for you will outshine them all. And,' he winked, 'think how much pleasure I will have when I remove them later.'

James had changed into a fresh shirt and lightweight grey suit. Anne's body was encased in a graceful dress of peach flowered cotton with puffed transparent sleeves to the wrists. She had donned her favourite large straw sunhat that dipped mysteriously low over her brows to shield her from the strong Australian sun.

Wandering outside onto the lawn to join the other house guests, Ettie caught sight of them and rushed over. 'There you are. Where have you been?' she insisted, dramatic and breathless. 'There are so many people to be introduced.'

After her initial slur on their arrival, Anne wondered why she now suddenly considered her worthy of introduction.

'My fault, Ettie.' James did not look at Anne but squeezed her hand in conspiracy, mockingly serious in his apology. 'I insisted Annabella ... rest.'

Anne smiled at her husband's carefully chosen words, and the remembrance of their shared and passionate lovemaking bolstered her courage.

Over Ettie's shoulder, Anne saw a striking raven-haired woman approach, drifting graciously to Ettie's side. She was breathtakingly beautiful and knew it, her gleaming hair as black and gleaming as a moonlit night, elegantly upswept beneath an exquisite wide-brimmed lacy hat. Her slender body was defined in a matching white lace dress contrasting her dark beauty. Like night and day. Anne felt positively rustic beside her.

Her perceptive dark eyes scoured Anne in a single sweeping glance from behind long eyelashes.

'James.' She uttered his name with familiarity and reverence, boldly kissed his cheek and embraced him, her dark eyes smothered with adoration. 'I've missed you dreadfully,' she whispered dramatically but loud enough for those nearby to overhear.

'It's good to see you again, Charlotte,' James responded warmly.

'Only good, James?' She pouted, teasing. 'You didn't pine.' She linked an arm through his. 'But of course you didn't.' She bathed Anne with another stripping gaze. 'You're married now.'

'If you were so smitten,' James teased with warmth, 'you should have responded to my advertisement.'

'You know me better than that.' She flashed a creamy smile and tapped her fan on his sleeve. 'I expect to be wooed.'

Anne had begun to feel quite forgotten when James slid his free arm about her waist and drew her closer. 'Annabella, may I introduce Miss Charlotte Burroughs, Albert and Ettie's oldest daughter. Charlotte, my wife Annabella.'

'So, this is your little secret,' Charlotte drawled. 'You're very ... young.' Her lips pulled into a tight smile.

And you're jealous, Anne stiffened, the retort almost burst from her mouth until James sent her a pleading glance of understanding.

'You caused quite a scandal in the district with your outrageous scheme to acquire a wife.' Charlotte reached across and touched the strands of barely visible but distinguished grey hair at his temple. 'Has she given you these already?' she taunted.

James smiled wryly. 'Unfortunately, as you are well aware, they have been there for a number of years.'

If Charlotte Burroughs was such a catch, why was she still a spinster? The woman was a shrew and Anne disliked her on sight, pressed close to James, her lacy gloved hand gentle but possessive on James' arm as though she owned him.

Suddenly, a dashing young man approached across the grass and burst rudely among them. 'Don't monopolise our new neighbour, sister dear,' he leered, ogling Anne from hat to hem then raising her hand to be kissed. 'James, from what garden did you pick this delightful English rose? Introduce me,' he demanded, his watery grey eyes never leaving Anne's face.

He was tall and thin, hair dark and slick, a gaunt version of his chubby mother. Anne stifled her amusement. James was right. This one would need to be watched.

'Laurence Burroughs. My wife, Annabella.'

'Your humble servant.' He bowed low, artificially polite.

Anne inclined her head and smiled, unimpressed by his slick well-practised flirtation.

Their recent appearance from the house and growing knot of company about them, soon drew attention. A blonde girl, perhaps fourteen or fifteen, Anne thought, with a bunch of ringlets bobbing about her ears, broke ranks from a younger group and hesitantly sidled closer.

Anne immediately recognised Albert in her. 'You must be Bessie,' she acknowledged the plump young miss with a warm smile.

The girl smiled shyly and nodded. 'I am pleased to meet you, Mrs. Barratt.'

'Oh, please do call me Annabella,' she said confidingly.

The girl beamed. 'I should like that.'

Her joy was short lived when Charlotte snapped, 'Bessie,

you should be with the children.'

'Elizabeth!' the girl corrected, her smile fading, eyes lowered with hurt. Quietly, she slipped away, outshone by cruel nature that favoured her radiant older sister.

Anne made a note never to call her Bessie again, regretting her ignorant slip.

'James,' Charlotte pleaded, her crushed sister instantly forgotten, 'I insist on a game of croquet.' Without waiting for his agreement, she caught his arm and drew him away. James raised appealing eyebrows toward Anne but, politely, did not resist.

'I shall look after your wife, James,' Laurence called after him, leading Anne into the deep shade of a nearby spreading oak. 'Boring, isn't it?' he said with lazy distaste. He looked back toward the house at the small tittering group of young women idly floating about in pastel gowns. 'What's worse, I'm expected to marry one of them. Hardly a sporting choice, eh?' he sneered.

Using his moment of confidence to her advantage and tapping Laurence's inside knowledge, Anne casually posed the question on her mind all afternoon. 'Ah but I understand you have other visitors from overseas. No one there to tempt you?' she probed, holding her breath for his reply.

'Hardly,' he said and his narrow distracted gaze roamed about the garden. 'Just one gent, I think. A horse breeding Londoner. Can't remember his name. He's around somewhere.'

Anne scowled in thought. She had never been to London and certainly didn't know anyone who lived there.

'But let's not talk about him. I find you far more fascinating.' He took her hand and caressed it. 'Hard to believe, my delicious Annabella,' Laurence's voice lowered and he leaned closer, 'That you are a thief?'

Despite the hot day, Anne went cold and her heart leapt with fright, horrified to believe Laurence could possibly know anything of her flight from Devon. Her mouth went dry and she could barely utter, 'I ... am?'

'Yes,' he smirked, 'You stole Charlotte's beau and married James.'

Once her mind had absorbed the words, Anne's body sank with relief. 'I shan't apologise,' she forced gaiety and a smile, 'because James chose me.'

'And we can all see why,' he replied smoothly, still holding her hand when she wished he would let go. 'Charlotte was desperate to marry James. Did he tell you?'

Not surprised to hear it for James Barratt was indeed a handsome catch, Anne shook her head and wisely remained silent.

'But my selfish sister doesn't exactly have age on her side any more, does she? All the same,' he continued briskly, 'She's a worthwhile prize. Father will settle a considerable dowry on her.' He pulled a tight conceited grin. 'She and mother were appalled when they learned of Barratt's scheme and green with envy when they heard he'd up and married such a charming young thing fresh off the ship from England.' He threw back his head and gave a malicious laugh. 'Mother was positively livid that yet another potential son-in-law had been whipped out from under her fat little feet.'

Anne was shocked by his openly blunt criticism. 'I'm surprised to hear it. I would think Charlotte could choose any man she pleased.'

Laurence sneered. 'Only if they don't know her. James had a lucky escape. Had he succumbed, he'd doubtless have been nagged into rebuilding his homestead to my sister's more ambitious plans. Or been begged to return to England to live in style in London.'

Anne could muster no respect for a son who publicly and shabbily maligned his own family, even if it was the heir apparent of *Rosevere Hall*. What had James said? Lazy Laurence. It seemed he was merely biding his time until Albert died and he could claim his inheritance. Unfortunately, both he and Charlotte had inherited their mother's sharp tongue.

The number of guests on the lawns had thinned but a buxom girl deliberately slowed, flirting at Laurence as she passed.

He smoothly released Anne's hand. 'Excuse me, my lovely Annabella. I see an old friend. Until dinner time.' Laurence strode off and caught up to the young woman who pretended surprise that he had followed and simpered as he kissed her hand.

Anne shook her head in amazement and glanced toward the croquet lawn where James and Charlotte still played. When he caught sight of her, she returned his wave and her heart swelled with love. As if in response to their private exchange, Charlotte's mallet hit the ball with a sharp crack that echoed across the grass on the still afternoon air.

From the corner of her eye, Anne noticed Ettie descending upon her again, trailed by a tall striking gentleman, vaguely familiar. Apprehensive, she smiled at their approach.

'Annabella, our English guest has asked to meet you.'

At her baffled frown and without waiting for their hostess to introduce them, the visitor eagerly clasped her hands. 'It is only six months but I see you have forgotten me. I bought your horse in Plymouth.'

His infectious smile prompted Anne's memory. 'Charles? Mr. Montgomery,' she quickly corrected with a nervous laugh. It was all right. The visitor from Devon was only Charles. She almost collapsed, not from her stiff corsets and hot petticoats, but with a sigh of relief.

'Indeed,' he beamed.

'Sir Charles Montgomery,' Ettie amended in horror.

'Oh, I'm sorry ... I didn't realise ... '

Ettie smirked at her mistake and discomfort but Charles seemed unconcerned and enthused, 'What an incredible coincidence. You're much changed.' He looked her up and down with approval. 'And I understand I must congratulate you on your recent marriage.'

'Thank you.' Even as she smiled in greeting, Anne's mind assessed the situation so that when she realised Charles would know nothing of her background, her panic eased.

'Did you emigrate with plans to marry?' he asked.

'No,' Anne flushed. 'I met James soon after arrival but I did leave Plymouth soon after I met you. The *Result* was in harbour and I sailed out on her.' She kept the details vague. 'How long have you been in Australia?'

'Since last October actually. Came out on the Cairngorm with my fiancé and her mother.'

'Ah, congratulations.' She was delighted for him and guessed such a caring and intuitive gentleman would have chosen nothing but the loveliest of ladies. 'I look forward to meeting them.'

'They've retired to rest before dinner but my fiancé came from Devon and by merely such a tenuous connection alone expressed a passing interest to meet you.'

James had mentioned that not all guests attending the afternoon garden party had been invited to stay on for dinner and the ball that night. It seemed only close neighbours and friends remained or, in the case of Charles, those who because of distance were too far from home. Anne knew that the pretentious Ettie would only too gladly extend her hospitality for aristocracy from England.

'We came out for the spring racing carnival and to run my eye over the horses I've heard so much about,' he beamed. 'We've become so enamoured of the colony we've stayed on. Had planned to be home for Christmas but extended our stay. Took the train to Geelong on Corio Bay, bowling along at over twenty miles an hour to enjoy the sea air, then took the steamer around the coast then back to Melbourne.'

'Australia's an easy country to love,' Anne agreed. 'When do you plan to return?'

'Next month on the Prince of Wales.'

From the corner of her eye, Anne saw James and Charlotte approach, their croquet match obviously at an end, and Ettie took charge of introductions between the men. Charlotte seemed bored, made murmured apologies and moved indoors.

By the time James and Anne walked arm in arm upstairs a short time later, she had briefly explained to him how she and Charles had met.

On the landing, they met Bessie sitting on the top step looking miserable. James hesitated but Anne, sensing the girl's distress and not wanting to embarrass her, gently pressed his arm and smiled. 'You go on. I won't be long.'

James read her tactful caution and said brightly to Bessie, 'I hope you're keeping a dance free for me this evening, young lady?'

As he moved on, the girl gazed up at him, her sad eyes lit with an idolatry spark of hope. 'I should be honoured, Mr. Barratt.'

'The pleasure will be mine,' he called back to her, flashing one of his devastating smiles, leaping the stairs two at a time until he reached the upper hallway and disappeared from view. Anne glowed with pride at the compassionate man James had allowed himself to become again.

Bessie hugged her knees as Anne sat down alongside. 'You're not dressing for dinner and the ball yet, Elizabeth?'

'I'm not going.'

'Why ever not?' Anne pressed gently.

'I hate my dress but Mother insists I wear it,' she announced, her pretty mouth thinning with blunt dislike.

Anne studied the insecure young woman who apparently received no self-esteem nor encouragement from Ettie and Charlotte. 'Can you choose another?'

Bessie's eyes widened in horror. 'I couldn't.'

'Why not?'

'Mother would only make me change,' she said gloomily.

Anne shrugged. 'Refuse.' An impish smile tilted the corners of Bessie's mouth. 'What's the worst that could happen?'

'Ban me from dinner and the ball.'

'At the moment you don't want to go so you have nothing to lose.'

She turned to Anne, wide-eyed, as realism dawned. 'No,' she breathed in wonder, heartened.

Even as Anne dared this impressionable young lady to disobey her mother, somehow the vision of Henrietta turning puce with rage was exciting and to be pursued.

'How old are you, Elizabeth?' Anne asked.

She beamed. 'Fifteen.'

A decade younger than Laurence and Charlotte. A late child perhaps? Unplanned and therefore unwanted? Either way, clearly neglected and ignored in favour of her older siblings. Anne found it hard to believe Albert would treat his daughter so.

She contemplated the sweet round face, compliant nature and, with Albert Burroughs' wealth behind her, enviable marriage potential. 'The moment we face our fears, Elizabeth, they don't seem half as bad, and often disappear.' When the girl remained unconvinced and to encourage the despondent child, Anne suggested, 'Perhaps I can help? May I see your dress?'

'Never.' Bessie looked appalled. 'It's hateful.'

'Please,' Anne cajoled, grinning.

The girl cast her a wary glance. 'Promise you won't laugh.'

Anne laid a hand lightly on the girl's arm and nodded. 'Elizabeth,' she confided, lowering her voice, 'don't tell a soul but I can assure you I'd much rather be riding a horse myself than attending a ball. If a lady must dress up, it should at least be in a gown she loves.'

She clasped Bessie's hand and drew the girl to her feet.

Bessie's room was even grander than the guest rooms. At least Henrietta hadn't stinted on her daughter's comfort and accommodations. But the contents of the poor girl's wardrobes were full of childish inappropriate clothes.

'Elizabeth,' Anne shook her head in dismay, 'Summon your maid. We have work to do.'

Bessie's face lightened with hope and she dashed over to the fireplace to pull the bell. Presently, Dolly appeared, a timid inexperienced mouse, obliging in the extreme, whom they swore to secrecy. The poor thing trembled in her thick black shoes, clearly fearing Henrietta's wrath and dismissal until Bessie assured her she would assume complete responsibility.

'She'll know you had help, Miss,' the maid's tiny voice quavered and she wrung her hands in anguish.

Anne stepped forward. 'Then name me. I shall gladly confront Mrs. Burroughs and explain.'

Finally if not completely convinced, Dolly helped Bessie into the despised aquamarine gown. At the mere sight of it, she verged upon tears. 'I can't wear it. I simply can't.'

'No you certainly cannot, Elizabeth. Not like it is. Dolly, I presume you sew?' The awestruck maid nodded. 'Good. We haven't much time but we can make a few basic and simple changes.' Anne prowled around Bessie pointing out the alterations to be made. 'We'll remove all these bows, here and here. Unpick the flounces around the hem so the dress falls down and flows out instead of hugging you like an over-decorated cake.' Anne frowned in thought but Bessie giggled. 'And all the lace around the neckline must go. Off, Dolly. Every inch.'

The maid nodded furiously and Bessie's eyes sparkled with animation as she began to imagine Anne's suggestions.

'What plans for your hair?' Anne asked.

Bessie showed her miles of blue satin ribbon and explained the usual style of ringlets and curls Henrietta preferred.

Anne shook her head. 'Never.'

She edged the gown lower off her soft pale shoulders and the young woman gasped. 'I couldn't.'

'All the other women will. It's summer, Elizabeth. Quite

acceptable,' she argued with delight. Anne gripped her shoulders and turned the girl toward the cheval mirror in the corner of the room. 'Look at yourself, Elizabeth. Imagine all this down and straight.' She stretched out the springy curls. 'Dolly will brush them out for you. Perhaps some tiny jewelled pins catching it to one side of your face?' She addressed the maid, the servant's eyes gaping like a scared rabbit, her head bobbing furiously, too terrified to disagree.

'It might make a difference,' Bessie reluctantly admitted.

With the dress stripped of its hideous frippery, the watercolour blue of Bessie's gown would, ironically, become her best feature and highlight the young woman's soft blue grey eyes.

'Oh, Elizabeth. It will be perfect. You shall look very grown up. Your card will be full tonight.' She squeezed the girl's shoulders in excited collusion.

Bessie blushed. Seeing the girl's face turn pink with heat, Anne pounced. 'You have a beau?'

'No,' she denied far too swiftly.

'Someone you like, then?' When the girl remained silent, Anne coaxed, 'Every young woman has her fantasy. It's no shame. In fact, it can be quite fun.'

Bessie hesitated and sighed. 'He would never consider me and Father would never approve.'

'He'll be good enough if you like him. I'm sure any young man you preferred would be a wise choice.'

With Dolly's help, Bessie began removing her gown. 'A school teacher is highly unsuitable,' she muttered.

'A teacher?' Anne seized on the snippet. 'He's here?'

Standing in her undergarments looking sweet and vulnerable, Bessie placed a hand to her red cheek, her eyes sparkling. 'Yes,' she breathed, barely above a whisper, 'He's a Scotsman. His name is Angus Ross. He's here because he's employed as a tutor on a station forty miles away but the household is at the seaside for a month so they asked father to look after him while they're gone.'

Anne clasped Bessie's hands. 'You're still young, Elizabeth. If Mr. Angus Ross isn't to be the one, there will be others. Just make sure, whoever he is, it's a man you love. I can't tell you the happiness it will bring.'

Anne hugged her and turned to Dolly. 'You remember all the changes to Miss Elizabeth's dress and how her hair must be done?'

The maid nodded, already seated at a side table and equipped with scissors, needle and cotton thread, Bessie's potentially beautiful gown spread out reverently across her knees.

'I'll see you downstairs.' Anne opened the door and smiled. 'No one will recognise you, tonight. You shall be quite the beautiful young swan.' For a moment, she stood in the long empty hallway and sighed with deep pleasure before hurrying back to James in their room.

'All well?' He looked up from the bath tub as she entered.

She pushed out an exasperated sigh and shook her head. 'What a crisis. If I had a daughter as gentle as Elizabeth, I should cherish her. Henrietta's treatment is shameful. She can't see her daughter is not a baby anymore.'

Distracted and stirred by the sight of James' sun browned body half exposed above the bath water, Anne began to remove her clothes. She slowly peeled her gown from her body and it floated to a pile at her feet. She stepped out of it and began untying her petticoats. 'Did you enjoy your afternoon with Charlotte?'

'I would have preferred your company. Did you mind?'

Anne sauntered across to the bath, perched on the side and playfully flicked soapy water into his face. 'Laurence entertained me. He mentioned Charlotte's affection for you. Why didn't you tell me?'

'I married you, not Charlotte.'

'She's very beautiful.' Anne unlaced her corset.

'Yes but she doesn't love the country life as you and I do. She wants someone to whisk her away from here.' James sponged his chest and shoulders, watching her, teasing her with visions of water trails slowly running over his broad bare skin. 'You seemed very friendly with Sir Charles Montgomery.' Anne shrugged, delighted to sense a hint of jealousy. 'Amazing that you should meet him again here on the other side of the world, don't you think?'

Anne rose from the tub and paced the floor in front of him, his comment making her unsettled. 'Yes but he has a fiancé now he told me. It just shows how many people come out here to the colony from England.'

Despite her reasoning, it did set Anne wondering if Charles' appearance could possibly be more than a happy chance. He seemed genuinely surprised to see her and his fiancé merely curious to meet someone also from Devon. She wondered how they came to know their hosts and be invited to *Rosevere Hall* at this particular time.

It was all too confusing to fathom. Anne's attention was distracted when James gripped the sides of the bath and pushed himself from the water, stepping out and wrapping himself in a towel.

'Shall I help you undress?' he murmured, sliding a wet arm about her waist. He eased the open corset from her body and untied the ribbons of her chemise while Anne unpinned her hair, shaking it free to tumble over her shoulders. A sensuous gaze burned between them. 'Shall we try out the bed again when you're finished bathing?'

Anne closed her eyes, awakened at the touch of his warm lips on her bare skin and breathed, 'I can't wait that long.'

His hands slid beneath her garments and found her breasts. Gasping with pleasure, she asked in a whisper, 'Why did you choose me, James?' As always, she was impatient to make love, yet craved the unhurried pace with which he seduced her anew each time.

'Because you are irresistibly wild and undeniably beautiful,' he growled, dispensing the last of her clothes and dropping his towel. 'And because you are young and wholesome, and I love and want you, not only to bear my children but because you will be the shining light beside me throughout our life.'

Anne flooded with emotion to hear his words of love. With their bodies pressed together, James firm and damp, Anne cool and soft, she sighed, 'I hope that I shall never disappoint or disgrace you.'

'You may frustrate me,' he chuckled, 'But you could never do that,' he promised before taking her mouth to kiss her.

Anne shivered, uneasy with premonition, as James swept her into his arms and carried her across the room to the bed.

CHAPTER 21

As was customary at *Rosevere Hall*, Anne learned that all weekend guests gathered in the grand drawing room before dinner. Because Anne was delayed helping with Bessie's dress and further diverted by James' lovemaking, they were among the last to appear and made an impressive handsome couple framed in the doorway. Anne standing erect and gracious beside James, like all of the men resplendent in a dark suit and waistcoat with a lavish cravat despite the evening heat.

Anne glanced around the gathering. Elizabeth was nowhere to be seen and she hoped Dolly finished the dress alterations in time. Charles Montgomery and his fiancé had also not yet appeared. Most women had chosen gowns of vivid turquoise, crimson and emerald silk, their gowns lavishly displayed across plush settees and chairs. Charlotte was radiant in scarlet, the colour striking against her dark hair and pale skin.

James and Anne moved among their fellow guests making polite conversation and sipping the wine and sherries offered to them by a parade of attentive servants. A ripple of interest rolled through the gathering and caught their attention. When Anne turned to see the reason for the disturbance, a transformed Elizabeth stood expectantly on the threshold, flushed and nervous.

Freed of her childish frills and flounces, the young woman looked remarkable, her blossoming young figure revealed, sweet round face glowing, eyes alive and hopeful, infused with colour from her watered blue silk gown.

Anne sighed over the difference and filled with pride as if

Elizabeth had been her own sister. The girl curtsied a slight respectful bob toward Anne who inclined her head in acknowledgement of the gesture and stepped forward in support.

'My, my. Who is this beautiful stranger in our midst?' Anne beamed but Elizabeth's moment of glory was short-lived for Ettie gaped at the sight of her youngest offspring as she self-consciously approached her parents.

Anne could have gagged Ettie when she rustled forward and hissed, 'Bessie, what on earth have you done to your dress?' Her shrill voice carried around the room.

Her daughter's brave smile faded. 'Improved it, mother.'

Ettie huffed. 'And your ringlets.'

'More suitable for a child, mother.' She openly challenged, if in a small voice. 'After all, I am fifteen now.'

Anne well knew the courage it took to be so defiant and sent up a silent private prayer of support. Her plea was either swiftly heard and granted or there was no need for concern for, even as Ettie spluttered with horror, Anne caught Elizabeth's gaze over the speechless woman's shoulder and they exchanged a victorious smile.

Albert on the other hand, as Anne expected, charmed to smitten devotion by this new chrysalis that had emerged in his household, kissed his nervous daughter on the cheek and said, 'New dress, Elizabeth?'

'Yes, father.' She ignored her mother's gasping protests and basked in her father's pride.

Albert turned to his wife. 'Splendid, Ettie, isn't she? I had no idea how much our Lizzie had grown.'

Outwitted, Ettie's nose lifted and, forced in front of every eye in the room, gave a sour smile, still apparently unable to speak. All the while in the background, Anne noticed Charlotte glowering with envy at the attention her little sister was receiving, an honour usually reserved for the older darker beauty.

Then Anne's happy world abruptly shook to its

foundations and her body turned to ice. Charles Montgomery and his fiancé appeared in the doorway, an older woman half hidden behind them. In that devastating moment, all Anne could think of was that she would be exposed and lose James forever.

Although it had been months and Anne had only met her a few times, she would have known the petite perfectly-groomed conceited woman with the dark blonde curls anywhere. Her narrowed and gleaming blue eyes immediately settled on Anne whose shocked gaze remained riveted upon her.

The instant Charles and his lady companions arrived, Ettie swept to their side in greeting and, to Anne's horror, drew them toward her. She knew it would be inevitable, of course, but Charles and Ettie remained ignorant of the tense undercurrent flowing between the two younger women.

Anne could have wept for wonderful Charles, clearly naive as to the true nature of the woman beside him, said so proudly, 'Annabella, may I present my fiancé, Miss Susan Wilson and her mother Harriett.'

How could such a distinguished and worldly gentleman have been fooled and fallen for such a vixen? The last vision Anne remembered of her was a half-naked body wrapped around Arthur in the woodland hut. She kept the image firmly in her mind to remind her of this woman's wickedness.

'I don't believe it,' Susan enthused in an affected hypocritical tone, all cordiality and warm smiles, reaching out and clasping Anne's hands in her own as though they were friends and not enemies. 'Little Annie. Annabella,' she corrected pointedly with a knowing grin. 'My, how you've changed.'

'You do know each other!' Ettie crowed in delight, clasping her hands over her ample bosom as though the reunion was all her own doing. 'You did say you had a feeling, didn't you, Miss Wilson? A woman's intuition indeed.'

Susan turned to Charles. 'Isn't it amazing, darling? Annie and I have indeed met before.' Anne stopped breathing until she smugly added, 'At a ... mutual friend's wedding, wasn't it?'

Anne smiled until it hurt. 'I remember it well.'

'Mother, look who's here?' Susan turned aside as if surprised to see Anne who had not a shred of doubt in her mind that this match between her and Sir Charles was a calculated manipulation in an attempt to find her.

As Harriett Wilson emerged into view from behind her insincere daughter, Anne well remembered the older woman's bitter condescending words on the day of her marriage at Combe Hill. The woman had been ambitious for her daughter yet somehow Anne thought they would have aimed higher than Arthur Westcott.

Despite the chaos whirling through her head and the stone weight in her heart, Anne gathered what poise remained. 'Mrs. Wilson. How interesting to see you here,' she emphasised, holding the older woman's hateful glare.

'We could say the same thing,' she replied stiffly.

Anne threw out a challenge. 'Yes, you could, but perhaps our meeting is more than a happy coincidence,' she subtly pointed out, deciding to play their own game. 'More like fate.'

Poor smitten Charles, so openly adoring of his fiancé, no doubt ignorant of her true purpose and origins, spread an encompassing smile around the women and said, 'I shall leave you ladies to catch up.'

He headed toward James and Charlotte. Anne panicked. How much had Susan confided in her fiancé? How much would he know and tell her husband? The men smiled and nodded in their direction. Charlotte, Anne noticed, selfishly preened to have the men all to herself.

'Come and sit, Mrs. Wilson. Dinner won't be long.' Ettie mercifully drew Harriett away.

'I shan't detain you from your ... husband,' Susan emphasised, glancing in his direction. 'But you did disappear rather suddenly last June, didn't you?'

Anne determined to remain impassive until she discovered Susan's purpose. It was difficult to imagine but the situation might not be as ruinous as she feared.

'Perhaps later tonight you might care to explain,' Susan suggested.

'I have no need to explain anything to you. Ever.'

'Ah but we do have lots to talk about, don't you agree?'

'Perhaps.' Anne knew a showdown was inevitable but her forehead wrinkled in puzzlement. Why had Susan gone to such lengths to find her? And where did Arthur stand in all this? Did he know her whereabouts too? If so, why wasn't he with Susan to presumably expose her? How had Susan found Charles and made the connection? The only possibility was through the sale of Arthur's horse. Somehow, she must have traced it to him which emphasised her desperation to find her. But why? No doubt she would soon find out. In the meantime, it was best not to panic.

With a deep calming breath, Anne controlled her nerves. Susan would expect her to crumble but the last six months had taught her much and she would not be easily intimidated or bullied. She must carefully guard her every single word.

'Until later.' Susan pulled a thin smile. 'I shall let you know where and when.'

'As you wish.' Anne refused to reveal a single indication of her raging distress. 'Excuse me.' With a gasp of relief, she moved across the large and sumptuous room to join James. Unfortunately, Susan followed to claim Charles.

Throughout the conversation that followed, James gave Anne strange questioning looks when it was clear she was highly strained. He knew her too well. Anne lost concentration, her thoughts wandered and she grew quiet but her reticence was hardly noticed for the stunning Charlotte brilliantly amused them all with her lively banter. Unable to do little more, Anne merely nodded and smiled.

Despite her promise to do otherwise, Anne could not

avoid worrying over Susan's intentions and grew increasingly afraid for herself and James, covering her alarm with a broad smile that was difficult to keep in place. The lovely evening that held such happy promise now threatened to become a nightmare.

None too soon, a white-aproned maid entered the room and curtsied. Ettie caught her husband's eye and, in turn, nodded to Albert. From his place near the unlit marble fireplace he raised his glass and addressed the room at large.

'I propose a toast to the New Year of 1862 and the twenty-fourth year of our esteemed Queen Victoria's reign.'

Hearty rounds of, 'Here, here,' followed.

'Dinner is served,' Albert announced in a booming voice, crossing the room to Ettie's side, offering his arm, and leading the glamorous entourage across the spacious entry hall into the massive dining room.

With relief, Anne welcomed the breakup of their falsely cordial group. With her attention momentarily diverted from the devious Susan and lovingly tucking her arms into James', they followed their hosts.

As a brief reprieve from her deep apprehension over Susan, Anne noted that, perhaps because Elizabeth smiled at him with such sweet appeal, a boyish-faced young man, probably Angus Ross, offered her his arm. Elizabeth looked as though she would faint with idolatry at his feet. Even better, in the dining room, Anne was pleased to see the young pair were seated together at the opposite end of the table, far removed from Ettie's disapproving gaze.

Anne estimated that the *Rosevere Hall* dining room was four times as large as the one at *Barratt Downs*. Three large French windows along one wall, which in daylight would have overlooked the front lawn, were all thrown open to admit the languid evening summer breeze. The long polished table stretched the length of the room. Chandeliers and heavy silver candelabra sparkled over the white damask cloth, glassware and gleaming cutlery, breathtakingly impressive.

Albert assumed his seat at the head of the table, Ettie on his right. Place cards defined other seating in strict order of etiquette. To her dismay, James and Anne were seated halfway down the table directly opposite Charles and Susan, Mrs. Wilson having been placed further along. All very formal and grand but agony to endure. Anne acknowledged them across the wide table with a cold smile.

Champagne was poured for most but some of the older men preferred whisky. Food was brought in by a parade of servants and, over entree and soup, a genial but restrained festivity settled upon everyone.

Anne focused on eating, ignoring Susan, although unusually she had no appetite from the fearful sickness churning in her stomach.

Conversation flowed around her over the change of courses. Maids trailed in again bearing silver platters of lamb and beef, roast duckling, hams and vegetables. Mellowed by wine and sumptuous food, the older squatters held court, reflecting with fierce pride and nostalgia on their early days and the simplicity of life back then.

Talk ensued of early runs and the need for each to be three miles from the neighbour's furthest outstation; the despotic Crown Lands Commissioner, Foster Fyans, who apparently rode up and down the countryside settling land disputes.

'They were rough times those early days,' Albert shook his head. 'Cutting and clearing timber just to build those damned draughty huts.' His comment raised a wave of laughter and more memories as the older men, including James, mused over early tracts of unoccupied land, gaining fourteen-year leases and finally being able to construct decent homes for their families.

'We fared well enough on mutton chops, billy tea and damper, eh men?' James said. 'And look at us now.'

'Gold certainly boosted our progress,' one old squatter said.

Then followed sombre recollections of Black Thursday in the summer of Fifty-one when bushfires had swept the colony in a broad and horrifying front across three hundred miles of pastoral land.

Albert plunged his fork into a thick slice of poultry.

'Fifty-one was a year to remember. Greatest drought ever known, wettest season in memory then the discovery of gold.'

Albert tore a meaty chicken leg between his teeth. 'Old bullocky Bill made his packet out of that,' he muttered. 'Shrewd old blighter refused to load his wagon unless we paid him treble!'

James laughed. 'We made handsome profits, Albert. Half the diggers ate our meat.'

'All our sheep runs in the Western District are envied now.' Albert continued attacking his meal with enthusiasm, clearly to Ettie's alarm. When he finished, he pushed his plate away and burped. Ettie glared at him in horror. 'And now we must endure this army of ragged selectors invading our land.' He wiped his mouth with a napkin.

'Remember last year when that angry mob attacked and stoned Parliament House over the debate on the Land Bill? Blasted unruly rabble.'

'Government's trying to break our power,' James agreed.

'I don't hold out much hope that even the new Premier, John O'Shannassy, in his third term will see us right and not release too much more land for selectors,' Albert added.

Disappointed in her host's unfair remark and thinking of her new friend, Mary Munro, Anne blurted out, 'Some selectors are very nice people.'

At a table filled with a number of original squatters, many heads turned in her direction and silence fell around the table.

'Surely you're not referring to that Scotsman and his family?' Charlotte's spiteful tone dripped censure.

'All new settlers began somewhere,' Anne replied crisply. 'Squatters years ago. Selectors today. What difference does it make? As pioneers you worked hard and deserve your wealth and comfort now but shouldn't you give the newcomers the same opportunity?'

Murmurs of dissent rumbled around the table. James groaned beside her and Charles' gaze sparkled with amusement from across the table. Anne was mildly self-conscious at the disturbance she had caused but unrepentant, for her unsettled mood had made her irritable.

'We've spilled blood and faced danger,' Albert frowned, red-faced from drink, thriving on the company but clearly in disagreement with a new chum's view. 'We earned our land.'

'We hold the power in Government, Albert,' said another. 'We'll keep them out as long as we can.'

Speaking of struggles, what about this American Civil War that's broken out? Fighting over slavery.'

'Disastrous business,' someone agreed.

'Nearly as bad as losing to the English cricket team though, eh?' Bawdy laughter diffused the serious mood. With nodding heads and swigs of drink, they commiserated over Melbourne's loss to the first players ever to visit Australia in a recent four-day contest.

Albert patted his ample stomach. 'Well, who among us would exchange all this for the Old Country, eh?'

'Well,' Charlotte interrupted quickly, 'I would gladly return Home as you know, father. London is much more civilised.'

'But, is England still our home?' James quietly posed the question, giving everyone cause for thought. 'Australia's been good to us.'

'Yes,' a squatter agreed. 'These are prosperous times. The telegraph is already at Ballarat and the railway from Geelong is due to open in a few months. Progress eh?'

Conversation grew animated with arguments on both sides.

'The Peninsular and Orient mail steamers are making the journey from Southampton in less than two months,' one of the other wives commented excitedly. 'England is growing closer all the time.'

'Recent seasons have been good to us,' James said. 'There's no shortage of pasture and we're getting bumper prices for our wool.'

As they dined, the table had been efficiently cleared and was now laden with jellies, fruit charlottes, pies and crèmes. All glasses were refilled with sweet wine and stemmed glass dishes filled with rich desserts.

Albert pushed his chubby frame out of his chair and looked down the table toward the younger ones. Raising his glass, he made a toast. 'To the generations to come.'

With a loving glance, James turned to his wife, echoing Albert's words with a romantic murmur, 'To the generations to come,' leaving Anne in no doubt what was on his mind.

Outwardly smiling but heartbroken inside, she hoped James meant what he said earlier before they made love. That she could never disappoint him. But what if she hurt or betrayed him? How would he react then? How deep must love be to forgive all?

Eventually, she supposed she might be forced to confide in him and confess her past. With Susan glowering at her from across the table, she saw no possible chance of avoidance.

CHAPTER 22

As dinner drew to an end, Albert rose, a signal for the menfolk to retire for shots of Scotch whisky, the pleasure of a pipe, and billiards.

After they disappeared into the library, the ladies gathered in the drawing room again, fans fluttering in the sultry evening warmth. Revealing yet another hidden talent, Elizabeth entertained them on the piano.

As Anne sipped a refreshing glass of cold lemonade, Ettie, with the fawning Harriett Wilson at her side, dourly received compliments and glances of admiration on her youngest daughter that floated across the room like her music.

'You must be so proud, Ettie.'

'The girl promises to be quite the centre of attention.'

Charlotte hovered on the opposite side of the room, talking with another younger woman in green silk and Susan moved to join them, deliberately leaving Anne sitting awkwardly alone to endure pleasantries with other older squatters' wives.

She presumed Susan was deliberately making her wait for the suggested rendezvous, squeezing the most misery from her evening before they met.

When the stately ballroom, occupying one entire wing of the house, was eventually opened to echo the first strains of lovely music through the house, the guests filtered in, the women's wide skirts whispering on the polished timber floor, shining beneath three giant chandeliers, the French doors at one end thrust wide onto the broad veranda.

Velvet chairs lined the walls with potted palms at

intervals between, the small orchestra seated on a raised dais at the far end.

With bitter sweetness, Anne allowed James to draw her close and be one of the first couples to sweep out onto the floor. She knew a brief moment of happiness and love with his strong arms about her, his captivating smile only for her. He became her respite, her protector. She choked back tears, knowing he was the love of her life and she would die without him, something she may yet be forced to do.

She crushed the thought but not the growing contempt for the calculating woman who had trailed her from England. To what end, Anne did not yet know. What was worse, it appeared to be at Charles' expense. Anne took exception to Susan's deliberate exploitation of an innocent man, too much a gentleman by far to be involved in her scheme, whatever it turned out to be, or have any knowledge of his fiancé's pretence.

As the night progressed, Anne was never left wanting for a dance partner, a small token she believed of her acceptance in the district and her heart ached with sorrow. James, of course, monopolized her time and half-filled her tasselled programme but, when Charles whirled her about the floor for a waltz, she bit her tongue against the impulse to reveal Susan's deceit. Of course, he would probably not believe her. It was each woman's word against the other.

Anne's attention was diverted with pleasure from time to time to see Elizabeth, charming and bright with newfound confidence, danced around the room more than once, not only with the sedate school teacher, Angus Ross, but Laurence and other young men.

Later, during a quadrille, Charles and Susan were one of the four couples in the square dance formation that included James and Anne. It meant she was forced to touch gloved hands when it came the ladies turn to circle in the centre and walk by her as they crossed to their partners. With a growing sense of doom, she endured Susan's superior air and falsely sweet smile.

Halfway through the evening, Anne felt crowded. 'It's very warm. Perhaps we could take some air out on the veranda?' she suggested to James who readily agreed.

She had just begun to sip her cool punch and enjoy James' private company alone for the first time all evening without Susan's image always hovering in the background, when Charles and her nemesis joined them. Annoyed, Anne's partly-revived mood sank lower again and she felt shadowed. I wonder whose idea that was, she thought bitterly, plastering yet another grim smile on her face.

Susan laughed and chatted idly as though they were friends and no undercurrents simmered between them.

When the men drew apart to one side, their conversation inevitably turning to the topics of sheep and horses again, Susan stood in front of Anne, shielding her from their view. 'Are you avoiding me?' she muttered viciously.

'Hardly,' Anne scoffed, unsettled at the depth of her aggression. 'I have been in full view all evening.'

'Midnight,' she announced curtly. 'At the lake.'

Later, when they returned arm in arm with the men to the ballroom, James dipped his head to whisper, 'Are you all right?' When Anne shrugged in puzzlement, covering it with a carefree smile, he added, frowning in concern, 'You and Susan seemed to be rather deep in serious conversation.'

Anne laughed. 'Susan's life always seems accompanied by some drama or another. She was confiding. We have planned to have a chat after the ball. Do you mind?' She turned her most pleading gaze up to him, feeling as deceitful as Susan.

'Ah, good,' a mischievous shadow of relief crossed his face, 'because Charles and a couple of others have arranged a few hands of cards. For stakes.'

'Then I hope you win.'

'Ah, Annabella,' he said softly, 'with you by my side, how can I ever lose?'

The remainder of the evening with supper and more dancing passed far too quickly for Anne, desiring to postpone her fate, terrified that her new life was in jeopardy. That it should be at Susan Wilson's hands was a bitter pill.

But soon the gathering laughed and clapped at the end of the last lively galop, signalling the end of the night's entertainment. Chatter and music faded, groups thinned and the ballroom gradually emptied.

Anne stood on tiptoe in the hall and kissed James. 'Go and enjoy. You deserve it.' But not me, her heart cried out in agony, knowing the next hour would reveal Susan's intentions, the extent of her malice, and the course of Anne's future.

Anne observed Susan standing half hidden behind a veranda column glowering, waiting. Anne flashed her a brief stiff smile and walked by. Her adversary could follow. The two women sauntering off together would not be deemed unusual since many individuals and couples had also streamed outdoors into the warm summer night to mingle or loiter under the veranda and on the grass before retiring.

Tired and tense, Anne kept walking across the lawn toward the lake in the darkness ahead until she heard Susan's swishing skirts alongside her. She forced herself to remain composed and kept silent. Could not bring herself to speak to this woman who had the potential to ruin her contented world far removed from the miserable existence she had been forced to endure in England.

Susan knew who she was and what she had done. Left her husband and wrongly remarried. Whatever revenge and exposure Susan sought, Anne had secret ammunition of her own that she could use to her advantage. Susan would think she had control of the situation but Anne believed she had enough knowledge to equalize the other woman's power.

'I believe this is far enough.' Susan glanced back over her shoulder to the faint light emanating from the homestead some distance behind them. 'We will not be overheard.' She hesitated and ran a condescending eye over Anne. 'Mrs. Annabella Barratt. We've both come a long way from Devon, haven't we?' She paused before suddenly demanding fiercely, 'Why did you leave Arthur?' her sweet façade discarded, all pretence gone, her eyes glinting with fury.

At her abrupt and frightening change, Anne stepped backward and tried to remain unruffled. 'He threatened to kill me.'

Susan threw back her head and laughed lightly. 'Liar. Arthur would never do such a thing.'

'Come now, Susan, you knew Arthur much better than anyone realised, didn't you?' she said slowly, pleased to see the other woman's attention sharpen at her steady tone. 'You knew what he was capable of.' When the wide-eyed Susan fell silent, glaring with suspicion and hatred, Anne continued, 'I had no wish to end up the same as the first Mrs. Westcott.'

Susan's mouth thinned. 'She died in childbirth.'

Anne shook her head. 'We both know that's not true.'

'How do you know?' she snapped. When Anne did not reply, she hissed, 'Stephen.' Her eyes glittered. 'That's why Arthur let him go. You should have stayed.'

'And meekly wait around until I was beaten to death?'

'We had it all planned. You ruined it.' Her eyes narrowed. 'Now I will ruin you.' Her cold stare sent a chill through Anne's body.

Trying to sound braver than she felt, Anne said, 'You threaten me yet you have revealed no reason. What is your purpose?'

'To destroy your life the way you destroyed mine.'

'Whatever your motive, surely there was no need to involve Sir Charles. He's an innocent victim.'

'Ah.' Susan turned away and smiled in reflection. 'He became a convenient foil for my plan. And he most certainly was not innocent. In fact, he has been most willing and pliant in my hands.'

'You traced me through the horse.' It was a statement not

a question for Susan could have found her no other way. She also felt compelled to ask, 'How is Arthur?'

Susan whirled on her. 'What about Arthur? Forget him!'

Anne frowned, puzzled. 'But you … cared for him.'

'Once,' she pouted. 'When we had a future but he doesn't matter anymore because you destroyed our plan, and now you shall pay.'

'What have I done?' Anne asked in frustration. 'Except marry Arthur? Unwillingly. I never understood why he didn't marry you.'

'No, you naïve little country girl, you wouldn't. You had no idea what was at stake.'

'Then tell me.'

Susan regarded her carefully for a long while, breathing heavily in agitation. 'You knew nothing of Arthur's background, did you?' she sneered then lifted her chin and proudly announced, 'Arthur William Maybury was his full and proper name.'

Anne could not remember what had been written on the marriage papers and couldn't recall even bothering to look but her mind hesitated over the surname.

'He was the bastard son of Earl Maybury and a servant girl at Devon House.'

Anne drew in a gasp of surprise at the revelation. She had heard of the reclusive wealthy Devonshire landowner at the other side of the Tavy valley who, as far as Anne knew, had always lived alone and about whom not much was known.

If Susan's claim was true, all the traits Arthur possessed could conceivably have been inherited from his father.

'He was raised by a childless couple on the Earl's estate by the name of Westcott. The Earl never married but four years ago after the Westcott's died he made Arthur a proposition. If he sired a son, the Earl promised to make the child his legal heir to inherit and educate him as his own. Arthur could go and live in the manor house.'

Susan wrung her hands together in growing excitement.

'We had it all planned. At my suggestion, the Earl agreed that Arthur could marry and bring his wife and child to the estate with him. Make it look more respectable and the local people more accepting of an unusual situation.'

Anne frowned. 'I don't understand–'

'Of course you don't.' Susan turned on her in fury. 'He could marry me but–' her voice trailed away and she glanced longingly away across the dark lake, 'I can't have children. We tried. Oh, how we tried. For two years, so any baby would be our own. But nothing happened.' She quickly seemed to collect her thoughts again, continuing brightly, 'Then I seized on the idea that Arthur could marry someone else, to make it respectable, of course. We chose Mary and she was instantly with child but it all went wrong.' She scowled in childish surprise. 'Near the end of her time, she wouldn't agree to give us the baby. Stupid woman wanted to keep it but we couldn't let that happen.'

Suddenly, she recalled what Stephen had told her and the pieces of Arthur's past life began to fall into place. 'That was the night they argued.' Anne gasped. 'And Arthur pushed her down the stairs.'

'It was an accident,' Susan blazed. 'Stupid woman tripped. She should have taken more care in her condition and so close to her time. We almost had the child,' she whispered almost to herself then flashed her attention back to Anne. 'If you'd stayed and had a baby, Arthur would have let you go and set you free,' she whined, sounding anguished. 'But you ran away. We would have taken your child and Arthur would have inherited everything and lived the life he deserved.'

Susan's wild eyes glittered with madness and Anne could see her sense of control had snapped. 'Four years.' She trembled with rage. 'Four years we waited and planned, and it all came to nothing. The Earl's getting older, we're all getting older. How much longer should we have to wait? With you gone, Arthur couldn't remarry. We couldn't say you were dead because your family knew you were alive when you left.'

'I went to see Richard,' she informed Anne smugly. 'He wouldn't tell me anything but I knew you would need money and you had Arthur's horse. It was easy to guess you would sell it and go where there were crowds and you could hide. I asked questions and traced Charles back to London. I bewitched him.' She gave a coy smile. 'And flattered him and pretended I adored him. It only took him months to propose. He's horse mad, of course,' she smirked wryly, 'as you know. So I encouraged him to come out here and investigate the prestigious horseflesh being bred that he'd heard so much about. I pretended it would be such an adventure for us both.'

Anne's heart went out to the man who must surely soon discover Susan's true nature and purpose in his life. It seemed his fiancé would stop at nothing to use or destroy everyone in her path who stopped her from getting what she wanted. But now she had the wealth and position she craved, why did she need revenge on Anne?

There seemed no point and she voiced her confusion. 'But if you have Charles-'

'A means to an end.' Susan shrugged carelessly. 'He was easy prey. I loved Arthur,' she declared miserably, 'and you took away our chance for a happy life together.'

'But Charles is-'

'Nothing to me!' she hissed between clenched teeth. 'How many times must I tell you? He only enabled me to reach you out here in this wretched hot and dry and godforsaken colony.' Her mouth curled in cruel derision. 'Trust a tenant's daughter to be happy living in such a miserable place.'

Anne shook her head and wondered how she could ever hope to influence this mad woman and stop this lunacy. Her twisted love for Arthur it seems had driven her to desperation and distorted her mind.

'Make no mistake, Mrs. Barratt,' Susan snarled, 'I shall tell James you are already married and had no right to marry again. Bigamist,' she accused, raising her voice.

'You have no proof,' Anne tossed out frantically in defence.

Susan grinned. 'I have a copy of your marriage certificate to Arthur in my possession,' she softly revealed.

In frustration, Anne now realized that because Susan had openly admitted to being Arthur's lover, her secret weapon of information against Susan's threats was now useless and she had nothing with which to bargain. It was only Anne's word. She could prove nothing.

By the second, Anne could see her life with James crumbling into dust. In desperation, she gasped, 'I can pay you.'

Enjoying her anguish, Susan's gaze turned hard and she laughed in her face. 'I don't need money. I have Charles. Enjoy your last night with your … husband,' she sneered, 'for I shall come and visit you at *Barratt Downs* and reveal the truth.'

Bad enough to endure Susan here on neutral ground but to have her visit and invade their home, their private sanctuary.

While Anne was sunk deep in thought, and as if from nowhere, Susan suddenly flung back her arm and brought it forward to smash across Anne's face. Before she could take evasive action, the blow hit her with such force, she unbalanced, lost her footing and fell heavily onto the grass.

She raised a hand to her stinging cheek but, by the time she collected her wits, Susan was striding back to the house. Anne had fallen with such force, it was some time before she overcame the shock and struggled to her feet.

Standing alone in the dark, watching Susan reach the house, Anne knew only an utter sense of hopelessness and that her future with James was doomed. After all she had been through, her spirit broke at the thought, and she dropped her head into her hands and wept.

She couldn't bear to see the look of disgust she was sure to see on James' face when Susan told him of her deception.

Knowing how much and deeply James had battled for years to recover from Caroline's betrayal and cruel treatment of him, Anne could only imagine his reaction when he learned of her own disloyalty and breach of trust she had fought so hard to gain.

CHAPTER 23

Desolate at what she knew she must do, Anne wiped away her tears, brushed the grass from her gown and with a shudder of resignation, walked unsteadily back to the house.

Hiding her face, she ran up the staircase and quietly let herself into the bedroom, relieved to see James not yet returned from his card game. In the bathroom, she dashed cold water on her face but there was still a nasty red welt where Susan had struck her.

Anne removed her dress, pushed the windows open and sat in her undergarments on the wide sill, hugging her raised knees, looking out at the soft tranquil night, all gaiety and noise long past, all guests having wearily sought their beds for what was left of the night.

The barely-cooled air drifted like a gentle caress over her skin but Anne felt no peace, only a drained sense of exhaustion and despair, frowning over what she could do and where she could go after James banished her from his life.

Cowardly, she knew, but she simply could not be present to watch James' face when Susan revealed her previous marriage to Arthur and the doubt it would cast over their own. Knowing now as she did, he would be crushed at her deceit. Oh, if only she had confessed before they were married. She was so in love with him, she had spinelessly not wanted to jeopardise their future. And now it didn't matter. She would lose him anyway.

Anne swallowed hard against the disgrace of what she had done. As always, without really contemplating the consequences and who she would hurt. This time the man she loved more than anyone else in her life. Not to mention her own deep sufferance of pain. How could she have been so foolish as to ignorantly believe her past would never emerge again to haunt her?

Too late now to dwell on the biggest mistake of her life but she had instinctively known from her first glimpse of James as he'd turned to face her in the Albion Hotel in Melbourne and her heart stirred with a strange awareness, that the course of her life was about to change and it would include him.

She fought back tears against the risk of James returning to witness her distress. She must give no indication of her misery and pretend all was well. Bad enough she had a mark on her cheek to explain.

Just then, Anne heard James quietly return and the door softly click shut behind him. She hesitated in the darkness, her bleak heart bursting with love for him.

'It's all right, James. I'm still awake.'

Her heartbreak erupted with a fresh surge and she stifled a sob with a sigh. She slid from the windowsill and walked toward him.

'Annabella?' James whispered. 'Are you all right?'

'Yes. Just enjoying the night.'

'I'll light the lamp.'

'No,' she said, alarmed he would see her marked face, 'there's no need. Were you successful at cards?'

'I'm afraid not,' he groaned. 'Charles is a damned fine player and old Albert is as cunning as a fox,' he chuckled. 'Charles expressed great interest in Princess and her bloodline. I promised to write a letter of introduction to Thomas Chirnside at Werribee and invited them to *Barratt Downs* if they have time on their return to Ballarat and Melbourne in a few days.'

'Our first house guests,' Anne tried to sound pleased. Ironically, with James' invitation, at least she would not need to explain Susan's demand to visit.

'Since you and Susan are acquainted, I thought you might enjoy her company for a few days.'

Never. 'That was very thoughtful of you but now I really think we should get some rest.'

'Yes, it's been a long day.' He stepped closer, eyeing her state of undress with interest. 'You shouldn't have waited up for me,' he murmured, drawing her against him. 'Sometimes the gambling goes on all night. But I'm glad you did.'

How could she sleep? Still tense from her clash with Susan and tormented over her dwindling time with James.

When they made love, it was with a desperation and urgency born of Anne's passion and need of him one last time. Her distress was pushed to the back of her mind as she responded to his exciting touch. Later, cradled in his arms, Anne drifted into an uneasy troubled sleep.

In the morning, strained from the moment she woke at the thought of facing Susan again, Anne rose before James and quickly dressed, padding extra powder onto her red cheek to conceal the worst of the damage. When James stirred and rolled over in bed to watch her, hands behind his head, he teased her haste.

'I'm eager to return home,' she made light of her ordered preparations. 'It promises to be hot again and we should leave early to gain as many miles as possible before the worst of the heat, and to spare the horses,' she suggested hopefully.

The Gods of good fortune for once had smiled on her because Charles and Susan were not in the dining room for breakfast, Anne relieved to be spared the humiliation of fronting her enemy again. Few other house guests had stirred so early, it seemed, some apparently preferring to take a light meal in their rooms.

So Anne was not subjected to any embarrassing questions about her cheek although, when James enquired, she brushed off his concern with the excuse that, 'I must have scratched myself with a button when I undressed last night in the dark.'

Feeling sick with worry over what she must do, Anne

forced herself to eat but, underneath, was desperate to leave.

By mid-morning, other guests were also preparing for their long journeys home. Wagons and buggies pulled up on the gravel in front of the house. Servants loaded baggage, farewells were taken and thanks to their host and hostess proclaimed. Footsteps crunched on the driveway and parasols snapped open against the already stinging sun with Ettie and Albert standing in attendance as the first of their weekend guests prepared to depart.

Anne sensed James watching her closely. Once in their buggy and barely underway from the Hall along the tree-shaded avenue, he addressed his concern.

'You're sad to be leaving?'

'In many ways, yes. The weekend was certainly memorable.'

Deeply moved by his perception and caring, knowing she didn't deserve him, Anne slipped her arm through his and turned to admire the countryside, hiding her tears.

The horses drew them along at a spanking pace but Anne only half-heartedly shared his lively talk of Bessie's transformation, among other things, as they drove, her concentration lying elsewhere.

Perhaps in an effort to brighten her reflective mood, James suggested, 'If you'd like to escape the heat, we could travel down to Geelong and take in the sea air for a few weeks. I could write to the licensee of Mack's Hotel and secure a room.'

Susan would find them wherever they went and a holiday, as lovely as it promised to be, would only delay the inevitable.

'Oh, no,' Anne swiftly reassured him. 'I'm happy just to be with you.' But not for much longer her heart cried out in silent agony.

She rested her head against his shoulder to avoid the concern in his eyes. She loved him with all her heart and was not sure she could bear to leave after all but James would despise her and she could see no other way.

She lifted her head. 'James…'

He turned and kissed her nose. 'Hmm?'

'I love you,' she said simply teetering on the verge of confidence but failing, drawing comfort and courage from his presence beside her for what lay ahead.

'I know.' He freed one hand from the reins to give her a loving squeeze.

By early afternoon, they sighted the familiar bulk of *Barratt Downs* homestead with the soaring backdrop of her beloved blue Grampians mountains behind, their ragged peaks jutting into the clear blue summer sky.

'Let Sarah unpack for you later,' James commented as they drew up before the house. 'You should go straight to our room and rest.'

Feeling little more than a ghostly shell, she nodded as he helped her down from the buggy, feeling guilty that time alone would give her a chance to think and plan. Anne hid her private distress during the warm welcome and, with distracted patience answered Bridget's eager questions as they bustled indoors to escape the heat.

In their room, Anne nervously paced, finding it impossible to sleep and refusing the evening meal. As dusk fell, Anne realized at the sound of James' heavy departing boot steps fading down the hall, that his absence visiting Will at the stables and meeting with his overseer to check on his stud rams, provided the perfect opportunity to accomplish what she must before she lost her nerve.

The thought of never seeing her husband, friend and lover again tore her apart. Now the moment had come, she wasn't sure she could give him up forever. He had become her life, the air she breathed, her sunlight each morning waking up beside him.

Desolate with cowardice, she sank onto the bed, covered her mouth with a hand to stifle the sobs and gathered her wits. She fully accepted she had brought her present predicament upon herself and, taking deep calming breaths, her fumbling fingers somehow managed to change into a simple cotton dress.

Her gaze settled on James' coat draped enticingly over a chair. It was too easy. Burning with humiliation, she slid her hand into the silk-lined upper pocket and found the key.

Casting furtive glances up and down the hall, she hurried to the study. With a pounding heart, she closed the door behind her and lit a candle. Urgently, she unlocked the bureau and shuffled among the papers. Nothing. There had to be money here somewhere.

Anxious and listening for every sound, she turned her attention to the desk. At last, in the bottom drawer, her trembling fingers discovered a long leather pouch. Anne prayed as she opened it, feasting her eyes with relief and shame on the notes inside. Because her future was so uncertain, she withdrew them all.

She returned to their bedroom and replaced the key then hurriedly stuffed a few essential basic clothes into a small carpetbag. She ran her hands over the blouses, hats and pretty floral dresses James had bought for her all those months ago in Melbourne and that she must now leave behind.

Because time was running short and she needed to leave before James' return, Anne dithered over whether it served any purpose to leave a note of explanation or plea for forgiveness. With an unsteady hand and tear-filled eyes, she scrawled a few vaguely plausible lines.

Sick with fear and hollow longing, for one last time her eyes scanned the cedar dresser, the washstand with her favourite blue and white ewer, the frothy lace curtains drifting in and out with each breath of warm night air.

With a shaky sigh, she blew out the candle, gathered her meagre belongings and tiptoed across to the French doors leading directly out onto the veranda, the quickest way out and least likely direction she would encounter any of the household staff.

The house and garden was quiet as she crouched low behind shrubs and the cover of trees heading toward the stable. Ensuring there were no lamps on anywhere and no one in sight, she deftly slipped a bridle over Princess' neck and led her from the stall.

Wanting to run but forcing herself to walk, she kept to the cover of buildings and pockets of darkness until she gained the nearest belt of trees before she mounted and settled the carpetbag before her.

A strong pull far beyond her control made her stop and turn to take one last look at the homestead, its roof looming darkly against the night sky. Princess moved restlessly beneath her and softly nickered.

Oh James, forgive me, she whispered, but I'll always love you. Her lips quivered and she choked back a sob. She would miss Bridget and Will, even Sarah. And it twisted her heart that she would not see Mary and the children again nor baby Helen grow up.

How unobtrusively, in only a matter of months, this house, its land and people had woven themselves into a tapestry around her heart. But her idyllic time here, the happiest days of her life, was destined to be nothing more than a painful memory. Cherished transient days. Days she had spent living and loving with James. She had no idea how she would go on without him but, despite knowing she had done wrong, did not regret a moment, only the way it was forced to end. Anne lamented only the wisdom of her decision not to confide in James earlier and avoid this inevitable outcome that she had always feared.

'Dear God,' she murmured to herself, realising the extent of what she was conceding and cursing Susan Wilson to her grave. 'Keep him safe. Help him understand and perhaps one day forgive what I have done.'

Tears, unchecked now, rolled down her cheeks as she turned Princess toward Wickliffe and, once they were safely distant from the homestead, pressed her into a gallop, already yearning for the man she was leaving behind, tortured with misery. She hoped the note delayed him long enough to ensure her escape.

Anne arrived at Wickliffe just before daylight, exhausted. Alex Farrell, the innkeeper, eyed her dubiously, James Barratt's wife travelling alone but accepted her story of urgent business in Ballarat, He agreed to stable Princess until her return. The horse sensed her melancholy and whinnied softly as she walked away.

As she awaited the Ballarat coach, glancing warily about, trusting no one, Anne felt bereft and lost. The early morning sky was washed with pink as the passenger coach rumbled to a stop. Hardly aware of her fellow travellers, she clambered aboard, squeezed into a corner and lapsed into a numbing trance.

After a change of horses, the coach rattled east toward her destination and she gazed out through the tiny window at the summer browned landscape, thinking how different and exciting it had seemed all those months ago when she arrived, witnessing the glory of the early spring and unfamiliar countryside unfold around her. Accompanied by a man she had then barely known and who had become the centre of her life.

On this journey, the dust and heat of midday stifled her in the coach. Numb and sore, Anne's back ached and she grew hungry. Despondent and lonely at Wickliffe, she had not eaten. Now, grubby and tired and confined, she longed for the simple comforts of home. James. Their big soft bed. Fresh air and open spaces.

At the next stop, Anne gratefully left the cramped coach to place firm ground beneath her feet. She ate her meal, appalled to discover from overhearing complaints that she and the other coach passengers would be forced to pay two shillings instead of the usual one shilling for the privilege. She grudgingly paid the exorbitant price, praying her money lasted until she found employment. To that end at least, she had a plan.

Through the uncomfortable endless miles that stretched ahead, she leant back and tried to sleep. Occasionally, she dozed but, at every changing station, took the opportunity to alight for exercise and to quench her thirst since the summer day was scorching hot.

On arrival in Ballarat, she made enquiries at the coaching office and bought a ticket for the businessman's coach that left at night, arriving in Melbourne in the early morning. With no time to waste, she joined the coach and, with a familiar lurch, was once more underway.

When Melbourne was finally gained before dawn, Anne wanted to cry with exhaustion. She had slept and eaten little and desperately needed to rest. She found a small hotel and stumbled upstairs to a barely-furnished depressing room. But it was neat with clean sheets, cool and inviting in her fatigue. She dropped her carpetbag onto the floor and crawled onto the bed, almost immediately falling asleep.

When she awoke later and sat up, barely refreshed but hungry, a sudden giddiness made the room spin. Clutching the bedpost, she waited until the sensation passed, then washed and tidied her appearance to go out and eat. She discovered a small restaurant nearby and ordered an appetising meal, washed down with two cups of tea, and felt better.

In the early afternoon, Anne gathered up her bag in case she was able to stay, hailed an Albert cab for the distance was too great to walk, and rode to *Belvedere* in South Yarra, the Rochester mansion where Jessie and Cissy were employed. As the vehicle rolled along the streets, Anne clenched her hands tight in her lap and prayed she might be hired, too. She had to earn a living now and make her own way.

The anticipation of seeing Jessie and Cissy again coupled with the passing landscape of elegant residential suburbs distracted Anne's underlying strain. Mansions set in formal spacious grounds with sweeping lawns, rosaries, statuettes, vases and conservatories were visible from the road as she passed. It wrenched her heart to see such comfort so that visions of her beloved *Barratt Downs* crossed her mind, the home she had thought she would share with James for the rest of her life, reminding her to expect no such luxury in the future. How swiftly life changed.

Anne hardly pined for the loss of the comfortable surroundings, only the wonderful man she loved and, because of her own blunder, had foolishly lost. Even if she had taken him into her confidence, the outcome might still have been the same. In retrospect then, taking up James' offer to inspect his home and unthinkingly responding to his newspaper advertisement in the first place, had been her undoing and the unnecessary cause of the anguish and forced separation into which she had plunged them both.

The cab jolted to a stop before a mansion as grand as all the others, settled securely behind a high iron fence. Anne paid the driver and tried to open the closed gate but it was plainly locked. She pressed a bell to one side, twice, before a male servant answered. She gave her maiden name and asked to see Jessie and Cissy on the pretext of being a friend newly arrived in the country.

Although the man was wary and aloof, he admitted her inside and she trailed wearily after him among leafy shrubbery along gravelled garden paths to the rear of the house. She waited at the back door in a wide paved courtyard and, moments later, her heart lifted with delight when Jessie burst through it, her face beaming at the sight of her shipboard friend.

'Annie.' She endured a warm hug of welcome. 'What on earth would you be doin' here, then?'

Amid Jessie's excited chatter, Anne struggled over a brief explanation, ending, 'It didn't work out.'

Her friend's gaze doubled in amazement. 'But I thought you were happy. We got your letters. Maggie the kitchen maid read them out to us.'

'Something happened ... I couldn't stay. I don't suppose-' Anne's voice trailed off in appeal.

'Is it work you're meanin'?' Anne nodded. 'For sure, I wouldn't be askin' the mistress now,' Jessie clutched at her apron, frowning in thought, then brightened, 'but I could try the housekeeper. If there's a job here, she'll be knowin' somethin' for sure.

Anne found herself bustled in through a rear hallway, past a huge kitchen alive with a large troop of white-aproned staff toiling in the heat, then along a narrow passage turning left and right until Jess thrust open the door to a small room in a side wing.

Anne glanced around. Two single beds, a small table between and a cupboard for clothes. Sparse but comfortable.

'Cissy and I share. Stay here and I'll go fetch her. She's cleaning upstairs. If I'm careful I'll not be noticed and I'll bring her back.'

Anne sank onto one of the beds in relief at seeing a familiar face and hoped her visit proved fruitful because she was anxious to have her future secured. The money she took from James would not last long and she urgently needed work.

When Jess returned with Cissy, there was another excited reunion. Jess must have explained her circumstances because Cissy, ever pessimistic, said, 'I always knew goin' up country was foolish.'

Remembering Cissy's constant pessimism, Anne ignored it and tried to sound brave. 'I'll be fine. I'll find something. And we can meet on our days off.'

'Not many of those. Only half a day more like,' Cissy muttered gloomily.

'Oh to be sure and when we do we go for lovely long walks around the lake.' Jessie quickly redirected the conversation to a more positive note. Then to Anne, 'It's morning call and everyone's busy so I'll ask in the kitchen first. Cooks talk. They know everything.' She was about to dash out the door when she added, 'Cissy, you best get back to work. Don't want nobody noticin' you missin'.'

They left Anne alone to wait and think, her stomach churning with anxiety. If she didn't get work here, she had no idea where she could go. It had shaken her confidence to be suddenly cast into such upheaval with Susan's appearance in her life again, her revelations and threat.

Eventually Jessie returned. 'Now,' she perched on the bed beside Anne. 'There's nothin' here at *Belvedere* but Cook said Mrs. Gannon at Dr. Harwood's house in Emerald Hill told her they've just let a kitchen maid go. It's worth a try.'

'Oh, Jessie.' Anne's hopes rose. 'Do you think I'd have a chance?'

'You'd be workin' in the kitchen.' Jessie emphasised, probably concerned that Anne had just been mistress of her own home and would now be forced to work for someone else. 'You wouldn't mind?'

'I'll do anything,' Anne declared desperately. 'As long as I make some money and have a roof over my head.'

'You won't have any references then?' Jessie looked sceptical. Anne sighed and shook her head. She'd never done any paid housework before. 'Never mind.' Her friend eyed her up and down. 'You look really respectable in those clothes but Cook says Mrs. Harwood's a refined lady, so we can't be sure she'll agree to meet you. But if you say you've got friends working here, it might help. Me and Cissy haven't never got into any trouble. We work hard and do as we're told. All the ladies in the big houses gossip about their staff. Word gets round. Mind you,' Jessie sighed with frustration, 'Cissy complains but she don't mind the work. I don't like it here. I'd much rather work in the country.'

'Oh, Jessie.' Anne clasped her friend's hands. 'I'm so grateful for your help. Is Emerald Hill very far? Can you tell me how to get there?'

'Only a few miles. You could walk it but if you've got enough coins for a cab, there's always one trottin' past and you could go around straight away.'

Heartened by her prospects yet sad to leave her friends again after such a brief reunion, Anne took her leave and was soon jaunting away from *Belvedere* toward Emerald Hill, passing a lake en route. It must be the one that Jessie said they visited on their half days off.

As her cab slowed, Anne's spirits lifted at the sight of open spaces and parks. It looked to be a really nice area. When they entered St. Vincent Place, she was impressed to find a large residential square of terrace houses and large private homes with a central area of gardens.

Filled with a renewed confidence, inspired by meeting Jessie and Cissy again, she paid the cab driver, pushed open the wrought iron gate and strode up the paved pathway to the front door of a two storeyed red brick terrace house. After wielding the heavy brass knocker and a lengthy wait, a young maid answered. Anne stated her business and her name, to be left alone briefly until the girl returned, ushering her through a wide central entry hall from which a single flight of stairs rose from one side, the narrowed passage continuing toward the back of the house.

In a front drawing room overlooking the front garden and street, Anne found herself in the presence of a tall elegant woman in her thirties, standing in the centre of the pretty parlour, hands serenely folded, thick dark brown hair gracefully upswept. Wearing a dark cotton skirt, cream silk blouse with a high lacy throat over which dangled multiple ropes of pearls, she was the image of femininity and grace.

'Miss Gutheridge?' Her voice was soft and low.

Fully aware she was under the strictest scrutiny from the lady's perceptive gaze, Anne dipped a curtsy and nodded, remembering her place as a potential servant. 'Yes, Ma'am.'

She beckoned Anne into the room and, with a slight wave of one hand, indicated she take a seat. 'Mrs. Adeline Harwood,' she announced serenely.

Anne sat still on the edge of her chair, hands folded in her lap and was rewarded by Mrs. Harwood's compliment on her admirable appearance, who then queried her about why she wanted the position.

Anne murmured, 'I lived at home with my family up country but we came upon ... reduced circumstances, so now I need to work.' A distorted account of the truth and not entirely untrue.

Mrs. Harwood, still standing, eyed her keenly. 'Indeed. No references?'

Anne shook her head and said humbly, 'As I said, I lived and worked at home.'

With a deep sigh of what Anne interpreted to be frustration, perhaps, Mrs. Harwood rose and paced. From time to time, she looked across at Anne and frowned.

For good measure and influence, and because she was desperate for the job, Anne mentioned being referred from staff at *Belvedere*. Mrs. Harwood's fine eyebrows flickered slightly in acknowledgement. After an unnerving length of time, during which the doctor's wife flashed sharp eyes over her caller at every turn, Anne was subjected to rigorous questions and informed with crisp and brutal honesty the strict rules and conditions she would be expected to obey and under which she would be employed.

Still hesitant after further deliberation, Mrs. Harwood announced reluctantly, 'You have arrived at a most opportune moment, Miss Gutheridge, and although you are without references, appear to be not without experience so I am willing to accept you as a kitchen maid under a one month trial at a wage of ten shillings a week including all meals and a single room.'

Anne breathed a sigh of relief, beaming her acceptance. 'Thank you, Ma'am.'

She would need to be frugal compared to the luxury that she had known at *Barratt Downs* but only had herself to blame for such reduced austerity. Not so long ago, she would have been accepted in an equal social capacity as Mrs. Harwood. In her changed and penniless situation, she would accept anything as long as it meant paid work and a place to sleep.

On Mrs. Harwood's enquiry, Anne assured her she was available to start immediately and the lady seemed not at all surprised when Anne pointed out all her worldly goods were contained in the carpetbag at her feet.

The new mistress rang a bell and summoned a servant, the same petite girl who had opened the door earlier. 'If you work hard and are conscientious,' Mrs. Harwood advised, 'You will be considered for permanent employment. Kitty will show you to your room and then take you directly to the kitchen to help Mrs. Gannon,' her slight nod an indication both young women were now dismissed.

After being led behind the front staircase and along narrow servants' halls, Anne was shown into a small neat room at the back of the house, not unlike the one Jessie and Cissy shared at *Belvedere*. It contained an iron bed with a thin cover, a small cupboard, a chair, but most wondrous of all, was the tiny square-paned window that offered glimpses of the formal rear garden.

She was not given time to enjoy the tantalising view for Kitty supplied her with a dark dress, two full white aprons and two starched caps from a hall cupboard. Once changed into her working clothes, Kitty then ushered her into the large well equipped kitchen to meet Mrs. Gannon.

'Call me Emily,' she insisted sternly.

Her service began immediately chopping vegetables for the evening meal. The cook talked as hard as she worked. The middle aged woman had kept her figure and caught her greying hair back into a plaited bun. Both she and her husband, Daniel, the butler, Anne learned had worked in the respected Harwood household for over ten years. The staff, although apparently small, also included a nanny, Hilda, and an upstairs servant, Grace. Anne was to learn that her lady's maid's pinched face reflected a nature to match.

'Dr. Harwood,' Emily informed her, 'is a busy man and

rarely seen and he has three lovely well-mannered daughters, Amelia, Margaret and Sophia. Known them since they were babies.'

Anne's days passed swiftly and she cautiously settled into her new life. She mostly worked in the kitchen alongside Emily, watching the older woman perform miracles with pastry the equal of Bridget at *Barratt Downs*, and transform a roast of mutton into a sumptuous tender meal. She respected and admired her skill and sincerity, flourishing in their simple friendship. Kitty slowly emerged from her shyness but didn't live in like all the other staff so there was less opportunity to become friends.

In the evenings, everyone but Grace gathered in the kitchen after dinner, the aloof above stairs maid mostly keeping to herself.

As February advanced, news arrived of the death of Queen Victoria's husband, Prince Albert. According to Daniel, who read out snippets in the evenings from The Argus to the others seated around the big scrubbed kitchen table, he had died of typhus at Windsor Castle before Christmas but news had not reached the colony until recently because of the late arrival of the December mail.

When Daniel had finished reading, a hush settled over the room at the sad news. The Queen's apparent misery and grief only served to emphasise the deep love Anne still felt for James and the aching regret that always plagued her mind.

Even Anne's long and busy working days could not stem her constant fretting for James and what she had done. She anguished over what he would think of her abrupt disappearance. Would he try and find her? Care what had happened to her? Did he still love or hate her? She couldn't imagine that, now knowing her past as he must, he would possibly still care. Her humiliation and despondency was absolute. And what of Susan? She shuddered to think.

Anne found the empty nights the worst, creeping into her cold small bed alone, surviving on the memory of James' strong arms around her, his warm body pressed to hers. It was many weeks later with the summer heat at its zenith that Anne grew suspicious when her monthly bleeding did not come that she might be pregnant.

Her first reaction was delirious joy and an untold longing to share the happy news with James, then guilt at depriving him of what was rightfully his. How often and passionately he had spoken of a son and heir for *Barratt Downs*.

Just when it seemed that with her job in the Harwood household her security was assured, the implications of her predicament surfaced. She would lose her employment and accommodation and be forced to find somewhere else to live. The enormity of it all, Anne found overwhelming and the weight of responsibility for raising a child alone encumbered her previously carefree days.

One evening as she and Emily settled down in the kitchen to share a pot of tea, the cook, normally chatty, was unusually quiet as she set out the cups and saucers and sliced cake.

As she poured the strong brew, she asked, 'How far along are you lass?'

Anne froze, almost relieved that someone else knew. She sugared and sipped her tea, gazing calmly across the table at the older woman but saying nothing.

'Mrs. Harwood won't be pleased,' cook muttered.

'Mrs. Harwood need not know. And it's not all bad, Emily. I'm married.' Although she had removed her wedding ring before reaching the Emerald Hill house weeks before, it was safely tucked away among her meagre belongings in her room.

Emily gaped, clearly astonished and said in profuse apology, 'Why, I hadn't thought ... I'd never have guessed ... I mean ... '

'I know.' Anne managed a weak smile. 'It's all right.'

'But why aren't you with your husband?' Emily spluttered.

Anne lowered her gaze and crumbled off a corner of cake.

'Circumstances.'

'He didn't beat you?' cook demanded fiercely.

'No, nothing like that.' Anne shook her head in brisk reassurance.

Emily grew indignant. 'He threw you out when you're expecting a babe?'

'He doesn't know about,' Anne admitted.

'You haven't told him?'

'I didn't know when I left.'

'Well, he must be told so he can take care of you.' Emily's firm advice was well-intentioned but impossible to consider.

'He wouldn't want to know,' Anne said miserably. At Emily's bewildered expression, Anne tried to explain. 'I did something back in Devon he wouldn't have been happy about. I can't say more than that. Promise me, Emily, you won't tell?'

Emily shook her head and straightened. 'I declare, it's a strange story lass.'

Both women turned at a faint muffled sound from beyond the kitchen door in the hallway outside. Emily struggled to her tired feet to investigate but returned puzzled. 'There's no one out there.'

'You don't think someone overheard?' Anne whispered anxiously.

Emily patted her hand. 'Of course not lass. Probably just the wind rattling something. Your secret's safe with me.'

Frowning, Anne repeated, 'No one must know. I need to work as long as possible. You do understand?'

The kindly woman gave her a reassuring smile and nod but, that night, although Anne was comforted that someone else now shared her burden and she carried James' child beneath her heart, she lay awake with an uneasy mind.

CHAPTER 24

Because she desperately missed riding and her regular country rambles into the Grampians foothills on *Barratt Downs*, Anne often walked around Albert Park lagoon not far from Emerald Hill on her regular half day off. She watched boys groping in the sludge at the water's edges for eels, smiling politely at fellow strollers and returning their greetings when she must but mostly keeping her face averted. On Sundays, it was a popular place for picnics under the trees.

As she strolled and lifelessly gazed at the warm summer wind billow the sails of yachts out on the water, she wondered if her life would always be like this. Living alone, hiding from the truth of her past. What kind of life would that be for her child?

Anne's shoulders sagged under the burden of constantly questioning whether or not she had made the right decision. Then she would take herself in hand and remember that she must take one day at a time for it was certain nothing was ever achieved by worrying.

The following Saturday, the Harwood household feverishly prepared for an important dinner, one of many the family regularly held inviting distinguished guests.

While Anne bustled about the kitchen, sorting silverware for polishing with cook absent picking herbs in the vegetable garden, Grace swept in. The haughty upstairs maid's presence stifled the room. The women glared at each other.

After a deliberate pause, Grace took a further step into the big warm room but remained at a circumspect distance. She was what people regarded as an old maid, her normal attire a crisp white blouse and black skirt that always rustled so that everyone knew when she was near. Not that the downstairs staff endured her presence often which made her appearance now all the more intriguing.

Her thin eyebrows arched and a smug smile hovered across her lips. Hands clasped sedately at her waist, she said, 'Mr. & Mrs. Harwood wish to see you in the drawing room, Miss Gutheridge. Now.'

With an arrogant tilt of her head, she turned on the heels of her polished black shoes and disappeared as swiftly and silently as she had arrived, leaving Anne gaping as to the reason for her summons. It must be important on such a busy day. She hoped she hadn't forgotten to do something and frowned as she tucked a strand of hair back up beneath her cap, instinctively straightening her starched white apron, trying to think what it might possibly be. Usually, only cook was sent for when she and the Mistress had their weekly consultation about the meals.

Anne frowned at the door, still swinging since Grace had left, and set down the cutlery and her polishing cloth. She shivered with an unwelcome premonition but hurried directly to the drawing room.

She hesitated at the door, placing a calming hand on her stomach, and knocked. Bidden to enter, she offered up a silent prayer and went in.

Adeline Harwood sat serenely by the window stitching a tapestry in an upright wooden frame blessed by her usual tranquillity while all about her buzzed with preparations for tonight's grand event. Her husband's distinguished silver hair and spectacles were all that was visible over the top of The Argus as he read but, as she entered and closed the door, he glanced up and folded his newspaper. His wife looked up from her needlework but without her usual smile. Anne frowned. Their demeanours were too casually posed.

'Good afternoon, Anne.' Mr. Harwood spoke first.

'Good afternoon Sir. Ma'am.' She curtsied, filled with foreboding, fearful of what she might have done wrong.

Thomas Harwood, rarely seen but adored by his womenfolk and highly respected by his staff, eyed her directly. 'Is there anything you wish to tell us, Anne?'

She shook her head, bewildered. 'I'm sorry, Sir. I don't understand.' But already suspicion filled her mind. Surely not!

'We shall be brief Anne.' Adeline Harwood said gently from her seat by the window. 'Your condition has been brought to our attention.'

Anne's body grew cold, her mind went blank and her world crumbled. Emily would never have broken her confidence and no one else knew.

'Did you know when you sought service here, Anne?' her mistress asked crisply.

'No, Ma'am,' she assured her quickly. 'Definitely not.'

'It appears some young man has misled you,' the Doctor said in a stern voice.

'Oh no, Sir. It wasn't like that.' Anne shook her head desperately and a strand of hair fell from its place.

Mrs. Harwood politely intervened by uttering a gentle sigh of disappointment. 'What matters now Anne is your future with us.'

She imagined her secure world quickly disappearing and, for the first time since she had fled *Barratt Downs*, feared what her future might hold. 'Oh, I beg you to keep me on, Ma'am. Please.' Seeing her impassive face, Anne appealed, 'I could work right through and, afterwards, I wouldn't let the baby interrupt my work. It could stay in my room or the kitchen. I wouldn't let it interfere with my service and I would be most discreet,' she implored, a growing knot of anxiety tightening in her stomach.

Anne held her breath but could see her pleas were useless and no amount of persuasion would change their mind. Both held her with implacable stares. She had never seen Mrs. Harwood's face so strained.

'Having three children of my own, Anne, even with nanny's help, I can assure you that babies are highly demanding and need constant attention.'

Humbled by the older woman's wisdom and unable to clearly recall anything of her little sister Emmy's baby years, Anne suddenly felt young and no words came to mind for her own defence.

'We could retain you,' Mrs. Harwood continued graciously, glancing across at her husband, 'But we have never kept servants in your condition before and, having discussed the matter at length, do not propose to set a precedent.'

'Please keep me on, Ma'am. At least a few months longer,' Anne pleaded, growing desperate and furious that they even knew about her baby so soon and that such a final and binding decision for her dismissal was so hastily reached.

Having allowed his wife to direct the conversation, Dr. Harwood now leaned forward in his chair. 'Miss Gutheridge-'

'It's Barratt, Sir. Mrs. James Barratt,' she snapped, overcome with fierce rage at her betrayal.

At her sharp announcement and change in demeanour, her employers visibly straightened. 'Mrs. Barratt?' the Doctor repeated, raising grey eyebrows and sounding sceptical. 'Then might we suggest you return to your husband without delay?'

'I cannot. It's an ... impossible situation.'

A stunned silence descended over the room save for the delicate ticking of an ornate china clock on the mantel and the sounds of the other servants scurrying about outside in the hall between the kitchen and dining room.

Dr. Harwood shook his head. 'Then our decision still stands. Mrs. Barratt,' he added carefully after a pause.

Angered by his slight and disbelief, Anne clenched her teeth and hands, biting back a retort. It wasn't their fault she was in this predicament but it was someone else's for their disloyalty, and she was beginning to suspect exactly who that might be.

'Since your service here has been entirely satisfactory,' Mrs. Harwood was saying although Anne barely listened, 'I am prepared to furnish you with a recommendation to obtain employment elsewhere. At a later time.'

Meaning after she had the baby. 'With respect, Mrs. Harwood, I need employment now, not later,' Anne said stiffly, heedless of the consequences of her sharp disrespectful tone. She was being dismissed anyway and her fate, in this household at least, was already sealed. She dared not think where she could go next.

'We must ask that you make alternative arrangements as soon as possible. Normally, we would ask you to leave immediately.' Anne silently gasped at the news. 'But, under the circumstances, we are prepared to grant you a further two weeks in which to resettle yourself elsewhere.' Mrs. Harwood's tone was uncompromising.

Anne caught her breath at their rigid stipulations. If only they knew... And where could she go from here? In her condition with winter coming. Even with a reference, any future employer was sure to ask the reason why she left and she would be bound to tell the truth. It would be impossible to find another job, unless she lived on her wits in the streets. Her stomach sickened at the thought.

Refusing to show any distress, Anne's back straightened. 'Is that all, Ma'am?'

Her employers nodded stiffly. Seeing the depth of presumed disgrace in their eyes, Anne fled the room.

Back in the kitchen, cook eyed Anne's pale face and distress, setting down the knife that had been chopping through a huge bunch of fresh parsley. 'Whatever's the matter, Annie?'

She cast her friend a bleak stare. 'They know,' she said in a small voice. 'I've been given two weeks to leave.'

'No!' A hand flew to Emily's cheek, her genuine shock sincere but Anne still felt obliged to ask.

'Do you swear you didn't tell?'

'How could you even ask, child?' A look of hurt crossed her face. 'On my word, I've not told a soul.'

'Then how?' Anne fumed, pacing the kitchen. 'We only discussed it the once.' She halted and whirled about to confront cook again. Gripping the sides of the table and leaning forward, she whispered, 'Do you remember the noise we thought we heard that night? You went to check?'

Emily slowly nodded and, as realisation dawned, her face grew stricken and incredulous. 'Never!' she breathed.

'Don't you see, it would never be Kitty. She'd already gone home. It could only be Grace,' she said bitterly. 'I wouldn't be surprised. Her heart is as cold as a Devon winter. I shall never forgive her. Never,' she added fiercely. 'I shall go upstairs this instant and-'

'No you won't, child.'

Emily moved around the table to her side. Her gentle voice and comforting arm about her shoulder was Anne's undoing. Suddenly, all the trials of her recent past grew overwhelming and she collapsed onto a chair. She dropped her face into her hands to hide the tears filling her eyes that she had so far refused to let fall.

Arthur and Susan. Leaving England. Finding James. Being forced to leave him. And now this. It was all too much. How on earth could she go on?

'Oh, Emily,' Anne sobbed and sniffed, removing her hands from her face and looking up at cook with beseeching appeal. 'I shall be run off my feet every Saturday seeking lodgings and new employment. In my condition, I shall never find anything else.'

'Of course you will, child.' Emily moved closer and wrapped her in a reassuring hug, pulling her against her apron. 'We'll think of something.'

Anne heaved a shaky sigh and shook her head. 'Thank you, Emily. I know you mean well but you're wrong. This time,' she said bleakly, 'I see no way out.'

All courage and spirit drained from her thickening body. Where was the girl, she thought ironically, who fearlessly left home to sail across the world, escaping a poor life in the hope of a better one? With her forthcoming child, she could no longer afford to be so spontaneous and carefree. She had responsibilities now and must make all her future decisions accordingly. The first was to find a new roof over their heads.

But that night, despite her firm intentions, Anne curled up in bed, weeping, terrified for her homeless future when her warm security was gone.

Next day, she moved passively about her chores, troubled with an urgency to find new work. Her life with a baby would vastly change but Frances Gray had ensured she received a reasonable education, even if she hadn't paid full attention.

Emily had kindly offered to ask other cooks she knew in big houses if there were any live-in service openings available. With the cooler days of autumn on the horizon and winter only months away, dwelling quarters for Anne's developing condition were vital. For the moment, her size was not yet obvious so cook, at least, remained positive of finding something.

Anne felt marginally cheered when seized with the idea to consider employment as a private companion or tutor. With an agreeable employer, the possibility gave her hope. She could ask Kitty, always brimming with gossip despite her timid nature and seek the girl's help.

'Hurry up.' Kitty flew into the kitchen later that afternoon during morning call where she was washing plates. 'They need another tray of cakes.'

As she obliged, she contemplated the wealthy drawing room guests in their elegant finery, sipping China tea, engrossed in idle chat. With a twinge of envy she couldn't stem, Anne nostalgically wished she could join them, just for a moment. She yearned to wear a beautiful dress again and longed to be pampered. Just a little. But such fancies were pointless.

Her coming child was her important priority now and, in truth, despite all the difficulties involved and potential hardships ahead, Anne treasured the new life inside her, a reminder of James to love and cherish, enough for both of them.

A short time later, a noisy disturbance captured everyone's attention. Harwood guests were far too well-mannered to cause such a commotion. Pausing at their work in the kitchen, cook and Anne listened to the loud raised voices growing closer.

Suddenly, a wide-eyed Kitty hurtled through the door and said breathlessly, 'Oh, Annie, there's a fearsome person causing a stir out there. Demands to see you.' She tugged at her uniform sleeve, timid brown eyes drowning with fright.

Anne's heart went cold. Susan Wilson? But even that wanton wouldn't make such a fuss. Her methods were usually far more calculated and subtle. She would first charm and ingratiate herself with Mrs. Harwood then loftily state her purpose. In a moment of panic, Anne worried that she might have informed the police.

She wondered whether to bolt or stand her ground. With a deep sense of impending fate, knowing her moment of accountability had finally come, Anne calmly dried her hands and prepared to confront her past. Everything that had happened back in Devon, her reason for leaving England and disguising the truth about her past since coming to Australia, and stealing Arthur's horse to flee was about to be determined here at this moment in this place. Whatever happened, she would face it with courage and bear the consequences. So much had happened lately, she was growing too weary to fight.

Anne placed a protective hand over her stomach, fearfully eyed the door and waited. Suddenly, it was flung open so wide, it slammed against the wall. A man erupted into the kitchen, his blue eyes wildly transfixed upon her. Across the room, husband and wife stared at each other.

'Annabella!'

'James!'

Anne almost collapsed in amazement at the sight of him

for he was the last person she expected to ever see again. Pale faced and dashing in his dark grey suit, he looked tired, his face lined, eyes bleak and he had not shaved for some time because a bushy growth of beard covered his chin. His hair had grown long and needed to be cut. Any wonder Kitty was alarmed. He looked wild and dangerous.

She peered over his shoulder. No policemen.

Anne yearned to cross the kitchen, hungered to declare her love, throw her arms around his neck and never let go. But of course she could not. She tried to read his mood but saw only haggard disbelief on his drawn face.

'Annabella.' He thinly rasped out her name again.

Deuce the woman, James swore to himself. How could he have forgotten her beauty? Even in a servant's uniform, she glowed. Wisps of errant golden hair spilled from beneath her cap. It had only been months. Such a short time that had seemed like years and during which, at times, he had wanted to concede defeat, surrender, depleted, and abandon all hope of finding her.

But she stood before him now, as nervous as the first time they had met, hands clutching her apron, eyes fearful. He stared at her as though he had never seen her before. She blushed and glanced away. Ashamed, yes, but also pleased to see him he was sure.

He grasped the table ends for support, sagging with exhaustion from weeks of endless searching wanting to yell at her for causing him such torture. So much had happened. Where to begin? But first, to take that edge of uncertain terror from her face.

James glared at her so ferociously as though he wanted to place his hands around her neck and squeeze.

Daunted by his thunderous face but clearly protective, the butler Daniel hovered close. 'Sir, I must repeat what the mistress has said and ask you to leave.'

'When I'm ready,' he growled. In two giant strides, he whipped around the table and confronted his wife, gripping her arms.

'Annie!' Kitty wailed from the door.

'It's all right, Kitty,' she assured the trembling girl in a steady voice, holding James' cold blue gaze. 'This is my husband.'

Kitty gasped, Daniel blustered indignantly and, from the corner of her eye, Anne noticed Mrs. Harwood hovering nervously in the background beyond the open doorway, now crammed with spellbound servants.

Ignoring their protests, cook ushered everyone from the door. Anne blessed and cursed her at the same time for there was no telling what James might do but she knew he would never hurt her. Clearly, he had only come for the truth.

'I see you are in good health and safe.' His gruff voice was rife with concern.

Anne swallowed over her dry throat and warily eyed the knives on the table. Just in case.

'Deuce it woman, why did you run off?'

'I left word,' she mumbled.

'Visiting Mary Munro indeed,' he scoffed. 'At that time of night.'

'You weren't supposed to find me.' She slowly recovered scraps of composure and spirit. Nothing would endanger their child.

'A short ride soon proved your note false. They had no idea where you were or what had become of you any more than I did. Dashing off to the Munro's was nothing more than a wild chase and a waste of time.'

'You actually visited Munro?' Anne gaped in amazement. He had always vowed he would never cross their threshold.

Helplessly, he released her and threw his hands in the air. 'Deuce it, woman,' he bellowed, 'I had no choice. One of many actions for which you shall answer when we return.'

Return? Anne was confused. She furiously shook her

head and her cap tilted. She reached up to adjust it and, frowning, said, 'I can't go back with you.'

His eyes narrowed and his face darkened with threat. 'Indeed you shall, Mrs. Barratt, if I have to tie you up and carry you kicking and screaming in a sack.'

'But ... you must know all about me and that ... I can't,' she said in a fluster. She must have missed something. She didn't understand.

James hurled aside a chair in irritation. Alarmed by his action, Anne backed further away around the table. She thought he would be crushed when he learned what she had done, but she had not expected this nor seen him in such a temper. Did he not know of her past?

His gaze fixed upon her and his loud voice boomed around the kitchen. 'Woman. I have scoured hotels and boarding houses in Ballarat and Melbourne, pressed the doorbells of wealthy men and travelled the length of Victoria.' He advanced on her and glowered. 'You will come with me. Now.'

'You have?' Anne shook her head in amazement, then whispered, 'Why?'

James lunged forward and seized her arm. Anne grew frightened but also disarmed with his body so near. The familiar scent of him lingered in her senses, that faint aroma of his favourite tobacco. She savoured the fleeting moment before it came to an end. He pulled out a chair for her to sit. This was surely the calm before the storm so she seated herself in preparation for his tirade.

Standing akimbo, looming over her, James slowly shook his head. A captivating lock of hair fell across his forehead and with an impatient hand he pushed it back. Then he perched on the kitchen table beside her and, to her amazement, his voice softened.

'It's all right, Annabella. You don't need to run or hide any more. I know everything.'

He knew? Her head pounded. 'Then why are you being

so nice?'

'You should have told me,' he growled.

'I know,' she said in a small voice and caught a sob in her throat. Her eyes brimmed with tears. 'But you would have sent me away and I should have died if you did that because we'd only just met and when I first saw you in the hotel-'

'I know.' He leaned forward and, with loving slowness, brushed his thumb across her damp cheek. 'I felt it, too.'

'But-'

He pressed a finger gently over her lips and bent forward to kiss her forehead. His warm mouth lingered before he pulled away. Anne closed her eyes in reverent pleasure. Was this false heaven before he cast her into hell? Still wary, she opened her eyes, drew in an uneven breath and prepared to listen.

'I knew something was troubling you when we left *Rosevere Hall* but I couldn't understand why because we'd made love and you seemed so happy.'

Poorly stifled giggles issued from the hall. Wide eyed at the eavesdroppers, James and Anne shared a mischievous grin.

'I guess something must have happened to change that,' he continued. 'When I returned to *Barratt Downs* later that night after returning from the Hall, discovered you missing and found your note, something didn't feel right. For one thing, your actions were so sudden with no warning. You have disobeyed me in the past but always after a request of me.' Anne cast him a sheepish glance. 'And you hadn't told Bridget. Just mysteriously left. But I needed to check your tale for myself so I rode over to Munro.' James sounded annoyed at the inconvenience. 'You weren't there, of course, and I had no other leads.'

'I'm sorry.' Anne realised now how his anguish must have been as great as her own.

'I paced the rest of the night, trying to think. Next day, Charles and Susan arrived.'

Anne clutched her throat. 'What did she tell you?'

He pulled a wry grin. 'Her version of everything. Charles was deeply ashamed and distressed by her accusations. She spoke with such spite, he told me later it was as though she had become a different person. A stranger to him. As plausible as her claims sounded, I couldn't help sensing she wasn't quite telling all the truth and that there was more. The heartless woman she painted you was not the beautiful caring wife I knew.'

Anne's heart burst with joy. Her deepest anxiety had always been the fear of losing James if she confessed. She had not believed any person could love and forgive that much. And now he was telling her exactly the opposite? Oh, if only she had stayed with him, all this separation and anguish need never have been endured.

'So, I deliberately baited Susan.' Larrikin mischief played at the corner of his mouth.

Anne hardly dared ask. 'What happened?'

The kitchen door creaked ajar and Emily's anxious face appeared from behind it. 'Annie,' she hissed. 'Mrs. Harwood's ringing for more tea. How much longer will you be?' Her brows furrowed and her concerned gaze flashed to the china comport laden with cakes still standing unserved in the centre of the kitchen table.

Absorbed in James' explanations, Emily's interruption suddenly jolted Anne back to a remembrance of time and place. She jumped to her feet. 'Oh, Emily, I quite forgot.' To James, she gestured toward the rear of the house. 'Perhaps we could continue out in the garden?'

'Of course.' James briskly took her elbow and nodded politely toward cook. 'My sincere apologies, Ma'am.'

'All in a good cause, I'm sure.' Mrs. Gannon beamed, one hand raised to a flushed cheek, plainly smitten with this male intruder.

Anne led her husband outside and they sat on a wooden garden bench draped overhead by the trailing leaves of a young willow tree.

Impatient at having been interrupted just when James' story was growing exciting, Anne asked urgently, 'You were telling me you challenged Susan. How?'

James gathered her hands into his own. 'Brace yourself, Annabella, for some of what I am about to tell you is ... unpleasant.' He waited a moment before continuing. 'Susan felt it her duty, of course, to reveal you were already married,' he said wryly. 'And I admit I was shocked to believe that you would knowingly commit bigamy.' His eyes sought an explanation of her.

Anne dipped her head in shame. 'I only did it for love of you. I couldn't bear to lose you. You promised such happiness that I'd never known before.'

'I understand,' James scowled and squeezed her hands, 'but if circumstances had not turned out as they have, and your illegal actions had been discovered, you could have been sent up before the courts and imprisoned.'

Anne swallowed at how narrowly she had apparently avoided detection. What James had not yet explained was how. She frowned with irritation.

'What has happened to change that?' she probed, afraid, but needing to know.

He paused, studying her, a deep compassion in his gaze. 'I kept questioning Susan, insisting there must be more. She grew ever more frantic in denial until she revealed your allegation that Arthur had been abusive to you and threatened your life. She brushed it off as lies but when I defended you and suggested there might be some truth to the charges, she grew angry then hysterical and called you names. In a rage, she asked how I could trust the word of a penniless tenant farmer's daughter.'

Looking downcast, James absently stroked his scruffy beard and, with a deep breath, let his gaze roam about the garden, but Anne guessed, unable to appreciate its green beauty.

'You can imagine that, through all this, Charles was bewildered. I knew, of course, he had met you briefly in Plymouth and bought your horse. He told me he sensed some mishap had befallen you and that, to your deep regret for some reason, you were forced to sell such a fine animal. At the time, he judged you to be of upright character.'

Anne cast her eyes down at the compliment. 'You can imagine Susan's reaction when he dared to speak kindly of you,' James continued, shaking his head. 'That moment actually was her undoing. She hurled more abuse and began to reveal wild snippets that set Charles and I to exchange glances and have our growing suspicions about her confirmed. He was distraught and embarrassed over his fiancé's highly unladylike and malicious behaviour. Not what one expected from a well-bred woman at all.'

James frowned and shuffled uncomfortably in the seat beside her. 'She turned on him and, in her madness, screamed abuse, revealing she had only used him after all. As we now all know,' he ended softly.

'Poor Charles,' Anne breathed, sorrowful that Susan had claimed yet another unsuspecting victim.

'The blow left him speechless and humiliated. I could see the deep hurt and revulsion for her on his face. The woman was clearly beyond all sense and wits.'

'No decent person would have mistreated such a noble gentleman,' Anne murmured.

'From that moment on, neither of us could believe a single further word she said. She attempted to explain her way out of it but when we refused to listen, it drove her into a frenzy during which she boasted of her worst deed. Annabella-'

James gathered up her hands again and gently caressed them and a deep furrow of wrinkles creased his forehead. Anne was at a loss to explain what could cause such agony on his face.

'Apparently, Susan was so livid and not of a clear mind when Arthur told her you had left. In her insanity, believing

all hope of the future wealth and comfort she craved was lost
to her, she … used one of Arthur's guns … to shoot him.'

Anne gasped. 'Is he-?'

She guessed even before James slowly nodded and placed
a hand over her mouth to stifle her sharp intake of breath,
stunned to hear and believe that Susan could be driven to
such lengths.

'Susan fled Tavistock,' James went on gently, 'Sought you,
was led to Charles and-' he pushed out a harsh sigh, 'you can
possibly guess the rest.' He drew her firmly against him and
kissed the top of her head. 'Although his death is a terrible
tragedy, it means you weren't married to Arthur when you
and I wed at Christmas, for Westcott had been killed months
before, not long after you left and while you were still aboard
ship to Australia.' When she remained quiet for some time, he
murmured, 'Are you all right?'

'I can't believe it,' she mumbled sinking against him, so
horrified she was unable to shed a tear. 'Arthur's dead? Susan
killed him? But … I saw them together. I believe she loved
him. She must have been out of her mind.'

'It looks that way. She determined to search for you to get
her revenge for not inheriting the Earl's estate through Arthur,
and find an unsuspecting man rich enough to give her the
grand life she craved.'

Anne felt the deep vibrations from James voice as he
spoke. 'Thank God Charles had not yet married her.'

She pulled away from him, almost afraid to ask. 'What of
Susan?'

'Charles escorted her to Ballarat police. I believe she will
be returned to England and tried.'

'Mrs. Wilson will be destroyed. She had such high
expectations for her daughter. I often wondered why she
pushed Susan and Arthur together. And poor Charles, to be so
deeply deceived. He may never desire to consider marriage
again.'

James gazed off across the garden. 'Charles truly adored

her, you know. When she was rational, she could be delightfully charming, if a little overdone. When I danced with her at *Rosevere Hall* she seemed genuine but of course it was all a front. Pity.' After deeper contemplation, James suddenly grew uneasy and stood up, running a hand across his forehead, frowning.

Anne's mood plummeted. 'Please don't tell me you have more bad news. Is Bridget all right? Will and Sarah?' she added hastily, hanging on his reply.

He held up a hand to silence her and grimaced. 'No, nothing like that but I do have a confession of my own regarding a ... minor deceit.'

Anne waited. Unusual for the unshakeable James Barratt to squirm so uncomfortably. 'Go on,' she urged with trepidation, wondering what further news he was about to reveal.

'When Farrell from Wickliffe had Princess returned to the Downs when you didn't claim her yourself as promised, he also delivered timely mail from England. When you seemed reluctant at my suggestion to write to your parents and reassure them you were safe and well, I ... er,' he cleared his throat, 'I wrote to my father and asked him to find them and make contact. You've always been vague about the real reason for emigrating and I did not know the true circumstances why you left, so I asked my father to be discreet in his enquiries. It took some time,' he admitted wryly, 'but he eventually found them. Of course,' he quickly added, 'this was all before our visit to *Rosevere Hall* when Susan appeared and the details of your life at Combe Hill were revealed.'

Instinctively, Anne placed a hand across her chest and stifled a light gasp.

Then James smiled and said, 'You, my dear sweet impetuous wife, have a letter from a Mrs. William Gray of Bridge Farm, Devon.' He allowed her time to absorb his words then withdrew an envelope from his coat pocket. 'I believe you know her.'

'Ma,' she whispered, accepting it, James' warm fingers brushing hers. She ran a hand over the paper with reverent hands and looked up guiltily at James. 'I never thought I should hear anything of my family ever again.'

Excited, yet afraid to read it, Anne slowly lifted the flap and slid out the thick pages. She unfolded them and eagerly scanned the lines penned from so far away.

CHAPTER 25

My dearest Anne,

How I thought to never write those words or hear anything of you again. You will never know our anxiety all these months, wondering over your fate.

Richard, cheerful as always and knowing you best, was confident you would come to no harm. He told us all soon after you left.

Your father was outraged at Arthur's behaviour and ashamed that our wish for you to be taken care of and make a good marriage, caused you such misery and the need to take such drastic action.

Your father immediately rode to Combe Hill where he learned the most dreadful news of Arthur's death.

Mr. John Barratt, your husband's oldest brother and a lawyer, states firmly that there will be no charges of any nature against you for taking the horse and making another marriage when you were likely still wed.

Your father and I deeply regret and humbly apologise that, because of our decision for you, well meant, you felt it necessary to leave Devon in order to be safe.

We eagerly await news of you from your new life in Australia. Your father-in-law, Mr. Alexander Barratt, assures us your husband James is of exemplary character and will take good care of you until we meet again. This has lightened our worry for you.

Anne dear, Mr. Barratt Senior is anxious to deliver this letter to Southampton today to reach the Peninsular and Orient mail steamer for Melbourne before his return to Sussex.

So I must be brief but know you will want news of your brother and sisters.

Upon learning you are well and happily married, Elizabeth consented to wed Edward Stokes and they took their vows in St. Eustachius last week. They will live in Rose Cottage along Back Lane.

I am sure you remember it, Anne dear, on the village green with rose bushes in the front garden every spring. Edward secured it for Elizabeth knowing she always admired it so. They are fortunate to have it since old Mrs. Marshall died last autumn and the cottage has lain vacant over the winter ever since.

And now, Anne dear, to Richard. Against my strongest wishes, he talks now only of emigrating to Australia and your father encourages him, saying, 'Look at Annie. There are boundless opportunities in the colony.'

So, with your father-in-law, Mr. Alexander Barratt's help, we have learned of an immigration scheme for people with relatives or friends in Victoria. For a Passage Warrant of five pounds, Richard can emigrate without delay.

Mr. Barratt has set it all out in another letter to James so, as soon as we can arrange it, Richard will sail for Melbourne where it is hoped you can meet him.

Anne, you must promise to write and keep us informed of events with you. We love and miss you, our dearest first born child.

Mr. Barratt is waiting and your father is impatient for my letter which I hope finds you well and happy.

With deepest, fondest thoughts and love from us all,
Mother, Father, Richard, Elizabeth, Edward and Em

Anne beamed up at James with tears of sadness and joy glinting in her eyes. She sprang from the bench and strode across the damp grass. 'I can't believe it. Elizabeth is married and Richard is coming to Australia.' She clasped the letter to her chest.

'Well, then,' James rose, too and approached her. 'Only two things remain undecided. The first is your name.' Anne grew warm and sheepish waiting to hear what her husband had to say. 'To me, my beautiful lady, you will always be Annabella and with your permission I shall continue to use it.'

'You may,' she whispered, smiling. 'I left Anne Gray behind in Devon almost a year ago.'

'My darling Annabella,' he growled low. 'Do you realise how you have tortured me these past months?'

She moaned softly and felt herself blush. 'I know and I am truly sorry for the heartache I've caused you. I had no idea how much you loved me. It is still a mystery and a miracle that you found me. How?'

'Ah. All will be revealed very soon, my dear.' He flashed a teasing smile.

'And what is the second thing you mentioned?'

He dipped his head and tenderly kissed her. 'When shall we go home? Let's leave for the Downs tonight,' he suggested. 'I will happily explain the situation to Mr. Harwood-'

'There will be no need,' Anne began awkwardly. 'Since I have been dismissed from my employment here, we can leave as soon as you like.'

'Dismissed! What on earth for?' James looked aghast but not unduly concerned for he pulled her against him.

Anne closed her eyes and held fast as they longingly kissed, leaving her breathless. Now was the perfect time. She must tell him or she would burst. 'James, there won't be two of us returning.'

He held her at arm's length and scowled. 'What do you mean?'

With a cheeky knowing smile, she placed a hand on her stomach. 'We have another ... smaller passenger.'

She looked up at him with smug contentment and wound her arms around his neck. His instant broad smile of recognition was full reward. 'I hope it is a son for you,' she whispered.

'Is it true?' She nodded. To her surprise, James unwound her arms, dropped to his knees on the grass and placed his hand on her waist, kissing her slightly swollen stomach.

'You shall give me many sons, my beautiful wife.' He rose to his feet again, grinning.

'And if it is a daughter?' she teased.

'Then we shall try again. And again.' His words rumbled against her mouth as he claimed another kiss. When they broke apart, he stated wildly, 'For every Munro, there shall be a Barratt.'

Anne gulped in shock. With five in the Munro clan already. They had much catching up to do. Then she was swept up into his arms and danced about the garden.

Anne clung to him, laughing, giddy with delight. 'James!'

He lowered her to the ground but still clung tight. 'We'll spread our heirs across this land to carry on the pioneering work that we've begun. Our children will grow as the country grows and they'll love it as much as we do.'

Anne absorbed his ecstatic mood then sobered. 'Oh James, I do love you so and I bless the good fortune that brought us together and gave us such happiness.'

'Our future happiness, Mrs. Barratt, is assured.'

He nuzzled her ear and her neck. Unable to resist each other, they kissed again, dissolving into their own private world, unaware of all about them. Anne's passion flowed back to him and her heart sang, knowing this was the only man she would ever love. But what filled her head to bursting was knowing that her love was returned in even greater measure without reserve.

In a whirlwind of activity, James made explanations to Mrs. Harwood while Anne packed her simple belongings. It seemed almost everyone in the household as well as the last lingering tea guests, besides the mistress herself and all the staff, gathered in front of the terrace house that Anne had called home in recent weeks.

Distracted by a flurry of farewells, she took no notice as James loaded her carpetbag into an Albert cab for cook was crying, dabbing at her eyes with the corners of her big apron and Kitty was jumping up and down with excitement and beaming. Mrs. Harwood, gracious and respectful, bade them a safe journey home. She shook hands with James, chatting to him easily. Anne saw curtains twitch as dour Grace, no doubt, spied on them from an upper window. On a parting prayer, Anne hoped she received far less than she deserved for her troublesome spite.

Then, as she turned to climb into the waiting hired vehicle, a familiar and beloved friendly face appeared from behind it.

'Jessie!'

'Annie!'

The two young women flew into each other's arms for a hug of reunion.

'What on earth are you doing here?' Anne frowned, perplexed.

James ushered them aboard. 'Plenty of time for explanations on the road. It's a long way home.'

They scrambled inside, both brimming with excitement, Anne's sadness at leaving her Emerald Hill friends now overshadowed by her delight at seeing Jessie again. As the cab pulled away from the house and lurched into the street, Anne called out, promising to write to Emily and Kitty.

As they circled the square and turned out of St. Vincent Place, James smiled at his wife. 'It will be so good to have you home. The house is in chaos since Sarah left and Bridget keeps threatening to leave.'

'Sarah's gone?'

James nodded. 'But I believe I have found a replacement.' He glanced across at Jessie.

Anne's mouth gaped. 'You're coming to *Barratt Downs*?' Beaming, Jessie nodded. 'Never!' she laughed and they hugged again, her heart exploding with happiness for the love of her husband and the blessing of friends.

'To be sure I'm not believin' I'm goin' up country at last.' She gushed with awed delight at her new employer. 'I'm most obliged to you, Mr. Barratt for givin' me a chance.'

'I only hope you will be happy with us, Jessie.'

'Cissy didn't mind you leaving?' Anne asked cautiously.

Jessie leaned confidentially closer. 'I've not seen her in months. I left *Belvedere* before Christmas. She's right keen on the gardener and nothin' would make her move now. And you know how she hates the wild bush,' she exclaimed in mock humour. 'All the same, 'tis the first time we've been apart since we was ten.'

'I can help you write letters. Maybe she'll come and visit?'

'I'd not be holdin' out me hopes,' Jessie said wryly. 'Guess it's the way of life that there comes a time for us to all be movin' on in new directions.'

Anne squeezed her friend's hand, seized by a moment of brilliant inspiration, secretly hoping her lively friend would help bring Will out of his shyness. Jessie couldn't write but Will could, and Anne reckoned some private tutoring would not go amiss between the two of them. Brimming with happiness in her own life, she held great hopes for Jessie and Will's future, hopefully together. It certainly never hurt to give fate a nudge.

'So, tell me, Jessie,' Anne eagerly prompted, desperately wanting to know more. 'Why did you leave the Rochester house?'

'Tis a long story.' Jessie's posture straightened and she puffed with importance.

'Tell me everything,' Anne begged, 'and don't leave off a single thing.'

Jessie heaved a long dramatic sigh of reflection. 'It was grand and all working in such a big fancy house for important people,' she admitted seriously. 'But it weren't the country you see?'

Anne nodded, fully understanding, for though she had loved Devon and always would in a nostalgic way, her heart had been equally captured by Australia with its wide open spaces and strange animals. Not to mention the wonderful handsome man at her side.

'You'll not be knowin' my brothers' good news,' Jessie

continued, a depth of excitement and pride in her voice.

Anne straightened, giving her friend her full attention in anticipation of exactly what the good news might be.

'While they were workin' on the station run up country near Sandhurst, they took up minin' licences. They did so well, they bought eighty acres of land over near a town called Daylesford,' she announced.

'God help us, Annabella,' James groaned. 'More selectors.'

Anne whipped a glance at him in shock to approach him for offending Jessie when she saw the twitching corners of his mouth and realised he was pretending. Amazed that her formerly dour husband was beginning to mellow, she threw back her head and laughed.

'The coming years will see many changes. Some old squatters,' she gave him a playful nudge, 'will just have to accept them and adapt to the new times ahead.'

Jessie glanced between them, frowning, clearly having no idea of the meaning behind their conversation. 'Well, eighty acres is seventy-eight more than we had in Ireland,' she said indignantly. ''Tis a grand start for them, sure it is.'

'That's a magnificent piece of good fortune, Jessie,' Anne said warmly in appeasement, pleased to notice her friend's bewildered and hurt expression had eased.

'That's where I was, you know. Up country on the boys' farm when Mr. Barratt found me.'

Anne turned to James. 'How on earth did you know where to look for her?'

He shook his head, grinning. 'Jessie can explain. I'm exhausted just listening to your women's talk.'

'Now we've made you cross, Mr. Barratt,' Jessie said reverently, seemingly mindful of her employee status and the conflict of the master's wife being a friend.

'Not at all, Jessie.' The new housemaid smiled warily in the wake of his genuine reassurance reflected in his warm deep voice. 'I'm afraid my wife may lead you astray once we get home. She has an independent spirit and you'll need to help me keep an eye on her.'

'I'll do that for you, Sir, for sure. That I will,' Jessie promised.

'So you best catch up on the news now before we reach the Albion. Once we arrive, I expect Mrs. Barratt to take a rest,' he said pointedly.

'I'm resting now as we drive,' Anne argued. 'I'll be fine, James. You mustn't fuss,' she added, although she privately glowed at his concern. 'Jessie,' she turned to her friend. 'How did James find you?'

'Well, as he told it to me,' she began importantly, 'It started in Wickliffe. You'd left your horse there and the innkeeper told him you'd taken the Ballarat coach. But as luck would have it for poor Mr. Barratt, no one in Ballarat remembered seeing you or where you'd gone next,' Jessie explained, barely pausing to draw breath. 'Mr. Barratt had a friend in Ballarat but she'd not seen you. Then he remembered you mentioned meeting me and Cissy on the ship and that we'd gone to work for Mrs. Rochester in South Yarra. So he travelled down to Melbourne and visits the lady of the house but, of course, she had to tell him I was gone and only Cissy was left. But Cissy weren't no help apparently. Can't hardly remember anything these days since her brain's pure addled and she's moping about in love. Isn't that right, Mr. Barratt?'

James had begun the ritual of lighting his pipe so he merely nodded his agreement sagely between puffs once it was lit, his concentration on the dusty road ahead, his eyes squinting against the late afternoon sun.

'Cissy did know the name of the run up country though where Johnny and Michael worked so off Mr. Barratt goes again on Cobb & Co. to Sandhurst travelling north to the station on – what river was it again, Mr. Barratt?'

'The Campaspe, Jessie.'

'Exactly. And of course all this travelling to find you is taking days and weeks, surely showing his devotion to finding you, Annie.'

'It certainly did,' she murmured, impressed by Jessie's memory and the extent of her recall in such detail. But the girl possessed a fierce interest in people and she seemed to soak up and retain every piece of information.

'On the sheep station, Mr. Barratt was invited to stay over and rest up for a few days. They must have seen he was weary but he was anxious because he knew he was gettin' closer to findin' you so he pushed on. They'd told him Johnny and Michael had set up on their own selection over at Daylesford so that's where he headed. And that's where he found me,' Jessie announced happily, 'on Wombat Flat in my brothers' cottage keeping house.'

'Indeed I did,' James readily agreed, still looking ahead as they trotted steadily closer to the city and the bridge over the Yarra River that they would soon cross.

'I was right worried when Mr. Barratt told me you'd run away. We'd not heard from you since September when we left you at the boarding house but one look at Mr. Barratt, if you'll beg my pardon, Sir, but I could see he was a right decent man and I weren't at all surprised to hear that you were wed. Praise the good Lord and fate,' Jessie hurried on, 'I was able to tell him exactly where you'd gone last month and was probably still there. Well,' she leaned closer in whispered confidence, 'I thought Mr. Barratt was about to cry. He grabbed both my hands tight and squeezed 'em and kept thanking me. Saying over and over how he was just right glad you were safe. And then he put his head in his hands and sat right still for such a long time.'

James cleared his throat, Anne sensing his discomfort at being so openly and personally discussed for Jessie's voice was never soft, even at a whisper and he'd plainly heard every word she said. She slipped a comforting arm through his and turned to press a gentle kiss on his whiskered cheek.

'How come you returned with James?' Anne asked Jessie.

'Oh, when he recovered, we got talkin' over a pot of tea and he said that Sarah had left and he'd need another housemaid and he'd not had time to arrange it while he was searchin' for you. So I put myself forward for the job. Mr. Barratt could see I kept my brothers' cottage neat so he took me on right then and there. I nearly fell off me chair with gratitude I can tell you. At least I'll be gettin' paid again. I know I was a help to the boys but I was workin' for nothin' seein' as they've no spare money gettin' the farm goin'.'

As the cab turned into Bourke Street and headed toward the hotel, familiar memories came flooding back for Anne from the first visit after her arrival from England and meeting James. It seemed only yesterday but so much had happened in the last six months.

Anne looked down at her lap where her hands twisted nervously together. 'I'm so sorry James for causing you so much distress. I didn't think-'

'It's over now.' He slipped his hand into hers and spoke warmly in the familiar deep tone she had come to know and love. 'We're going home tomorrow, although I'm not sure I'll be happy to let you out of my sight for a while.'

When they were safely settled in their hotel rooms, and since the summer daylight stretched well into the evening, Anne begged James to allow she and Jessie to make a brief visit to Cissy at *Belvedere* after supper for they would have no time before they left on the coach early in the morning.

Although he adamantly refused her plea at first, world-weary from his travels over recent weeks, he soon crumbled beneath his wife's insistent pleading that they might not see Cissy for months or even years.

When he finally agreed, she threw her arms around him. 'Oh, thank you James.' She pressed a bevy of kisses over his clean shaven face and lips.

'Do hurry back,' he growled suggestively.

'Yes, Sir,' Anne replied in mock obedience.

So, before sunset and promising to return before dark, the two women set off in another Albert cab to surprise Cissy. Jessie was equally excited for she had not seen her lifelong friend in months.

They warily retired to Cissy's room at the back of the house, the same one as before but which she now shared with a new under housemaid. Anne marvelled in surprise at the noticeable change in Cissy. Their previously mutual timid friend was much stronger and more confident, positively blossoming as they gossiped excitedly, which she could only attribute to the girl's new-found love of the gardener.

When Anne confided the news of her forthcoming child, Cissy and Jessie both gushed with joy. So parting seemed easier between them in the wake of such happy news and prospects ahead for them all.

Next day, the light hearted trio headed by coach for Ballarat.

'Is Will going to meet us?' Anne casually asked. James nodded. 'Wonderful.' She beamed. He eyed her with suspicion but remained silent. 'I'm just looking forward to seeing him again after all this time,' she explained innocently.

Recounting the events of recent weeks occupied much of the journey.

'You could have knocked me down when Mr. Barratt told me all about your troubles in Devon, Annie. No wonder you left,' Jessie said, wide eyed as they chattered. 'And poor Mr. Montgomery to be tricked like that. That Susan woman was devious for sure.'

A secret smile played on James' mouth. Anne gently nudged him. 'What?'

'There have been ... developments in Charles' life. Don't give up hope yet for a happy future for him.'

When no further details were forthcoming, Anne pressed, 'Don't leave it there. You must tell us what you know.'

'He's staying at *Rosevere Hall*.'

'Oh, how wonderful of Albert and Ettie to have him.'

'I hear he intends to delay his return to England.'

'He has some plans?'

'In the short term, I suspect he's merely enjoying the

Burroughs' hospitality and Charlotte's company in particular,' James idly dropped into the conversation.

Anne whirled on James and gaped. 'Charles and Charlotte?'

'Ah, don't be dismayed. It's for certain she will need a firm hand but,' he predicted confidently, 'in the light of his recent unfortunate experience, he will no doubt be up to the challenge.'

'Just as well he also has a large purse,' Anne muttered, 'and, I presume, a house full of servants.'

James chuckled. 'Indeed. I understand his London house is quite grand. And then there's his country estate in Berkshire. Of course, Ettie's crowing. Charles has invited them all to England for a visit.'

Anne chuckled. 'Ettie will love it. She hates Australia.'

'Rumour has it that Albert plans to leave the Hall under the care of Laurence as Manager while they're away. Who knows, it might be the making of the man. Give him a purpose and some responsibility.'

'Faint hope,' Anne muttered, 'but we must certainly hope so. I'd hate to see Albert's lifetime of work squandered.'

Seeing the bewildered look on Jessie's face, for the coming miles Anne proceeded to elaborate on their own household, their neighbours and each personality.

As the cramped passengers bumped against each other in the hot stuffy coach while it rattled and jolted across the parched brown summer countryside, Anne contemplated the roads she'd travelled since leaving Bridge Farm in Devon, the seas she'd crossed in the hope of escape to a better life, and sent up a silent prayer that her courage had been rewarded with James.

That, all being well, the first born in his dynasty would emerge into the world later in the year with strong and lusty cries. A playmate for Helen Munro, perhaps, Anne pondered in mischievous amusement.

She sighed and laid a hand over her growing child, cast

her husband a loving glance that he returned, and watched contentedly as, seated opposite, Jessie's head drooped in sleep.

Surely the gap between classes, squatter and selector alike, would narrow. Perhaps society would mellow and the generations to come would see changes their ancestors could not have imagined and be part of a young country filled with harshness and beauty and adventure.

She was sure many challenges and adjustments lay ahead for all of them but she was equally certain their family would increase under James' fearless guidance and they would continue to prosper in this wide and wonderful sunburnt country.